NATURAL
SELECTIONS

NATURAL
SELECTIONS
GLORIA NAGY

VILLARD BOOKS   NEW YORK   1985

Library of Congress Cataloging in Publication Data
Nagy, Gloria.
  Natural selections.
  I. Title.
PS3564.A36N3 1985   813'.54   85-40176
ISBN 0-394-54428-5

Manufactured in the United States of America
Designed by Ann Gold

TO RICHARD

The best way out is always through.

—*Robert Frost*

I would like to thank Susan Wallach for her invaluable guidance, Peter Ginsberg for believing, and Ann Thomson for being there.

NATURAL
SELECTIONS

PROLOGUE

She would always remember the night before he died, because of the eclipse. It was December. He set his alarm and went to sleep in his clothes to make the awakening less painful. He put on his heavy sheepskin jacket and walked to the Charles River and watched the moon disappear, leaving only a fine halo of platinum light in the sky. It was very cold. He shivered and began to cry. He cried for his family and his lost childhood. He cried for his name, calling to himself softly as in prayer, "Adam."

When he stopped, the top half of the moon was back, like a bloated egg sitting in an ebony cup. He breathed in deeply, wiping his swollen eyes with his cold white hand. He had always been alone, but he had never been this alone. He closed his eyes and saw his parents, his baby sister, his brother, standing in front of the mansion on Great River Road, smiling in white summer linens as if all on earth was safe and fine. He smelled *beignets*, chicory roasting and wet warm air. He heard porch swings and mosquitoes. A sadness so deep it knotted his stomach,

overwhelmed him. Tomorrow he would cease to exist.
As if instead of Adam he was Adam's rib, torn from his
body without the dignity and beauty of his own birth,
sprung whole and plopped down on the planet. Adam's
rib. Eve. So it would be then. After it was over, he would
call himself Eve.

When he opened his eyes again, the full silver moon
was back.

PART ONE
RICHELEAUS:
THE PAST

My name is Nathan Poe, though I call myself something else now. If you live in America and watch television, you'd probably know my face, or my voice. I covered national and international news for CBS for almost fifteen years. Before that I covered anything they told me to for a variety of newspapers, including some now dead and some that should be, ending with *The New York Times*, which gives me the chutzpah required for this task.

If you remember me, it is probably a blurry vision of a middle-aged guy with thinning gray hair parted too low on the left side to be convincing, standing in the wind, rain, sleet, snow, or dead of night in front of some government building, airport runway, or convention center, looking cold, tired, and hungover (but ironic and serious), telling it to Walter, or more recently Dan, like it supposedly really is.

I was the one with the slightly puffy and jaundiced eye, the too prominent Hebraic nose (never an anchor, always a rover), clutching the microphone with nicotine-

tinted fingers, the collar of my square-cut L. L. Bean
raincoat slightly askew, looking, as I mentioned before,
cold, tired, and hungover. That part was the truth. I was
cold, tired, and hungover for almost thirty years. I didn't
know there was any other way to feel until last year, and
part of me will always miss it, like any familiar not too
uncomfortable hurt that we get used to.

I still keep a photo of me on my desk in that preten-
tiously simple WASP raincoat, hunching forward to speak
earnestly and hoarsely to America. I didn't always like
that guy, but I really understand him and will always think
of him fondly. After all, he got me here, to this lop-eared
state of grace from which I will try to tell a true story
that you may have great trouble believing.

This is not *my* story. If it were I would have begun
with something far more dramatic, borrowed from one
of my literary heroes and certainly not in the first person.
This is not my story, though I am certainly a character
in it. This is the story of a person named Eve whom I
love. And whom I believe to be a saint.

It is not, however, the gushings of a Jewish Abelard
(though Abelard is a fairly ironic choice of metaphor
here). It more closely resembles King Arthur, the reliable
literary standby who sipped from the Grail and regained
his soul. I seem to have done that, and that is why I am
offering this tale. Because it might help. Me. You. Or
our increasingly terrified populace, which was, when I
actively left it, bounding over hill and dale as far from
the now dusty and deserted Round Table as the most
rascallious knight-errant. Farther than the noble king could
have ever envisioned.

It seemed a good time to tell a story, a true story about
love and goodness and, of course, evil. Using my cynical,
unredeemable self as living proof that even for one not
Percival born, a sip of the sweet juice can still be found.
I raise my goblet and give thanks. Let me begin.

CHAPTER 1

New Orleans, Summer 1953

O n the sweet, wet-hot August morning that Adam
Richeleau was born in the master quarters of his
grandpappy's mansion near New Orleans, a political cartoon by Herblock appeared in the *Washington Post*. It showed
the bottom parts of a huge, bureaucratically attired male
standing on a dune above Uncle Sam and President Eisenhower. Written on his coat flap in large white letters
was the word *H-BOMB*. In front of Sam and the president
was a serenely happy sunbather dozing beneath his striped
beach umbrella, his paperback novel lazing at his side.
Uncle Sam is nervously whispering behind his hand to a
grim-faced Ike. "Think maybe we'd better say something
about it?"

This badly dressed boor of a bomb was Adam's birth
announcement, reflecting the mood of the country; planting himself right beside the happily sunning citizens and
clouding an entire generation. No one knew it yet, but
the guy was not going to leave and he would affect us in
ways that are only just beginning to come clear.

This Southern baby of the Cold War arrived, like the

9

happy sunbather, unaware of the H-bomb or of the smaller
model waiting for his family on the fallow green acres
surrounding his new home.

Adam's mother, Hillary Proust Richeleau, was not new
to childbearing. She had produced a son, Alexander, seven
years before and, after a series of miscarriages that took
her small surplus of physical strength and half her sanity,
she gave birth to a little girl, Clara. Three years later
Adam appeared and with this blessing and her wifely work
complete, the doctor mercifully tied up her child-making
machinery and let her be.

Child-making was very important to the Richeleaus.
They bore the romance-novel burden of old Southern
tradition, and unfortunately for the Richeleau women,
took the whole load much too seriously. Not that the
men married women as if they were horseflesh. If they
had, life would have probably been far less tragic. No,
they married for love and then *expected* horseflesh.

The Richeleau dynasty began when a young French
captain from an old French family sailed across the Gulf
of Mexico up the Mississippi, landed somewhere around
what is now the Toulouse Street Wharf, removed the
Spanish flag from the spire of the St. Louis Cathedral,
and replaced it with the French tricolor. But the triumph
was short-lived. Two weeks later the fifteen stars and
striper went up, ending the hat dance between the French
and Spanish, forever changing the course of history in
the bayou.

The young Frenchman, however, fell in love with New
Orleans and stayed. The year was 1803 and the oppor-
tunities for a bright young man of good family were vast.

With the already thriving French and Spanish aristoc-
racy, the arrival of the Americans, and bullion from his
father, the young Frenchman had a ready foundation for
trade. He began to import fine silks, perfumes, and an-
tiques from his native land. To house the goods, he bought

a piece of land on the waterfront and built warehouses. To sell them, he bought several plots on Royal Street and built shops.

Eventually he would own a large part of the Vieux Carré and the waterfront. With his mounting riches he bought two thousand acres of land, previously ripped from the hands of the Houmas Indians, and built the most magnificent plantation in Louisiana. The house was of the Greek Revival style, surrounded by white stone columns and upper and lower verandas, with a watchtower on the roof, twenty Italian marble fireplaces, satiny maple floors, and encircled by live oaks, magnolias, crepe myrtles, and exotic plants and flowers of every imaginable sort. His property included a working thoroughbred horse farm, a dairy, commercial orchid greenhouse, and flowing fertile acres of sugar, cotton, and peppers.

By 1873, when Adam Richeleau's grandfather was born and the Civil War destruction on the mend, the surviving wealth of the family was great. Its tentacles were deep and spread throughout Louisiana, and its history was filled with its share of interlopers, slave traders, cowards, madmen, and thieves as well as solid Southern citizenry.

Anton Richeleau, the young captain's great-great-grandson, was strong, driven, cunning, paranoid, addicted to absinthe and virile as a ram in heat.

He ran two wives into the grave, leaving him with a gaggle of daughters, before meeting his match and his downfall—an exotic mulattress, a "woman of color," named Aurelia by whom he had his only son, Adam's father, Louis.

Mulattoes are people of mixed Spanish and Negro or French and Negro ancestry, born in the new land. Theirs is a proud, fierce, and ritualistic heritage, the subject of many adventure stories and B movies with Yvonne DeCarlo and Linda Darnell wearing too much pancake makeup and tatty black wigs.

Unlike old movies, Anton Richeleau was not Errol Flynn and to marry Aurelia rather than to follow the accepted custom of concubinage—or as the French called such women, *placées*—cast a shadow over the Creole family's good name and gave the decadent *riche* New Orleans society something to keep them awake all summer.

Aurelia was a hot-tempered, sensual woman keenly aware of her good fortune and power over Anton. To Anton, she was a vixen tempting him toward evil and not to be trusted. He was obsessed with her, filled with jealousy, lust, and rage at his inability to penetrate her muscular reserve. He drank more absinthe and retreated for days at a time into his dark, hot study where he wrote the family history and polished his Derringer.

By the time Louis had reached his tenth year, the household situation had deteriorated to the point of mutual madness. Anton, who had guided his legacy with the zest and zeal of a warlord, was neglecting the Richeleau empire, delegating important decisions to his chargé d'affaires (who calmly proceeded to embezzle bits of bullion into his own purse), and ignoring his once impeccable personal appearance.

As Anton grew weaker, Aurelia seemed to grow stronger and more beautiful. It was as if she became the bodily icon of all the half-breed righteousness and despair, as if by destroying her husband she would pay back the Creoles for the pain of her people. It was, Anton knew in the recesses of his absinthed paranoia, a battle to the death.

The devil was in her, he believed. She need only open her pink silk robe, flashing a whisper of satiny olive flesh, and he was helpless—poisoned, out of control. He would mount her, with the weary passion of an aging rodeo rider, knowing that the price for the ride would be too high but unable to stop; burying his graying whiskers in her soft round belly and screaming with pleasure while she would lie motionless, long firm legs spread wide, head back, smiling in triumph.

Their child, Louis, was an outsider in his parents' *folie à deux*. He was a dark, quiet, sensitive boy with bad eyes and frail bones, lonely and confused, but not without character. He was afraid of both of them and kept to himself, and he would most likely have developed rather severe emotional problems if not for his nanny, Maybelle, nicknamed "Maybe" when Louis first spoke her name. Maybe was a large Cajun orphan woman, Cajuns being of German descent but French-speaking, raised by Negroes. Her blue-eyed, red-haired heritage was covered in black dialect and slave philosophy. The effect was disconcerting to outsiders and seemed, in some beautifully sardonic way, to mock the prejudice and silliness of the rich Creole value system.

Maybelle Carver was one of the rare humans blessed with the gifts of wisdom of the spirit and an almost vicious common sense—a remarkable combination. She knew Cajuns and she knew "free men of color" and she knew Creole rich men. She understood very quickly that this was a house covered in darkness and her job on earth was to save the child. If she had been anyone else, Louis would never have survived.

Maybe understood the insecurity that forced Aurelia to behave as a parody of mistress of the mansion. Maybe was the only one to offer solace, but it was an offer that Aurelia was too defensive to accept. Aurelia's only refuge was the natural world—a world of weather and creature—jungle laws that she lived by; she needed nature. She was bound to the earth and its creatures like a Caliban in lace, and without guile or motive she passed this love and knowledge on to her only child during long early morning walks. It came from the healthy part of her, the love and joy in being, in mud and sun and ant that had been pushed aside by the entrance of Anton into her bourgeois young life.

Half-breeds like Aurelia learn to manipulate early; they learn to stand aside, watch carefully, test all waters, be-

cause they belong nowhere. Set adrift in a society that
fears and disdains them, they learn to fear and disdain
back, but invisibly. Aurelia was filled with things held
too long inside, warping her view of her fellowman and
cutting her off from the finest parts of her own nature.
Her mother had been the *placée* of a Cajun merchant, and
she had grown up protected, haughty, ambitious, and
totally incubated in the distortions of her own mother's
rage. Her son was a further dilution of her own plight,
but with the protection of money and power. It was this
fantasy of safety that her husband represented and to
which she latched herself, forsaking the pleasure of tree
and grass, except on the outings with her son. It was the
only real time they spent together, and Louis loved these
walks and talks with his mother above all else in his life.
Covered with layers of light clothing and hats to keep
back the sun, they would set off at dawn with a lunch
packed by Maybe.

Frail though he was, Aurelia took Louis out in the
summer sun and taught him to endure it. Beside his lovely
mother he hiked over his father's land, his shirt and hair
soaked with sweat while his mother worked her magic.
Her eyes were remarkably fast. She could spot a katydid
at ten feet, snatch a butterfly from the air faster than
flight, and hear a lark miles away.

"Do you know of the scarab beetle, Louis?" she murmured, bending over to plop a caterpillar into a mason
jar.

"No, Momma," he whispered, watching her work with
weak-eyed wonder.

"Well, it is the ugliest, evilest creature on God's earth.
It is so dreadful to see that other insects flee it in horror
and many a naturalist has shuddered and been sick to his
stomach when attempting to examine one."

Louis blinked in awe, visions of the terrible creature
darting behind his thick wire glasses.

"Someday I will find you one and it will keep you from harm, scare away all the nasty goblins forever!"

Louis blushed. His mother knew, without a word ever having been spoken, of his night fears: goblins and ghosts and giant soldiers (who looked like his father) riding through his window to chop off his head.

When they returned from their walks, flushed and exhausted, Louis would take the mason jars filled with his spoils and set them on an old oak table in the laundry room. Maybe and Aurelia let him keep his collection there: a battered old table filled with spiders and moths, worms and beetles, and bugs of every sort—all carefully pinned, pressed, jarred, numbered, and tagged. His father had never seen the table, since the kitchen and the laundry were parts of the house that were of no interest to him and chances of discovery were slim; still, Louis lived in fear that one day Anton would enter, see the bizarre array, and throw it all in the trash.

The Collection, as he called it, was the only thing that was of himself. It was his friend, his passion, and his link to his mother, something he and he alone shared with her. After her death it became an obsession.

Summer might have been the finest season for insect gathering, but summer in New Orleans before the glory of air-conditioning was a merciless prison of humidity from which there was no escape; no door to fling open releasing fresh air, no room to enter filled with the whir of conditioned coolness, no escape but sleep or death. The heat held the body and the mind in an airless coffin of lethargy. Custom, dress, manner, and fashion exacerbated the dilemma, forcing brocade draperies, corsets, petticoats, gloves, dress suits, hats, and ties on the stifled, sweating gentlefolk.

The ramifications of this weather helped shape the personality of an entire society, struggling to survive the motionless wet drain of Southern summer. Life for upper-

class New Orleanians was like a frieze of grainy old photos: languorous ladies and gents stopped in time, lolling
on porch swings, sipping mint juleps, speaking slowly.
Minds crawled. Drink increased. Nerves snapped. Pas-
sions boiled. Sensuous, lagoian instincts born of too many
hours lying and fanning; idle minds and heated bodies
fermenting social mischief on wicker-filled verandas.

The heat had much to do with Anton and Aurelia. Even
in 1933, with corsets gone, electric fans whirring, and
the primitive glory of the new invention, air-conditioning, summer was hell; but summer was Aurelia's time of
strength, her mixed blood ran cooler, her body bred to
withstand it, to serve the Creoles, like her husband, who
rotted in it. She would rise up and he would sink down,
drinking to supplant his waning energy and quiet his
itching nerves.

The pace and personality of the South seem tied to
the summer, molded by its demands. Life moves slowly,
people move slowly, progress is resisted. Years pass, nothing changes, nothing happens. No one seems to be born,
no one seems to die. Drunks get drunk, old grow older,
misery stays miserable; but so slowly, within the confines
of such rigidly callow tradition that it is easy to believe
that, like the citizens of Brigadoon, one day of life comes
every one hundred years and any alteration from wakening to wakening is imperceptible.

Tragedy, then, when it enters, is such a shock, so
aberrant to the pace of daily life and, consequently, so
grand, astonishing, tearing, and exciting, that it forever
brands those who observe as well as those who participate.

After years of creeping delusion hidden within the cool
white majesty of Richeleau House, tragedy happened.

Aurelia and Anton had lived side by side for a dozen
years, their mutual seething distrust pumped like a bellows
inside their minds. With every slight from Anton's so-

ciety, every smirk on the faces of jealous Southern belles,
every sidelong look from her husband, Aurelia's rage, fed
by the memory of her mother, grew. Anton saw her with
the collective eyes of his Creole past, resenting his need
for her, trying to conquer it by demeaning and sexually
abusing her. She began to believe that she had a mission
on earth and that mission had led her to Anton Richeleau.
His desire for her had brought her up from the half-caste's
wire walk through the world. If she and her quadroon
son could defeat the Creole master, they could bring
mulatto power to Louisiana. Her conviction made her
clever and pushed her away from the beauty of the earth
and into the world of night demons and darkness. Her
son would soon be a man and he had been raised without
any knowledge of his black ancestors, without resentment
and fire to unite him to her cause. Anton stood in her
way. She believed that the justice trail led to Anton's slide
into madness and death. Jealousy was her weapon. She
knew it was his fatal weakness, and when it filled him,
he was powerless and out of control. She could drive him
mad with it. From the distortion of her reality, triumph
seemed certain.

The vehicle she chose to carry her down this unpaved
road to vengeance and power was Anton's chargé d'affaires—whom Aurelia knew to be a womanizer and a
thief. She had evidence of his petty embezzlements of
Anton's gold with which to blackmail him, but to begin,
seduction seemed enough.

Anton watched the dance of his queen and her drone,
sensing its purpose and yet drawn toward the poisoned
honey by masochism and lust. At night he sat in his study,
absinthe fogging his mind, listening to his wife and her
lover, groaning in sin through the paneled walls. He
would wait, blood rouging his cheeks, his penis hard,
until he heard the door to her suite open and close. Soon
after he would rise, naked under his monogrammed robe,

and unsteadily make his way to her. She was always waiting for him, knowing that Anton knew, knowing that each journey down the Persian-carpet-covered hall was longer and slower.

He would enter and throw himself upon her, a sotted sobbing relic stripped of his arrogance and hubris, trapped by his own bigotry and fear. But, as in all tragedy, people are not only what they seem, and Aurelia took Anton at his worst and herself at her best, which is not a true test of reality. She underestimated him and grew overconfident and impatient.

For the day of Louis's tenth birthday, Maybe had arranged for a party, a picnic on the grounds by the river for all the neighbors and workers. Louis had no friends, except the children of the servants and employees of his father. He led a sheltered, narrow life that gave him asthma, eczema, and self-doubt, which he covered in sporadic bursts of bravado and snobbishness—a pattern that despite Maybe's guidance would reemerge in times of stress throughout his life. "I am a Richeleau and I must carry on my great-great-grandfather's work," he announced to Maybe, pouring homemade maple syrup on buckwheat cakes and grits.

"You is a wheezin', sickly little quarter horse and don't you be forgettin' it," Maybe would shout back. "No man is better than no other, and if we never left the jungle, we all still be monkeys!"

Louis would go to her then, a pale pigeon of a boy with his scrawny wings clipped, and bury his face in her dry, warm, flour-smelling lap. "I'm sorry, Maybe. The devil made me say it."

"Don't you be blamin' the poor devil for your flappin' gums! He's got enough to atone for as is. Ever since the Lord tossed him down the chute, he's had to pay for everybody's evil and even he don't do it all. He'll never get back up there if every little Southern boy blames his own dirty work on 'em."

He would squeeze in closer to her, inhaling her truth, trusting completely her words and they would hold one another, hearts beating in tandem, until his mother rang for her tray.

On this dog day summer morning of his first real birthday celebration, Louis awoke long before dawn, eager for time to pass. He loved Occasions, for on them his mother smiled and held his hand and his father came out of his study clean and smelling of Bay Rum and soap and patted his head and let him light his Cuban cigars. His half-sisters came and spoiled him with candy and life felt happy and filled with hope and he always believed that each Occasion would change everything and would go on forever.

But the next day, life would darken, slow down; the beautiful memory would begin to fade like his mother's glistening smile, and within a fortnight he would have an attack of asthma so severe that Maybe would bring him to her bed, shoot him full of Adrenalin, and cover his tight white face with an oxygen mask.

On this Occasion, as he lay in his great-grandfather's hand-carved mahogany bed waiting for the sun to shoot stripes of lavender and persimmon across the dawn, he did not feel the familiar excitement reserved for such special events. He felt frightened. Elated without joy, anxious. He had felt that way before, more often in the past year. He felt it at dinner, watching his mother and father, talking politely behind straining smiles, delivering double whammies that he could feel but could not understand.

"It seemed a bit cooler today, don't you think, Anton, dear?"

"Hadn't noticed. Could be just your ancestral tolerance at work, my love. Those ancient genes of Afrique, coming to your rescue."

"How regretful, Anton, dear, that you do not share in my genetic good fortune; fortitude is the key to survival.

Would you like a damp cloth, dear; I see your brow is wet again. The heat does so drain you."

Louis moved his potatoes about on his china plate, inhaling the hate under the perfect diction and genteel conversation, sick to his stomach.

He felt it in the middle of the night as he lay half-asleep dreaming of soaring down long corridors, shooting through tunnels of neon lights, whizzing toward a figure far in the distance; a child, out of control, faster and faster until he could see the figure, a glowing skeleton, smiling at him. He would wake up, wheezing and wet with cold sweat, arms outstretched, pushing away the face of death, and then he would hear the sounds coming from his mother's room. Asthma sounds, foul sounds; pigs and beasts, and he would feel it, again. Elation without joy. Fear.

He sat up and turned on his bed light. He heard the old Federal hall clock chime four times. He yawned, wishing he had a dog to play with. Instead, he picked up the new book on Charles Darwin that his mother had bought for him. He tried to concentrate, but the tension stayed.

For Anton and Aurelia tension had passed. One hour earlier Anton got to his feet, having sat in his study all night, drinking and waiting for the adultery to end, waiting to make his ritual march down the creaking halls of his family home to his wife's musky bed. But this night was different. This night, after the animal moanings, he heard different sounds. Laughter. Aurelia's soft throaty giggles. Her lover's gruff chuckle.

The laughter ignited him with paranoia and dismembered pride. They were mocking him, plotting against him, planning his death. They would take over his house and murder his son. No, the boy had her evil blood, he would do her bidding. It might even be Louis who would kill him, today at the birthday picnic. How easy to pass his unsuspecting poppa a piece of poisoned cake, a glass

of tainted lemonade. But he would outsmart them. He
was Anton Richeleau, not some blind old fool, and this
was war.

He waited, sizzling with rage until the laughter ended
and the door closed. He put his pistol in the pocket of
his robe and made his way down the dark hall and opened
her door. He stood, tall and steady, not whimpering and
lust-blinded as in the past, but marble hard, silent, and
completely insane. Aurelia sat up, her body outlined beneath the pale blue satin sheets, and beckoned to him.

"Come, darling," she whispered.

Anton moved toward her. He stopped at the foot of
her shiny blue lair, his face breaking slowly into the grin
of an ignited jack-o'-lantern. The glowing grin of his
madness moved skin from bone, and she felt herself
shrinking like a cannibal's victim—her skull tightening in
terror.

The smile spread. The smile was too fast and she had
not prepared for it. She raised her arms to beckon him
and felt her limbs weaken. Her arms were too heavy to
hold, they fell to her pillow and she could not move
them. The diamond was cracked. She was afraid. "What
is it, darling?"

"Something new," said Anton, his eyes bright with
secret voices. "Turn over on your stomach and just relax."
Aurelia obeyed.

She had underestimated the ferocious energy of her
husband—the insanity had not fragmented his power,
but conversely, he was monolithic, larger in his paranoia
than he had ever been. She was astonished and so weak
that the act of turning depleted her. A Delilah with rusty
scissors, defeated by suddenness. Anton had found the
missing link. He had simply changed the rules of their
game, reversed the engine without a warning bell; a change
of pace, a second wind cooling the air, shattering the
long-range plan.

He crawled onto the bed using his knees to hold her

legs in place beneath him. With one rough hand he
pulled back the sheet, revealing her soft, warm naked-
ness; with the other he pulled the satin pillow down over
the back of her head. She stirred. "I can't breathe,
Anton."

"So sorry, my dear," he said, withdrawing the gun from
his pocket and sliding it up between her legs into her
body. "The devil will stay in hell," he hissed as he pulled
the trigger.

The bullet went through her, crashing against bone,
lung, and heart, smashing into her head, the pillow muf-
fling the sound of its exit. She never moved. All the years
of patient, steady scheming seemed to have taken her
energy for the battle.

It had almost been too easy. One fierce moment, then
nothing. No one heard, no one came. Anton lay on top
of his defeated tormentress listening to the soft sucking
gurgle of death. He heard the clock strike four and he
crawled backward away from his wife and left her room
for the last time. There was still the war to be won. Down
the empty hall he moved, with steady, zombielike grace,
his silk robe coated with blood, the gun—smelling of
Aurelia's private places—still held in his hand.

When he reached Louis's room, he stopped. The voice
in his mind grew softer. He shook his head to clear it,
to bring back his guide. "The boy is hers, he must be
stopped," it said at last. He turned the knob. The door
was locked.

Louis and his goblins, keeping him out. He pushed at
it, juggling and twisting the handle.

Downstairs, too far away to hear a knob jiggle or a
bullet smash into a satin pillow, Maybe sat up in her
single bed. Something was wrong. She put on her robe
and slippers, led by instincts as old and as sure as the
ground on which she stood, stuffing her wide bare feet
into furry old slippers. She made her way in the dark,

knowing the path as well as a blind man: across the cavernous old kitchen, through the aroma of biscuits and the pot roast from supper; out into the dining room, already set with fresh linen and silver for breakfast; through the music room and into the vast formal parlor smelling of roses and furniture polish; into the checkerboard marble entry and up the circular staircase to Louis's room.

Before she reached the landing, she heard him scream; a gun went off and she ran; a fat red-headed woman sprinting like a wildebeest toward its calf. She reached the splintered door and ran through it, fearless and unhesitating. Louis crouched in the corner behind the door, the book on Darwin still in his hand, shrieking in terror. His father stood over him, smiling the same brilliant mad-eyed smile that had drained Aurelia of her energy. His robe fell open revealing his graying pubis and blood-stained genitals; the gun, still warm from Aurelia, pointed at his son's heart. "The devil will stay in hell," Anton said quietly.

Maybe lunged, knocking Anton backward, discharging the gun and shattering Louis's left leg. Maybe and her master rolled over each other, nightclothes parting, revealing soft white flesh; they grappled like clowns of Eros for survival.

Anton was stronger. He pinned her beneath him and pointed the gun at her forehead. Their eyes locked, the sound of Louis's agony above, a deep cavern of empty timeless space between them. Maybe relaxed beneath him. "The devil is in *you*, in you, sir. It's his voice you hear, tricking your mind. The child is innocent."

It was the proper thing to say. Anton shuddered and with the shudder the madness fell away and he saw what he had done. He lowered the pistol and climbed off his servant and onto his feet. He turned toward Louis, who lay bleeding, sinking into shock, no longer crying; quiet in his escape from pain and terror. "Dear God," he said as he stumbled out of his son's room and down the corridor to his study.

As Maybe tightened a tourniquet made of pillow slips around Louis's thigh, there was one final shot and she knew it was over.

CHAPTER 2

At the time the Derringer was popping off in New Orleans, I was three years old, a motherless Jewish boy with an unemployed father, sharing "two eggs, toast, and coffee for ten cents" in the Bowery.

Outside the fraying Camelot of Richeleau land, the country was in wreckage. Master Hoover got dumped, leaving only his Hoovervilles (of which my pop and I were sometime inhabitants), some twenty thousand suicides the previous year, a 25 percent unemployment rate affecting directly or indirectly thirty million people, children starving and grown men fighting to the death over bags of garbage.

One family made the news by walking nine hundred miles from Arkansas to the Rio Grande to apply for a job in the cotton fields.

In Washington, D.C., much to the chagrin of H.H. (who was just about to be defeated by F.D.R.), General Douglas MacArthur himself, accompanied by a cherubic young major, Dwight D. Eisenhower, marched into a Hooverville set up by World War I veterans appealing to

the mercy of the government for an advance on benefits
to help them through the Depression, on the very night
the tattered vets were packing up, and attacked the paper
and tin shacks, destroying everything and chasing helpless women and children across the Potomac and into
oblivion. The Richeleaus screamed in private, the country
wailed publicly.

The good news of 1933 was the repeal of Prohibition
(the government must have known I was coming) and
F.D.R., though there are those who will disagree about
both choices.

By 1934 the mood had brightened and recovery began.
From the despairing dust bowl survivor—who told the
press, "I have worked hard my whole life and all I have
now is my broken body"—to the article in a popular
magazine that proclaimed the Depression good for family
life—enthusing, "unappreciative wives who were indifferent to their husbands and neglected their homes have
become tame and cautious"—we moved into the mid-
thirties with the supreme father figure in power offering
a New Deal and bringing back the grin to American daily
life. As the country climbed hand over fist out of its first
real bump with vincibility, Louis and Maybe were climbing out of their own personal Depression.

Anton Richeleau had produced six daughters. By the
time of The Tragedy (as it was to be known in local
history), three had died from a variety of childhood diseases, one was mentally retarded and institutionalized
somewhere in Mississippi, one was a Catholic nun, and
one the mayor's bride. Since their own finances had long
since been settled on them by Anton, with the clear
understanding that everything remaining would go to his
only son, and since Anton and Aurelia had not set out to
win the parents of the year contest, the news of the
disgraceful massacre met with cold shock and not much
further concern from Louis's half-sisters. They knew him

only from his christening, Thanksgiving, and Christmas
parties, and though fond of him, they resented the loss
of the scraps remaining of their father's love to him and
That Woman. Louis had the attention and the bulk of
the family fortune, and that did not endear him or provoke
these neglected women toward his side. But two of his
surviving sisters did answer Maybe's call for help: Laurel,
the oldest and the wife of the mayor of New Orleans,
and Suzette, the nun.

When the smoke cleared, Anton and Aurelia were buried side by side in the family crypt (though having committed every sin in the Old Testament), and the news
retreated from the front page of the *Picayune*, Maybe had
time for the messy reality to hit.

Louis was still in the hospital. He remained in the
hospital, mentally and physically shattered, for almost a
year, undergoing a series of painful and only partially
successful operations to repair his mangled leg. The leg
would not heal. It was almost as if on some barely con-
scious level, Louis held on to the injury as his only link
with his mother and father, as if healing meant death,
finality; scar tissue on his heart. And he felt guilty. He
did not know what he had done, but he knew that somehow it was his fault.

At night, alone in his private room he would lie, eyes
blinking back sleep, resisting the medicine they gave to
take him away from consciousness, terrified of his dream.
It came again and again, zooming along in blinding light
toward the face of death. It had been a dream and it had
come true, so now nothing was safe, and that meant it
could happen again. This fear haunted him, but he told
no one. He was afraid to go home, back to that house
of anger and murder, and so he did not heal. The leg
was his memory, and for the rest of his life, the crippled,
scarred, scrawny limb was his penance for his unknown
crime.

Maybe came to him every day, huffing up the stairs,

fruit, homemade raisin cookies, pralines, and fresh milk
in her ample arms. She was all that he had left, and he
clung to her with a fearsome desperation that brought
tears to her eyes and worry to her soul.

"Lissen here now, boy, you got to pray harder for the
Lord to heal you. We got work to do. You're the last of
yo' line and the folks needs you. You don't have no more
time to be a chil' now, darlin', you got to come out of
this place a man. Drink yo' milk now, Louis, we got to
build them bones up good. Can't be waltzin' at the Mardi
Gras cotillions with a puny bent-up old leg."

"Good, then I won't have to go! I'm only ten years old,
I'm of no use to anyone, crippled or not crippled."

"Oh, Louis, baby, now you stop that pity talk. No one
is gonna rescue a quitter, they just dance on by and step
right over yo' self-sorry quarter-breed hide. Yo' daddy
left everything he owned to you and if you don't get well,
I'm just gonna have to give it all to the state, now you
don't want that?"

"I don't care, just don't give them my Collection."

"That's the first thing I'll give 'em. All those ugly critters. 'Here,' I'll tell 'em, 'this here's the Collection of a
spoiled little rich boy who wouldn't get his behind out
of bed to save his home. Here, give 'em to some other
crazy boy!' "

While Louis was mending, pondering Maybe's threat,
she had other difficulties weighing on her. There she was,
a crewman on a massive, deserted vessel, with the captain
dead and no first mate or life raft in sight. She knew it
was only a matter of time before the big wave hit, the
submerged reef cut through the rolling hull, and the vul-
tures and starving sea birds descended. She could not lose
her balance for an instant, or they would be shark fodder.

She began to investigate. First, she set up headquarters
in Anton's study, sorting through his ledgers, his key
rings; opening and examining the contents of the safety

boxes and the wall safe, poring over wills, trust deeds, mortgages, balance sheets, and insurance policies. She was uneducated, but quick-witted and highly motivated. She managed. She studied and restudied, knowing that the lawyers and bankers and welfare workers would soon be knocking at the polished oak doors. What she found was most interesting. It was obvious that Anton did not expect to go mad and commit murder and suicide. His main legal obsession had been to keep Richeleau land in the hands of the male line, no daughters to bring in unsavory sons-in-law and squander his ancestor's holdings. Louis was to inherit everything. There was only one paragraph, handwritten and seemingly added recently, that dealt with guardianship:

> In the event of my demise, my son, Louis, is to be raised in his family home in the care of his nanny, Maybelle Carver, and his estate shall be managed by Mr. Proust, president of the Bank of New Orleans, until he reaches the age of twenty-one years. At that time, it will be transferred into his hands, with the fear of God and the memory of his great-great-grandfather to guide him righteously and with the understanding that it is his blessing and his burden and must never leave his domain or be passed to any but his male heirs. The Richeleau name must be preserved forever. If this condition is not met, I will meet his soul in hell.

Maybe shuddered as she read and reread this. A rich father's domination, reaching out even from the grave to frighten and control. She put the piece of paper in her pocket, knowing it was a double-edged sword and a dull one at best. It was not witnessed, and his daughters or the sharks in the sea could challenge it in court. Her only hope was Mr. Proust, whoever he be, and Louis's sisters. After a week of phoning she reached Laurel and Suzette who agreed to come home. Then she called a meeting of all the workers: the foreman of the horse ranch and the apiarist, the managers of the orchid business and the import-export operation, the keepers of the Royal Street establishments, and the captain of the cargo vessel. When all the meetings had been arranged she went to her room, knelt down on her rag rug, and prayed until her legs fell sound asleep.

Laurel was the first to arrive. Laurel Richeleau Poisson (or "Miz Fish," as the servants called her privately) was the oldest daughter, the product (as was her sister Suzette) of Anton's first union with the heiress to a small Kentucky tobacco fortune. It was a marriage arranged for Anton, and he suffered through it, fulfilling his conjugal duty by closing his eyes and thinking of the little coquette who worked in one of his antique shops and had the softest, sweetest breasts he had ever encountered.

After two daughters and no male heir, Anton's patience grew thin.

When Suzette, the second born, was just two months old and before his poor wife had recovered mentally or physically from her second birth in two years, he impregnated her again. The third daughter was born prematurely and mentally retarded, his wife hemorrhaged and died two days later from shock and loss of blood. The unwanted baby was placed in an institution, his wife's fortune placed in trust for "her girls," as he called them, and Anton went off to find another mate to bring him a son.

Laurel grew up fast. Even as a baby she protected her little sister and kept watch over her. She was a strong, large, athletic girl who looked exactly like her father (much to his annoyance), and she used her physical strength and a dry waspish wit to fend off her loss and hide her vulnerability. She did well in school and excelled in tennis, swimming, gymnastics, and horsemanship. Later she discovered golf and became a local champion, winner of the New Orleans Country Club's cup year in and year out. She grew into her body, a large-boned, horsey, tweedy sort of woman who always seemed to be holding an invisible golf stick or tennis racquet. She married a local politician named Philip Poisson, a male clone of herself, while still in her teens and put together a complex and robust household, marred only by their inability to produce children, which her analyst would later diagnose as a severe fate neurosis, a terror of repeating her mother's karma rather than any physical disability. Whatever the psychological reasons, she desperately wanted children to fill her life and possibly to please her father, whose quest for a male child continued onward. Eventually they adopted a Creole orphan boy, around whom they focused their love and energy. He died of pneumonia when he was three years old and Laurel seemed to die with him. Her tall sturdy body bent with grief, and she sank into a depression so severe that her husband finally agreed to have her hospitalized. There fate intervened.

The afternoon nurse who tended her inquired one day if she had a relative by the name of Richeleau, for there was a retarded woman with that name who had lived there since infancy. The next morning, for the first time in months, Laurel got up out of bed, washed her face and teeth, put on clothes, and ate some breakfast. When the afternoon nurse came on duty, she was sitting, dressed and with her hair combed, waiting for her. "Please, will y'all take me to the woman you told me about. She's my baby sister."

The nurse nodded. A call to the supervisor was made, and Laurel was led through the dank green halls that smelled of stale urine and boiled meat, out across the lawn to the cottages where permanent residents lived.

Her sister was sitting on the floor playing with two rag dolls, one white and one black. She spoke to them with the voice of a small Southern child of maybe four though she was a full-grown woman, slightly overdeveloped, with fair skin and short light brown hair. "Now, Missy nasty, girl. Play nice. Give Ruby the cookie or I spank yo' bottom."

Laurel stood in the doorway, unseen by this rejected baby-woman, and her heart filled with a love and compassion so deep that she felt it burn into her being, healing her wounds, soothing her. When Laurel went home, her sister, whom the staff had named Kate after the "Southern Songbird" Kate Smith, came with her, and Mr. and Mrs. Poisson resumed their place in community life.

Suzette Richeleau also grew up with a numbing emptiness. She did not have Laurel's wit or physical strength. She was a small, elfin woman like her mother, with a childlike appearance and a pathological shyness. In the presence of her father she was benumbed with fear. This fear was not altogether unfounded.

One night, when she was eleven years old, Suzette heard a noise outside her window and went to find out what it was. As she tiptoed down the long wide corridors of Richeleau House toward her sister's room, the door to her father's bedroom opened and he stood before her in his silk pajamas looking slightly drunk and affable. He beckoned to her.

"Where are you headed all alone and half-naked in the dead of night, girl?" Anton whispered, weaving and motioning her toward him.

Suzette turned pale with apprehension. "I heard a noise, Poppa. I was just going to see if Laurel heard it, too."

"Come on in here, now, there's no boogeymen on Richeleau land. It was probably a jackrabbit chasing a squirrel. Come on in and let your poppa warm you up."

Suzette followed him into his vast, golden suite glowing with fire and shiny velvet couches. Cherubs danced on the gold-leaf ceiling, Sheridan chests, and Queen Anne chairs; beveled mirrors in hand-carved rosewood frames reflected the fire and her father's face. "Climb in here with your poppa and go to sleep, girl, you're shiverin' like a doe in a blizzard." Suzette obeyed, so overcome with the awesome, seductive majesty of her father's attention. Her father, who had never spoken her name or held her hand or told her she was pretty but whom she loved fiercely and in silence, was inviting her into his sacred room, to his sacred bed, to be warm and safe. In she climbed, afraid to breathe or move or break the magic. The room was lit only by firelight, luminating her small white body and her father's handsome face. "Here, child, have a drink of this, it will warm your bones." He handed her his brandy glass and she gulped it down, feeling the liquid kindling her insides, unable to catch her breath. In moments, the brandy and the excitement had worked their magic and she was asleep.

In her sleep she felt something. Her father behind her, his breath against her back. Deep in sleep, she tried to swim up above the waters of unconsciousness, to understand what was happening, but she felt herself sinking deeper, farther from the surface. Her nightgown was sliding up, and she felt his large, rough hands turning her over, opening her slender legs; felt heaviness upon her, physical weight, heat, and then the heat moved, entered her, tore her open, drowned her with pain; heat and pain and she swam in it, embraced it, opened to it, sunk down to the bottom of it, straddled it, pain, heat, evil, love, Poppa.

When she woke the next morning she was back in her own room, and if it had not been for the blood on her inner thighs and the sticky wetness seeping slowly from inside her body, she would have convinced herself it had all been a dream. Part of her wanted it to be true, to know that he had chosen her, and part of her recoiled from the depravity of her wantonness with a force so

searing, so cauterizing, and so complete that she turned
to the only thing that seemed to offer guidance—God
Himself. When she was twelve she convinced her governess and her father to send her off to a convent school,
where she became the first serious Catholic in the Richeleau dynasty, and there she remained atoning and
escaping from the secret parts of herself, forever blotting
her memory and the undercurrent of her nature. Poppa
was replaced by Jesus Christ, an acceptable selection given
the alternative.

And so it was that when Louis finally regained enough
mental and physical balance to return to the scene of the
crime, and thereby saving his fortune (and, more importantly, his grasshoppers), he was greeted by Maybe, a
red-headed Cajun who thought she was Negro; Laurel,
a female jock with formidable biceps and a rolling, sarcastic conversation known to wilt grown men; Kate, a
twenty-three-year-old woman with the intelligence of a
barely toilet-trained child; and Suzette, a tiny abused nun.
It was a quartet of matriarchal March Hares that only the
South could lay claim to. All in all, however, this band
of emotionally ragged survivors managed to maneuver the
lurching vessel through the tidal wave without running
aground. Family meetings were held during which Louis's
interests and future course were charted and entered suc-
cinctly in Maybe's daily log.

One afternoon Louis hobbled in after the daily ac-
counting and found Maybe's file left untended on the
shiny dark table. His curiosity overcame his fear and he
opened it, feeling as if it were his father's coffin under
his trembling fingers. Right on top was the note. "The
Richeleau name must be preserved . . . I will meet his
soul in hell. . . ." Louis closed the file and stumbled from
the room, his lungs filling with asthmatic panic. The past
now pressed more firmly into his destiny. The note con-
firmed his worst nightmares. He was still a prisoner of

his father's will, trapped in his duty to his ancestors, and burdened forever by his parents' sin.

"All ready now, girls," Laurel announced, pouring a large bourbon and branch water for herself and tea and milk for the others, all positioned around the dining room table for their daily afternoon meeting. Thunder and lightning clashed behind them, washing their faces with a deathly green light. "I should warn y'all that the radio report says the delta is flooding and the goddamn ol' muddy river is pouring out all over. Half the crypts in the Metairie cemetery are floating around and Christ only knows what's going to happen to our crops, *pardonnez-moi*, Suzette. Anyway, our crackbrained sea captain tells us that the *Richeleau* cannot leave port to deliver its wares and is bobbing around the dock like an apple in a barrel. Too bad old Captain Richeleau didn't settle somewhere *above* sea level. In addition, I have been unable to participate in a single set of tennis or round of golf and my nerves are tighter than a whore's garters, so let me just bring y'all up to date and then after the bourbon takes effect, I'll give the floor to whoever the hell wants it.

"Now, Philip and I have had a rather tedious but productive luncheon meeting with Señor Proust of the First Bank of New Orleans, and it seems that the combined effect of the Richeleau name and sharing fried catfish tidbits with the mayor and his *formidable spouse* has melted whatever latent paranoia and avarice the pallid little man may have had. He also, by the by, has an adorable little daughter, Christian name Hillary, whom I have invited to play with Louis, should he ever again be up to normal boyhood divertissement. Anyway, Señor Proust has offered no opposition to Louis being placed in Maybe's custody with Suzette and yours truly as co-trustees. So unless some bastard son from dear Poppa's infamous past comes forth, I see fairly smooth sailing.

"Proust will draw up certain documents that will basi-

cally set up an allowance schedule for Maybe to run the
household and provide for Louis's medical and personal
needs, and she will receive a check on the first of each
month. All incomes and the running of the estate will be
entrusted to the bank with Philip as overseer, and he will
in turn set up a troika of one lawyer, one accountant, and
himself. He will be present to keep the good ol' boys
honest until Louis is twenty-one. Hopefully, Philip will
have pounded enough of the *merde* into Louis by then that
he can run it himself with our help. The main job after
we get things in running order is to see that Louis heals
and doesn't turn out like his scum of a father or that
nigger whore of a mother, and that the shysters and
moneylenders are kept under control. Frankly, I think it
would be far better to sell this pretentious relic and get
Louis out of here for good, but Señor Anton made damn
sure that that doesn't happen. If Richeleau House leaves
Richeleau hands, Louis ends up with only a gimpy leg
and his goddamn caterpillars. Any questions?"

Suzette raised her hand.

"Suzette, darlin', this is not grade school; you will not
be sent to spend lunch hour facing the spider webs in the
corner if you speak without permission."

Suzette sighed. "Yes, Laurel. But being a younger sister
and the victim of years of sisterly lecturing it comes nat-
urally. I just wanted to ask one thing. There are still almost
eleven years until Louis is of majority, and since only the
Lord knows which of us will still be here, what can we
do to protect him if we are gone?"

Laurel looked first at her sister, then at Maybe, then
she took a long sip from her drink. "Well, darlin', I suggest
that you call upon your catholiconic armor and pray those
Vestal Virgins keep the fire going, and we all forswear
cigarettes, chitlins, and gin, 'cause that little lad is going
to need all the help he can get. I, for one, have a four-
year-old to care for, who will never be getting any older,

so I have already told His Holiness that I am not going anywhere and I suggest y'all do the same."

Suzette sighed, bracing against the power of her sister. "I'll do my very best, Laurel, but just in case the Lord has other ideas, I think we should draft our own little will, just to keep the 'shysters' and the 'good ol' boys,' as you so aptly put it, in line. God is often too busy to attend probate hearings."

"That sounds right to me, Miz Laurel." Maybe sat forward. "I'll sleep better if I know that boy is safe no matter who's here. You weren't there that night—that boy saw his daddy standin' over him crazy insane, his *own* daddy tried to kill him. Now he's a cripple on top. I worry so 'bout him. Miz Suzette's got a good point. Let's make sure he's seen after no matter what the Lord has in mind."

"Lo be it for me to interfere with the Divine plan. All right, girls, we'll write it ourselves and send it over to the shysters, make it all legal. Amen. Now I think I'll go run up and down the stairs for an hour or two till dinner. Court is adjourned until four o'clock tomorrow afternoon."

And so, right smack in the middle of this maternal maelstrom, Louis resumed what remained of his boyhood. As might be expected, Kate became his friend, the only person around in worse shape than he was, or at least so he thought at first. Later he realized that she was in just fine shape, her mind not clouded with memories or pain, her world simple and protected with absolutely no pressure or other folks' expectations weighing on her. Hers was a spirit filled with love and sweetness and being with her helped Louis relax his death grip on Maybe and begin to look out the window at the birds and butterflies. Eventually, he was able to journey across the grounds, his leg held steady with a brace, keeping his balance with a cane, hand-carved by one of the servants. He could now walk among his trees and creatures without doubling over in

grief, shadowed by his mother's ghost, tormented with
memory. When he felt strong enough he invited Kate to
join him. "Please, Laurel, I'll take care of her. I know my
way all around. I can teach her things."

Kate stood at his side towering over him. "Pleez, pleez,
Lal, I be good. I won't cry."

"Y'all are both hardly able to *stand up* alone. You just
make sure, Louis Richeleau, that you have her back by
lunch or I'll break your other leg, hear me?"

"Yes, yes, Laurel, we'll be back at the stroke of twelve."
Off they went wobbling down the meadows and into the
woods, Louis and his first companion, the baby sister he
had always wanted, holding his hand and listening to him
with wonder, that same old wonder he had shared with
his mother.

A sort of normalcy began to return to Louis's and Maybe's lives. After a time, Suzette departed, leaving him her
antique golden crucifix, which he wore around his neck
for the rest of his life, and the knowledge that he was
cared about. Soon after, Laurel and Kate left, breaking
his heart. "I'll write you every week and send you spec-
imens," he said, sobbing.

"No crying, Lou-is, or I'll spank yo' bottom," Kate
replied, crying right along with him.

Every Friday, Philip would come to visit, sitting with
him in his father's old study and explaining to his growing
young mind whatever he was old enough to grasp about
his enterprises. Louis liked this. In his own way it was
his revenge at his father, the Oedipal triumph complete:
a skinny, horn-rimmed, cripple-legged boy sitting in his
giant poppa's chair, the scrappy-tailed survivor of the
dogfight. Some of it went to his head, much to Maybe's
annoyance, but his asthma stopped and she was wise
enough to know that somehow these *business* meetings
with his elegant, educated *brother-in-law* had something to
do with it.

Louis grew, and his Collection grew. The Zephyr, the world's first stainless steel train, was introduced and Louis added a model train mania to his interests. "Someday Richeleau will include a railway," he announced to Maybe as she buckled up his brace before school.

"Yessirree, then we can send your worms and spiders first class deluxe, no mo' creepin' around the garden."

The thirties passed and before Maybe had let out her breath, it was 1939, Louis was sixteen, and German tanks were rolling into Poland.

While England and France were busy declaring war on Germany, Philip and Mr. Proust were frantically trying to keep a rein on Richeleau & Co. in a world and a country feverish with the infection of war.

The Depression was more or less over, leaving small reminders like Amos 'n' Andy—"I is flat as a pancake . . . I ain't got no money friends; all my friends is sympathy friends . . . dey listens an' feels sorry fo' me, but den . . . de's gone."

Louis's role model of the moment was Jack Armstrong, the All-American Boy who resembled a young version of Uncle Philip and had simplified his goals down to eating Wheaties, fighting bad guys, and bringing athletic glory to Hudson High. As war was being declared, Jack Armstrong sought the advice of a Tibetan monk who counseled (according to a poster in Louis's room), "Tell the boys and girls of the U.S. this world is theirs. If they have *hearts of gold*, a glorious new age awaits us. If they are *honest*, riches shall be theirs. If they are *kind*, they shall save the whole world from malice and meanness." Louis took this to heart, expounding on it at Laurel's house over fried chicken and hand-churned buttermilk.

"Why don't y'all send a copy to Señor Hitler, Louis, darlin', just in case he's missing his Wheaties these days, running around conquering Poland like he is. I'm sure he'd be grateful."

Louis flushed. "We've got to believe in something. We need our principles to fight for right and justice, that's what this country was founded on."

"Louis," Laurel teased, pausing to swallow an entire glass of buttermilk in one gulp. "I think you should telegraph this information to Suzette at once, tell her that Jack Armstrong will soon be replacing Señor Jesus Christ himself; she'll want to know, dear."

Everyone laughed, even Kate, everyone but Louis, who left Laurel's even more convinced that this was the only philosophy to follow.

To Louis it seemed a man's way, not brutal like Dick Tracy, bringing violence even into the comic strips— "I've got a tommy gun in my hand and it's in a barking mood." Honesty and hearts of gold, that was the ticket. As far away from the memory of his father as he could get.

CHAPTER 3

Louis and Maybe decided to celebrate the principles of *golden hearts* by opening Richeleau House for the first time since The Tragedy to all the workers, friends, neighbors, and employees of Richeleau & Co. for a grand New Year's Eve gala, bidding good-bye to the gloom and poverty of the thirties and welcoming the new decade, which was poised on the brink of trading bread lines for aircraft assembly lines and margarine for guns.

Maybe had never seen Louis so excited. He had grown into a large, square-bodied, good-looking young man with his mother's auburn hair and olive complexion. His sturdiness seemed to balance his impairment, giving him a rolling heavy gait and an air of sophistication far beyond his sixteen years. His eyes were dark and weak, covered still by the thick horn-rimmed glasses that were by now so much a part of his face that he seemed incomplete without them. He was quiet, partly because of the scar tissue still caking his spirit and partly because he had so many things filling his mind. First, there were his bugs, his library of entomology and nature books, then there

was his schoolwork and his involvement with Philip, Mr.
Proust, and the "shysters." He barely had time to sleep,
let alone talk. He was also shy, for his new manhood and
attractiveness were overshadowed by his vision of himself—frozen in time on the day of his tenth birthday.

When he was overtired, he would succumb to his
loneliness, and this combination of physical and emotional overload would lower his resistance to the constant
aching pain in his leg. The pain was always there, like a
baby picture kept in the well-worn wallet of an aged man.
Somehow he needed the pain to remind him of who he
was. The aching kept him from disappearing, from admitting that he was an orphan. His leg had become his
baby picture, his locket with one blond curl, his Purple
Heart. When the melding of pain and loneliness overwhelmed him, he would rise from his studies or restless
sleep and hobble, without his cane or brace, across the
house and down the stairs to Maybe's room, kneeling by
her side and lowering his tear-streaked face into her lap
as if time had stopped. Maybe never chided him for this
regression. "We is all lonely, frightened chillen lookin'
for that fat warm lap at least one-half of the time."

After one of these outbursts of need, Louis would armor
himself in bravado, cloaking his vulnerability in boorish-
ness until he could balance himself, put his Pimpernel
suit back in the closet, and relax. "Kindly disregard my
show of weakness. I am the master of this house and it
is best that we not forget the difference between us, Miss
Carver."

When it passed, Maybe would quietly but certainly call
it to his attention. "Louis Richeleau, sir, it is so nice to
have you home; there's been some terrible little pig's tit
of a boy passin' hisself off as you. I was fixin' to run him
right off—what a relief!"

This part of his personality worried her most, and she
saw danger in it for him and for his future wife and

children. She knew that it came from his fear and that it was his vilest enemy, for when he was in it, he was blinded by pomposity and illusion and could not see or hear the truth, struck blind and mute by his own self-doubt.

Among the guests invited to Louis's first gala event to sip French champagne (brought in by the Richeleau cargo ship) and feast on Maybe's Cajun delicacies and Creole cooking—platters of jambalaya, the rabbit steaming and the sauce so hot it watered the eyes; black-eyed peas; red beans and rice; hand-stuffed Portuguese sausage and okra; crayfish bisque and pompano en papillote; fried catfish; real turtle soup with rare Spanish sherry; kidneys and braised sweetbreads in cream and brandy; corn bread with red chilies; oysters so fresh they curled when you blew on them; crab cakes and berries as big as fists; French pastries and chocolate cake and coffee thick and black as night—were Mr. Proust and his daughter, Hillary.

Louis had met Hillary Proust only once, shortly after Laurel and Company had alighted to take charge of his future.

He was ten and she was twelve, and the scorn with which she entertained him, coupled with his rather severe ignorance of social protocol, left such an indelible and negative impression that Louis absolutely refused to repeat the rendezvous no matter how loudly Laurel protested.

Hillary Proust was as much an outcast in her own way as Louis was in his. Not by any violent waving of fate's hand or physical disability (though she was never to reach beyond five feet one inch in height, which enraged her to the point of frenzy—"How in hoary hell can I be powerful and intimidating if I'm a goddamn midget!"). Hillary's impairment came from her singular, hypnotizing originality, her manic bohemian temperament, and a total inability to adjust to the form and content of daily life.

"You were born under a shooting star and so every day

must be Bastille Day. You think your entire life should be a holiday, with none of the mundane concerns that occupy the rest of the world," her father would say as he wrote still another check for her latest project or passion.

Like Louis, she was an only child, raised in the strict, narrow bourgeois tradition of a banker and a housewife. Her mother died (Hillary always said of boredom) when Hillary was eight. By her thirteenth year she had reached puberty, her full height, and her limit with the slow, stifling sameness of her father's world. She was already a beauty: a tiny, small-boned, tightly packaged wire of a mademoiselle. She had a shiny cap of jet-black Betty Boop bobbed curls, creamy fair skin, and enormous gray-blue eyes, which she batted and rolled to effect. "I am wonderful; I will change the world," she told her mirror, her father, and whatever governess managed to last more than a month.

Finally, after weeks of Hillary's unrelenting outpouring of charm, tears, temper, and tease, Mr. Proust agreed to let her spend her teenage years abroad. Off she went, a tiny shooting star in an unknown galaxy, to her aunt's château in Deauville seeking excitement, adventure, and an alternative to real life.

On this New Year's Eve night, she had been back in New Orleans for just a month. She was now eighteen, superficially adept in French and Italian, speaking English with an accent extracted from the International Set, a sort of high English with Southern infusion, liberally sprinkled with foreign phrases. The plan had been for her to stay with her aunt until she adjusted and then to go off to a proper school in Switzerland. Somehow, she and her aunt, who was too much like Hillary herself to supervise with any authority, never got around to the Swiss school, and so underneath the patina of worldliness there was a young woman with a thirteen-year-old's schooling, a fact that never bothered Hillary one bit. "Le monde c'est mon école," she would announce, as her father pounded his head in frustration. And so it had been. She and her aunt had traveled Europe, the Orient, and India; she knew music and food and wine and could hold a rather enchanting conversation in various languages on a wide variety of subjects for approximately five minutes. "That's all you ever need to make an impression," her aunt counseled, and Hillary readily agreed. On the night she entered Louis's house and changed his life, Hillary Proust was a supremely self-confident eighteen-year-old woman with radiant charm, sexual experience, and a vast veneer of knowledge of Le Beau Monde, with no future plans, commitments, career incentives, or proper suitors.

From the moment Louis saw her, shimmying across the marble dance floor, a cigarette holder in one hand and a bottle of champagne in the other, he was finished, dumbstruck, addicted, entranced. He had never seen a girl like her. She was everything that he was not and he wanted her with all of his golden heart.

He followed her every move till almost midnight, watching her flirt and wiggle and posture and pose, patting her hair, powdering her straight small nose, afraid to approach her.

"Laurel, who is that black-haired girl with the pink, I think it's pink, some sort of pale color, satiny material, small built, dancing over by the stairway?" He had finally raised the courage to inquire.

Laurel, who was wafting slightly leeward after an excess of bourbon, locked him in piercingly meaningful eye contact. "The color is *mauve* and the name is Proust, Miss Hillary Proust, from whose company you ran screaming like a pickaninny many, many years ago, and who was so downcast by your rejection that she ran away to Europe and has only just returned. Would you like me to introduce y'all? I am sure her wounds have healed by now."

"No, no. I was just curious, so few new faces around

here. No, some other time . . . well, maybe, yes, I think
I should, rather rude not to, being her host, this is my
house after all. . . . Yes, if it's not taking you out of your
way."

Laurel weaved toward him, grinning wickedly. "Why,
I would be delighted. The stroll will do me good, help
evaporate some of the alcohol. Come along."

Louis took his sister's arm and let her half lead, half
push him through the parlor, into the cavernous entry
where Hillary reigned, sitting cross-legged on the stairway lecturing one of the shysters on monetary concerns.
"If you were smart, monsieur, you would take all your
clients' assets and buy DuPont stock! Buy, buy, buy! Look
at my legs, do you know what that is on my legs? That
is nylon, *cara mia.* Nylon stockings from Mr. DuPont's
company. They have just released four thousand pairs
onto the market and I will gladly wager that they will be
snapped up before you can say *à votre santé.* Nylon is the
wave of the future and you may quote me." She patted
her head, her eyes moving from her audience of one
around the room, searching for new challenges, just as
Louis and Laurel emerged from the crowd heading toward
her. She saw them and waited, recrossing her legs and
puffing furiously on her French cigarette.

"Hillary, dear, I would like to present our host for this
ambitious evening of drunkenness and gluttony, my baby
half-brother, Louis Richeleau. Y'all met many years ago
before puberty, when boys and girls still regarded one
another as objects of scorn, which has all changed now
that lust has entered, and will only reappear after marriage. Louis, may I present Miss Hillary Proust."

Hillary offered her free hand, smelling of smoke and
French perfume, warm and soft as moss, and he took it
and put it to his trembling lips. "So glad you could come,
Miss Proust, it is an honor."

Hillary felt the trembling in his hand and on his lips

and the stiff wet-coldness of his fingers and knew that he
was hers. Knew it instantly, calmly, without arrogance.
Men had sought her, made love to her, flattered her, but
no one had ever adored her or loved her before. Now
suddenly, this dark, husky boy-man, with his cane and
his thick foggy spectacles, Lord of all New Orleans, was
hers.

"I'm very glad that I could come, Mr. Richeleau. I must
say that your villa is *bellissima*, as fine as any I saw in
England or on the Continent, and I would adore a personal tour at your earliest convenience."

Laurel yawned. "Well, now that that's done, I think I
have oozed enough bourbon out of my Southern pores
to reload, so if Scarlett and Rhett will pardon me, I'll
leave y'all." Laurel curtsied and turned to go, thought a
minute, and leaned into Louis's shoulder putting her lips
to his ear. "Go slow, darlin', this here is a hellcat and
y'all never even had a kitty."

He barely heard her. "I would be happy to show you
Richeleau House, if you would be so kind as to follow
me, we can start in the garden."

"*Très bien,*" said Hillary, smoothing her new nylon stockings and batting her cat eyes at Louis. "May I take your
arm?"

Louis blushed; he had never held a beautiful girl's arm
before. "Certainly."

She smiled at him, looking directly into his eyes, telling
him that she understood what was happening, even though
he didn't then, nor ever would quite understand it himself.

CHAPTER 4

O n December 7, 1941, shortly after Louis's eight-eenth birthday, the Japanese invaded paradise. Flying in low and fast over the breathtaking beauty of the ancient volcanic mountains, which during the course of several million years had broken through the surface of the sea to form the archipelagos, isolated in the North Pacific two thousand miles in any direction from civili-zation, the Japanese ripped the Hawaiian Islands from their bovine innocence. They screeched into Oahu along with the lavender sunrise and blasted the warm, wavy aquamarine port into the future, sending most of the U.S. fleet and shipboard villages full of young American men to deep, kelp-tangled death.

For Louis, the shock of the news was exacerbated by his personal despair. Here was the keeper of Jack Arm-strong's flame, wanting beyond all else to fight for truth, justice, and the American way and physically unaccept-able to all branches of the armed forces.

It enraged and humiliated him, and with these feelings came nightmares from the past: a terrified boy crouching in the corner, pointed pistols, agony, endings. Bitterness began to form around the sac of his golden heart, tightening his jaw and adding a cynical edge to his voice. One by one the young men went while Louis watched and stayed.

The only consolation was Hillary, who had replaced his Collection as the sacred obsession of his life.

The two years since they met had been a funhouse maze of ecstasy and angst for Louis. What, after all, could a sixteen-year-old boy-man do? He was too young to court her properly or request her hand. She played with him, letting him escort her to Mardi Gras cotillions, only to leave him standing in the corner as she waltzed and jitterbugged with the eligible young scions of Southern society. "I don't know why they're all so stuffy about their precious 'Mardi Gras.' They should just call it 'Fat Tuesday' and stop taking the whole silly thing so seriously. All those old horny toads and their secret Krewes! As if anyone cares who they are! Don't you ever get caught up in that 'fine family' silliness. The only Krewe for me is the 'Zulu Krewe'—put a golden coconut on my head and let me go. Oh, pardon, Louie, I see someone I must dance with."

In Hillary terms, the war worked rather well for Louis. No more young men, no more merriment, no more nylon stockings, French champagne, jaunts abroad, or couturier clothes. The government issued decrees limiting the length of hems, the yards of fabric per garment, width of shirt collar and cuff, and number of buttons. Zippers were rationed, creating the wraparound skirt craze; narrow hems brought shorter dresses, less fabric made them narrower, and military chic was born.

Hillary took all of this quite well. Off she would go in her Katharine Hepburn trousers, General Eisenhower jacket, and Royal Air Force–inspired chapeau, to fold bandages at the Red Cross headquarters on Canal Street.

With little difficulty, she managed to convert the in-
dignity of war to one enormous Clark Gable movie. She
hostessed at the Louisiana version of the Hollywood Can-
teen, wheeled a Cheerfulness Cart up and down the dismal war-tainted corridors of the V.A. hospital, and held
teas at Richeleau House to help sell war bonds. She was
not without sensitivity and she knew instinctively that
Louis was suffering his isolation from the heat of the
storm. After all, she was, though she would never admit
it, waiting for him to catch up to her. She knew that
someday he would ask her to be Madame Richeleau, and
this idea was highly attractive to her. She could see herself presiding over galas and garden parties, running the
import-export enterprise, ruling side by side with Louis
in business and society. She would have power, money,
a position from which to fulfill the promise to her mirror,
"I will change the world!" How she would do this had
not occurred to her as yet, but regardless, her future shone
before her as bright as the neon lights on Bourbon Street
and as clear as the sweet wail of a Dixieland sax.

Louis's malaise deepened, and Hillary took pity. "Louie,
chou, you must stop this moping! Do you think I want
you off in some god-awful place like Rumania or Guam
getting malaria or stepping on a land mine! We all need
you here. Just think of poor Maybe and Richeleau House,
what would become of everything without you?" She would
hold his cold hands and kiss his forehead, and for a while
he would be better, but only for a while.

Hillary knew that there was one more thing she could
try.

It was time to let him make love to her, and it was her
duty to help him through his depression. She approached
the task as a combination Mata Hari and Eleanor Roosevelt.

One evening after a war bond cocktail soiree at Louis's
house, when they had both consumed far too many mar-

tinis (Hillary's new World War II drink, borrowed from
a Franchot Tone movie that left her with the impression
that the war was being fought over martinis and fox-trots
in the British officers' club bar), she led Louis upstairs to
his mother's old suite, which was now his own. He sank
down on the bed, motionless with excitement and tension, watching his tiny goddess remove her black,
shoulder-padded cocktail suit with the golden eagle ap-
pliquéd on the right sleeve. She stood over him smiling
softly in the moonlight, stripping garment by garment
until she was naked: firm, pointed, rose-nippled breasts;
small, tapered waist; graceful, slender legs. "Now you,
Louie," she whispered, lying down beside him and feeling
his body stiffen.

"I can't. My leg, it's ugly, you'll be frightened, no one
has ever seen me, I've never . . ."

"I know, *chéri*. I'll do it for you." Gently, efficiently,
she undressed him. When she reached the brace, she
unbuckled it, freed his leg, pulled off the long heavy
stocking and sat naked and silent, looking at it, running
her finger over the wound, feeling the scars and knotted
bones. "Is this where the bullet entered?"

Louis nodded, so overwhelmed by her sensual warmth,
her unexpected tenderness, that he knew if he spoke he
would begin to sob and never be able to stop.

It was at this moment as she sat beside him, understanding for the first time the depth of his loneliness, that
she knew she loved him. Her eyes filled with tears of
compassion and she bent her head to his naked, mauled
limb and kissed the place the bullet had torn.

They made love together with a sweet, tearful sultriness
that only occurs on a pure moment of emotional surprise,
when there are no defenses, just total trust, surrender,
need, openness. It was a moment of such closeness that
neither of them would ever forget, and it bound them
forever.

Soon after the night of Louis's deflowering and Hillary's avowal of love, the office of the secretary of the navy contacted Philip, who in turn contacted Louis about the possibility of converting the Richeleau cargo ship for wartime service. This involvement lifted him from his black hole and gave him a sense of service and purpose. Before it met its heroic end, sunk by German U-boats on its tenth Atlantic crossing, Louis had gained self-confidence and the respect of his fellow citizens, and this in turn helped him as a lover and a suitor.

On June 7, 1944, the day after what remained of the 176,000 troops who had landed on the historic Normandy coast waded onto Omaha Beach sealing the fate of the Krauts' Crusade, Louis asked Hillary to be his wife.

"*Oui*," she replied. He had for all intents and purposes caught up with her.

The timing was right. He was soon to turn twenty-one and the control of the estate would fall into his hands. A smart and energetic helpmate could only make the difficult and heavy burden lighter.

CHAPTER 5

Exactly five years to the night of their first grown-up meeting, December 31, 1944, Louis Richeleau married Hillary Proust (which turned out to be fortuitous, since she was at the time six weeks pregnant).

Their first child, Alexander, was born amidst the manic, romantic turmoil that surrounded V-J Day and the end of the war.

It was not a romantic time for Hillary, however, who was so snugly built that childbirth was a three-day night-mare that she would later refer to as "the Siege of Stalin-grad, Southern style."

All of the negatives of the experience were soon ob-literated by the presence of her first, fat, handsome, black-haired boy child. He was her. A male replica from nose to dimpled knee. Her creation, the first productive release of her bridled energy; the first thing of substance in her life and her connection was instantaneous and too pow-erful to be good for either of them.

"Now I know how I'll alter the world, Louie. My chil-dren! I'll give the world the most magnificent children it has ever known, and they'll do great things, historic things!"

At the time, she passionately believed what she said, ignoring Louis, who was half-frozen with terror at this new responsibility and his fear of repeating his father's parental pilgrimage to the underworld, and consequently paid Hillary's messianics little mind.

"When he stops sucking and screaming, we'll see about his changing the world, sugar."

They played house and were happy as long as they stayed in the game, away from disturbances.

Maybe took to the care of Alexander with the same wistful ease she had brought to Louis, only this time tinged with the sadness of memory.

She felt at times as if no one had grown up, just merely multiplied, so that now she had three children to care for: Louis, Hillary, and Alexander. She had been as close to Louis as his conscience when he was a boy, but now that he was a man, they did not quite know how to treat one another. She knew that he often needed her and fought his desire to hobble across the dark night-shadowed halls and bury his face in her warm fragrant lap, and this made her sad with longing for the past and worried for his future. He loved Hillary, but Hillary was also a child, though a spunkier and wiser child than Louis, and so Maybe guided her gently, helping Louis through his wife, teaching her about him and how to help him be a man.

Maybe and Laurel continued to support him with the business, and Philip still came every week, although Maybe worried about this, knowing that he leaned too much on Philip, and that this made him insecure and arrogant. She would have to speak to Laurel and Philip about it soon. The shift of power was necessary for Louis to remove his father's presence from the house and for him to truly respect himself. He had a son of his own to consider now, and from what Maybe saw, she knew he would need

all the self-esteem he could grab to handle his child properly.

Hillary knew a lot of what Maybe knew about Louis,
but on a more romantic level of reality. She saw him as
a heroic warrior, a maimed but valiant hero. He had
survived his father and thus he would always overcome
adversity. This view allowed her to wade around the same
worries that sank Maybe. She let Maybe do the unro-
mantic thinking for her. Besides, Hillary had a lot to keep
her mind occupied. First there was the joyless task of
regaining her slender figure. Then there were the endless
thank-you notes, christening arrangements, and visits from
the "ooh and ahers" as she called them. She was at the
same time immersed in what would later turn out to be
a pathological dedication to the redecorating of Richeleau
House in accordance with the trend of the moment. There
was the shopping for new clothes, linens, silver, and baby
paraphernalia and courses and books on child psychology,
toilet training, and new developments in preschool education to ponder.

"That baby can't even sit hisself up and you've got him
off to college," Maybe muttered as she followed Hillary's
latest dictum.

"If he's going to be great, there isn't one moment to
lose. Why, I read that he can learn French from records
by osmosis. I just sent away for a complete set. Just
imagine, Maybe, dear, he could learn French, Latin, Italian, even German, now that all that mess is over, before
he even goes to school! He'll be the first president from
New Orleans—you can quote me."

"I'd like to see 'em stand on his hind legs first, if you
don't mind." Maybe would shake her head at this silliness,
knowing that once again she would have to put in a lot
of time undoing well-intentioned maternal whims.

Hillary began all of her maternal and decorating plans
with steely determination and energy, convinced that she

had found her calling at last and that her passion would
never wane. Unfortunately, the fatal flaw in her character
was her restless search for the next magic something, and
it was stronger than all her good intentions. Her figure
returned and her attention wandered, and it was a fine
time for wandering attention. The war was over and the
good guys had won.

Probably to offset the horrific aftermath of Hitler and
the moral fallout from Hiroshima, and to make digestible
the hacking up like a caveman's dinner of Eastern Europe, the young survivors were tap dancing and roller-
skating away from the horror faster than the sound of a
nickel falling into one of the newfangled jukeboxes.

Hillary time-stepped right into the center. She was now
almost twenty-four years old and already satisfying her
womanly requirements, having given up her carefree youth
before she was finished with it. To compensate, she took
to dressing in the style of teenage girls, complete with
bobby sox, Louis's rolled-up jeans, and saddle shoes; jit-
terbugging to the miraculous new music. She worshiped
Frank Sinatra. "I read in Robert Ruark's column that 'The
Voice' was seen in Havana, Cuba, having supper with
Lucky Luciano—isn't that the *très* evilest news! J'aime le
Mafia."

She styled her hair like her favorite New Orleanian,
Dorothy Lamour, knitted argyle socks for Louis and the
baby, and scorned her fellow young matrons of good
family who were rapidly turning into younger versions of
their mothers. Hillary refused to join them, the club-
women and do-gooders with edemaed ankles, flowered
hats, and stone martens crawling around their shoulders
in bewilderment; fighting the Red Menace and playing
bridge during the week, and hoeing up their abandoned
victory gardens on the sabbath. Not for Hillary. The war
was over, she was young and pretty, rich and adored,
and the party was back on. No more hoarding bacon

grease and empty toothpaste tubes; no more "Point Values," ration stamps, and narrow lapels. Mr. Dior unfurled his bolts of taffeta and Hillary was first in line. She sported the widest hems, the fullest skirts, twirling inside her first Dior like a tiny ballerina set atop a crystal ball.

Norman Rockwell retired Willis Gillis, Joe Palooka went back to the ring, and Audie Murphy took his medals to Hollywood. Hillary bought a wired strapless bra, a nylon drip-dry dress, and ten thousand shares of jukebox stock.

"See, Louie, no one listened to me about nylon, now just look at this dress!" she demanded, dunking it dramatically up and down in their marble bathroom sink. "Now, I am *not* going to wait for you and the shysters to catch on to jukeboxes. Did you know that Americans are currently popping *five billion* nickels per year into the ugly things? I'm buying now!"

As with everything Hillary wanted, Louis acquiesced. It was really quite simple; he worshiped her. She brought him out of the darkness and into the light. She threw away his brace and his crutch and refused to allow him the morbid safety of his cherished wound. "Hobble, waddle like a goddamn duck—but no more braces!"

She massaged his leg with Spanish turtle oil and made him exercise. She taught him to tap dance. She lit him up. He carried a heavy weight on his young shoulders and too much of his time was spent role-playing for others' expectations. He sat in his father's study surrounded by evil spirits, thinking that he could conquer them, never understanding that with ghosts, goblins, and poisonous persons, the only way to win is to lock the door and leave the premises.

He was bent on proving that he was not his father, yet he was driven toward becoming his father by wrestling with the mad bull; it was his spirit that was being gouged. As he had as a boy, he hid in his postures and lost the ability to trust himself. He played the role of scion, busi-

nessman, father, and leader. It was only with Hillary,
who had kissed his mangled shame and offered her love
and her light, that he was himself.

Louis turned his old room into a laboratory for his
"critters," as Maybe still called them. All of the furniture
was removed, the wood floors covered with rubber mats,
the ceiling hinged with fluorescent lights. In the center
was the old oak table from the laundry room laden with
spoils, a microscope, pins, knives, formaldehyde, and
other exotic accoutrements of the avid entomology buff.
The bookcases, windowsills, and corners were stacked
with Louis's library of animal, vegetable, and mineral books
and it was in here that he relaxed, without stiffening self-
consciousness and doubt. Hillary would sit with him,
cross-legged on one of his tall laboratory stools, a bottle
of French champagne set neatly between jars of spiders
and beetles, teasing him gently as he instructed and shared
his obsession with her.

"Someday, hon, I will take you to the Galápagos, just
like Darwin. We'll take Alexander, too. You can wander
among the iguanas while they sun themselves, as if you
had stepped back in time, back before the dinosaurs.

"These marine iguanas are remarkable, Hil. They're
cold-blooded, like all reptiles, but they cannot generate
their own heat, they rely totally on the sun, like batteries
recharge, they sunbathe until their body temperature rises
high enough for them to go swimming to hunt for food.
They have to be careful about getting chilled or they lose
their strength and can't swim, so they concentrate their
heat in the center of their bodies, like solar conductors.
After they feed, they scramble back onto the rocks to
recharge their bodies with the sun. Isn't that amazing?"

"I don't see anything amazing about it. I do exactly the
same thing, all summer long, and I'm a lot easier on the
eye than one of those horrible old lizards. Why, they
would frighten our little baby to death."

"No. If he learns like I did, like my mother taught me, from when he's small, he won't be afraid; he'll see their wonder. It helps understanding what life means, where it all began, how much greater nature is than we are. It builds spiritual awareness and humility."

"Well, we could probably achieve the same thing with a good hot bowl of real Southern-style turtle soup, shell and all, explain about ancient creatures right in our fine old house. Now take a sip of this icy old bubbly and a bite of these reptilian malossol eggs and tell me about the dinosaurs, again. I love the dinosaurs."

If it is true that a well-lived life leaves no loose ends, that before the journey on into mulch or oblivion, peace demands the tying of all the bits of string, the trudging back over every skipped step, spiritual shortcut, and self-deception of our lives, then what happened to Hillary and Louis may possibly be accepted as the price for the refusal to take the high road. The one of truth of self. This is one possibility, though God knows their dues paying, their final reckoning seems undue punishment for the sins of messy emotional housekeeping by well-meaning people. It may just have been the luck of the draw. Hillary and Louis drew the joker.

Hillary's passion for Alexander was fierce when he was smiling, happy, powdered, and dry. She would swoop down, snatching him up in her sweet perfumed arms, smothering him with kisses and declarations of devotion and homage. "You are the most beautiful baby boy on God's earth; you are perfect; you will do great things, great, great things! My darling, sweetest, precious boy. Momma adores you. Kiss me, kiss me, Zander, my joy, my rex—my Mardi Gras king!"

This passion had a way of deserting her, and consequently him, when he wasn't smiling, dry, happy, or otherwise perfect. When her ecstasy was disrupted by the pragmatic reality of motherhood, her panic at the void in her daily world propelled her into more and more frantic flights of make-believe. A new wardrobe. A more au courant color scheme for the ballroom. A hot new business to champion. Hillary, scoring her quick fixes of fantasy, adrenaline pumping through her veins, flushing her cheeks, keeping her up for a while longer.

Other things were happening. Her darling baby grew, moving into personhood, speaking and demanding and seeing more clearly. It frightened her and Louis to death. She had nothing to replace her conviction that in her children lay her road to glory, and neither did Louis, who was committed to replaying the role of the Richeleau Man, sprouting heirs like corn stalks to build the empire. Hillary's body fought back as if knowing that she could not really cope with the demands of mothering real growing beings who did not stop frozen like bugs in ice at babyhood, but pushed forth to demand and question. She conceived and aborted, conceived and aborted until finally, when Alexander was five, she gave birth to a little girl, Clara Aurelia Richeleau. "We'll call her Clara after Clara Barton, Louie, and she will have courage and convictions, not like one of those rancid belles of our day."

For a short time she was rapturous, filled with the same magic gauze of romance that shrouded her after Alexander's birth. But the years and the miscarriages and the growing emptiness within had taken her energy and defenses from her, and she gladly turned her daughter over to Maybe's waiting arms, staying in her room, reading *Forever Amber* and the Kinsey Report, and watching her miraculous new addiction, television. "They're selling a hundred thousand of these marvelous things every week; now, Louie, tell the shysters to order us twenty thousand shares of Motorola stock, at once. This is the future!"

Meanwhile, Louis's loose ends were all tangled up inside his handsome, troubled head like a kitten in the knitting yarn. His night terrors returned, the old dreams of whizzing toward the death head—Anton and Aurelia grinning down at him. Life was moving too fast for him. His son was a boy, not a baby, looking at him with love and uncertainty as he had looked at his father. He longed to hold him, tickle him, coo with him, sniff in his child scents, and hold him close. But he could not. He acted the role of father using the only pathetic role model he'd ever had—his own. He sprinkled this with bits of Maybe, Philip, Laurel, and Suzette, creating an erratic proselytizing caricature, a costume hiding a frightened and overburdened young man.

One morning, when Alexander was three, Laurel came, bringing with her Kate and the lawyers. "Louis, Philip's had a stroke. He can't talk. He can't see. He'll be of no more help to you now. I'm sorry, darlin', but now I have two helpless children to care for. You're on your own, baby."

Louis felt as if he had been attacked by bandits, thrown to the mud, beaten, and robbed. Pain shot up his bad leg, tears spurted from his eyes. Kate saw at once. "Lou-is, sad, LaLa. Make Lou-is happy. No cry, Lou-is, or I spank yo' bottom."

Laurel took his hands and held them tight, forcing him to meet her hard, steady eyes. "Now, you listen here, Louis Richeleau. You are fine, just as you are. You will do the best that you can. You are not Anton or any of our sordid, lunatic old forefathers. I said long ago, the best thing for you to do would be to sell this whole goddamn kettle of snakes and get out of Louisiana. But I don't think you will. No one can take anything from you now. For God's sake, Hillary's father is the only one outside of us who's ever *seen* Anton's will! Do what makes life safer for you and your family. You have nothing to prove to us. Don't waste your life on a herd of whitewhiskered apparitions. Let go, Louis."

"Yeah, Lou-is. Let's go," said Kate, resting her graying head on his shoulders.

But Louis could not let go. He began to venture out into the public world more, gave speeches for the chamber of commerce, was elected to the board of the New Orleans Country Club, and spurred Hillary on with her childbearing efforts. "Hil, we've inherited the Richeleau responsibility to reproduce." Their lovemaking became technical, formal, distant. With each of Hillary's failures, her return to merriment took longer and dwindled faster and so Louis could no longer rely on her light to warm him and pull him out of himself. He was too old to lean on Maybe and afraid of how much she saw into him. He did not want her truth anymore; he was afraid of her truth.

By Clara's second birthday, Hillary mustered her energy together and joined an amateur theater company. She was just thirty, still lovely though too thin and without the vibrancy of her young womanhood. In her daydreams, this was the start of a serious career in the theater where she would find herself at last. To her delight, she was cast as Blanche DuBois in her idol Tennessee Williams's Pulitzer Prize—winning play, and she threw herself into the role to the point of hanging out on Decatur Street, soaking up atmosphere, neglecting her children and Louis. She recited her part while Louis dissected swamp frogs. "I don't want realism! I want magic! I try to give that to people. I misrepresent things to them. I don't tell the truth, I tell what ought to be the truth."

When the play was over and no New York agents flocked around with offers of glamour and glory, she grew bored and decided instead to redo the music room in the brand new modern look.

She and Louis clung together now more like lost siblings than man and wife while Maybe held the family in place, a solid human dam set against the rising delta.

CHAPTER 6

Alexander worshiped his baby sister. He became her champion, teacher, and protector. With Maybe and baby Clara he could give love without fear of his father's rejection or his mother's hysteria. Clara was his baby as far as he was concerned, and he would save her from the Commies, the Bomb, and all the other scary stuff he heard his parents talking about when they thought he wasn't listening.

By Clara's third year, she and Alexander were almost identical in coloring and features, photocopies of Hillary in visage if not spirit. Alexander was serious, like his father. He was quiet, cautious, and self-critical, as if he supplied his own parental disapproval whipped up from a quite efficient and sinister machine inside him, punishing and criticizing even when Louis was not, which was rare. Louis harped at Alexander; Hillary suffocated him.

Clara had a younger sibling's ability to observe and learn from the travails above—and, after Adam's birth, below. She had inherited her mother's energy and charm, but it was enlarged by a rock-hard sense of reality. She

was not flighty and she was not afraid to see what was.
She gazed at her beloved and troubled family and what
she saw gave her purpose and made her love deeper. She
had her mother's missing piece.

Alexander was a pre—Cold War baby in a hothouse
climate, where the problems of the country often seemed
remote and unimportant. But Clara entered in time for
the June 25, 1950, White House cable from the United
States Embassy in Seoul. North Korean forces had invaded the Republic of Korea and even the Richeleaus felt
the heat.

Louis submerged himself in his old World War II
depression, watching the war from the sidelines with resentment and guilt. Hillary rallied enough to commission
a bomb shelter/rumpus room for all the neighbors and
Richeleau workers. This ambitious and timely project
brought her to the attention of the press and the local
television station. She began to appear, offering dramatic
elegiac speeches on the "responsibility of Southern women
to stop the war and ban the bomb." She was quite successful and had power of her own for the first time in her
life and she clutched at it. She dragged Louis, Zander,
and baby Clara to the station, pleading to New Orleans
from the heart of her perfect family.

"If the H-bomb were dropped on New Orleans, a cloud
of radioactive dust would rise twenty-five miles into the
stratosphere and spread one hundred miles across the sky.
Then a fireball four miles in diameter would vaporize
everything from the airport to the Garden District, from
Jackson Square to the west bank of the river, incinerating
everything in its path, leaving a giant, molten crater in
place of our beloved city, and destroying the Mississippi
forever. Whatever was left alive would die of radiation
poisoning." Delivering these chilling words, her fine family surrounding her, was heady stuff.

Hillary received a personal, handwritten letter from

Mamie and Dwight, thanking her for her work and "concern for the American family and the land we love."

Talk started about Louis running for governor. Louis was thrilled and horrified by the attention and the idea of running for office, but he also knew that being governor would prove his worth; stuffing Anton's ghost back up in the attic. Hillary loved the idea, it resoled her magic slippers and brought her out of her room. She turned off the TV, canceled her subscriptions to *Vogue, Collier's, Vanity Fair*, and the endless ladies and fan magazines with which she passed her days, and became more active in the lives of her children and husband.

"Louie, *chou*, I think we should sit down with Laurel and have a good, straight talk about this governor thing. Philip was mayor a long time, I bet she knows the ropes. Let's do it soon, it takes eons to plan a campaign, create an image, and all the rest."

"I already know what Laurel will say. She'll say I'm dead crazy, she hated all that phony, avaricious nonsense."

"Honey, she doesn't have to approve to give information, now does she?"

"No, I guess not. Hil, do you really think I could? It would be wonderful for the family, for our children, but I don't know anything about politics, I could get in way over my head. I wouldn't want to do anything to disgrace our name."

Hillary put her hand over his mouth. "Now hush up! You're as smart as Mr. Eisenhower or any of those old wind bags. If you can learn all about nature, you can surely learn all about the Louisiana legislature! Who's up there in Baton Rouge anyway but a bunch of bayou hillbillies and Creole fops. You'll be divine!"

Louis glowed in the reflected light of her praise. "Well, it's something to consider."

While he considered, Hillary proceeded to have three more miscarriages, finally producing her last child, Adam, and ending her ordeal. "One more pregnancy, Hillary, and your innards will be down around your ankles," said the doctor after she signed the tubal ligation consent. But the toll of motherhood had already been taken. She had lost her luster and her strength, and she knew it. What was left was her frustration and nervous energy, which she used like the powder that covered her fine aging face, as a prosthesis for enthusiasm.

When Adam Richeleau was born, his brother Zander was eight and his sister Clara three. Maybe hired a full-time nurse and cook to help her, but from the moment she set eyes on Adam, watched him push forth from Hillary's tiny tortured body, she knew that he would need her more than anyone since Louis was born.

PART TWO
ADAM'S
BOOK

CHAPTER 7

Adam was born calm. His midnight-blue eyes were open as soon as his perfectly shaped head poked out from between his mother's slender legs; he never cried. He was already breathing and he smiled at her (she swore), though everyone but Maybe, who was at her side, said this was not possible. He was so physically different that no one ever quite got used to him. His hair was pure white gold, his skin as pale and smooth as Ivory soap. Louis teased Hillary about the "milkman" and if it hadn't been for Adam's striking structural resemblance to his grandmother Aurelia, Louis probably would have believed that someone else had fathered his last child.

If Louis was stiff and intimidated by Alexander, he was paralyzed by Adam. Even as an infant, Adam was so serene and delicate and self-contained that Louis felt the child could see into his mind. Only with Clara, as with Hillary, could he let down, relax, allow himself the incomparable beauty of paternal love.

Clara was a saucy, chunky, easygoing little girl, perennially dressed in Hillary's baubles, waddling about the vast house, her fat little feet stuffed into Hillary's shoes, with Hillary's earrings and hats bedecking her round dark head.

"Clara purty. Me, Momma. Me cute. I love me. Zander loves me, too. I hate the baby, the baby's yugly." Her jealousy toward Adam was amusing to everyone but Clara and Maybe. Maybe slept in Adam's room, terrified that Clara would make good one of her countless threats. "Shush, Clara, lamb, Adam's sleeping now, you go play with Zander." Maybe would intercept her sneaking up beside Adam's crib.

"He not sleepin'. He died already. We gonna put him in a jar on Poppa's table."

Maybe took to locking the door when Clara was around, just in case.

For the next few years life at the Richeleaus moved calmly, the ebb and flow of gentry life rising to storm now and then, but quickly settling back into windless seas. Hillary kept working on Louis about politics and got him to go so far as enrolling in several government and political science courses at Tulane and joining the Young Democrats. She kept up her media efforts, writing "A Mother's View" column for the Sunday family page of the *Picayune* and holding anti–H-bomb luncheons at Richeleau House. Alexander and Clara were in school now, and Hillary had long, empty hours to fill. Louis was so overwhelmed with running his business that he was rarely home till late and preoccupied when he was. "Sell the damn business. We don't have any fun, Louie. We never travel anywhere. I'll rot in stinking Lusiana just like I always feared."

Louis would have been delighted to sell everything and spend the rest of his life with his wife and children and his bugs, but first, he had absolutely no idea how to go about it, and second, he was still haunted by his father's warning. To sell was to fail or be met in hell, and he could not accept either possibility. He had kept his father's note. It had burned into his heart and branded him. The image of his father, whiskers flying through the hellfire—watching his every move, waiting to smite him—had never left his consciousness.

"I can't do that now, Hil. But things will slow down, we'll take a cruise on the S.S. *France* this summer, I promise." When summer came, he had crop troubles and so, for the first time since their marriage, Hillary went off without him, taking Alexander with her to her aunt's old bastion in Deauville. She felt young again, free and carefree. Alexander had never seen her so relaxed.

"Zander, baby, your old momma used to be some hot cookie. Why, when I was just fourteen I was speaking Italian and sipping French champagne. I even went to *India*. You listen to me, now, you make damn sure that just as soon as you can, you get your gorgeous self out of Louisiana and see the world. We're going to give you the finest education any boy ever had. Have you been workin' on those new French words I gave you? You're almost ten years old now, you haven't a moment to waste. You're going to be president or at least a United States senator. I know it as well as my own face. I'm counting on you, my darling boy."

"Je voudrais un table pour deux, s'il vous plaît," replied Alexander, desperate to please her, to measure up to the accelerating expectations all around him.

"Poppa says I must learn about nature, that that's more important than anything. I'm trying, but everything makes me sick. He says it shouldn't, that it never made him sick, but it does. It makes Clara sick, too."

"Well, your poppa loves his Collection very, very much, and you must try not to let him know that it makes you ill because it means so much to him that you children share his interest. I'll tell you what I do when he's working on something real horrid and slimy. I pretend that it's a beautiful flower, I just make the awful thing go away. If you concentrate you can do it, and then you won't even see what's really there. Now, enough of this. I'm going to take you and Auntie to lunch and teach you all about fine food—you must know about food to be a senator."

"*Mais oui*, Mama," said Alexander, taking her hand, flushed with the glamour and his singular position in her company.

"Très, très bien, Zander, mon amour."

While they were gone Hillary's father died and ended Louis's last bulwark of support. Hillary sailed back, looking pale and frightened, throwing herself into Louis's waiting arms.

While Hillary and Louis huddled together, Maybe and her brood began to get out and around. She was determined that the children would not grow up as Louis had, hidden away from the world and reality. They loved being with her, finding nothing unusual about her speech or manner, even when people would smirk or stare at her.

"That there's a colored lady trapped inside a Cajun body," they heard the old black man who washed the cars saying to the housekeeper. It made no sense to them.

Into the French Quarter they would march, Zander, wide-eyed and just eleven, holding six-year-old Clara's warm pudgy hand, three-year-old Adam wheeled before her in a cast-off stroller (so as not to be conspicuous). Women stopped them on the street to gaga over Adam. "What a beautiful little girl, look at those eyes, I've never seen eyes that color blue. Why, they're aquamarine, I swear."

"He's a boy, lady!" Clara would shout, still coiled with jealousy though edging slowly beyond the murder stage. Maybe would tighten; somehow, she knew it wasn't right, now that he was growing, that everyone took him for a girl. In spite of Hillary's protests, she cut his golden curls

short and kept him in dark-colored clothes, but still it
happened.

This odd foursome would always follow the same route,
starting at the produce section of the French Market,
wandering through, picking peaches and melons as big
as basketballs, sniffing garlic hanging in coiled strings
from the walls and ceiling. Then they'd march down to
the Café du Monde and eat *beignets* blizzarded with powdered sugar until their bellies puffed out. "Not as good
as yours," Clara always said (after she was finished), and
Adam and Zander loudly agreed.

They would sit for a while in Jackson Square Park
watching stick-skinny black boys tap dancing in the moist
afternoon air; stiff-kneed, solemn. Zander was fascinated
by these boys, on their own, out of school, bringing
home quarters and nickles to help out. Children's bodies
with ancient faces, out in the street with no one to answer
to, soft-shoeing in the heat until their shirts ran with
sweat. They saw drunks on Bourbon Street, and hobos
picking in the trash cans and everywhere was the sick
sweet smell of sewage and garbage kept too long in the
sun, an odor they had never smelled before and one that
they would never forget. They heard about the black
bottom and shotgun houses ("So narrow one shot pass
right on through,"), Bessie Smith and black vaudeville.
They gobbled fried oysters and "po' boys" and stared in
gap-mouthed fascination at the pictures of near-naked
girls on the strip joint billboards. Then off they'd march
to hear Maybe's black foster uncle, who played piano in
a Dixieland band on St. Peter Street. They saw crazy
people, poor people, even a lady with orange hair and
hardly any clothes on wearing bright fluorescent pink
shoes that Clara fell in love with and a red feather hat
and carrying a tiny battery-operated fan that blew the hat
feathers around like dancing flames.

"Now, you use your lucky eyes, chillen; I want you to

see what the rest of the world is like. Life is lots more
than Richeleau House and don't you never forget it." She
told them tales of the old Storeyville section, where bor-
dellos flourished and jazz was born. Of the Casket Girls
brought by the Ursuline nuns to provide proper wives for
the French—how every New Orleans matron claimed one
in her ancestry—but no one claimed the prostitutes and
saloon girls who had been everywhere.

Of course they liked life as she showed it to them a
whole lot better than home, so much so that Zander even
wrote a short story for his class essay contest, "Real Life
Is a Place for All Kinds of People."

One Saturday afternoon, Maybe and Hillary took them
to the ballet. It was a gala occasion because Dame Margot
Fonteyn, the brilliant British ballerina, was in town and
would be dancing *Swan Lake*. They were all dressed in
New Orleans summer cotton finery, umbrellas tucked under
their seats in case of a sudden downpour, hushed and
awestruck at the beauty of Saenger Center, described in
the program notes as "an acre of seats in a garden of
Florentine splendor." The curtain went up and the dancing
began.

"When do they start talking?" demanded Clara.

"Hush up, sugar," whispered Hillary, her breath warm
with the two Rum Ramseys she'd had at lunch. "This is
ballet, darlin', there *is* no talking. They talk with their
bodies."

"Pretty dumb," Clara said and passed the word to Zander. "There's no words. They wiggle the words out with
their bodies, that's what Momma said. Got any gum?"

Zander and Clara endured it, fidgeting until the first
intermission when they could gather candy to ward off
their boredom.

Adam, however, was not bored. Five-year-old Adam
was entranced. Hillary later told Louis that he watched
the dancers as if "he was seeing Jesus Christ, the Father,

and maybe even the good old Virgin." He would not leave his seat, refused all offers of candy and orange soda, never moving or taking his eyes from the miracle he was watching on the stage.

The next day, when Maybe was giving him his bath, he turned to her, his beautiful face stern and solemn.

"Maybe. I want to dance like the swans. Teach me. Please, teach me."

She put down his towel, feeling something harden in her stomach. "Sweetheart, your poppa would never allow it and that kind of dancin' is really for little girls."

He looked at her steadily without wavering. "I *am* a little girl. Inside me, I am." He reached down his small slender body and took his penis in his hand. "This doesn't go here, it's a mistake. Please teach me."

Two years passed. It was the beginning of the new decade and America was walking in shaky shoes. The Russians not only had the Bomb but also an intercontinental missile, capable of annihilating any spot on earth, as well as the first artificial satellite, a tidy little package of radio transmitters, whirling in orbit and bringing American superiority from a standing to a sitting position. The country went to see *On the Beach* and listened to Tom Lehrer's antiwar folk songs. Korea was over, but the aftershock was a bitch. "We will bury you!" shouted Soviet Premier Khrushchev, and we believed him.

The anxiety of this new pressure front in the American Dream worked on the nerves and the digestive systems, and to compensate, as they always have, Americans looked for escape—they turned to "Gunsmoke," "The $64,000 Question," James Dean, Marilyn Monroe, hula hoops, and rock 'n' roll. Of course, the South had Martin Luther King, Jr., and the Civil Rights movement for distraction. Maybe went to Alabama for the march on Selma, and though privately Hillary and Louis supported her, they knew that these views would not help Louis's budding

gubernatorial campaign. Maybe returned shaken and confused. "Folks spat at me, called me 'Nigger lover.' I got
knocked down and punched about. All of the hate out
there, Louis, it's so bad! What a terrible way for the chillen
to grow up, with bombs and fear all around 'em. If you
run for governor, you gotta help those poor people."

"It's a very complicated issue, Maybe. I don't really
know what can be done, but we're trying to find out." By
this time Louis had a campaign committee and was preparing to officially declare for the 1960 election. He had
spent two years as a state representative learning his way
around state politics, building confidence and comrades.

In order to do this he had, with the help of Hillary's
father's successor at the bank and the shysters, finally
begun to consolidate and divest himself of Richeleau &
Co. Hillary had ultimately swayed him with the argument
that if anything were to happen to him, with Philip and
her father now gone, it would be impossible for her and
Maybe to carry on and the children would be the victims.
They read and reread Anton's will until Hillary convinced
him that there was *no* enemy—no one to challenge his
right to sell—after all, the main condition was the male
line, which was safely assured. He wanted to hear this,
and in spite of his anxiety and his by now regular bouts
of insomnia and depression, he proceeded, taking on his
father's ghost headfirst.

One evening shortly before Louis officially declared his
intention to run, he brought a young minister, who was
a church lobbyist, home for dinner.

Maybe and the children loathed him on sight. Harley
Kurtz was a small, stocky, red-faced fellow with acne-
scarred cheeks and oily, slicked-back, mud-colored hair.
His eyes were his most distinctive feature, not for their
beauty but for their darkness. They glowed like jet-black
marbles, into which you could not see. He had a wide,
surprisingly white smile and even, large teeth that he used
to charm his small sullen audience.

Surprisingly, Louis and Hillary did not seem to see him as Maybe and the children did. Hillary was especially intrigued, almost enraptured, playing with her black curls, batting her eyes, and flushing slightly when he turned his glittering stone-hard eyes on her, which he did too often to please Clara or Alexander.

"Why's that bullfrog lookin' at Momma like that? It gives me the creeps. I don't care if he is a preacher, he's got an evil mind, I can tell it."

"Maybe he's important in politics. Don't worry, Clar, I'll check it out with Momma after he's gone. I'm sure she's just being polite, 'cause Poppa wants her to."

But Hillary was not just being polite. Hillary was hypnotized, as was Louis. They had never known anyone like Harley Kurtz with his poor-boy street-wise knowledge and his religious rhetoric. Kurtz knew people the way a snake oil salesman or a gambler does. Professionally. He knew black people and poor people and lonely folks and greedy folks, and he knew how to manipulate them to get what he needed. He was a master at it, though he was not yet thirty years old, and he had seen instantly that Louis Richeleau was opportunity, and Kurtz was nothing if not an opportunist. Kurtz also saw Hillary, saw her nervousness, emotional frailty, and the wantonness she did not know she possessed. He played to her.

Soon he had an office next to Louis's in the main house and had left his lobbying activities to become Spiritual Advisor and Political Analyst to Louis's campaign; an outrageous move for a Catholic, however lapsed.

One evening Laurel, Suzette, and Harley Kurtz were invited to dinner. Laurel brought Kate, Philip being too ill to leave home. She had heard about this preacher with power on his mind and was concerned about his influence on Louis. Her concern was heightened by Maybe. "This is a bad man, Miz Laurel. He smells money and he wants somethin' here and if he gets it, Lord help us. I don't know what's come over Louis and Hillary; it's like he's put a spell on 'em. The chillen sense it, too. Come see with your own eyes, I don't know what to do."

Laurel, as usual, led the conversation. "Tell me, Reverend Kurtz, how do y'all find the time to combine your gospel duties with your political activities? I would think that would try y'all. Why, it takes all of my sister's time and energy just serving Señor Christ and us sinners. You must have special powers."

Harley Kurtz turned his fathomless eyes on Laurel, his smile widening. "When you grow up poor, dog-dirt poor in Lusiana, you don't have much choice but to develop 'special powers,' Miz Poisson. The only way out of the bayous for a poor man is with the church or the alligators. I chose the Lord. But the church understands that it needs its champions in the real world as well as in the world of the spirit and that is how I can best serve. I am sure the sister can understand a poor boy turning to the Lord as salvation from his daddy's dismal fate?"

Suzette blushed, her small hands toying with her crucifix. "How we come to God isn't important, all that matters is that we do His will. The Church has certainly understood well the need for its spokesmen in the 'real world' as you put it, Reverend Kurtz, but I must say, I would find such a path without the joy of spiritual peace. But that is only my opinion."

"While y'all are serving Jesus, could someone please serve me the corn bread," said Clara, with her mother's instinct for changing the subject and revving up a dying conversation. Everyone laughed. Hillary laughed a bit too loud and too long, and it made Alexander and little Adam uncomfortable.

"Now, Laurel," giggled Hillary, pouring more champagne for herself, "don't you dare give Harley a bad time. Harley, Laurel is a black angel sometimes, and she would argue with the Holy Ghost himself if he came to supper."

Kate's eyes filled with tears. "LaLa not angel; LaLa real."

The Reverend Kurtz turned his smile on Kate. "Of course she is, but someday she will join the angels if she is good, and the devil if she is bad, just like all children of the Lord, and that is why we must flee from temptation and repent each day for our sins, or we will face the hellfire!"

Kate began to sob and Louis rose, instinctively reaching to protect her. "Now, now, Harley, we don't want to frighten the children."

Adam rose, too, and came up beside Harley Kurtz, his perfect face red with anger. Maybe gasped. Everyone turned toward him. No one had ever seen him without his sweet, calm smile; no matter what happened, he forgave whoever or whatever life presented. It drove Clara so crazy that even she finally surrendered her weapons and became his protector. Now he stood, his small body shaking with rage, his wide-set azure eyes blazing at this intruder, a six-year-old crusader for right. "You're a liar! There isn't any devil! There's only God. God doesn't want children to be afraid. You shut up!" His body shook with sobs.

Maybe reached him before anyone could move. "He's all tuckered out," she muttered, sweeping him up in her arms and carrying him upstairs, Kate lumbering up behind them, holding Louis's hand. Far below, she could hear Laurel's booming voice.

"Well, now that we've done religion, y'all, how about politics?"

From the evening in the bathroom when Adam had made his confession, Maybe had not slept through an entire night or spent a single peaceful day. Adam had trusted her, instinctively and completely, with a secret that he himself could not have yet begun to comprehend. She had given her life to this family, living without man or children of her own, gratefully hiding from the snickers

and suspicion that she engendered, not fitting into the
black world or the white world, but fitting perfectly into
this strange old family, who needed her, loved her, and
accepted her with open and often trembling arms. Their
care was her life as simply and peacefully as Kate was
Laurel's and God was Suzette's, and she had never doubted,
wavered, or longed for anything else. But she had been
given a sacred trust and she could never betray this angel/
child by telling his mother and father. There was no one
to tell. She was all alone with something that she could
not control and did not understand. She had never even
heard of such a thing. At night, his clear soft voice echoed
in her head. "I *am* a little girl. This doesn't belong here.
Teach me." Once their bond was sealed, he began to let
her into his world of angel hairs and loneliness.

"When I grow up, I'll wear pretty white dresses like
Momma and dance on a stage with roses in my hair," he
would tell her, twirling around his room in Clara's cast-
offs.

She sat, rigid with fear, not knowing what to do or
say; saying nothing at times, telling him the truth at
others. "Adam, baby, you can't ever be doin' what you
say. You is a boy child. That's how the Lord made you
and how you will be. You can't be tellin' anyone but
Maybe such things or terrible sorrow will fall on us. And
that's the truth. Baby, you must turn yourself to Jesus and
ask his help."

Adam walked to her, taking her honest round face in
his slender hands. "I've already done that, Maybe. Don't
worry about me. I won't tell. I know it's wrong. I just
can't help it. But please teach me. Please." She did. She
found an old Russian Jewish woman who lived in an attic
on Chartres Street and had worked with Nijinsky and
Pavlova. These were names that Maybe had never heard,
but she read books and found the best teacher she could,
saving money secretly from her household allowance to

pay for them. No one noticed her comings and goings with Adam, so it was not too difficult to arrange. She kept his ballet slippers and tights hidden in her closet and even learned to drive so that no driver would ever question where she was going.

The first time she went to see the teacher, Madame Zhanna, she was so nervous her left eye began to twitch and her hands ran sweat down the sides of her black patent leather purse. "I have a boy, ma'am, he wants to dance, like in the ballet, but his poppa and momma wouldn't understand. He wants to, so bad. Can you teach 'em? I'll pay cash money every lesson. But you gotta swear not to never tell nobody 'bout it, or there'd be terrible trouble for my boy."

The Russian woman listened quietly and without shock. "If he's possible, I teach him. Bring him."

Adam walked into the old dancer's apartment as if he had always been there. He smiled at her and curtsied before her, like a budding ballerina of the old school. His beauty and sweetness moved her. "Dance for me. I play music. I play Tchaikovsky. You will remember that name. I play, you dance."

The music started; gravelly echoes of *The Nutcracker Suite* sputtered out of a dusty old record player and Adam began to dance. He knew only what he had seen on the stage, in movies, on "The Ed Sullivan Show," or in the books that Maybe brought him, but he moved with the grace and flexibility of a natural dancer, his arms shaping his movements, floating beside him without bone or weight; his body straight and strong; his legs, steady and limber. He did not dance like a boy, he danced like a girl. Maybe and Madame Zhanna watched without speaking. He danced and he danced, sweat glistening on his small face, his eyes almost closed with ecstasy; no one moved. When the record finished, Madame rose and handed Adam a towel. "Wait outside, little one," she said.

She stood beside Maybe watching him duck walk in perfect classical form across the polished bare wood floor
and into the parlor beyond, closing the door quietly behind him.

She turned to Maybe, her face solemn. "This child has
the soul of great dancer, but he will never achieve this.
I know one other like him, in Moscow. He cannot be
male dancer, he dance like prima. His body and mind
are like prima's. It is a great tragedy."

Maybe felt her heart stop in her body. "Oh, please,
ma'am, please, teach him, don't tell 'em that. It'll break
his heart. Lord knows what happens by the time he's
grown, just for now. You said if he was 'possible,' you'd
teach 'em and he is. I know he's not like other boys, but
he's the sweetest child on God's earth and he wants to
so bad." She was sobbing, all of the secret anguish freed
by this wise old woman's acknowledgment of Adam's
strangeness.

"Yes, yes. I teach him. But I must teach him to dance
like prima. Do you understand what this means? It means
he will never dance for public."

Maybe nodded, wiping at her tears with the back of
her large freckled hands. "Just teach 'em. Please, ma'am."
She stopped crying and met the old woman's watery gray
eyes.

"You said, you knew a boy like Adam. What's wrong
with my baby?"

The old woman shook her head slowly and motioned
to Maybe to sit down. "It's called gender dysphoria; in
simple words, unhappiness with one's sex. It is God's
mistake. Girl trapped in boy's body. Sometimes boy trapped
in woman's. It is great, great tragedy. He is a beautiful,
kind child. It is a great sadness and it will be worse when
he is grown. A life of lies and pretense. Better for him in
some other country. Here there is no tolerance."

"What about the boy you knew, what did he do?"

"He threw himself in front of railroad car."

Maybe stood up, a mother crocodile, swooping up the helpless calf in her huge ancient jaw. "Not my boy. He's no tragedy. He's gonna find his way."

Adam learned to dance like a prima, working every day after school until new muscles formed in his petit body and he could hum all of Tchaikovsky's ballets by heart. He glowed, and he was happy even though he had taken a further step away from his family and into his lonely, painful private world.

CHAPTER 8

While Maybe battled her personal anguish to keep Adam safe and the rest of the family in order, and Louis fought to build his political career and consolidate Richeleau & Co. before his campaign consumed him completely, Hillary found herself, at age thirty-nine, with a new obsession. Only this one could not be sated by a shopping spree, or a new coat of paint, or lived out through her children or Louis; this one was rammed up inside her belly, clouding her eyes with want and her senses with rapture. It was a perverse rapture to be sure, but since she had never known the power of rabid, physical desire, never thirsted, lickerish, with lust for any man, she had no experience of it, no way of distinguishing good hunger from poison, no basis of comparison. Harley Kurtz was the desideratum, the object of this new compulsion, or so Hillary thought. In fact, he was the hunter, the hawk, the aggressor, leading her slowly out from the velvet cradle of Louis's devotion, into a world of night sweats and witching hours, of sensual abandon and moments suspended in illusion, without time or conse-

quence, without, as she had always hoped to live, reality.
He stalked her and she fell, doe before coyote, wide-
eyed and stunned by the force of the blow. She was drawn
to him, will-lessly and witlessly. She sank into lust like
a chicken in quicksand, with feathers flapping.

That blinding rush of physical attraction, that connection that starts in the groin, glazing the eyes and
moistening the glands is always, as Hillary would say, *très
miserable*. This reaction, in fact, is often the only road sign
that there is a big fat unpaved ditch up ahead. Turn and
run like hell when those bees start buzzing Eroica in one's
bonnet. Most victims don't, and until they've learned the
hard way enough times, they won't trust instinct and
abandon the tainted honey pot. For someone like Hillary,
who had little such worldliness or experience, what was
in fact a reaching from her most primal, dark, neurotic
instinct toward the alter ego which was most likely to
bring her down, looked like love—opera style. Bigger
than life and filled with magic potions and ecstatic moments. Hillary never had a chance.

Harley Kurtz was ugly. He was hungry, smart, devious,
and magnetic. Women had been drawn to him since
boyhood, and he had learned long ago that there was
not a one of them that he couldn't have in spite of his
rather obvious limitations. He was a Southern Svengali,
a Don Juan without the paint and polish, but even then
it served him well enough. It was his gift and his power
and it would take him further than he could imagine. He
was part of the Richeleau empire, the power behind the
throne of the governor-to-be—and governor he would
be, too. From there, it could go on—the Senate, even
the White House. There were no small dreams in Harley
Kurtz's life or in Hillary's.

It began fast, high, without thought. A match too near
the curtain, a crackle, then flames. Later, local folks would

say that it was Aurelia's ghost taking revenge, and for all we know, maybe it was. It began in Louis's mother's bedroom one rainy afternoon when Louis was in Baton Rouge and Harley was going over plans for a press conference at Richeleau House with Hillary. He had waited for it, he wanted it, and he knew that she was dying for it. He touched her hand.

"Take off your clothes," he said and she did. He stood over her fully dressed. She was transfixed. She had never known feelings like this, never been the blind man and not the guide dog. They played Simon Says and she hopped along behind.

He dropped his shiny black pants, under which he wore no underclothes. He had a large thick penis that was stiff between his short heavy legs. "Put it in your mouth, beauty," he commanded her. She fell to her knees, all sense and insouciant flirtatiousness gone, crazed with a part of herself that she never knew existed and had no idea how to control.

When it was over, he straddled her and took her head in his hands. "You have a real man now; you will always be mine and you will never tell. if you ever tell, I will go away and you will never see me again. Do you understand?"

Hillary nodded, her beautiful childlike eyes wide with apprehension. "I'll never tell, never."

Life went on. Maybe knew and Hillary knew that she knew, and so they became polite and distant with one another and it broke Maybe's heart; first Louis and now Hillary, lost to her by their fear of themselves. Adam had his secret and she had hers; now Hillary had one, and the house grew quiet and tense.

Even Alexander and Clara were affected. Alexander grew more withdrawn, angry at both his father, for his distance and his blindness to this hobgoblin who had taken over their lives, and his mother, who had abandoned him and Clara with her preoccupation and her increasing absences.

"Funny, don't ya think, Zander, that whenever Momma's not here, the ol' armadillo isn't here, neither?" Clara whispered to Alexander one night when Hillary had called home to say she would not make it for dinner for the fourth time that week.

Alexander flushed with anger. "Momma's working on the campaign. You have an evil mind, Clar, I swear you do!" But he lay awake all night, sick with doubt. Even they had their secret. Alexander knew one thing for sure, something was going on, pulling his family apart. He knew something was wrong with his brother and now something was wrong with his mother, and there was no way his father would listen to anything he had to say.

But the next evening, after Clara had read his thoughts out loud, he went to his father's laboratory after dinner. The door was closed and he knocked softly, afraid to disturb him and begin his visit with disapproval. Louis was sitting on a stool, concentrating intently on the monarch butterfly carefully spread out on a cut of glass before him.

"Do you see this, Alexander?"

"Yes, Poppa."

"Well, tell me what it is, then?"

"It's a butterfly, Poppa."

"Of course it's a butterfly, son, now don't talk foolish! I have spent years teaching you lepidopterology and that's the answer I get?"

"I'm sorry, sir. I can't remember what kind."

"I'm ashamed of you, son!" Louis stared at him. "It's a *monarch butterfly*. Now do you remember?"

Alexander felt tears building in his throat. "Yes, sir."

"And what can you tell me about the monarch butterfly?"

"They migrate every winter to Mexico. They're the only ones that do that. To the mountains."

"And why do they do this?"

"Because they need to rest in the winter, to preserve their body fat."

"Very good, Alexander. Do you remember why they go to Mexico, to this particular place?"

"No, sir. I'm sorry, Poppa, I don't remember."

"They go because it's high enough to be cold, so that they can become dormant, but warm enough so that they will not freeze; moist enough so that they will not die of thirst; and the forest is thick enough to protect them from winter storms. You really should write these things down, Alexander. You will need them for your biology courses next year."

"Yes, sir." Alexander slid slowly onto the stool beside his father, almost afraid to breathe, feeling at once as if he wanted to take a great hammer and smash everything on the sacred table to bits and at the same time aching to throw himself in his father's arms, as his father had once ached for his own father to stroke his back and let him cry out his sorrow and concern. They never said I love you to each other, and the words stuck in Alexander's throat now and made him cough.

"Not coming down with something are you, son?"

"No, Poppa."

"Well, then, to what do I owe the honor of this visit? It's been a long while since you came and sat with me here."

"Yes, Poppa. Remember when I was little and Momma would bring me and make you tell me about the dinosaurs over and over again?"

Louis smiled. "I surely do. They were the only damn things she could stomach and they still are. I used to give you picture books filled with the creatures and you would be scared silly, but if we dared to take one away, you bawled your eyes out."

"I guess people can be scared of something and still be interested in it, too."

"They certainly can. Most things are like that."

"Remember the stories about the end of the dinosaurs? How they ruled for 130 million years, how they seemed so strong, so frightening, as if nothing could harm them. And then they were all wiped out, just because their skin couldn't stay warm."

"Retain heat."

"Yes, yes. The earth grew colder and colder and they couldn't stand the cold nights and so just like that in about ten thousand . . ."

"A hundred thousand," Louis corrected.

"Right, a hundred thousand years, which isn't much compared to 130 *million*, they just crumbled up and died and their dead, rotting carcasses would float downstream; all shapes and sizes, Brontosauruses, and those three-horned ones; you said you'd take me there one day. To Montana . . ."

"Utah."

"Yes, Utah, where the quarry is, where the giant bones are. Maybe, could we go this summer? Clara and Adam would love to go, too, and so would Momma. A trip would do her good. She, uh, she seems kind of funny to me lately, have you noticed?"

Louis stiffened. "I would love to take you and the family, Alexander. But I am running for governor and you must understand, as I understood at your age, that we are Richeleaus and we have a duty to our heritage. When I was your age I was already an orphan and taking charge of our ancestral obligations. I never had time for trips and games, I had school and business concerns, so I am sure you can understand about priorities. One day we will go. I give you my word."

Alexander felt the excitement, the moment of closeness, the promise of intimacy fade before him. "Yes, Poppa. It was just an idea . . ." He paused, catching his breath. "About Momma, though, have you noticed, she seems a bit, uh, different lately?"

Louis put down his magnifying glass and looked quizzically at his son.

"Whatever is or isn't the matter with your momma is
hardly a subject for our discussion. It is a subject for your
momma and me, and as far as I'm concerned I have *not*
noticed anything different, except that she has been very
busy helping Reverend Kurtz with my campaign, and
that's been good for her, getting out more and doing
something productive. It cheers her up. Now, I don't
want this conversation to go further, it isn't proper, son.
I would never have dared approach my father with such
a personal subject."

Alexander felt his emotion steam up, boil over, and
splatter against the lid of his control. "Your poppa was a
fiend! He killed my grandmother and he almost killed
you! Maybe if he'd let you talk to him, let you tell him
things, he wouldn't have hurt everyone. You never talk
to me! Never! And Adam. You hardly even *look* at him!
We're not bugs, we're people! Everyone's unhappy here,
something bad's going on here and you won't talk to me!
You don't care if we're unhappy. All you care about are
your damn bugs and your *family name!* I hate what you're
doing. I don't want us to be governor. I want us to be a
family. I want Adam to be happy. I want Momma to
brush Clara's hair again and take us to plays. I hate this
room. You love these ugly disgusting things more than
you love us. And I hate that preacher; we all hate him.
And I . . . I hate you, too!" When he finished, he was
gasping for breath. A tortured, handsome, swollen-eyed
boy-man, spitting out truth from all the sore, tender,
hidden places of his soul.

Louis was stunned into silence. Unable to move, to
reach out, to comprehend. He was frightened, overwhelmed by the direct, open, unvarnished honesty of his
son. His son had overpowered him with truth, broken
through his posture, and left him with nowhere to hide.

He longed to reach out and pull Alexander into his arms, to give what he had never gotten, but he could not move. He was cold. He was stone. Before he could find his voice or the power in his now heavy body, his son pushed past him and ran out of the room.

He did not know it then, but he would never have another chance to do it right.

The night of Alexander's outburst Louis did not sleep. He wandered the halls of his house, limping past memories, his leg throbbing as it did more and more often these days, trying to keep himself from descending the stairs and stumbling into Maybe's loving arms to pour out his fear and doubt. He had betrayed his son and he had betrayed Maybe and God knows he had betrayed himself. But he could not find the courage to rectify things, as if by admitting he had been weak he would be forced to be strong. Somehow he knew that that meant looking at Hillary and himself clearly, and that was impossible. He knew in his gut that what Alexander had tried to share with him was true, some things were very wrong. He was becoming more and more aware of Harley Kurtz's aggressiveness with him and Hillary, of his family's dislike of this brilliant but unsettling man, and of the tension and quiet within his family.

Hillary spent almost no time with him lately, and when they were together, the ease was gone, the trust broken. They pretended that this wasn't true, but he knew it was, and so the one person he had been able to confide in was now estranged from him. His loneliness burned like a white-hot hole in his heart. He was lost and there was nowhere possible to turn without risking exposure, and his fear prevented that.

He hobbled to Adam's room, gently opening the door, and knelt beside his strange, beautiful boy's bed, smelling his freshness, tracing his rose-lipped smile with his finger. He was so afraid of this boy. He had always felt that

Adam was the father and he was the child, which made it unbearable for him to look into his eyes or hug him close; always waiting to lose control and sink in a sobbing mass at his tiny boy's feet begging forgiveness. Adam was too beautiful, too feminine, too honest. Louis took his hand and held it gently against his cheek, his glasses stopping his tears before they splashed onto Adam's white wrist. He sat for some time, listening to the child's breathing, feeling small and lost in the friendly room.

His bad leg fell asleep and he got to his feet, clumsily, knocking against a chair. Adam opened his eyes, looked at Louis, and smiled. "I love you, Poppa," he said and went back to sleep without waiting for a reply.

"I love you, too, Adam," Louis said, tears now streaming under his glasses and down his cheeks. He wandered again, downstairs, out into the moonlight, inhaling the crepe myrtle and magnolia, staring into the stars, praying for an answer. He felt haunted, old, alone. Suddenly, all his goals, his campaign, his *name*, seemed meaningless, empty. A wild urge to set fire to his house, grab his children, and flee into the night, flooded him.

"Poppa?"

Louis turned, startled.

Clara was standing beside him, barefoot, her eyes still puffy with sleep, a ten-year-old version of her mother. "I heard something. I thought maybe it was Zander heading for the cold fried chicken, but it was safe and sound just like Maybe left it. Then I thought maybe it was a prowler or a Russian spy, so I sure was relieved to find you out here. Is something the matter?"

"Nothing, sugar. I just couldn't sleep. Got a lot on my mind these days. Go on back to bed now."

Clara stared at him, not budging. "You and Zander had a fight. He was crying and carrying on. It made me feel so bad. Why don't you like Zander? He's a real nice person."

The white-hot hole burned deeper. "I do like him. I love him. He's my son."

"Maybe says that talk is cheap. That it's not what people say, it's what they do. You don't do much with him. It makes me sad for him and Adam, 'cause you're so nice to me and Momma. We're no nicer than them. In fact, most of the time we're a lot meaner." She stopped, watching him for signs of reaction, testing with the unerring instinct of children the boundaries set by adults. "Are you mad at Momma, too?"

"No, sugar. I am *not mad* at anyone. I love all of you very, very much."

"Where's Momma? She's not in her room, I looked."

The color drained from Louis's face. "She's probably in the bathroom."

"Probably," Clara replied evenly, her dark blue eyes never leaving his face.

"You go on to bed now, sugar. You have school in the morning."

"Unfortunately"—Clara rolled her eyes—"but only for three more years and then it's off to Europe—like Momma—'the world will be my teacher' just like her."

"The state of Louisiana will be your teacher for at least *seven* more years, so you just put those crazy thoughts in your bureau drawer and slam it shut. Your momma shouldn't feed you that foolishness; that was a different time and it was also a great mistake. We have other hopes for you, miss."

"What hopes? The H-bomb is gonna blow us all to hell sooner or later anyways, so the way Zander and I figure, it doesn't make much difference if we graduate or learn algebra and Latin or not, since we won't be here for long anyways."

"*Anyway*. There is no such word as *anyways*. And that's a lot of existential rubbish."

"What's exissential?"

"Existential. It's a philosophical idea, much admired by French intellectuals, based on the premise that since death is at the end of life, life is absurd, and therefore goals, commitments, and discipline are meaningless."

"Sounds like my kind of thinking."

Louis laughed in spite of himself. "Except it breaks down quite quickly if bombs don't drop and one has seventy or eighty years to hang around, caring about nothing. Now, to bed with you. We will continue this discussion, however, in the near future. Your outlook is not in keeping with a proper example of a future leader of Southern womanhood, to be sure."

"I'm not an 'example' of anything. I'm an original just like you and Momma. Can I—"

"May I."

"May I take a chicken leg upstairs with me before Zander eats them all?"

"Yes. But quickly and quietly. Some persons in this family are still asleep."

Clara wrapped her long skinny arms around him and rested her shiny dark head on his broad, thickening chest.

"Night, Poppa. Please try to be nice to Zander tomorrow, he's so sad."

"I'll try, sugar."

When she had gone, he stood for a while torn by three impulses. The first was to reclimb the stairs, wake his oldest son, and attempt to undo the damage. The second was to cross the hall, walk through the kitchen, knock on Maybe's door, and pour out everything inside. The third was to find Hillary, who had kissed him good night in his lab hours earlier and said she was going right to bed.

He chose the third. It was not a good choice.

She was not in bed and she was not in the bathroom. Instinct led him back downstairs, out of the house, around the rose garden, past the greenhouse to the guest quarters

currently inhabited by the Reverend Kurtz. There were
no lights on inside, only the glow from the small pink
porch light and the moon. He could not see in. He moved
closer. Then he heard it. Sounds. From the festering,
cobwebbed cankers of his childhood; from the middle of
long-forgotten nights—wheezing pigs and beasts. His
mother and someone. Now his wife, his adored, perfect,
for-life wife and Reverend Kurtz.

He turned, gasping for breath, stumbling across the
Bermuda grass, his lungs shut down like storm windows,
blindly groveling on his bad leg in the balmy moonlight,
like a maddened animal fleeing ambush.

He threw himself against Maybe's window, his air gone,
the old rattling shaking his chest. A light went on. He
saw her plain, white, freckled face, red curls now washed
with gray.

"Asthma," he wheezed. "Help me!"

Two days later on a cool, surprisingly dry late spring
Saturday, while Louis was being driven home from the
hospital by Laurel, Maybe was in the kitchen baking sweet
potato pies and home-cured ham for the Richeleaus' first
official campaign dinner and Adam was in his room practicing his *relevés*, life began mercilessly tying up Louis and
Hillary's loose ends.

Clara and Zander decided to go fishing, taking their
bikes, poles, and one of Maybe's famous picnic lunches
down the river road to the clearwater pond at the far end
of their property. It was a perfect, private, hidden place
that could only be reached by climbing a steep mossy
incline and sliding down the other side onto the swampy
bank. Because it was so much work, it was even more of
an adventure, saved for rare days of energy and freedom.
Adam had been invited, but declined, leaving Clara shaking her head in disbelief. "He just stays in his room playing
those weird old ballet records and doing God only knows

what! I hear all of this jumping up and down in there—
he's probably putting voodoo spells on me," she told
Zander, as they whizzed down the driveway and set off
for the day.

They were feeling especially close, sobered by Louis's
asthma attack (for which Alexander felt responsible).

The ride cheered them up. They rode hard, as children
do, not thinking of anything but the joy of the moment,
not pacing their energy or anticipating its end, throwing
themselves into life without hesitation.

When they reached the hill, they were hot and thirsty
and dripping wet. "Zander, I think you should carry me
up, I'm too, too tired to make it on my own. Men are so
much stronger than women, you know."

"Carry you, hell; you'll climb and you'll bring the picnic
basket or sit and rot with the toads." Alexander grabbed
the fishing gear and, sweating and panting, began his
assault on the hill. "Last one up is a Communist!" He
crouched low, using his new man's body, his fresh physical power to outsmart his baby sister. "Stay low, you'll
move faster," he called back, never able to resist pro-
tecting her in spite of his rivalrous intentions.

And so he reached the top first, low to the ground,
panting and pleased with himself. He lay there, his head
in the moist, silky moss, catching his breath. His eyes
were closed and he opened them slowly, treasuring the
first view of this beautiful place. Beauty of live oak and
lily pond. Of rock and reed and liquid. Of raccoon and
water fowl. Of cricket and guppie and quiet. Here he
understood his father's passion. Zander focused his eyes
on the sky and let them slowly drop toward the water.
Something was wrong. Something ugly and horrible was
in his way. He shook his head, but it did not disappear.

Across the pond, crouching on her hands and knees in
the moss, was his mother, her face lowered, her mouth
hanging open, black hair covering her tightly shut eyes.

Her shorts and panties lay discarded on the bank beside her; she was bucking backward, naying like one of Maybe's pet goats. Behind her, his red hands clasped around her tiny bare hips, was Harley Kurtz, naked from the waist down, thrusting his penis inside his mother's small buttocks, a wild swine in heat.

Zander's stomach filled and he vomited, a single spasm so intense and fast that he could not even raise his head.

"Hey, Mr. Superman, y'all help your delicate little sister with this crap." Clara pulled at his pant leg with her free hand.

He slid backward, pushing her down before she could see.

"We're going back, right now!"

"Back? You crazy, boy. We haven't even gotten there yet!"

"I said we're going. Now!" He grabbed her arm and pulled her down the hill kicking and yelling behind him.

"Zander, what in hell is wrong with you? What's up there? An H-bomb? A crocodile? Tell me!"

"Get on my bike, goddamn it! I'll tell you later!" He half pushed her onto his handlebars, leaving her bike, the picnic basket, and the fishing poles—vomit still running down his chin.

"But I'm starving! Zander—Jesus H., you stink! Tell me!"

"Later. Now just hush up!" He rode, as fast as his new muscles could take him, back over the gravel path, down along the river fleeing monster truth as his father had just days before.

Only Maybe's window was nowhere near. Instead a piece of metal was near. One small jagged metal bit in the road. The bike hit it hard, tearing the front tire and flinging Clara off the handlebars and into the stone wall damming the riverbank. Her skull cracked; Alexander heard it. His sister was dead.

CHAPTER 9

Guilt. Five little letters. Fourth-grade spelling word. The third definition in the dictionary says "remorse for a real or imagined crime." The backbone of psychoanalysis. Original sin. When you say "no" you feel it. You suffer it when someone dies; when someone leaves, gets sick, gets better, gets mad at you; when you lie, sleep late, have sex, masturbate, abort, consort, cheat, think *bad* thoughts; when you feel anger, lust, feel too good; when you make money, lose money, fall in love, buy something expensive, forget to call a sick friend, manipulate a child, run a red light; when you pass by a hitchhiker, the blind man's cup, or the Crippled Children's box in the supermarket; when you get married, get divorced, take too many deductions on your 1040, sell a house without telling the buyer the plumbing stinks; when you succeed or when you fail; when you're loved and when you're not.

Guilt. A wise guy once said, "People make mistakes in life, but life never makes mistakes." Then why do we have so much guilt? Ask a Fundamentalist. Ask a psychiatrist. The worst sinners suffer the least of it, saints and children

drag the biggest bag. I have known decent people driven
to drugs, drink, and death because of it; and maniacs who
decapitate young women and keep their heads in the
fridge, who set babies on fire, and poison their widowed
aunts for Bingo money, who have never spent a sleepless
night. You figure it out. The fact of the matter is we've
got it and while it may well keep us from the devil's work
and on the path to righteousness, it also does damage,
terrible, exceptional damage, with the least guilty parties
often paying the severest penalties. It settles in on people,
like invisible mist; a toxic fog that lingers long after the
sun comes out.

Guilt got the Richeleaus more than anything else. It
ravaged Alexander, tormented Louis, and ruined Hillary.

Grief and guilt covered Richeleau House like an ex-
terminator's tent. Each member of the family suffered
alone. Alexander turned from his mother in disgust and
rage. Hillary sat stunned into an awareness that she was
not equipped to handle, and Louis blamed himself for not
going to his son that last night. No one knew the other's
secret and so they were unable to confront, comfort, or
cleave together and heal. Adam wandered among them,
a pale wisp of forgiveness, offering his love and keeping
his personal confusion private. It was a thankless job,
consoling the inconsolable.

Laurel came and tried. "Clara is gone and you're not.
And I don't rightly think she wants y'all to join her, so
let's open the windows and resume living." They blinked
at her like calves trudging toward the slaughterhouse door,
unable to intercept their fate.

Suzette tried, too. "You must believe that God has
taken her for a higher reason. You must not punish your-
selves for His will. It is time to ask forgiveness and let
Clara go. The Lord has His plan for you and you must
find the courage to go on." She may as well have been
selling Fuller brushes for all they cared.

Maybe fed and cleaned, not speaking, knowing it was

useless, knowing that the unspoken things went deep,
that there could be no healing without boiling water,
sterilizing the wounds. For that to occur truth must be
present, feelings lanced, rage offered, rage accepted. It
would only come in its own way and its own time and
she could only pray that it came before the freeze, before
the feelings sunk deep inside, away from the heat of guilt
and grief, down inside where the sun could not reach,
where lives were lost to cold lies.

And so it went. History dying to repeat itself; the war
to end all wars, the bomb to insure peace. Irony and
repetition. Kurtz left Louisiana and Louis withdrew from
the governor's race. Hillary crawled into her bedroom,
closed the curtains, turned on the TV, filled the sherry
decanter, and gave up. Zander refused to go back to
school and would not speak to his mother (though no
one, not even Hillary, knew why). Louis retreated into
his lab for days at a time, his father's shadow falling across
his aching heart. His business was in disarray and he did
nothing to intercept it, retreating as he had after The
Tragedy, into the delusive safety of the maimed, the
grieving. Life dragged on.

Adam bore his loss in silence, sobbing at night in Maybe's arms. And he danced. He found release when he
danced. Comforting him, transporting him out of his
sadness up to where he was strong and loved and could
accept his fate. The harder he stretched his body, the
stronger he grew within himself. Physically he was growing, too; he was almost eight now and his secret was
growing with him. Alone in his room he danced in his
dead sister's clothes, feeling the first stinging heat of shame.
It helped in a perverse way that everyone was so preoccupied with themselves. It took their eyes off him, away
from his strangeness. It helped, but it did not stop it.
And it did not stop his anguish about Zander. He could
feel his brother's anger at himself and Louis and Hillary.

Zander did not seem able to forgive anyone for Clara, but most especially himself. He had been her protector and he had killed her. Period. That is what he told Adam and that is what he believed. He reacted (though he never would say to what) like an hysterical child and he had killed his baby sister.

This guilt was his cherished wound—his bullet hole— and nothing would break him free of it. He would not eat at the table with his parents or return to school or talk to his mother. He spent his days wandering around the French Quarter smoking cigarettes and tossing pennies into the hats of the poor black street dancers and student musicians who played the blues for the tourists ("I'm gonna shake it, break it, hang it on the wall"), and spent the spoils on kegs of beer. He met a prostitute named Miss Missy and lost his virginity against a brick wall off Magazine Street.

At home, Adam would follow him, offering the comfort of his love, asking nothing, expecting nothing. Sometimes he would reach out and place his small cool hands over his brother's angry, sad eyes, as if to say, "Let it out, let it go," and Zander would allow it, accepting the silent communion, understanding the advice, though unable and unwilling to follow it.

Time passed, Christmas came and with Maybe's guidance, and "for the sake of the children," Hillary and Louis emerged from their private purgatories to attempt to rejoin the living.

Alexander would still not speak to Hillary, and alone at night in her room, filled with sleeping pills and sweet wine, Hillary, from the twilight of her consciousness, knew why: Zander and Louis had seen the shameful truth. The reality of what this required of her was more than she could bear, her daughter was dead and she was dead, too. Life was not magical or safe anymore. But at Christmas she tried. She put on her best clothes and her brightest lipstick and sweetest smile. Laurel and Kate came with Philip, wheeling in his half-dead body as a dare to self-pity. Suzette came, more quiet than even she had ever been, sitting in the corner, teaching Adam about Christ.

After Christmas, the pulse of Mardi Gras took over. For Louis and Hillary, it was torture, the gaiety of their past, the agony of their present. The Louis Quatorze table in the hall was filled with invitations. The elite Mistik Krewe of Comus Ball, fancy envelopes bearing Roman, Greek, and Egyptian mythological names cluttered the table, beckoning them. This "Krewe" wanted them for one thing, that "Krewe" for another. Floats, parades, balls, tourists, bacchus before atonement. New Orleans at its best and worst. They were besieged with requests to use Richeleau House, and Maybe and Laurel pleaded with them to accept. Adam begged, too. "Please, Momma, Poppa, I've never been to a ball." Finally Alexander interceded, speaking to his mother for the first time since the accident.

"Give Adam the ball," he said. Hillary flushed. She would have done anything to regain her son and they both knew this. "May we, Louis?" She spoke as softly as a timid child. Louis looked at her, testing himself for vulnerable places, for the risk of leaking some of his anger and hurt. He had spent so many months burying it all, pounding it down inside, looking behind him for bits and scraps, not trusting himself to return to his wife until all of the remnants of betrayal and grief were stored neatly and he was back in charge. And there she was. His girl-wife. Gaunt, sobered, humbled, guilty, alone, terrified, his. "Yes, Hil. For Adam."

Hope began to reappear in Maybe, Adam, Hillary, even Louis. The beginning of renewal, the life force providing a reason to be there. But it did not return for Alexander. All of his despair was turned inward, bile over his energy, pulling him toward darkness. His withdrawal gave him power over his family, and as this power grew, so grew the self-loathing it engendered. He could bring his mother and father to their knees, destroy them with one paragraph of truth. He could punish them forever with his silence. His mind bent into the wind of paranoia and capsized. He had cut himself off from his friends, and since no one grabbed him by the back of the neck and jerked him up from his depression and self-pity, he sank deeper into it. Louis was afraid to upset him and Hillary was terrified of his secrets, and so he sailed out of control, a half-grown man needing a rudder, a furious father, a container to hold him together, to keep him from spilling out all over himself—and there was no one.

The only relationship he had, besides Adam, was with the street boys and Miss Missy, who worshiped him. "I ain't gonna take no money from ya, Zander. It'd be like takin' money from a king or a movie star. If I go with ya for free, then it's like I was yo' girl, like a friend, unnerstand? Like y'all really chose me."

"But I did really choose you." Zander enjoyed her. He was safe with her. She was from the dark side of the moon, where he now lived. Whatever he said or did with her, it was okay. She was his revenge.

On the Saturday afternoon that Mardi Gras officially began, on the afternoon of the night of their ball, Alexander went to the Quarter and found Miss Missy negotiating a deal with a tourist from Fort Worth.

"I want to invite you to our party tonight," he said, watching her painted pink mouth fall open in amazement. "Here's some money, buy a costume, something classy-looking. Be there at nine o'clock."

"What'll you tell yo' momma and poppa? Zander, I don't wanna make no trouble for y'all, I got enough trouble here."

"You're my guest. And besides, you'll be in costume and there will be three hundred people there. Relax."

Adam would always remember the way Hillary and Louis looked that night. Like gods, divine creatures. His mother shined, a glimmer of silver beads, a mask of rhinestones shimmering across her nose. Louis wore his grandfather's Confederate Army uniform, his strong, serious face, slightly red-cheeked behind his ritual Krewe mask, both of them so tentatively back into life, so unsure of the next step, walking without help, wobbling toward one another on shaking limbs. Maybe had done a lot of praying and a lot of cooking. She had done it for Zander and Adam, mainly. She had even made Adam a dress like Hillary's, which he was only allowed to wear in his room with the door locked and only after he left the party for bed. She knew it was wrong to make it for him, but she could not bear to deny him; he *was* a little girl going to her first ball, and if it had been Clara, she most certainly would have had the very finest dress she could concoct. For public he had a Pierrot costume and, glory be, ballet slippers, which he would wear for the first time ever in public. He was as happy as she had ever seen him, more for what he hoped was happening to his brother and his family than for himself.

"Suzette told me that God has a reason for every single thing that happens, for Clara, too. I'm going to keep my eyes open and see if I can find out God's reason for our ball."

"That's not how the Lord works it, darlin'. You must trust His reason, but you cain't see it, you're not supposed to figure it out—that's where faith comes in."

"I wish Zander had faith."

"Give him time, chil'. Trust the Lord, He'll provide him with what he is supposed to have."

"Will He provide for me, too?"

"All His chillen."

"Maybe He forgot about me. He's got a lot to do, billions of people to provide for."

Maybe took his face in her dry, freckled hands.

"He's got special plans for you, baby, don't ever, ever, doubt that. You must always believe that, no matter what happens. You hear?"

Adam smiled at her, tears filling his lovely eyes. "I hear. I'll do my best. I wish you'd tell Zander that. I try to tell him, but he just looks right past me. He misses Clara so much. He doesn't believe in God, he told me."

"But God believes in him, baby. God believes in him."

By the time Miss Missy arrived, Alexander was drunk. Very drunk. As often happened amid the thick, anonymous luxury of very large gatherings, the party freed his demons. It was as loud as the screaming inside his head, as loud as his rage at his mother and himself, as loud as his grief. When Miss Missy clumped up the steps in her too-high heels and French wench costume (a whore costumed as a whore), he was standing on the veranda with a group of foppish young sons of the South, drinking straight bourbon and passing a highly illicit marijuana cigarette around the circle. He beckoned her and she tripped over to them. The boys looked her over, impressed by Zander's nerve.

"Allow me to present my dear friend Miss Missy. Please pass her the firewater, fellows." She soon joined them on the moon, high, the way only the young can be high, without worry of consequences, hangovers, car accidents, or image. Just high. Surrendered. Not responsible for one's actions. Alexander was very high.

"Come with me." He grabbed Missy's arm and led her into Richeleau House past the elegant dancers, the tables laden with food, the candelabras and the laughter, up the stairs to his mother's bedroom. He pushed open the door. The room was dark, quiet, smelling of Hillary's perfume; of soap and cream and female. He inhaled it. He had never been drunk before, and he was swallowed by its illusions: power, lust, fantasy.

"Get down on the carpet on your hands and knees, I want to do it to you different."

Miss Missy giggled. *"Different,* what y'all know about *different,* someone been teachin' my boy new tricks?"

"In the backside. I saw it once." He was panting. "Take off your undies and pull your dress up."

"I ain't got no undies, Mr. Richeleau. You be gentle now, don't go rammin' away or I'll scream."

"Quiet!" He had his pants down and he moved behind her, placing his hands on her hips, moistening his penis with his own saliva and pushing it slowly into Missy's wide soft buttocks.

She moaned. "Easy now, honey. That feels real good. Real good. Some ol' gal's been showin' you somethin'."

Zander could not hear her. Zander was moving out of himself, up and down into darkness and fire, flashes of Kurtz, Hillary, Clara, sparking his lust. He began to move faster, harder, not caring, not hearing Missy's moans and cries.

"Stop now, Zander, y'all's too rough, now just settle down, honey, please, now."

He pumped harder, sweat dripping down his face onto her back. "I'll show you . . ." he gasped, reaching up for his climax.

Light flashed into the darkness, light and noise. He opened his eyes. His mother was standing in the doorway, glittering in the darkness like a sculpture of fireflies. "I'll show you," he moaned again and passed out cold at his mother's feet.

Sometime toward morning, long after the ball had ended, Adam had hidden away his silver dress, Hillary had cried herself to sleep in Louis's arms, both of them reaching out without explanation; sometime, while the house slept and the ghosts wandered, gently rattling their crystal chains, Zander woke up in his own bed and remembered. Darkness surrounded him. Brick walls, dead ends; the polarized life view of the very young, banging on the sides of the box, not noticing that there is no lid. He got up, still drunk, and went next door to Clara's room. He felt sick with despair, anger, sorrow, feelings that he could no longer bear, and he crouched on his dead sister's bed until they overwhelmed him and then he hanged himself from her brass chandelier with the sash from his Jean Lafitte pirate's costume.

At seven that morning Adam tiptoed in to put back some of Clara's things and found him.

From the moment of Adam's scream that Mardi Gras Sunday onward, Hillary and Louis moved out of reach, trapped in a time capsule of their own augury. Even Laurel and Suzette backed off, overcome by the web of tragedy knitting through their brother's life and now accelerating recklessly. Maybe never let Adam out of her sight, terrified that he would be the next victim. But Adam seemed to have, as Robert Browning aptly observed, the ability to "count life just a stuff to try the soul's strength on." His soul rose to meet the onslaught. Not that he did not suffer. He lay awake for weeks on end, forsaking his dancing, his delicate face solemn. His body would shudder in spasms of grief. He would begin to shake, tremble, his teeth would chatter, his muscles would shudder as if the grief were purging him, working its way out into the air. It became a part of him, these attacks, and though they would stop for months on end, they continued to happen in times of great stress and pain from then on.

If Louis and Hillary had been able to continue wobbling back toward one another, it is possible that they could have survived even this unbearable loss. But the power of their mutual guilt was greater than their love of self or one another, and so the straggling survivors went off to search for salvation separately, Hillary never telling Louis about Zander's last night and Louis never telling Hillary about the cause of his asthma attack. Louis practically lived in his lab, selling off more and more of his heritage without thought or interest, as if his father's curse was now so alive in his life that he had nothing left to lose. He avoided his only living child as if his very presence was a scarlet flag before the bull-nature of a life stripped bare of its colorful masks and costumes. Zander's and Clara's deaths were threadbare truth; night fears escaping into the sunlight; the underbelly of reality no longer separated from them by good luck and illusion. They had been ripped from the dark warm womb and plopped in the shrieking, freezing water without a life preserver.

Six months after Zander's death Hillary got up one morning, dressed for the first time, came down to the kitchen, and called Maybe. Maybe was shocked when she saw her out of the dim rosy mist of her room. She was haggard, skinny, seeming even smaller than she was, shrunken in grief; her face hollow-eyed, dry, and lined; her lovely smile turned downward in two deep furrows. Her eyes were the only remaining light in her face, shiny and moist as if constantly on the verge of sobs, fighting for life, batting away the cruelty of her fate. "Maybe. I am going abroad. I am going to take Adam and visit my aunt in France. Please see to our clothes and make the arrangements. It's time Adam saw something of the world outside." She spoke calmly, softly, her voice without bitterness, but also without inflections, without her vernacularizing, mesmerizing Hillaryness.

Within a week the arrangements were made. Louis and Maybe took them to the airport, Maybe filled with a bloated mixture of dread and hope. "Adam, baby, now you remember to talk to the Lord, if you be scared or in trouble, he'll lead you right. And think about yo' momma 'cause she's not too strong, baby, she needs yo' love more than ever. And no dressin' up or private talk, now, you mustn't, you just pretend, like at home. And let the Lord guide you through it. Y'all never been nowheres without

me and it's time for you to be on yo' two feet, but jest
don't forget 'bout yoself, now promise me." Maybe held
him tight, whispering into his ear out of range of Hillary
and Louis, who were stiffly saying their good-byes behind
them.

For Hillary, it was a final flight from reality, back to
the mimosa and the music, the beauty of unfolded pos-
sibilities, of life at its peachiest; succulent, unpeeled, filling the head with passionate, perfumed fantasy. As with
all flight, it had about it a quality of desperation that
could be seen in her eyes and the nervous mania of her
haste and that Adam inhaled with her French perfume,
making him sit straighter in his seat and pray harder every
night.

But of course nothing was the same. Her aunt was ill,
the château cold and run-down, the suitors and sycophants who had surrounded her, enchanted by her beauty,
Southern charm, and wealth were now put off by her
desperation and tragedy. She and Adam were alone. They
traveled the countryside like two lost birds, wan wings
flapping at all the wrong nests.

They traveled faster, spur-of-the-moment journeys,
fleeing the dour sour smell of her ailing aunt, searching
for magic. "Adam, let's tour the Loire, you must see the
châteaux. An understanding of architectural history is so
important and the American schools never teach it. I took
Zander to Chenonceau and Valençay, and Versailles, of
course. He loved them. Clara would love them, too, she's
so poetic." She spoke now of Zander and Clara freely,
but always in the present tense, making Adam cringe.
She smoked constantly, drank compulsively. Her laughter
came too quickly, tinted with hysteria. Every day when
he woke up, Adam went directly to her room, tiptoeing
in to make sure that she was all right. He would lean
over her listening for her breathing and she would open
her dazed, sleepless eyes and smile at him.

"I love you, Momma. We're going to be all right. I asked God to make sure Zander and Clara are together and happy, and I know He's taking care of them. They smile at me when I'm asleep and they tell me things. They're worried about us, they want you to be happy, because they're okay, they're safe and sound. I love you so, Momma, please don't be sad."

She would take his face in her hands and look into his eyes quizzically, as if trying to fathom this odd, lovely being, her last child. "Let's take a train somewhere today, Adam, darling. Let's go as fast as we can, somewhere sunny."

As the time passed, more school was missed (which prompted Louis to send lengthy pleading letters) and Hillary's quest grew more desperate, emptied of expectation, Adam grew quieter.

He took to sleeping in the hall, his cheek pressed to the floor beside his mother's door, listening to her tears, her pacing, her life noises, so frightened that they would stop.

When they had been gone for three months, Hillary developed the flu and returned to her bed in her aunt's house seeming almost relieved, able to lay down the pretense of the life force and give in to her demons. Adam sat by her side, reading to her, making her tea and toast, mopping her narrow brow with damp French washing cloths.

"Oh, Adam, baby, you're such a good nurse, better than Clara, you should have been the girl, instead," Hillary teased weakly.

Adam flushed, longing to throw himself in her arms. His eyes filled with tears and his body shuddered. "Clara's *dead*, Momma, and I'm a—I'm a boy!" He had never raised his voice to her and they stared at each other shocked by his emotion.

Somewhere behind Hillary's stunned child eyes, somewhere between the rational and irrational, she heard him, she understood, she knew. There was no room in her being for old truth—*Clara's dead, Zander's dead*—let alone new truth, Adam's truth. A ten-and-a-half-year-old son who was more beautiful than any little girl, who was still called "mademoiselle" on the streets, whose sweet strangeness melted hearts. No more truth.

Hillary's flu grew worse. Pneumonia developed in her left lung, then moved to her right. She would not go to the hospital, and she hid her medicine under her pillow. The roles changed. Adam became the mother, nagging at her, threatening to send for Louis and Maybe, finally crying in helplessness in her arms. He slept on the floor of her room, refusing any attempt to move him, guarding her, like the loyal family dog, from intruders or harm, listening to her cough and wheeze beside him.

By the third week he knew she was dying. "I'm going to take you to the hospital. And I'm calling Poppa, today! You're not even trying, Momma. God doesn't want you yet. You must try!" Hillary covered his shaking mouth with her small white hand. "Let me go, baby. I want to go. Don't try to stop me, please don't. I'll just find some other way. This is best. No one will know how. Poppa won't have to live with that. This is the best way, baby."

Adam understood. "But I have to, Momma," he said quietly. Then he went downstairs and called an ambulance; he called his father and Maybe, then he went back up to Hillary.

"I called, Momma. If God thinks it's right, it will happen anyway."

Hillary smiled at him. "My little saint," she whispered.

That night at the hospital she ripped the oxygen tent open and suffocated. The official cause of death was pneumonia, but Adam knew and would always know that it was suicide. She had gone to join her children, off somewhere, where the magic was, where life would brandish no more pins to prick her magic bubbles.

Then there were two. A father and a son splintered and bent by loss living silently and separately, side by side and millenniums apart. Adam behind his closed door with his secrets and pain, and Louis behind his. Adam kept dancing and Louis kept collecting and Maybe kept holding what was left of the Richeleaus together.

Philip finally died. Laurel and Kate came home to live with Adam and Louis, bringing some energy back inside. "I hate this goddamn horror house, but Louis will never leave it now. It's probably as good a place as any for all us misfits to fight our monsters."

CHAPTER 10

Hillary Richeleau died in late October 1963. President Kennedy was assassinated less than one month later. The sixties turned out to be a banner decade for death, or as my old friend James Reston put it, "The worst in the nation prevailed over the best."

Adam Richeleau was in his tenth year and I was in my thirty-third, a hotshot tearing up the city room at the old *New York Herald*, dashing from Dallas to Washington, chasing the big news like a madman in the wind on the heels of his only hat. What was to whiz across our senses over the next seven years fit in perfectly with this tormented child's world view. Unfairness was the way life went, with the Angel of Death chortling at the martyred president and his "I look forward to an America which will not be afraid of grace and beauty" idealism. "What a crock," said the angel. Kennedy's light went out and the short circuit dimmed the brightness of all our lives.

I was there in the sixties. I was everywhere. I even liked the dimming lights, because the pain meant news.

Adam grew into his ambiguous manhood in the most

despairing decade in American history, or so it seemed
at the time. F. W. Woolworth's, Greensboro, North Car-
olina, 1960. Four black boys ordered a cup of coffee,
which never came, were abused, burned with cigarette
butts, and humiliated, but they changed Southern history.
In 1963 Dr. King gave his "I have a dream" speech before
two hundred thousand people in Washington, D.C., and
George Wallace promised "segregation forever" in Alabama.

The whole decade was locked in a struggle of good
over evil, with evil continually making the touchdown in
the last minute of play. The Cuban missile crisis forced
us to deal matter-of-factly with the real possibility of the
world's end. The Green Berets created a gladiator pit,
where trainees leapt in, sixty at a time, battling one another until a single victor emerged. L.B.J. smiled his approval while we "liberators from oppression" brought the
white man's medicine to Vietnam. In '66 and '67 we had
the Watts riots, Cleveland, Chicago; in '68 we had Bobby
Kennedy (I was there) and Dr. King; we had the Love
Children, Turn on, Tune in, Drop out, God Is Dead,
Peace, Don't Trust Anyone Over Thirty, Black Is Beautiful, Stoned. We had communes, draft dodging, free
love, body paint, hair, mescaline, LSD, marijuana, hash-
ish, nonviolence, the Yellow Submarine, Woodstock,
Dylan, Hog Farm, psychedelics, "tangerine trees and mar-
malade skies," venereal disease, hard drugs, Maharishi
Mahesh Yogi, Lee Harvey Oswald, Jack Ruby, James Earl
Ray, Sirhan Sirhan, the Warren Report, the Moratorium,
the Tet offensive, the singles scene, the Moon Landing,
Snoopy, Streisand, Huntley/Brinkley, Julia Child, the
Smothers Brothers, Betty Friedan, Helen Gurley Brown,
Agnew, doves, hawks, Twiggy, miniskirts, Leisure World,
Verushka, Southeast Asia. Camelot churned into chaos,
America testing the old "a house divided" theory to its
outer limits. Meanwhile, the Big Bad Bomb sat under its

parasol, legs crossed, soaking up some gamma rays and waiting for further instructions. The Commies were eating their *piroshki* with chopsticks and the Southern president was fighting for his life with crossed watermelon ribs and Hubert Humphrey's dimples. It was a decade of much shame and little greatness and though I thrived in it, I don't think anyone was sad to see it end, not even Adam, though God knows it was the end zone of his childhood and any fantasy hiding place from himself or the world.

Two years after Hillary's death, Adam made his first real friend, Duggan O'Toole. O'Toole's father owned a popular watering hole in the French Quarter known for its twin mirrored pianos, Dixie music, flaming fountains, and killer drinks. Duggan was in Adam's class at St. Martin's, the fancy boys' school that Louis had placed him in (despite his sobs and pleas) the year before. He wandered through his days among these boys like a creature from under the sea, blinking at the aliens, trying to imitate without benefit of predetermination. He used Zander as his guide: "What would Zander say now, how would Zander handle this."

He did well in his studies, but was teased and ridiculed because he would not play ball (Madame Zhanna forbade it) and because he was so pale and so feminine. For the first time he heard names like "sissy" and "fairy." He would look them up in the dictionary, trying to see if maybe, by chance, someone knew what, in fact, his problem was. Until Duggan.

Duggan was a lean, loose-jointed boy with a thatch of black, burgundy-tinged hair, small even features covered completely with freckles, and thick wire glasses that he rarely wore, avoiding the taunts of "four-eyes" and the like. Consequently, his face was almost always contorted into a squint, like a little old man looking into the sky. He was a fanatical hat collector, with a passion for military

chapeaus in particular and garb in general, and he was
something of a mathematical genius, with a passion for
prime numbers and all forms of electronic equipment,
especially the telephone, which he could take apart and
put back together as casually as some boys built model
planes. He could also tap in on people's lines; cheat phone
booths out of stacks of dimes, nickels, and quarters; and
call Tokyo free. He had courtly, somewhat antiquated
manners, a formal way of speaking, and the kindest,
friendliest green eyes that Adam had ever seen.

Duggan shared other things with Adam. His mother
was gone, having fled with his baby sister when he was
barely five. Why she had fled he well understood. "My
father has a temper and a great left hook," he would later
tell Adam, but why she had left *him* was not so simple;
in fact, it burned into his very soul like a permanent
ember, softly sizzling and causing him chronic vexation.

He had about him the loping angular posture of those
who mourn and the Irish sensibility that enhanced it.
There was a twinkle in his eye, an angle in his army cap
that somehow conveyed the charm of the underdog and
the winsome acceptance of one's role—the mutt in the
pedigree show, a clown in the opera.

Neither of them could ever quite remember how they
started, some words exchanged during class, the turning
away of a bully; daily events in both their lives, but
somehow, suddenly, they were friends.

On the first visit Duggan made to Richeleau House,
Adam was so excited he could barely slow his breathing
enough to introduce him.

"Calm yoself, chil', you'll fall in a faint," Maybe whispered to him as Duggan strode up the driveway to the
front terrace, where Adam and Maybe were waiting for
him. Duggan tipped his hat to Maybe and extended his
hand.

"This is my *friend,* Duggan," Adam panted, testing the

word out loud for the first time and causing a lump the size of a biscuit to fill Maybe's stout throat.

"Pleased to meet ya, Mr. O'Toole, I been hearin' a whole lot of fluff 'bout y'all and I be more than glad if half of it's the truth."

Duggan shook Maybe's hand hard. "Good afternoon, Madame Maybe, thank you for having me to your magnificent home. I will try to live up to my reputation."

Adam was rocking back and forth on his toes anxiously.

"Well, let's see if you boys can 'live up' to some fresh-baked peach pie and cream, first off."

Maybe prayed for Adam and his friend. She was afraid that Adam's affection for Duggan was not natural, that Adam loved Duggan like a girl would love him, and that Duggan would find out Adam's secret. Adam did love Duggan partly from his feminine self, with passion and romance. But much to Maybe's *and* Adam's amazement, what Duggan made him want most of all was to be a boy. Adam longed to be one with Duggan, to rip his secret from out of his body and his mind like a bandage off a healed cut; rip it off and throw it away. "I'm going to be a real boy, Maybe. Like Duggan." And he tried. Though they were the same age, Duggan had led a vastly different life, shunted around from barroom to barroom, baby-sat by B-girls and hookers, left on his own from the time he was old enough to reach a stove. In fact, his father had been shamed into sending Duggan to a good school by Duggan's sixth-grade teacher, who was shocked at his father's disinterest in this gifted student. The teacher had sponsored Duggan and used her influence (her uncle was the headmaster) to help Duggan past the rigid social requirements. It was the only money his father had ever spent just for him, and so it became his tangible proof that his father did love him after all.

Duggan's father managed to combine neglect with rigid behavioral requirements including an 8:00 P.M. bedtime, no television or radio anywhere in their French Quarter apartment, and perfect table manners and hygiene. An orange thrown into a neighbor's patio was punished by a kick in the groin and a black eye. So Richeleau House became a haven and visits there the highlight of Duggan's troubled life. Though his father hated to have him out of his control, the glamour and power of the Richeleau name made it impossible for him to refuse and the boys spent nights, weekends, and even vacations together wandering the fields and gardens of Adam's estate, telling stories and being boys together.

Often Kate would join them, and Adam, the only remaining heir and last of the male line, would lead his aunt and his friend on his pensive, tentative version of his father's nature walks.

"Will y'all look at that trio," Laurel would say with a sigh, resting her long, well-muscled arm on Maybe's pliant shoulder. "If only Señor Faulkner or that new fella, Capote, could be a flea in our ointment."

Tears would cloud Maybe's eyes and she would fall silent. She was quieter nowadays, tired and sleepless with dread over Adam's future and Louis's present.

Laurel and Kate were a good influence on Louis, and the combination of them and Maybe seemed to work like a human hydraulic, pumping up his will to live each morning, keeping the blood moving and the heart beating. He had aged, and though he was not yet forty-two his hair was gray, his eyes weaker, his limp more pronounced. In his depression after Hillary's death, he stopped shaving, and with his gray hair and beard, he truly looked like Anton's ghost. This irony did not escape Louis, who seemed to derive some perverse satisfaction from it. His Collection and his research continued to shelter him and provide the only positive thrust in his life, and he used his waning energy to put his thoughts and years of study on paper. He actually began this task when Hillary flew off with Adam to France, and he continued plugging into this lifeline every day until he had a manuscript as thick as his fist. The first concrete proof of his purpose on earth, an accomplishment all his own.

Laurel encouraged him to submit it to Tulane University for consideration and he froze, the dark angel chaining his will, moving him back from life. Finally, in frustration, Laurel broke into his lab, *borrowed* the manuscript, photocopied it, and put it in shiny blue folders. She wrote a serious and professional-sounding cover letter introducing herself as "Laurel Poisson, 'Literary Agent for Louis Richeleau,' the reputed Louisiana naturalist," and submitted it to the university and a selection of publishers in New York known for their scientific lists. Within a month, Laurel received a telephone call from one of the New York publishers offering $10,000 for hardback publication rights, with an option on Louis's subsequent work. Laurel accepted on the spot, not daring to wait for Louis to stop her or the Northern "shyster" to reconsider. "But the option is additional, sir," said Laurel, regaining her infallible composure in record time. When the contracts came, she forged Louis's signature and probably would not have told him until the galley proofs were in her tanned fingers had it not been for a letter, opened by Louis, from the dean of the life sciences department at Tulane inquiring as to the possibility of Mr. Richeleau accepting a guest professorship for the upcoming term and raving about his manuscript. Louis was enraged for all of an hour, railing at Laurel (who was speechless for once) and storming out to lose himself in the trees and birds.

After a while, as the beauty of his land calmed him, he relaxed, settling down on a stone bench in time to see Adam, Duggan, and Kate marching across the lawn, Adam instructing them in mock Louis rhetoric.

"Today we will try to locate the whirligig beetle, like

the one on Poppa's table. It is an amazing creature. Its eyes are divided into two sections. One-half of the eye stays above the water and one-half below—giving it superior vision and aiding it in catching food and spotting attackers."

"How neat! If I had eyes like that I could throw away my goggles and conquer the world."

"Conk the world, Duggle, take the bug eyes and conk the world." Kate clapped her hands and Duggan roared with laughter, chasing her in circles and putting his camouflage cap down over her forehead.

"That's me, Duggle, conk of the world!"

"Come on, now, I can't teach you if you won't be serious. Look, look here at the pond, quiet, now, look closely." They all peered over Adam's outstretched arm at a small shell-like object decaying on the side of a water reed. "That there is the old body of a red dragon or maybe a damsel fly. They begin under the water as eggs, then they turn into nymphs on the water, and then they move up on the land, onto the banks and attach themselves to something stable and wait until they're big enough to leave their old bodies. Then they just push themselves right through their skin like in a horror movie, crack it open, and leave their old body for a new life. They just have to lie still for five hours next to their discarded body until their wings are hard enough for them to fly and then they're off. They don't have much time to live and they're very hungry. They can eat their own weight in half an hour. Poppa showed me a moving picture of one, it was sickening, but real interesting." Duggan and Kate were quiet, impressed by Adam's expertise, seeing imagined damsel flies, breaking out of their own skin and flying off into the unknown.

"Wow, I wish I could do that!" Duggan whistled, squinting hard at the tiny remains. "That'd show my father for once."

"That'd show 'em," Kate agreed, hugging Duggan.

Louis listened, unseen by the explorers, allowing the
tender warmth of mercy to move slowly, meekly up into
his cold, sick heart. In spite of all, Louis could feel; he
was alive and there in the bushes, the fair blond head
bowed in reverence over an abandoned crust of primal
life, was the reason left to live. Tears dripped from his
tired eyes for the first time in years, blurring his sight
and fogging his glasses as they had when he was a child.
Someone wanted to publish his work. Aurelia laughed
and blew a kiss; his leg throbbed, Anton grew smaller,
shriveling inside his head. A second chance. The mercy
of God nodding at him one last time. He had one son
left, it was all he would ever have, and it would have to
be enough.

So Louis had a publisher and a professorship, and Adam
had a friend and Louis. Maybe sighed and slept through
the night for the first time in years. Laurel entered a golf
tournament and accepted a dinner date from a widowed
gentleman farmer.

Summer came and Adam celebrated his thirteenth
birthday. He and Duggan had been friends for over a
year and Adam trusted him completely.

One afternoon when he and Duggan were in Adam's
room changing into their swimsuits, Duggan reached down
and took his penis in his hand. "Let's whack off," he said,
winking through his glasses at Adam's shocked face.

"What?" Adam was stunned, feeling the blush of red
hit as Duggan smiled through his braces, squinting at
Adam's private parts. He was drawn to the wonder of
what Duggan was doing to himself, feeling his own penis
tighten, stiffen before him as it had so often in the past,
mocking him, invading his secret.

"Don't tell me you've never done it, ol' boy, even babies
do it—I've been at it since the cradle. Watch."

Adam watched, fascinated, filled with fear and excitement.

"Now everyone join in. Swing your partner."

Adam tried. Touching himself shyly, his face hot with embarrassment. He tried, expecting no reward, anticipating nothing. It was Adam's first such experience and the joy that filled him was radiant. The thing worked. It worked. Just like Duggan's. He *could* be a real boy. He could and he would.

Some weeks after they shared this new dimension to their relationship they were walking together through the Quarter after school when Madame Zhanna stepped out of Pirates Alley right into their path. "Good day, Adam. I see you at four today and do not be late. We have serious work on 'dying bird.' " She winked at him, their shorthand for the dying swan pas de deux that he was struggling to learn, and after nodding to Duggan, who stood crinkling his freckled nose at her from under his Red Chinese flyer's hat, off she went.

"Who is that old foreign woman? Do you have a secret, Monsieur Richeleau? Are you perhaps working as an undercover agent for the Reds? Do you have a private life that your one and only blood brother, Comrade O'Toole, knows nothing about?"

Adam swallowed, disturbed, but longing to expose this part of his secret, to be accepted as he was. He wanted to share his beloved world: music, dance, Madame, Odile, Odette, Giselle, grands jetés, arabesques, tondus, pliés, the barre, rosin, toe shoes, sweat, pulled muscles, ecstasy, grace, Tchaikovsky, aching shoulders, callused toes, Pavlova, Nijinsky, Balanchine, Stravinsky, himself. "She's a friend. I can't talk about it."

"You mean you *choose* not to talk about it."

"I *can't*. You wouldn't understand."

Duggan was silent for several blocks, his mind clicking behind his freckled brow. "I am a *very* understanding person, unusual for my age in that regard."

"Yes, you are, but I can't. Not ever. I promised Maybe."

"What if I told you a secret that I've never told anyone

and that I swore to my father on pain of death that I would never repeat. Would you trust me then?"

Adam stopped. They had walked in circles ending up almost back where they had started on the steps of the St. Louis Cathedral. "My great-great-great-grandfather raised the tricolor on this spire," Adam said proudly, trying to change the subject.

Duggan smiled at him. "What if we go on in and swear on your great-great-great-granddad's grave that we'll never tell our secrets? Then would you trust me?"

"It's not that simple. It's not just about telling. You just might not understand." Adam paused, taking a long deep breath. "You might not want to be my friend anymore."

"I'll always be your friend! There is no crime horrible enough to drive me away from you. You could come to me in the middle of the night, a bloody puppy, his guts oozing from his dead body, in your vampire teeth and I would still be your friend. I would know you must have had a damn good reason."

Adam laughed and gave Duggan a pat on the back. "Sometimes you really remind me of my brother the way you talk. I'm kind of scared."

"Me, too. Let's do it anyway."

"Okay, let's."

When they knelt inside in the quiet, humid, darkness swearing on the powdery old bones of Captain Richeleau, Duggan whispered to Adam.

"I'll go first, make it easier for you." He took off his glasses and rubbed at his eyes. "My father beats me up real bad and when he's finished, he puts his thing in my mouth and makes me suck it."

Adam gasped and crossed himself, picking up Aunt Suzette's comforting ritual in time of crisis. "Oh, my! Oh, Duggan, how terrible for you. What a terrible, mean thing to do. I, oh, my, Duggan, I'm so sorry. I'll never tell, never!"

For the first time since they became friends, Duggan cried. Short, wracking sobs, shaking his wiry body, breaking Adam's heart. Knowing what he now knew, it was almost a duty, a pleasure, a responsibility to share his secret place with his friend. He would have done anything to take away some of Duggan's loneliness, knowing so well his own intractable isolation. Adam stood up, pulling at Duggan's sleeve. "It's almost four. Come on. You'll see my secret."

Past the Pontalba Buildings they marched and up into the dark, dank hallways to Madame's creaky, wondrous attic rooms.

"This is my friend Duggan," he panted, leading Duggan inside and settling him down in Maybe's favorite observation chair.

Madame Zhanna eyed him hard. Adam strode over to her, confident, and now that he was this close to the forbidden release, proud and anxious to share his passion with his friend. He took her hands in his and looked steadily into her eyes. "It's all right, Madame. He's to be trusted."

For three hours, until the sky grew dark with storm clouds, until he was too tired to walk, Adam danced for Duggan, pouring out all of his love in his beautiful, strange, lyric artistry. Duggan sat speechless, drawn into this underworld of faun and fantasy, reaching for an empathy that would bond him closer to his odd, lovely friend.

Before they could discuss it all, reassure one another, promise fidelity, trust, secrecy, and allegiance forever, Adam heard Maybe's heavy steps on the stairway.

"Oh, no, Duggan, it's Maybe! Hide! Don't tell, Madame, please don't! I'll see you tomorrow. Hide!"

Duggan ducked into Madame's bathroom and Adam threw on his clothes and ran out to intercept Maybe, leaving Madame, startled and unsettled, with a freckled young stranger in her toilet.

The morning after when Adam arrived at school, there was a package on his desk. Inside was the London Philharmonic recording of *Swan Lake*, Von Karajan conducting. "Thought you might enjoy this, your friend forever, Duggan" the card read.

Forever lasted almost four more years. When Adam and Duggan were nearing their seventeenth birthdays, three things happened to change their lives again.

First, they met a girl. The girl's name was Robin Mathes, quickly nicknamed "Molasses" when Kate tripped it over her tongue. Robin "Molasses" Mathes was the only daughter of one of Louis's longtime shysters, a young lady of good New Orleans stock, fluent in French, tennis, needlepoint, art history, horses, and boys. She had the plain-pretty debutante look featured in *Town and Country* magazine and Junior League newsletters; a wearer of single strand pearls, Laura Ashley cottons, penny loafers, and Mark Cross leather handbags. Her hair was straight, light brown, uncolored, and worn loose or held behind her small diamond-studded ears with tortoiseshell barrettes. She was of medium height with small breasts and the sturdy, broad-hipped, square-legged shape of the all-American, perfect for childbearing, bride-to-be.

She had a laconic, mildly sarcastic personality, a bright but undisciplined mind, and a sensual insouciance that tightly masked her feelings of hostility and self-doubt.

Both Adam and Duggan were drawn to her from the moment she strolled up the steps of Richeleau House with her "Mums and Pops" for Sunday lunch. They were drawn partly by their boys' school longing, which made any female contact, from giggling sisters of fellow students to clumsy clutching at school dances, enchanting, rare, and rapturous excursions into the wilds, a sniff around foreign creatures, musky with odd smells and habits, and

partly by her haughty teasing sensuality. Soon they were
a threesome, meeting after school (she attended Miss
Potter's) and on weekends, baiting one another with sly
adolescent double entendres, warring Indians circling the
covered wagon of virginity.

Maybe had her doubts about Robin and her motives,
but Laurel reassured her. "Better that one here at home
than some street girl in the Quarter. Anyway, she'll get
bored and move along soon enough, that kind always
does."

But she didn't. "Did you boys ever see *Jules et Jim?*" She
yawned, stretching out between them in the sun, her face
shaded by magnolia blossoms, casting shadows on her
tan shoulders.

"I did," Duggan piped in, edging Adam out of the
competition.

"That's what we all are like. Only I am gobs more
desirable than that old French bag."

"Who's that?" Adam pushed his way back.

"Jeanne Moreau, silly. Really, Adam, you must get out
more, gain some sophistication."

"He's out enough," Duggan muttered, in conflict with
his ulterior motives.

"Let's go skinny dipping," Robin shouted, leaping to
her feet, seeing her control slipping, and racing toward
the vast lakelike swimming pool, the boys, eager and
flustered, scrambling behind her.

"You all go first!" she demanded, coyly removing her
sandals and Cartier watch.

"Okay." Duggan grinned, stripping off his shorts while
Adam nervously imitated him. When they were naked,
she began to laugh, covering her face with her long sun-
tanned fingers.

"Oh, my, now, what a sight! Why, a young lady could
lose her honor with this perverted motley crew! What
will your poppa say, Adam Richeleau? I'm leaving you

two sex fiends, instantly!" With this she scooped up their
shorts and took off, hair flying, leaving them, mortified
and naked, clinging to the side of the pool without a
towel or hiding place in sight.

"We'll get you for this!" Duggan shouted. But they never
did.

"Just like Jeanne Moreau," she murmured in Duggan's
ear when she finally let him inside her bra. Soon they
had progressed to more serious business. Adam watched,
confused and hurt, terrified of losing them both. But she
had bigger plans for Adam; Adam was the prize, Duggan
merely the ball used to knock over the kingpin and he
played his part with the eagerness of his innocence. Life
had not been kind to Duggan. He was too big for his
father to beat or molest anymore, and so the physical
and sexual sadism had ended, only to be replaced by a
constant verbal barrage of humiliation that left him in
blind furious turmoil.

"If I can just hang on till graduation," he confided to
Adam, "then I'm safe. Then I'm gone."

"You'll come here and live with us."

Duggan took off his sailor cap and scratched his head.
"Not far away enough, old boy. I'm gonna enlist. Go to
Nam and become an officer. I'll be too tough for him
then. He'll never get to me again. Never."

Adam could not bear this possibility, praying in the
dark every night that something would happen to stop
it, even hoping that Duggan's father would die and they
would be together forever. Even if Duggan married Robin,
they'd still be together and better that than the army.

The second thing that happened was that Duggan didn't
make it to graduation. One rainy Saturday night his father,
who usually didn't come home on Saturday nights at all,
staggered in to find Duggan and Robin petting on the
living room sofa. He was drinking, which always made
him worse, and the violence of his anger came fast, pro-

pelling him across the room toward the astonished young lovers, leaving Duggan just seconds to block his father's blow, fending him off until Robin could get into her clothes and out the door.

"Run, Robin, run!" he screamed after her as she stumbled down the stairs and out onto the wet blackness of Toulouse Street.

What happened from the time Robin left, hobbling into a tavern to call Adam ("Come quick, Duggan's daddy's gonna kill him, it's real bad this time, come quick, Adam!"), until Adam and Louis arrived, no one knew. But what they found was Mr. O'Toole, a bullet through his neck, paralysis already freezing his body for good and Duggan gone.

Adam's grief had about it the Talmudic majesty of collective suffering; the loss tearing into his past, assembling all his dead together, crushing his heart with anguish. Zander, Clara, Hillary, Duggan; dead, gone, lost forever.

He took Duggan's hats and his broken wire glasses (somehow abandoned in battle) and built a monument to his friend on the wall of his room. Each night he prayed for him to return. But he did not return and so Adam turned to Molasses to pat sweet sticky binding into his gaping wounds.

The third thing that happened was that Madame Zhanna left New Orleans. One afternoon, several weeks after Duggan's disappearance, he arrived for his lesson to find Madame sitting by the window looking out toward the Mississippi, her head lowered, packing boxes on the floor beside her.

"What is it, Madame? What's happened?"

Adam sat silently beside her.

"*Yingele*, my brother in Israel is ill. I have not seen him for twenty years. I am ready to go, Adam. But even if I would not go, darling boy, it is time we stop. I give you all I can. If you were real girl instead of dysphoric, you would have great career; but you are young *man* now and it is not right for me to let you go on like this, dancing like prima. Maybe and I may have done great harm to allow this, but you loved it so much. Now, you stop. You are not male dancer and that is the only choice. I feel so sorry, *yingele*; it breaks my heart after many years of hard, brilliant work; but it is right. You cannot have this dream. It is finished."

Adam's whole body was shaking, his grief a palsy, rattling his slender frame like an earthquake of the soul.

"What am I, then? What did you say I was? What was that word, tell me!"

The old woman shuddered. "You don't know? Maybe did not tell you?"

"Tell me what?"

"About gender dysphoria?"

"No! No!"

"*Yingele*, I am not God. Could be I am wrong or you outgrow tendencies; but I knew a boy like you in Russia. Dysphoric. Means mistake in gender. Unhappiness with one's sex. Girl trapped inside boy's body. It is God's mistake."

Adam was on his feet, his teeth chattering, his chest heaving in spasms. "No! No! I'm not anymore! I'm a man, like Duggan. I'm not what you say. I just dance this way, that's all!"

Madame rose, taking him in her arms to help him, to stop the shaking, trying to still his panic with the force of her compassion. She held him for a long while, her body vibrating from the force of his fear. When it was over, he wiped his face and took her hands in his.

"I'll never forget you, Madame. I'll find a way. I will."

"I know you will, *yingele*. I will pray for you."

Three things. The Grim Reaper and his scythe hacking at the frozen soil in Adam's withering garden.

For the occasion of Adam's high school graduation, Louis planned his long-awaited trip to the Galápagos. Adam was thrilled, more by this first excursion alone with his father than by the choice of destination.

For Louis, it was a life's dream come true. More and more, in recent years, he had begun to see his lot with some objectivity, blinking through the grief and loss and finding the sunset. He had survived. Bent, scarred, humbled, but alive and no longer just alive in body, but also in mind and heart. His work had been well received, he found teaching to be a source of continuous joy and renewal, and he had a relationship of some intensity with his remaining child. He had forged a bargain with life at last, buried his dead, and let himself feel the warmth and healing beauty of sun and light on his chilled spirit. He had a son to whom he could pass on his riches and his name, a son to reverse the cycle of negativity and doom, to bring new Richeleaus into the world screaming with life and hope.

Louis knew that it was almost time for Adam to move on into his own life, and that meant it was time for the sort of man-to-man conversation that both had skirted for too long. They were afraid to challenge their delicate new bond, to risk conflict where love and support now lay floating atop the troubled waters of the past.

Adam had done well at school and had been accepted at several universities, but beyond that, Louis knew nothing of his plans, goals, and dreams, and so they left the eerie safety of Richeleau country for the diaphanous mystery of Darwin land, to commune with nature and one another while they could still relish the bond between father and son, before Louis's advice was no longer welcomed.

Louis had never gone this far with his own father, and so he had put off this father-son communion, not quite grasping the rules, not seeing the landing strip as he clumsily guided their cerebral two-seater to safety; sliding gently into his son's dreams—his hand steady on the throttle, not jerking back and scaring him off; quietly in control, but not dominating. This was Louis's first solo as a father, and he was excited and jittery with the deepening of his responsibility.

Maybe sent them off armed with pounds of sunscreen, insect repellent, color film, sneakers, Lomotil, and straw sun hats; a hobbling white-bearded father and his flaxenhaired son off to the Equator, to the mystical land of blue-footed boobies and volcanic violence.

It was, it turned out, a very good trip. They stood on the deck of their cruise ship, binoculars pressed to unbelieving eyes, each feeling the primal ironies of man and maker, earth, fire, life, death, in their own way.

"The earth is four and a half billion years old. These islands are, at the oldest spot, three *million*; they're still babies, still erupting and growing. We're nothing in nature; just butterflies' lives, specks on the universe."

Adam listened, blinking his wide blue eyes at cactus grown as tall as trees.

"They grew that big so the tortoises couldn't eat them, so good old evolution made the tortoises' necks longer. Action-counteraction, adaptation. It's still natural selection doing its housework." Adam let his father's words flow over him like a comforter of familiar texture offering wisdom and protection.

The water below was swollen with creatures: penguins and dolphins, iguanas and pilot whales, sea turtles and sea lions.

"Quick, Adam, look there! It's the thirty-six-armed starfish from my book!" Louis shouted out, overcome by the ecstasy of his dream coming true. They sailed past lagoons of flamingoes, heads lowered, feeding on shrimp. "That's where their color comes from, you know, the shrimp. I used to tease your mother about that. Eat your shrimp, Hil—she hated shrimp—they'll make your cheeks rosy."

Each dawn they waited on deck, green herons and Galápagos hawks, finches and bizarre, unnamed sea birds whizzing above, waiting for the little rubber pangas to take them ashore.

"This is the only place on the planet Earth where life evolved in situ, without connection to any land mass or interference by outside influences. It's the purest place," Louis whispered in Adam's sunburned ear, tears often spilling into his glasses, moved beyond words by the arid, primal truth before them.

Adam inhaled it all, a young, skinny, sun-red tourist; eager to learn, drawn toward his father's obsession; knowing intuitively that through this he was coming to an answer of his own, finding, as he snorkled in a sea succulent with life, his body brushed by penguin and sea lion, his heart flopping in excitement, that his own truth lay here, too. Six hundred nautical miles from the dead center of the earth, in humid desert and arid jungle, straddling this, Horse Saddle over the Equator, bouncing up and down over the center of the earth's soul, somewhere between man and God, he was finding strength, a direction, a reason for his aloneness.

On the last night, Louis and Adam stood together on deck knowing it was time to talk. Adam was unusually quiet and Louis watched him, this handsome, shy boy-man without whiskers or chest hair, without Louis's hard, brawny maleness. Adam looked out at the night sea with the sad sweet smile of a rejected village maiden, a boy without malice or guile, as alien to Louis as the ancient, indifferent creatures they had wandered among, his inner life as private as the porpoises.

"What are you thinking of?" Louis spoke quietly, love for this foreigner touching him, pulling him forward away from the safety of his intellectual isolation, toward the ever terrifying risk of intimacy.

Adam looked into his father's tired dark eyes and smiled.

"I was thinking about the cormorants. Why they survived. Flightless birds. Can't fly, useless in evolution it would seem. But here they are millions of years later, running around on the ground, flapping those funny stunted wings, still trying to be birds. I think I'll remember them most. It's God's will, it's part of God's plan, beyond what we or Darwin or anyone can figure out. They're freaks, but they're here."

Louis stared at him, knowing that the answer to his next question was in that metaphor.

"God is very important to you?"

Adam nodded, his eyes shining, looking into the black night, his face solemn.

Louis sighed. "I've always seen that in you. The way you would follow Suzette around like a lost puppy asking questions. And that night, the night you got so upset at Harley Kurtz, do you remember that? You stunned all of us. You had never, ever yelled at anyone, and there you were, a tiny tow-headed little kid taking on a preacher about the devil."

Adam laughed. "I remember, all right. He made Kate cry. To me, he was the devil."

Louis's jaw tightened. "To all of us."

Adam turned and placed his hand on his father's broad shoulders, the act of touching, a sharing of truth.

"I want to thank you for this trip, Poppa. I'll never forget this place or this time with you, and being here's helped me to make a decision. I want to be a priest, Poppa."

Louis moved backward away from him. "Oh, dear God, Adam, please not that. It will break my heart. You're the last of us. When you die, if you never have children, we're all gone and all of this suffering, to keep this family alive, will be for nothing! Please, Adam, please don't!" Louis's shoulders shook with sobs. "It's our fault, your mother's and mine, we made you afraid to love and have a family. Oh, God, Adam, please!"

Adam shuddered, his father's pain unbearable to him.

"No, Poppa, it's not your fault! You don't understand. It's best for me this way. It's how I can live peacefully. Please try to see, it may be the only way that I can be happy."

"Do you think Suzette is happy? She ran from her fears and she only found a place to hide, not peace, not happiness! Please, Adam, please! You don't have to run away to serve God!"

Adam put his slender arms around his father's heaving back, trying to calm him.

"All right, Poppa," he said softly. "All right. Don't cry anymore, please, don't. I won't do it. I'll study for the ministry. I'll try to bring you an heir. I'll try. I understand how you feel. Don't cry anymore. I'll try."

They stood on the deck, holding each other, a son fathering his father, drying his tears and thinking of ancient birds flapping their useless wings.

CHAPTER 11

Adam and Louis went home and life went on. Adam was admitted to the Episcopalian seminary in the Garden District. "Catholicism without the Latin" Robin called it. He held the depth of the promise to his father within the loneliness of his life. He still mourned Duggan; the loss of his only friend and his dancing mingled together. His body rebelled, cramping him with repressed energy. He still did his barre work, using the Chesterfield chest in his room for balance, working his muscles and freeing his mind, fighting the end of his dream. He studied hard. Eastern religion, philosophy, Latin, ancient history, sociology. He read Bertrand Russell, Immanuel Kant, St. Augustine, Confucius, Martin Luther, Kierkegaard, Buddha, Gandhi, Jesus. He copied a line from Goethe and taped it to his bathroom mirror: *As soon as you trust yourself, you will know how to live.* The thought brought him comfort.

He had no friends but Robin, though he had cordial and polite relationships with the clerics and fellow postulants. He had never quite learned how to be with other

young men except Duggan, and the memory of that caused
him to shy away from new friendships. He was not strong
enough yet to risk another rejection or abandonment,
preferring to spend his time working, lost in the thoughts
of the great minds of the world.

At night he shared his studies with Louis over quiet
dinners, two lonely men in a vast empty house, turning
inward toward one another, afraid of the dangers outside.

Laurel, Kate, and Maybe provided the entertainment,
their feminine energy still juicy with hope and humor,
caring for their stricken men with the kindness and plain
sense that is the special domain of women. They were
all getting older and Kate was not well. Laurel knew that
it was a matter of time before she would have to put her
somewhere that could care for her permanently. Laurel
was nearing sixty and the strain of caring for a 130-pound
middle-aged four-year-old was getting to be too much
even for her. Maybe was close to seventy, but except for
her silver hair and solid frame, she was little changed; it
was almost as if she had decided that it was her job to
stay alive and well until there was no one left who needed
her. At the moment, her work was far from done.

As Louis and Adam grew closer, Maybe backed away,
wanting more than anything for her two beloved sons to
find friendship in each other. But she also knew that Adam
still needed her, that no matter how close Adam and Louis
became, there would still be walls between them.

Adam no longer talked about being a girl, that had
stopped with Duggan, but she worried about it, not able
to risk asking him, knowing that he still suffered enormous
self-doubt and uncertainty. They did talk about the dancing, and she had helped him through Madame Zhanna's
leaving. She could hear him at night, practicing in his
room, knowing that he suffered and that there was nothing she could do to relieve it.

Adam had blamed her at first for what she had kept

from him, what Madame had said, gender dysphoria, words that he could not find in the dictionary.

He went to the library and found a book about a woman named Christine Jorgensen, who had been changed from a man—in the year he was born. He read about transsexualism and transvestism and how the operation on the Swedish man/woman had been performed. His hands were dripping wet and he had to blot the pages of the book to keep them from sticking together. He put it back and shut it out of his thoughts.

He knew, however, in the depths of his being, in the middle of long empty nights, in the times between things, when his mind was not filled, when he was not running from the anxiety that shadowed his every living moment, he knew that Madame had been right. He had the body of a man, though a rather effete one, but he had the soul of a woman. To combat his terror at this truth, he repressed it fiercely. Masturbating compulsively and spending every available moment with Molasses, who affirmed his manhood by her very presence.

This was just fine with her. She had decided from the day she arrived at Richeleau House for lunch that Adam and his family name and all that accompanied it were just right for Ms. Mathes. It was the sort of life for which she was born and bred and certainly easier than following her contemporaries into the seventies full of slovenly self-indulgence, free love, pig farming, gurus, bra burning, and, most horrifying of all, a career. Not a chance. She knew Adam was odd, not like any boy she had ever known, and it bothered her that he was prettier than she was. But he was also shy and gentle, not grasping and snide like most of the other fine young fellows from the cotillions. He was serious and in awe of her and, besides, her mother had always told her that marriage is based on real things, not romance. She could always have romance, that was easy. Her greatest fear was that he would be sent off to Vietnam like so many of the other eligibles and get his head blown off and where would she be then? So she helped him with his studies, knowing that the seminary was his hedge against the draft board, and worked hard at making him desire her.

This was not an easy task because the usual feminine trappings seemed to have no effect on Adam. For a time she feared that he might like men and she watched him closely for signs of deviation, but it did not occur, even when Molasses set him up, dragging him to gay bars in the Quarter and studying his reactions.

"Could you ever do it with a man?" she teased him, sipping her rum and Coke and watching his discomfort in the steamy seediness of New Orleans's back-alley bistros.

Adam swallowed his fear, feeling the threat of her prying, knowing how close to the canyon rim he was standing, with her behind him, ready and willing to give a shove.

"No. Never. It's a sin, anyway. Could you?"

"Oh, Adam, you're silly. What if it wasn't a sin?"

"But it is. Let's get out of here."

She had not tried to seduce him yet, or tried very hard, anyway, because she was afraid of failure. Failure would ruin her plans for the future, and yet she knew that without any sexual power over him, there was no way of convincing him to marry her.

A year passed in this cajoling, platonic way. Adam studied constantly and was at the top of his class; Molasses halfheartedly attended Tulane, majoring in art history and putting as little effort into it as she could possibly get away with. She was bored. All of her friends were either off backpacking around Nepal or ordering wedding gowns. It was time to make her move. The summer of Adam's nineteenth birthday, with much the same forethought that Hillary had used on Louis so many years before,

Robin "Molasses" Mathes staged a seduction scene worthy of note.

One hot July evening when they were alone at Richeleau House—Maybe, Laurel, and Louis having gone to a concert downtown—Molasses suggested a swim. Adam agreed, feeling mellow with dinner wine and summertime, relaxing more than usual and slightly offguard. They ran from the porch to the pool and dived in, wearing shorts and T-shirts, not bothering to stop for bathing suits.

"Let's skinny dip!" Molasses shouted across the pool to Adam as he swam away from her. He stopped, turning on his back and laughing. "Oh, sure, like that time with Duggan. You're a rat fink, Molasses. I don't trust you."

"Oh, yeah. I'll show you!" She pulled off her wet T-shirt and threw it onto the grass, her shorts and panties sailing after. "Okay, big mouth, your turn!"

Adam felt his heart pounding. He knew what was coming, had known for months that it was time, that it was some final test of himself; a door that must be opened, no matter what truth waited beyond. It was time and he was terrified. He wiggled out of his shorts and threw them on the grass next to Molasses's.

She swam to him, her laughter echoing, floating over the shimmering moonlit blue water.

"Let's go in the guesthouse, Adam."

"Okay."

She took his hand and led him up the steps of the pool, a tan, athletically built young woman with a strong, determined stride and a small-boned white-skinned young man tripping along behind. From the back, it would have been easy to mistake who was the man and who was the woman, which is exactly why they worked.

Molasses had not been a virgin for some time and she easily took charge, confident in everything except her understanding of Adam's needs.

"Lie still and let me get you going," she murmured,

kissing him on the lips, her peppermint- and wine-flavored tongue touching his, then moving down his heaving chest across his narrow hips and stopping at his genitals, making him gasp with pleasure and anxiety. She began to lick him, gently massaging the skin of his testicles, feeling him respond, hearing him moan above her. Once this feat was accomplished, once she saw the hardening, the moans of pleasure, she relaxed. When he was ready, she mounted him, lowering herself slowly over his erection, filling herself. She squeezed down on him, holding him tight with the muscular force of her body, moving slowly, building slowly, until she could feel his climax coming, feel his hands pulling her toward him, feel her own juice moving down, working through her, pushing out; they came together. From out of their total self-absorption and total involvement—sweaty, groaning, breathless, sex.

For Adam, it was an experience so mingled between joy and sorrow that he could not quite understand what was happening to him. With his eyes closed, feeling the sweet muskiness of this woman, this person, who was caring for him, caressing, kissing, holding, touching him as a man and the sheer physical joy of contact, of being held and stroked by a woman for the first time since his mother died, with passion and raw feeling, taking this from a woman, mother, lover, friend. Yet lying beneath her, his eyes closed as she moved above him, he was a woman, passive, protected, being taken, surrendering as a woman, but from the outside, without invasion, without penetration, without completion. He had learned that it worked by himself and now he knew that it worked with a woman, like a man; like it was supposed to, like he had prayed for. But it did not fill the emptiness, the feeling of hollow dead space inside his body, that could not be filled in, that it seemed to be his fate to live with. It had been good and it had done wonders, but it had not done that.

The sexual bonding with Molasses changed Adam. Part
of the change seemed to be an acceptance of his discomfort, and part was a denial of the discomfort. He let his
hair grow and began working out with weights. He took
to following the fashion of the times, sardonic T-shirts
and blue jeans, shirts with rolled sleeves. He made the
track team and stopped his ballet practice. He even tried
to grow a mustache (which consisted of several pale strands
perched over his well-formed lips). There was an almost
bitter desperation in his attempt to accept the hollowness.
He went everywhere with Molasses as if she was the
missing link between him and his fate; the mammal before
the sea, the long-buried carcass holding the key to life's
meaning. She kept him from slipping off into dust, off
the face of the earth into despair. They made love often
and always in the same way. She on top, he below, eyes
closed, longing for the feeling of fullness, longing to be
entered, completed, forgetting who was who, becoming
her, losing himself; out of body and into space.

Laurel and Maybe kept their doubts to themselves.
Maybe was secretly relieved to see him with a girl, but
she sensed the frantic quality of his reaching for mascu-
linity.

"I admit it, señora!" Laurel said to Maybe one rainy
afternoon during Adam's sophomore year. "I was dead-
ass wrong. Miz Molasses did *not* get bored. She has marriage on her mincy little mind and ain't nothin' short of
arsenic in her rum punch gonna get her off now. You
wait. She'll be knocked up and waddling down the aisle
before Adam graduates."

"It be true, Laurel. I'm afraid for that chil'. He don't
understan' 'bout people like her. He's too good. It might
of been better if he'd gone off and been a priest. This
world's brought him too much trouble and Lord only
knows what the future's got. He's so loyal to that girl,
ain't nothin' we say make no difference. He don't even

speak her name to me anymore. Maybe Louis ought to
have a talk with him?"

Laurel shook her head and lit a cigarette. "Y'all must
be kidding. Louis doesn't have any more experience than
poor Adam. Just Hillary. She played the same siren song
that little Miss Mathes is strumming at this very minute.
He's as much a baby as his son, and besides, he's so
goddamn hysterical for Adam to marry and bring some
more misfit Richeleaus into this phantasmagoria that he
wouldn't much care who the lucky lady was. Also, darlin',
to be practical, if this horrible war goes on, a wife and
baby will be Adam's only chance of stayin' out of that
mess, and we both know there is no way in hell that kid
could handle the Viet Cong." Laurel sighed, dragging
deep on her French cigarette. "It may just be, señora, that
we are gonna have to be real practical about all this. The
fact that the poor baby is still alive at all is a bloody
miracle. So if little Miss Muffet is what we must live with,
well, so be it. It could be worse."

Maybe shuddered. "Yes, ma'am. That's the truth. It
could be worse."

As Adam moved closer to the end of his studies, Robin
was losing patience. She had given up on her own education and taken a part-time job as a production assistant
in an ad agency. She was more and more aware of time
passing, of Adam's growing commitment to his impending
career. She had hoped he would outgrow the religion
thing. Being a cleric's wife, even if it was a rich and
prominent Episcopal priest's wife, didn't much appeal to
her, but he had, if anything, grown more serious and
intense about it. However, there were compensations.
They got on well, he let her take charge in bed and out,
and that suited her just fine, and he was so nice, really,
truly nice, and he listened to her. He seemed to understand her feelings so well that sometimes she almost felt
like she was with her momma or a girlfriend. It was almost

weird. He didn't flirt, get drunk, gamble, or ignore her, and sex was okay, if a little staid. All in all, like her mother had always said, the real things were there. But she had waited long enough and she knew that his family, that horse-faced aunt and that weirdo housekeeper who talked like a Negro, hated her, so something had to be done. It certainly didn't take a genius to figure out what. During Christmas break, six months before Adam's graduation, Molasses stopped taking her birth control pills and waited for the accident to happen.

"The painter wants to know what things seem to be; the practical man and the philosopher want to know what they are. But the philosopher's wish to know this is stronger than the practical man's and is more troubled by knowledge as to the difficulties of answering the question." Adam was sitting on the steps of the Tulane library reading *The Problems of Philosophy* when Molasses sat down to inform him of the "accident" that had happened. It had taken a little more than three months, which was not at all bad, and she was anxious to unburden herself and get on with the future.

"Hi, there, your eminence, what wonders of new truth have you found today?" Molasses kissed him on the forehead and settled down beside him.

Adam put his book down and smiled at her. "I thought you were working today. Isn't this the shoot day for the 'Quaint Old New Orleans' brochure?"

Molasses nodded, unwrapping a piece of Juicy Fruit and plopping it into her mouth. "Yep. We're on a lunch break, so I thought I'd mosey on over and see how man and God were doing this afternoon."

"Just fine, speaking for the man part. Actually better than fine. I've been accepted as assistant pastor at Holy Cross on Prytania Street. Poppa will be pleased. It means not having to leave New Orleans."

"Oh, honey, that's just fine. Let's celebrate tonight.

Let's go to Antoine's and gorge out on crayfish and oysters Rockefeller. I know the captain there. We'll get free champagne at least. Besides, honey, I have some news of my own for us to celebrate."

Adam leaned over and kissed her high-boned cheek. "Great, what is it?"

Molasses crossed and recrossed her legs, building the suspense. "Well, Adamo, I don't know quite how to tell you. It's, well, it's not an easy thing to tell. I've been real upset since I found out yesterday. I mean I'm thrilled, but I just didn't know how you would feel about it. I don't quite know how to begin."

Adam cocked his blond shaggy head to the side, watching her, not quite knowing what it was she wanted from him.

"Just begin. That's what my philosophy prof always told us. 'Beginnings are the hardest part.' Just begin, don't think too much, just start anywhere."

Molasses lowered her head and looked up at him from under her long dark lashes. "Okay, then. I'll just say it right out. Honey. Adam, honey, I'm pregnant."

Sun and blue sky, warm concrete under his hands, the smell of Jungle Gardenia in Robin's hair. Mississippi stink blowing under his fine, sharp nostrils, papers rustling, lunchtime growling in his belly, philosophers and practical men, birth and death; storm clouds floating overhead, appearance and reality, ballet shoes, cormorants; fathers, mothers, sisters, brothers, sons, daughters, wives, husbands, lovers. A blond man and a healthy young woman sitting in the sun looking at one another, not smiling. "Well, then, we'll get married," he said and took her hand.

Readers of the society pages would have seen the picture of the handsome young couple, the scion and his pretty bride, beaming on the veranda of the young pastor's ancestral home, surrounded by family and friends. The fact that the bride was four months pregnant was not mentioned in the press and was nicely concealed from the guests beneath layers of chiffon and the tightest panty girdle in Louisiana.

Suzette came, as much to say good-bye as to celebrate her nephew's wedding. A scandal had rocked Suzette's school leaving her stunned with shame. Two nuns, her peers and colleagues, had been indicted, tried, and convicted of physically abusing a nine-year-old Spanish boy and a six-year-old black girl. The charges included punching the boy in the groin, pulling out hair, stepping on the little girl's foot and breaking her toe, lifting them off the ground by their ears, and verbal and racial abuse and intimidation. Suzette was the principal of the parochial school in Tuscaloosa and though she had no knowledge of the attacks until the charges were made, it was her responsibility. The humiliation brought her back to her own troubled childhood, to Anton's bed and her flight from the real world; she had run from her fear, seeking the safety of God and good, and it had followed her, jumping out from under her bed of thistles, reminding her that there was no escape from the webs of the world.

It was too much for her, now. She had lived her way for too long. To start mucking about in the attic of her defenses and choices at her age was just more than she wanted to do. To Suzette, the price for this kind of growth, new awareness, reliving the past, was higher than she could afford. She resigned as principal and accepted a position as assistant administrator of a Catholic mission in Guatemala. She was fleeing, flapping her stunted wings, running away from the world that insisted on tracking her down. The nuns were found guilty and placed on two years' probation and Suzette resigned, head bowed in shame, an elfin young girl following a sound down a freezing hallway, seeking comfort and finding the blackness in her soul.

Laurel was horrified. "Jesus H. Christ Almighty, y'all

might as well just jump on into the pine box and let us
nail you up. Guate-godforsaken-mala! Those hoary old
nuns are staying here and they're the guilty ones! Does
your whole life have to be lived on your knees?" Laurel
was crying and this stunned Suzette. She had not seen
her feisty, unbending, prideful older sister cry since she
was ten years old. It moved her deeply. She put her arms
around Laurel, standing on her toes to embrace her.

"Don't cry, Laurel. It's the best that I can do. I don't
have your strength; I only have what little God gives me.
I can't stay here now. I'm going where I can serve better."

"You're going where you can hide better."

Suzette backed off and looked at her sister calmly and
with love. "That, too. But we all do that one way or
another at least part of our lives. Look at Louis and Maybe.
And poor Hillary. And now, even Adam. He should have
been a priest, you know; he doesn't belong out there.
Sometimes we have to hide for a while to find our way."

"Sometimes we hide too long and get even more lost."
Laurel wiped her eyes and patted Suzette's narrow shoulder with her large damp hand. "I'm afraid for us, señora.
I bet y'all didn't think I had any of that pansy stuff in me.
I'm real afraid, now. Kate's gotta go soon and so do I. I
can't stay here in this mausoleum forever. I'm gonna be
sixty-five goddamn years old! I don't know what to do
next.

"Everyone's gone or going, Adam's married to that 'Maid
of Orleans,' and there is no way I'm gonna play the kindly
old aunt to that piece of goods. I need you. You keep
me honest. I know I've never told you that, I know I tease
you and I'm tough on you, but you're all I have left of
who I was. You're more than my sister, you're my friend."

They were both crying now, relieving themselves of
the distance between them so that they might say good-
bye and go on with what they had to do. Soon Louis
joined them, looking from one to the other and smiling

at these two unique and disparate women who had given him so much, who had helped save his life over and over. "Now, now," he said, putting an arm around each of them and leading them back toward the party, limping between them across the sun-filled gardens to his son. "Now, now, this is a great day for us. We've lived to see Adam become a man. He'll bring the light back. Everything hasn't been in vain."

His sisters' eyes met, a red-eyed connection of shared knowledge and misty melancholia. They wanted more than anything to share this fragile dream, for Louis to be the visionary seeing more clearly than they the truth of the future. "Yes, darling," Suzette said finally. "It hasn't been in vain."

CHAPTER 12

The newlyweds honeymooned on the Gulf of Mexico and settled down in the redesigned guesthouse (it had been enlarged, redecorated, and separated from the main house by a private driveway and black wrought-iron fence as a wedding present) while Adam threw himself into his work at the church, and Molasses did what all young mothers-to-be of her kind did in the seventies: read baby books, slept, took Lamaze classes, decorated the nursery, and waited. Louis was beside himself with joy over the baby and so was Adam. Part of this joy was at giving this gift to his father. He often felt now the way he had longed to feel as a child, watching his brother's pain, and then his mother's and finally his father's; he had longed to offer himself, give something that would take it away, and he would have gladly given anything, but he was only a child and he had nothing but his love (which was never enough). Now it was different. He had given his father the gift of hope and in his father's joy was his reward. More than this, this baby, who would never come from his own body, whom he could never mother as in his childhood fantasies hidden in Clara's closet with her dolls, he would not mother it, but he would parent it. It would be of him, filling úp a piece of the emptiness, a child to whom he could offer his love and protection and who might never know the loneliness of his own life. Daily, he prayed to be worthy, to be a good father, to live with his discomfort, to overcome it for the sake of this baby.

In his role as young priest in waiting, he was superb. A natural-born cleric, without ambition of self, filled with empathy, intelligence and integrity. He was so kind, so handsome, he seemed (and some of the more cynical seminarians agreed) too good to be true. But mostly it was true. He was not without pride, anger, and envy, but it was as if the dosage was decreased, as if he had been injected with a different syringe than the rest of us. Whatever the reason, he was quickly accepted, loved by parishioners (especially the ladies), and went about his studies and duties with ease and cheerfulness; he was a handsome young husband of fine background with a bright future and tidy new family to complete the portrait.

Some parts of the tidy family were not so joyous. As the reality of what she had done set in, Molasses grew uneasy and irritable. Both of them blamed the pregnancy and both of them knew that was a lie. She loved being Mrs. Richeleau, an honor that made saleswomen and maître d's courteous and got her invited to all the best teas and luncheons and asked to join more committees than she could ever respond to. She and Adam were still friends, easy in the slightly hostile, jocular way of their high school years, but it was clear already that this was no romance, no great love to last a lifetime, no passionate embraces and sensual abandon. They were strangers in spite of being friends, and in addition there was the child coming. Robin was discovering that having an "accident" to push Adam along into marriage was a whole lot dif-

ferent from really having a baby. It made her edgy and
bitchy toward Adam, who could not understand her changes
in behavior and mood. "You're the one who should be
having the goddamn thing. You're the saint!" she shouted
at him one night when he came home late with tales
of good deeds and good folks to find her sobbing on
their English chintz sofa, her belly heaving as she un-
loaded her resentment, bordom, and dissatisfaction with
her lot.

Adam tried everything he could to make her happy.
He cooked, he took her to dinner at Galatoire's and
Arnaud's, and bought her silk maternity dresses and French
perfume and Beatles albums and a new color television.
He held her hand and told her she was beautiful and
wrote down lists of baby names and planned a grand
christening. Nothing seemed to help.

"Sometimes women take poorly to it, chil'. Don't be
too serious 'bout it, it's a woman thing. She be fine when
that belly goes down, you see. Now, take her home this
fresh pecan pie, that'll cheer her." Maybe comforted him,
offering what she could, wanting herself to believe it.
Two children were having a child—it was certainly not
the first time nor the last—and as far as she had seen,
somehow it all worked out. What Maybe also saw was
that her work was not finished, that as long as there was
a breeding Richeleau alive, she could not lay down her
apron and put up her swollen feet and let go. Adam still
needed her and Lord only knew what the baby would
need.

In the middle of one of the worst storm fronts to hit
Louisiana in a decade, with howling winds and hurricane
watches and rain falling in opaque torrents across the
Pelican State, with Maybe, Laurel, and Adam in attend-
ance, Louis Richeleau's first and last grandson was born.
It was 1975, and this was a war baby, the beginning of
a boom of replacements to the fifty thousand American

boys lost in Vietnam. Adam named his son Alexander
Clare Richeleau, which brought tears to the eyes of everyone present. Robin, who gave birth with a robust ease
that was ironic in proportion to her abhorrence of the
whole production process, was so relieved to have her
body back to herself that Adam could have named the
baby Gunga Din for all she cared. She was elated, happy
with the attention and the health of her son, but more
pleased to be free of it. She had done it, and it had
worked perfectly, and now they would be The Richeleaus
and the fun would begin.

A year passed. Louis published a second work and
began to keep company with a pleasant scholarly widow
from the botany department. Adam and Maybe were thrilled
for him, basking in his newly wrought fulfillment with
work, child, grandchild (whom he adored), and now a
woman, an end to the years of self-imposed penance.
Maybe was starting to have hope that she might be able
to retire soon. She would get little Alex through his first
five years and then she could stop. Adam continued to
do well in his professional life and he and Molasses were
seen at church events, fund-raisers, and the ballet. In
private they spent less and less time together. He completed his day at the chapel, then stopped to see his
father, returning to the guesthouse in time for dinner and
playtime with Alex. In the mornings he got up with the
baby, fed him, changed him, and took him up to Maybe
for the day. Robin was caught up in her role: lunching
at the Bon Ton and Brennan's, attending charity fashion
shows, and shopping with her mother. It rankled her that
they lived in the *side house* but she knew Adam would not
move back into the main house until after Louis's death.
They were the only private family still occupying one of
the River Road mansions and that made them objects of
envy, curiosity, and scorn. She played tennis, had her

hair done, took Alex to visit her mother, and tried to ignore the widening gap between her and Adam.

They had just about given up the pretense of a sex life; it was as if all the steam had gone with Alex and neither of them could quite work up the enthusiasm or interest. That part didn't bother her too much; since the baby she hadn't felt very sexy and anyway she was bored with having to do the man's part, but not motivated enough to ask Adam to try something else. Laurel stayed out of her way and Maybe, though certainly not her mammy, was easy enough to have around and made her mothering duties almost effortless. She frankly didn't know what she would do without her and told her so often enough to keep her feeling responsible for Alex's survival.

Adam had managed to fall into the same sort of slow, numbing pace of life, fashioned by the summer South that carried over into spring and winter. He carried out his responsibilities, trying to stay away from introspection, being a husband, pastor, son, and father from the outside in, much as Louis had done two decades before.

Then something happened to remind him that there is no endless summer, no escape from the self for long.

One weekday night he picked Alex up, had a cup of coffee in the main house kitchen with Maybe, and arrived at the cottage to find it dark and a note from Molasses explaining that she had gone to the theater with some friends from the Junior League. He was relieved and guilty for it. It meant time alone, time to put down the backpack of expectations that he lugged about all day and night, time to be alone with his thoughts and his baby, where he could mother him without fear of ridicule, of Robin's sharp tongue.

"I really do swear, you should have been the goddamn mother! Just look at the way you hold him! You have the mother instinct, Adamo, *you* can have the next one."

Adam bathed his fat, healthy, gurgling, dark-haired baby boy, murmuring to him, burying his face in the sweet, hothouse warmth of his plump round belly, kissing the soft damp folds behind his knees and under his arms. He gave him a bottle and put him to bed, told him a story that he could not yet understand, and left him with his Brahms wind-up pillow and his Mickey Mouse night-light to his dewy-cheeked trusting sleep.

Adam fixed himself a sandwich and a glass of milk and carried them into the master bedroom. He flicked on the television, took off his collar and black suit, and turned on the shower. He soaked for a long while, eyes closed, letting the hot fresh water beat the fatigue and angst, which had been gnawing at him for weeks, out of his tense, tired body. When the water grew tepid he got out, dried himself, and reached for his robe. His eyes were still blurry from the shower and it was not until he had Robin's negligee around his back that he realized that it was not his robe. He paused, looking at himself through water-red eyes in the steamy bathroom mirror and then, as if entranced, carried away from right or wrong, con-scious and unconscious, dazed and methodical, he put it on. Then he put on her high-heeled slippers and her Chanel No. 5 bath powder. He closed his eyes and felt the silky softness next to his body and he did not want to take it off. When he came to, out of the forbidden garden and back to the bathroom, tears were running down his powdered cheeks. He was ambushed, captured by a silk wrapper, ferreted out of his disguise by a pair of slippers and a powder puff. Exposed to himself. It was the first time it had happened since Duggan. "It doesn't belong there, it's a mistake." The truth, lying in wait on a bathroom door hook, had found him. From that night on, there was no escaping for him. And from that night forward the bathroom trauma became compulsion. It was repeated in an increasingly ritualistic way, beyond his

control, clouding his every waking moment until there
was no peace and no place to hide.

One morning, shortly after Alex's second birthday,
Louis was putting on his socks when he noticed a small
reddish mole on the inside calf of his good leg. He didn't
think much about it, except that he had never noticed
anything that size or color on his leg before, but when
he went into town for his physical therapy visit (he still
had pain in his maimed leg), he mentioned it to his
doctor. His doctor did not take it so casually, and within
an hour Louis was in the hospital having a biopsy done.
The result came one week later. Melanoma, advanced.
Metastasis to lymphatic system. The irony of it being his
good leg crushed Louis's ability to fight back. They cut
off his good strong leg, leaving him with only the re-
minder of his neurosis without the balance of his healthy,
surviving, muscled defense. He was mad, bitter, anguished. Laurel, Maybe, and Adam watched him shrink
before their eyes, shrivel, and surrender to fate. His hair
fell out, his eyes grew weaker; within six months he was
too frail to hold his grandson on his lap or turn the pages
of one of his beloved books.

A cancer specialist from Washington was flown in—a
small, natty Italian with kind brown eyes and a brusque
Brooklyn-bred directness. "Make him comfortable," he
said to Laurel, who stood towering over him, her eyes
burning. "Don't let them use him as a guinea pig. Don't
let them give him any more of that chemotherapy crap.
Give him the morphine and let him go in peace. It's a
goddamn shitty disease and he's riddled with it. There's
nothing any of us can do but let him go without pain and
with some human dignity. Don't let anyone cut anything
more off of him. I shouldn't tell you this, 'cause the way
we learn is from experimenting on terminal patients, but
you're a nice strong lady and I can see a lot of anger in

you and he's your baby brother. So I'm telling you. If he was *my* brother, that's what I'd do. And if you don't mind eating with a short old Italian sawbones, I'd like to take you to dinner."

Laurel went to dinner and Louis died two months later. Adam was with him, holding what was left of his emaciated hand. "Save yourself," was the last thing he said to Adam. "Save yourself." It was unlike anything that he had ever said, it seemed to come from far away in the past, not from any role that Louis had ever played, not from the tragic rigidity of his unhappy life; it seemed to be a blessing, a release, an opening of the gilded cage; permission to fly, to be. "Save yourself," his father said and left him alone forever.

Louis was buried beside his parents, his wife, and his two children. Adam conducted the service, his voice steady and low, as he paid tribute to the last of his blood, the end of his childhood.

Three months after Louis was buried, Adam called a family meeting. He had spent long hours alone with his sorrow and his thoughts, reading and contemplating, his father's last words repeating in his mind. "Save yourself," Louis said. "Save yourself." Around his neck was Louis's filagreed gold cross—Suzette's gift to Louis when Anton died. It was as sacred to Adam as life and he fingered it constantly as if its presence was a conduit to his father.

Laurel, Maybe, and Robin were at the meeting, sitting solemnly around the great mahogany dining table with Adam standing before them in his father's place, in the place Laurel had stood after his grandfather's death. He spoke quietly, with a certain surety in his voice.

"First, I know that we must disassemble Poppa's laboratory. I'm going to do it myself. I think he would have wanted that. I'd like to give his library to the university, except for the special books that we want to keep for ourselves."

He paused, watching their faces, knowing that they were not prepared for his next pronouncement. "As you all know, Poppa left the bulk of the estate to me with a sizable bequest to the university and the Darwin Foundation, and provisions for Maybe and Kate. Anyway, the financial arrangements are pretty straightforward. Most everything had been sold off and reinvested long ago, so we shouldn't have many decisions or government tangles. Robin's father is handling the legal intricacies and so far he doesn't anticipate any problems. But there is something I need to discuss that isn't in the will. I want to give Richeleau House to the state of Louisiana to be used as a historical museum. It will be of much greater use that way and, I believe, a great relief to all of us. We can keep the guesthouse as our family residence and for Maybe to live in, if she so chooses, but the main house will be for others. It's more a monument than a home now, anyway.

"As for us, and Robin is hearing this for the first time, and I apologize for that, honey, but I was just officially informed this morning, well, I've been offered my own church. It's almost a miracle at my age. The pastor died suddenly and his assistant took another spot. I guess they're desperate! It's near Shreveport, at the army base in Boissier City, and I think it would be good for all of us to take a break from here; there's been so much sadness in this house, so much . . ." Tears flooded Adam's face. He stopped to regain control and let his words sink in. "I think it will be healthy for all of us to move on."

"Hallelujah," said Laurel.

"Amen," Maybe nodded her approval.

Only Robin was silent, her face hot with indignation. She was stunned, fists clenched, listening to them murmur and plan the details of the dismantling of her dream. "Shreveport!" she shouted, jumping up and knocking over her French Regency chair. "You're out of your cotton-pickin' mind! I'm Mrs. Richeleau! I live *here*, you pious, do-gooding fool! How dare you do this without even telling me! How dare you!"

Before Adam could reply she was gone, slamming the massive front door and leaving them open-mouthed.

Laurel stood up and put her arms around Adam. "You've made a wise decision, darlin'. Long overdue. Now go along home and mend your fences. We'll iron it all out later on."

Adam nodded, still shaken by his wife's outburst.

Late that night, after the baby was asleep and Adam had given up trying to apologize or discuss the situation with Robin, who chose to slug down double bourbons instead, Adam came out of the bathroom, damp and sleepy from the shower and the stress to find Robin lying naked and well into her cups on their bed, her legs spread and her voice mocking him. "Okay, Chaplain. If I'm going to give up all of this for you, then the least you can do is perform your husbandly duties." She crawled toward him, pulling his towel off, leaving him naked and vulnerable and frightened by her hostile, burning disgust. She lay down close to him spreading her legs wide and watching him. "Fuck me like a man, Chaplain. You do it to *me*. Put it in me, Adam. I want it, now!" She raised her hips provocatively, swaying before him, taunting and demanding.

Adam felt as if his body had been removed from him, severed, decapitated, gone; he stood over her, bridled, numb with self-loathing. He could not move, he could not do what she wanted and what she had the right to expect.

"Fuck me like a man! Take me, take me!" She closed her eyes, slurring her words, dizzy from too much liquor and emotion. Adam moved slowly, every movement draining his energy; he lay down on top of his fertile, angry, drunken young wife, his penis limp between his

legs, and tried to meet her need. But there was no way
that he could do it. "Oh, God, Robin, I'm so sorry. For
everything. I can't. I just can't." He rolled off her and ran
from the room, locking himself in the morose privacy of
the bathroom, falling to his knees and sobbing out all the
tortured, guilty longing in his orphaned heart.

Three months later, Molasses, Adam, and Alex left for
Shreveport, leaving Maybe and Laurel to finish closing
up the house. A new bargain had been silently struck; a
marriage like many, made of disappointment and reduced
expectations, of isolation and distrust; of hurt pride and
rejection. The smiling young couple on the grand veranda
was no longer smiling.

CHAPTER 13

I f New Orleans was poetic delusive fantasy, Shreveport was hard, crystalline reality. There was nothing here between Robin and her wifely chores, or between Adam and Robin. It was the first time she had taken care of Alex without Maybe and she found the task horrendous. She soon hired a slow-witted but good-natured black girl named Trewanna who loved babies, "The Edge of Night," and bacon-grease sandwiches, and moved with the lugubrious, flat-footed rhythm of native girls. Almost daily, driven to distraction by Trewanna's slowness, she sent notes to Maybe ("Hurry with the damn details and get down here. Alex needs you! We all need you!").

Their residence was a fine old Victorian-style house on a quiet street shaded with oak trees and much grander than the rectory residence that came with Adam's new position. That subject had not been negotiable with Molasses, and Adam chose not to push his luck, even though rejecting the quaint little parson's house did not endear them to their Boissier City welcoming committee. Adam worked hard and was gone for long days and evenings, and Molasses, once she had Trewanna in place and could reassure Adam that Alex was safe in her lackluster care, began to explore this foreign and pedestrian new life. It never occurred to her that their "excursion" in the provinces was anything but temporary, an adventure, a horizontal career move, a break for Adam from all the death and memory at home. As she began to settle in and surrender her outrage, her attitude improved. She got up in the mornings before noon, played with Alex, had coffee with the general's wife, set about fixing up their new home, planting flowers and ordering draperies. She enjoyed her power, the golden carp in the guppy pond, and she enjoyed the sidelong looks from all the hungry young soldiers, swaggering their maleness before her everywhere she went. Since the night she had thrown herself at Adam, they had not attempted any sexual contact, but she had been restarted, a button pushed, a subtle awareness of her body returned. And the idle was heard, like the sounds that make dogs jump, by the horny young men of the hinterlands.

By the time she had finished her home beautification project and the boredom of her vacant daily life reclaimed her, she had given in to temptation, to the rough, virile maleness surrounding her. In fact, the frustrated young clergyman's wife felt entitled to sample the local product, which just happened to be randy young men.

Sample she did. In motel room, jeep, field, supply truck, even the church basement. It was the talk of the base and accounted for the cool reception by the officers' wives and the sparsity of invitations addressed to Mrs. Richeleau from the local do-gooders.

What offset the gossip about Molasses was the fawn-eyed devotion of these women to Reverend Richeleau. His kindness and understanding of their needs and longings made him quickly indispensable. Even their husbands liked him (probably more because he listened to their

wives prattle than anything else). They would put up with
the snobbish little society slut if it kept him there.

One hot afternoon as Adam strode across the base to
lunch at the officers' club, he saw a young man in a
lieutenant's uniform, standing on the airfield beside an
army helicopter, saying good-bye to several soldiers. Adam
stopped dead; something in the man's posture, his coloring, the angle of his hat. Duggan. He blinked and
looked again. Duggan. The man waved to his friends and
jumped into the helicopter. Adam started to run toward
him, toward the men who were pulling away in their jeep.
"Wait!" he shouted over the whirring propeller noise.
"Wait!"

It was too late. When he reached the scene of the
farewell, no one was left. Adam spent weeks trying to
find him. But there was no record of a Duggan O'Toole.
He had, it seemed, seen a ghost.

Six months passed, Maybe finally arrived with Laurel,
and Adam was filled with joy to have them there, to see
him in his new life, with his own church. Maybe settled
in and took charge of Trewanna and Alex, who was rapidly approaching his fourth birthday. He was a shiny,
happy little boy; "fat as a flapjack and bright as sunlight,"
as Laurel put it. Adam could hardly look at him without
feeling his heart swell.

Laurel had come with news of her own, which she
presented after dinner on the last night of her visit with
her usual flair for the dramatic.

"I would like to make a small toast." She rose, towering
over the table.

"I love some toast, jelly, please!" Alex offered, giggling
into his fat greasy hands.

Laurel stared the smiling baby down. "Cute, darlin'.
That child is so damn cute, he should be in a Home for
the Cute. Now, Alex, close that drooly little trap and let
your aunt finish her act, please."

Molasses took a long sip of champagne and winked at Adam, both having no idea what to expect.

"Now, what I am going to tell y'all you may find amusing; in fact, I myself find it a bit bizarre and mirthful, but so be it." Her voice was steady and strong, but Adam could see her hand shaking when she paused to light a cigarette.

"Okay, now. I am sure y'all remember that wonderful little Eye-talian doctor from Washington, Joseph Bellio, who came when Louis was dying? Well, the romantic old señor has asked your crazy old aunt to marry him and I have accepted. I know we make a perfectly ridiculous couple on the surface of it, but y'all know me well enough to trust, I hope, that I'm no fool, and the truth is that we just happen to make quite a wonderful couple under the surface of it. So off I go, east, though still *southeast*, thank the Lord. Joseph has found a fine place for Kate very close to us and that's about that. I hope y'all will come see us and will learn to love the señor. He's a fine person . . . the only man I've ever known who's tougher than I am." She sighed, tears moving, against her will, into her narrow brown eyes. "He makes me feel feminine and, much to my surprise, it's a relief. So I leave tomorrow for Washington. We're not having a wedding, but we'll be spending several months in Italy on honeymoon as soon as we settle in and get Kate adjusted. She's crazy about him, by the way. She calls him 'Daddy.' " Laurel stopped, grinding out her cigarette and flicking away her tears. "I love y'all and I will miss you terribly."

Adam stood up and raised his glass to her. "God bless you, Aunt Laurel, may you and Joseph have a life together filled with love."

"May we all," Laurel said hoarsely and blew him a kiss.

Adam was not to share Laurel's blessing for long.

For reasons known to almost everyone but Adam, Molasses seemed to be adjusting to their move better than he would ever have dreamed. She beamed at him from the front pew every Sunday and invited the parishioners to Sunday lunch (prepared, of course, by Maybe). In private, they were polite with each other, living on opposite sides of a widening crevice, using Alex and Maybe as the bridge across. Since Maybe's arrival, Molasses had been forced to alter her ways. She gave up the basement floor and the nameless bodies and settled in with one bull-necked Alabama gunnery sergeant named Elmo, who had a paranoid, humorless personality and a seemingly endless erection.

Their rendezvous spot was the sergeant's mobile home, a cramped, filthy, dilapidated little trailer, perfectly suited to sordid encounters.

They met three times a week at noon. Molasses was always able to come up with a reason for her journey: hairdresser, shopping for Alex, household things to buy. But since she rarely arrived home with the stated goal of the outing accomplished, and because Maybe was no fool, Molasses soon gave up the phony excuses. She knew Maybe would never tell Adam, so why even bother. "I'm going into town" seemed to be all the information required. Into town she went.

Elmo would be waiting for her, sprawled naked on his one set of soiled sheets, his massive muscular body filling the space, a joint in his thick purplish lips, a beer can in his fist, the effort of sexual protocol never exerted. Molasses didn't care, conversation and chivalry were not why she came. She clambered in, threw off her clothes, and plopped down beside him, grabbing the cigarette from his mouth without uttering a word.

"Anyone folla yew?" Elmo always inquired, the military suspiciousness as pervasive as his crewcut and dog tags.

"Don't be silly." Molasses ran her hands over his long, hard body, his penis already stiff, a muscle flexed as easily as a bicep and as thoughtlessly.

"Yew should carry a pistol. There's all kinda Commie kook-koos round here—someone could blackmail yew or kidnap for ransom."

"You're right, ducks. I'll buy one first thing in the morning. Just touch me, baby, touch me and I'll buy a dozen great big ones."

He responded slowly, heavily, with an arrogant, base sensuality, his large thick fingers sliding up her thighs and disappearing between her legs. She moaned, pushing against him, visions of Adam's delicate, pale body speeding behind her sealed eyes.

"I gonna fuck yew real good, missy, and then y'all's gonna take care of Elmo like a good ol' girl." He mounted her, pushing her legs up onto his shoulders and sliding slowly inside her. She rolled her head and grunted with pleasure as he thrust himself deep within her. She came and she came again until she was soaked with sweat, begging him to stop, and he would, without emotion, as if he were a mechanical object and the switch had been turned.

"Now Elmo." He moved over her—his thighs like buttresses on either side of her face—and thrust his penis roughly into her mouth, gagging her. "Suck it, bitch. I'm gonna sprinkle all over yew."

She choked, gagging for air while he moved himself, smiling down at her in placid contempt.

"This is how those Commie whore bitches in Nam like it. Great big mouthful of American cock. Oh, yeah, I'm gonna sprinkle now."

When he was finished, she left without pleasantries, her mouth rubbed red, her insides raw, driving home to her perfect little life, the smell of his flesh carried on her own gardenia-scented body.

The day it all began to fade was a Tuesday morning just before Christmas. Adam was in the chapel preparing new signs for the rectory bulletin board: "Be humble lest ye stumble"; "I am the vine, you are my branches."

It was his first Christmas away from home without Louis, Laurel, and Kate and as it grew nearer, the dark lonely place within him grew blacker. His nights were haunted. He wandered the dark rooms of his alien new house fighting himself. On the nights that he lost, it ended in his study with one of Robin's stolen dresses, his face painted, lost in his fantasy picture show, strolling through town in his best dress, with his beautiful little boy beside him; smiling and happy on his way to ballet class.

After each slip came a backlash of despair so deep that it was only his faith in God and Alex that kept him from suicide.

Hidden in his library were books that he had collected—books on transsexualism, stories of others like himself. James Morris (now Jan), an investigative reporter for the London *Times* who had fathered three children and scaled Everest: "I knew I was a woman at age three, sitting under my mother's piano listening to Sibelius." Adam read about these men/women with horror and hope (he was not the only one, he was not all alone). But what they had done was not possible for him. An Episcopal priest. A husband and father. Alex, he would lose Alex forever. He remembered his mother's face that last tortured day in France. "I'm a boy," he had screamed and she looked into him, having already begun to let go, able to tell herself the truth now that it was almost over, the pain almost gone. She had looked at him and known the truth and decided not to live through it. He could not do it. He would overcome it with God's grace.

On this Tuesday he needed all the grace God had available. The night before, for the first time, he had left the house in Robin's clothes. Left in the moonlight and gone to a bar; like a werewolf or a vampire, he had come out in the dead of night, his agony cloaked in darkness, walking the earth as an enemy of his own soul. A man followed him from the bar, a strange man touched his arm and asked to take him home. He ran from him, tripping over his high heels and falling into the street, skin tearing from his knees, nylon ripping, bloodstained, terrified; he left his shoes and ran. A she-wolf howling in the moonlight, streaking toward cover before the merciless light of day.

He worked on the sign, closing his mind against the memory, his knees stinging inside his perfectly creased black pants, his beautiful face shadowed in shame. Someone was behind him. He turned.

A tall, dark-haired young woman with slanted gray-green eyes, wearing a crisply tailored lilac wool suit, with a matching hat, black leather gloves and pumps, and immaculately applied makeup was standing behind him, clutching her handbag to her ample chest as if it contained all her earthly belongings. She had the filmy, floating quality of the belle, a gauzy caricature, holding on to an antique idea of femininity like Scarlett O'Hara at an ERA rally. She stood before him, blinking at this brittle new world with the glazed schizoid eyes of the emotional nomad.

Adam rose slowly, wincing at the stinging ache of his skinned knees, and smiled at her.

"Good morning. I'm Adam Richeleau, welcome to our church."

"Thank you." She tried to return his smile, the corners of her bright red mouth twitching upward and falling quickly back, she offered her hand. "Lily Smith."

"Hello, Lily. I don't think I've seen you at services, I always remember the pretty ladies. Are you new here?"

She nodded, her eyes lowered. "Yes, sir. My husband's just been transferred here and I'm—I don't know anyone and, Father, I need to talk to someone, real bad."

Adam could see her trembling, the faint odor of cold sweat mingling with her perfume.

"It's all right, come with me. We'll go to my office and talk awhile." He guided her, his hand gently touching her arm, forgetting his own trouble and the burning in his knees, drawn to this frightened dove with a profound empathy he did not understand.

When she was settled in his study and he had seen to glasses of water and drawing of curtains, he sat down facing her across his desk and their eyes met for the first time.

It felt to Adam as if he were being electrified, frozen in flight by the searing bottomless vision in the oblong eyes of this wilting maiden. He entered them, Alice down the well, free-falling down an electric tunnel, a fairy-tale world of upside-downs and fun-house mirrors; whirling teacups and grinning gargoyles; falling into a pair of screaming eyes that felt like the inside of his own.

They sat facing one another in silence for several moments. Adam was stunned, unable to pull himself from the vortex of her face and she, shaken by the unexpected intimacy, wanting his strength but seeing only her own.

She broke it first. She withdrew her eyes and turned them downward; she removed her gloves and uncovered long, well-manicured fingers.

Adam breathed deeply, shaking himself free, knowing he was losing her trust and wanting nothing more at the moment than to have it. "What troubles you, Lily?" he said finally, hearing the quaver in his own voice.

She took off her hat, fluffing her shiny dark hair with her graceful hand, keeping her eyes slightly over his head.

"This is very hard, Father. I have no one to turn to. I'm an orphan."

"So am I." Adam leaned back, relaxing slightly.

She looked at him quickly. "How sad for you, it's very sad, isn't it? My father and mother were alcoholics. My mother was killed in a car crash and my father put me in an asylum because, well, because of something, and then he died a year later. I was only eight. Too old for anyone to adopt me, I guess, so that was that. The sisters were nice to me, but, you know, it's not like a family. When you got hurt or scared, there was no mother to hold you and make it better, there was just yourself."

"I was luckier. I had my father until two years ago. I grew up with family around me. Is this what's upsetting you?"

She shook her head fiercely and fumbled in her purse for a cigarette. "No, oh, no, that was all long ago and far away. I've traveled bumpier roads since then."

She lit her cigarette and sat back, her mood changing, growing tougher, more in control, testing him. "You've never met anyone like me. I can stand your pretty blond hair right up on end."

Adam met her eyes now, responding instinctively to her fear, the child's posture, the show-off with quaking boots.

"Good, that might be a nice change. Go on, let's see if I can take it. I'll tell you if I'm too shocked to listen. But the way I see it, if God's not too shocked, why should I be."

"How do you know He isn't?"

"Because that's not His job. His job is forgiveness."

She laughed, a fast, snickering cynical laugh edged with hostility. "That's not what the nuns said and it's not what my mother-in-law says, either."

"Is your mother-in-law God?"

"God forbid."

They both laughed. "Well, then?" Adam sat forward. "Maybe I should tell you a bit about my interpretation of Christianity before you tell me or don't tell me your awful deeds. I don't believe in a God of retribution. I don't believe in hell, brimstone, fallen angels, Catholicism,

Judaism, Protestantism, Mohammedanism, or any of the rest of that legacy of theological separatism and fear. Of course, I keep quite a bit of this to myself, as you may imagine, because people are not ready to hear a priest talk this way. They would rather listen to the Fundamentalist garbage that lets them function as mindless infants, acting out their parental fantasies of right and wrong and abdicating responsibility for themselves and their irreplaceable uniqueness and blaming, fearing, judging from cradle to grave.

"I believe in the endless omniscience of God's beauty and love. For all people. One God force in the universe, whom we can only trust despite pain, and injustice and massacre and the daily horrors of life on earth. We must trust with the full natural beauty of our humanity, beyond what we can see or what anyone can tell us. He is the only one with the sense of it, and maybe in death it is shared with us as His children. But it is beyond good or evil, it is pure love and cannot be manipulated."

Adam stopped suddenly, aware that he had just given a speech, a speech only heard by himself inside his head, now shared with this strange, unsettling woman.

She watched him, sipping water, as if making a decision. Then slowly she reached into her handbag and took out a small photo of a good-looking young man in swim trunks and army cap and set it down firmly in the center of Adam's lacquered oak desk. He looked up at her, feeling his heart beating in his fingers and the pulse in his neck, sensing danger.

"Is this your husband?"

She found his eyes again, locking into them, picking him up and flying him around the room. "No, Father, it's not my husband. It's me."

Adam would always believe that God sent Lily to him. She was his Angel of Mercy, his salvation, his guide through the darkness into the light, Magdalen with the packaging askew. He did not tell her about himself for several weeks, though afterward, he realized that she had probably seen right through him with her crazed laser eyes from the first moment. From that morning on, she was his first friend since Duggan. He had shared one secret with Duggan, but not this one. Only Maybe knew this, though it had been buried between them since puberty, when his flight from himself began.

Lily Ivers was put into an orphanage by her father after catching her (or rather the small overweight boy named Leo that she had formerly been) dressed in his dead mother's clothes. Adam absorbed her anguished, sordid life story in daily installments, delivered in a self-consciously pitched staccato voice ("They did a ton of work on my damn Adam's apple. It was as big as a beanbag, but my voice is not perfected yet"), reciting a voyage of wandering, lying, loneliness without emotion or self-pity.

"I saved for my surgery working as a bar girl. You gotta take hormones, estrogens, progesterones, for at least six months to a year and the shrinks make you live as a woman for all that time (some places it's up to two years, but Boston's not *that* sadistic). So there I was—with my softening skin, my tapering waist, my spreading hips, my growing tits, my disappearing body hair and the Thing, the goddamn Thing just kinda shrunk up and nonfunctioning, chemical castration is what they call it. Anyway, I was this hermaphrodite freak, living in total weirdoland and completely paranoid, or as I told the shrink at the time, 'I'm not paranoid, I just don't trust anybody.' I was terrified of being found out, I played 'I Love Lucy' all day long but I felt like something from 'Lost in Space.' I couldn't use my social security number, driver's license, birth certificate, or, God forbid, any of poor old Leo's job references, so go-go dancing and cocktailing were all that was left (anyway, I wanted a night job, dark places made me feel safer).

"One night some poor old redneck drunk grabbed my crotch, I was taped and little Leo was pretty measly by then, but not *that* measly. I lost my job and almost my jaw, too. I just clutched my photo of Christine Jorgensen and fled. I have a friend from the Gender Identity Clinic, just had her breast implants put in, sometimes the hormones aren't enough and you need them, but the skin there is real thin, doesn't have the fat a real woman's does, and some guy grabbed her for a feel-up on the dance floor and the damn thing popped right out of her chest and smacked the sucker in the nose! Well, anyway, I finally completed all the prelim stuff, saved enough money, trotted in, and they did the dirty deed—whacked little Leo right into the Glad Bag! I think I took the first real deep breath in my entire pathetic little life. Then, don't laugh now, while I was still hardly conscious, I asked the doctor to put little Leo in a box, I wanted to give him a proper burial. And the sweetheart did. When I woke up, there he was all packed in ice. The nurse wheeled me out, and I buried him outside on the grounds. After all, he was gone forever, the wimp deserved something. I'm all he had and look what I did to him! 'So long, kiddo, rest in peace,' I said. The nurse was crying like it was her grandmother!

"Well, then afterward, the adorable Gender Clinic folks went to work. They arranged for a new birth certificate, driver's license, social security number, college records— the whole potato. I was a person again. A real woman with her own credit card.

"And a vagina. Of my very own! I'd look at the cute little thing every single morning. It was miraculous! I just couldn't believe it was still there, that it hadn't disappeared while I was asleep.

"The whole procedure is amazing. They bring in a team of medicos; an endocrinologist—did you know that all fetuses are female for the first six weeks of life? There's a theory called the Eve Base View that says that men are

just women plus androgen, that since all life begins female, and needs nothing added to exist, that we were
God's original being. I just love that! So anyway there's
the endocrinologist, a urologist, gynecologist, and a plastic surgeon. The operation has four parts. First the pe-
nectomy, then castration (frankly, I never understood
how all those macho, ball-worshiping male doctors could
handle it at all!), then they do the reconstruction, forming
the vagina, they call it a vaginoplasty. They do it by
making a cavitylike thing between the prostate and the
rectum (I have pictures at home if you're interested), then
they form the V from a skin graft on the thigh. It's not
great with a bikini, but I had a little plastic on it. After
all that they line it, sort of like a designer dress, with
scrotal skin and penile skin, thus, you can have the big
O like other girls. *Then* they put a mold in to keep the
V from closing up—same principle as pierced ears. When
they take it out, you have to manually dilate it, which is
quite enchanting, or, if you're lucky, have penile insertion
two or three times a week to keep it from clamming up
again.

  "But the hardest part is learning all the other stuff. How
to walk and talk. When women become men, which is
much harder, anyway, the male hormones lower their
voices, but the female hormones don't raise ours. You
have to retrain your voice. You also need a role model,
some woman to pattern yourself after. I know I'm a little
sixties, out of step with the times, though it's not so bad
out here in the sticks, but my role model was Donna
Reed. They used to show an old movie of hers in the
orphanage and I was mad to be like her. I was too scared
to trust being a new-wave unisex type. Lily's style suits
me and my husband likes it. *He* still wants to be Gary
Cooper!

  "I was on the street for a while after my change. I kinda
ran amok, so being super fem and conservative makes me

feel safer, now. I met my husband like that, hooking out in Texas. He *took me away from all that,* married me, and brought me home to his goddamn mother, a woman redeemed. That's *all* he knows, the orphan hits the street, and he doesn't suspect a thing. Poor Leo. I told my husband I had a brother who died."

This lie was the source of Lily's turmoil and it was on this that Adam concentrated as they grew closer, before his own confession. Her mother-in-law was hostile, jealous, and suspicious, scavenging around the edges of Lily's past; probing, prying, pushing. "If he ever found out, it would be over in an instant. He'd probably kill me, but he'd definitely leave me and that old bitch will not give up till she finds something. She doesn't have any idea what she's looking for, but she won't stop till she hangs me. The day I came to see you that first time, she had called to ask me the name of the orphanage I was in, she said she wanted to 'make a contribution.' I wish I'd frozen little Leo, I'd wrap him up and send him to her with a note pinned on him, 'Here's *my* contribution.' "

They met almost every day, with Adam trying to help her overcome her panic and tell her husband the truth. "You can't live like this forever. If the love is strong enough, he'll forgive you and you'll find a way."

"Wanna take bets," she replied, her red lips pulled down in a clown's frown.

Adam hired Lily as his secretary, and so they worked together every day, growing closer and more trusting. One morning as they walked together across the base to buy supplies at the PX, laughing together about the rumors spreading around the base (that the young reverend and the new secretary were growing far too chummy) he stopped suddenly and turned to her, searching her hypnotic eyes for permission. "I must tell you something. I haven't been honest with you. I've withheld and put my pride between us."

She smiled at him, sensing what was coming. "Lighten up, Adam, it's all right."

"No, it's not. Lily, I can't begin to tell you what knowing you, listening to you, has meant to me. I hope I've given you something in return, that I haven't acted too selfishly, but I know what you've shared is more than I can repay. I'm . . . I'm"—tears filled his sad blue eyes, washing over his confessional, softening the fear—"I'm like you. I mean like Leo. I've fought it all my life, until you put that photo on my desk."

"I know, Adam." She smiled, gently touching his cheek. "Isn't it nice to say it out loud? It's going to be okay now. You'll see."

Just how it was going to be "okay" Adam was a long way from seeing. Molasses was jealous of Lily and made snide remarks every chance she got. One night, after a scene with Adam over his request that Lily and her husband be invited to dinner, she stormed out, fleeing to Elmo, bottle of bourbon in hand, bursting in unannounced, just in time to see him slide his prized penis into the craggy orange mouth of none other than the commanding general's neglected wife. She raced home in a rage of frustration and righteous indignation, slugging down Jack Daniel's and baying at the moon. She slammed into their driveway, stormed up the stairs to their bedroom, and shook Adam awake.

"Listen to this, you pompous, adulterous bastard. You think you can sneak around protected by your dirty white collar, or should I say *lily* white, well, you're just an amateur! I've fucked everything that moves on this goddamn hicksville base! I've even done it in your precious little church, you two-timing impotent hypocrite!"

Adam sat, pale and still, not knowing whether to laugh or cry. The Goddess of Irony winking at him from the ceiling, and Venus, who cried for the feminine soul lost

inside the unyielding body of man, weeping silently beside him.

If Adam was shocked by Robin's hysterical confession,
his guilt at his failure to perform as a husband overrode
his feeling of betrayal. His forgiveness only upset her
more. She played her ace and he simply put his arms
around her and told her that he loved her and it was all
his fault. What was the fun in that? It left her feeling
powerless and desperate and out of this desperation she
decided to try something new, a direct hit, and so she
called Lily and invited her to lunch.

The morning before this "Ladies Lunch" Lily came into
Adam's office. "Your Holiness, sir, are you free tonight?
My friend Sam is in town, and I want you to meet him.
It's important for you."

"Important? More important than spending the evening
with my son?"

"Equally. Meet me here at eight o'clock."

At eight that evening, when Robin had gone off to the
movies, or so she said, and Adam had bathed Alex and
helped Maybe feed him and put him to sleep, he met
Lily for what would turn out to be the longest night of
his entire life.

They drove into town, Lily in her best black dress and
Adam in his street clothes, minus his collar so as not to
attract any unnecessary attention.

"I'll go in first, Adam, just in case Molasses is lurking
in the lobby. Meet me in Suite Two Hundred."

Adam waited several minutes and then followed her.
He could hear the sound of Lily's high melodious laugh
and a hoarse male voice mingling and echoing under the
door and down the hall moving toward him. He knocked,
his heart beating fast, trusting her but uneasy about what
waited inside.

A short swarthy man in his mid-fifties with thinning
hair, a small pot belly, and a large stogie clenched in his

teeth stood grinning at him. "Hi, Adam. I'm Sam. Pleased
to meet you. Lily has told me a lot about you, it's an
honor. If you'll excuse me, I just want to run into the
bedroom and get my sister. Be right back."

"Certainly," Adam replied, looking quizzically at Lily,
who just winked at him and motioned for him to sit next
to her.

"Come sit, have a glass of wine, he'll be right back."

Adam sat down next to Lily and waited. The wine
relaxed him and he closed his eyes for a moment, releasing
the strain of his daily battle.

"So sorry to keep you waiting." Something in the voice
was different. Adam opened his eyes and gasped. Sam
stood before him, his coarse, heavy face covered with
makeup, his stocky figure squeezed into a floral summer
dress, hairy bandy legs splayed almost sideways in his
white patent leather pumps. A curly, bright red wig sat
precariously on his broad, lined forehead.

"My God," Adam whispered, in spite of himself. Lily
took his hand.

"Sam, do the dance for Adam; he needs the whole act."

Sam sat down across from Adam and lit another cigar.
"First of all, don't call me Sam when I'm dressed, you
know better than that. I'm Samantha. I used to be 'Hard-
Hearted Hannah, the Vamp of Savannah,' but some drag
queen from Chicago stole it from me. I admire your tact,
Father. Most people laugh when they see Samantha. I
appreciate your compassion. Now, let's get down to it.
Lily called me in Boston, that's where I come from. She
told me quite a bit about you and since I was coming out
this way on business anyhow, I agreed to take a little
detour and pay you a visit. Besides, Lily and I are old
friends." He pushed his wig back up on his forehead and
puffed deeply on his cigar. Adam sat dead still, in awe
of this strange creature.

"I'll start by telling you a little bit about myself. I've

been married for twenty-five years to a feisty little broad and we've raised three kids. I'm a grandfather. I used to be an electronics salesman, but I retired, went back to school, got an M.A. in social psych. Now I run the Gender Identity Clinic in Boston. I'm also a heterosexual male transvestite. I'm gonna throw some monikers like that at you tonight, just ask me to explain anything you don't catch. Anyway, I dress up; I've done it for years. It makes me feel good. My wife knows all about it (she bought this dress for me) and my kids do, too. We're an unusual family that way; most of the fellas have to lie and sneak, I'm blessed that way. Anyway, that's another story.

"Lily wanted me to tell you about the clinic. We're there to help people with sex identity or gender problems. We get guys like me, we get drag queens, lesbian feminist transsexuals—that's a guy who becomes a gal, but likes gals—and vice versa—gals who become guys, but like other guys—and regular transsexuals like Lily. We get kids and grandpas and psychotics and nice, intelligent leaders of major corporations who just happen to enjoy running around hotel rooms in their wife's panties. We are the Barnum and Bailey of gender dysphoria and everything in between.

"We've even got a group of lesbian feminists who think that guys who have sex changes are trying to destroy women and replace them altogether and a group of male-to-female transsexuals who believe that women are becoming obsolete. We got eunuchs, we got hermaphrodites, we got a pre-op female-to-male jockey who's scared to use the locker-room john, and we got 'Marilyn Monroe' who just happens to have a cock; high fashion models with balls; macho factory workers with ovaries, you name it. We're a haven for life's rejects, God's mistakes, nature's little jokes.

"From what Lily tells me, you're in a great deal of conflict, and I think what she hoped was that I could

show you that there are others, many much worse off
than you, a community of people and a place to go for
help. We have live-in facilities while you're waiting for
surgery, counseling, even makeup and modeling classes,
and shop, and electronics—stuff like that.

"Now, at our meetings I give a little speech, even done
it on TV, though poor Samantha had to stay in the trunk
of my car. I'll try to give you a mini-version of what I
say. I also have a little booklet available for a buck twenty-
five donation.

"I'm not a minister, Adam, but I consider myself a
spiritual man, and since the Bible is filled with references
to transsexualism and the reuniting of the male and female
parts of the self, I don't think that the guilt and shame
and anguish that the world proffers to those of us who
are different is fair or Christian. In your case, you don't
have a fetish, like myself, or a homosexual need—that
comes in the platonic model of finding the female within
the self but treasuring the male body. You are a being
trapped in the wrong skin. There's a psychiatrist, John
Money, who believes that we are wired for gender, hor-
monally wired prenatally, and that people like you blow
a chromosomal fuse or something. Others believe it's
because your mother put nighties on you. I don't think
it much matters. What is, is. If the mind doesn't fit the
body, why not adjust the body to fit the mind?

"We don't live in a society that understands its misfits.
The Orient celebrated transsexualism and transvestism for
centuries. There are tribes of Arctic Indians who raised
handsome boys as girls and married them off to the mightiest
warriors and chiefs. The Greeks worshiped Hermaphrodite; Ovid sang of male and female transsexuals; the
Amazons were idolized; young Roman men cross-dressed.
Philo Judaeus, the Jewish philosopher of Alexandria, and
Gaius Manilius, the Roman politician, even old Juvenal
wrote of them.

"My point being that history and literature are full of aberrants. The courts of Louis the Fourteenth and Fifteenth certainly made a vogue of cross-dressing, and the eunuchs at Scythia were adored. Even old Nero, after searching for a woman who looked like the pregnant wife he accidentally killed, finally chose a beautiful young slave boy, had him castrated, and married him.

"But the sad truth is, we haven't come very far in five thousand years. In fact, in many ways we've regressed, and even with homosexuality a new social order and more than thirteen thousand pre-op and post-op transsexuals, you're about as welcome out in the open in the straight world as infectious hepatitis.

"So, Adam, what I'm getting at is, this is not a new phenomenon; it's been around before old Athena jumped out of Zeus's head, the ultimate man-made broad, and it's also not a resolved theological, moral, or social issue. It still ain't okay to be this way, but it's getting a little bit better.

"At least now the preachers and theologists are getting into it. After all, it's supposed to be the soul that counts, right? The body's just the container. In the Jewish cabala, heterosexual lovemaking is described as the act of reuniting the separated male and female parts of the original being. And in a way, when you transsex like Lily did, spiritually, you could see it as a merging, a movement beyond the limits of the physical self, a freeing of the true soul. Christ was a pretty androgynous character himself, ya know.

"Your need speaks from your soul. Look at it this way. You take a straight-arrow, high-hetero chick, give her a double mastectomy, take out the uterus, the ovaries, the works. Is she a man? Of course not. But if she's a *transsexual*, she becomes manlike, because that's where her *brain* is, and her soul. You can't change chromosomal sex, only anatomical sex; the rest is in the person's mind. So they cut Lily's cock off, gave her hormones, some cosmetic surgery; anatomically she's female, but most of it's an inside job, from her head and heart, 'cause if she washed up in the Old Mississippi, the autopsy would still say 'male.' That's the fact, Jack.

"We are a fanatically gender-defined society; the first question Mom and Pop ask is, 'Boy or girl?' 'Little pink booties or little blue booties?' No more cute Roman youths running around the temple in Mommy's clothes. Boys are boys and girls are girls, in public, anyway, or unless you're a rock star.

"So, I tell my friends at the clinic, there ain't no one gonna understand, approve, or make room for you, so go for the soul. If you're wearing the wrong body and you can't live with the bad fit, take it off, but only for yourself, your own salvation. Christ was only up on the cross for three days, some of you've been up there for twenty or thirty years."

Adam stood up, his legs tingling, a slice of tension cutting across his forehead.

"What is it, Adam?" Lily put down her glass and moved to his side.

"Nothing. It's . . . this is very hard. I . . . Sam—Samantha—this has been most helpful, and fascinating, but I . . . you see, I can't 'take it off' as you say just because it doesn't fit. I wanted to be a Catholic *priest*. Serving God is my life. And I have a son who means everything to me. If I do this I'll lose my work and my child forever. That's a very high and, at the same time, self-indulgent price for peace of mind or maybe just a little comfort. I promised my father I'd keep our family together and . . . and . . ." Adam stopped, Louis's last words pulsing inside his aching head: "Save yourself." "I'm just not ready for this. Thank you, Samantha, I appreciate your concern."

Sam stood up, stamped out his cigar, and took Adam's hand in his. " 'Give thanks unto the Lord, for He is good:

For His mercy endureth forever,' I Chronicles. I do a little Bible reading, myself, Father. I'll pray for ya."

"Thanks very much. I'll pray for you and your 'flock,' too."

They drove home in strained silence, Lily afraid to speak, feeling that she had made a terrible mistake, frightening him and pushing him away. The tension filled the space, squeezing Lily's chest until she could neither breathe nor bear the distance between them a moment longer. "Adam? Are you mad at me?" she whispered gasping for air as they reached the rectory where her car was parked.

His slender fingers gripped the steering wheel, his cheeks burned red. The tendons of his throat stood out in knotted cords. He said nothing.

"I just wanted to help. I never had anyone like Sam or me around when I was going through it. I just thought it might help you. I'm so—I didn't mean to . . ." She was shaking, feeling the power of her friend's pain, the weight of his conflict. Because he was never angry, the rage he now struggled to contain terrified her.

He turned on her, his eyes burning. "Help me what! Help me what! Throw myself and my family and my work into the garbage can? Or live a lie like you're doing? Trade one lie for another? Help me what!" He beat his delicate fists into the dashboard until sweat ran from his forehead.

She had never seen him out of control and it overwhelmed her. She sobbed like a child, sucking air in with each thud of his fist, streaking her perfect makeup. Her tears ran in crooked black lines down her face, melting her mask. "I'm sorry, I'm so sorry. Please stop, Adam. Please! I didn't mean—I know how hard it is for you. I didn't have anything to lose, I know that, but you suffer so. I—I'm going to tell Joey. I'm going to, you're right about that. At the clinic they say, 'If they care they don't mind and if they mind they don't care,' so best I find out the truth. I—I just don't know how you bear it."

Adam stopped. He unclenched his bruised hands and
put them over his wet face. Lily fought for control, afraid
to move or breathe. After a while he opened his eyes.
For a long moment he sat staring over the steering wheel
at his little chapel, then he turned and took her in his
arms. "Don't cry, Lily. Please forgive me. I didn't mean
to hurt you. I've got some thinking to do. Dry your eyes
now. I'm no one to judge right or wrong. Don't listen to
me. Do what's right for you. I must find out what's right
for *me*, that's all. You'd better go on now. I'll see you
tomorrow."

She nodded, wiping at her melted face with a perfumed
linen hankie. "I love you, Adam. I'm so sorry."

"I love you, too, Lily. I'm sorry, too."

He waited while she fumbled in her oversized purse
for her keys and settled into her car. Finally waving good-
bye, he drove off in the opposite direction, too fast, his
fine-boned jaw clenched in silent fury at himself, his fate,
his God. . . . His mercy endureth forever. . . . He shook
his fist at the unyielding moon, speeding down a country
road heading home to his own lie, his words to Lily
mocking him. "How long can you go on living a lie like
this?" he had said to her. How long indeed. He threw
his head back and screamed out loud, discharging his
outrage and self-loathing into the sealed steel capsule
surrounding him. How long, indeed.

As it turned out it was not very long. When he arrived
home the lights were on and he could hear loud voices
crackling through the open windows down the sloping
driveway to the street. He looked at his watch. It was
after ten.

He walked slowly toward the disturbance, knowing
that whatever it was it would take energy he did not have.
Before he could turn his key, Robin threw open the door,
her face contorted with anger; behind her, crouching on
the stairs, tears streaming down her shiny black face,

Trewanna sat holding her knees against her body as if warding off Robin's voice. Maybe stood beside her, face white, one hand lightly touching the terrified girl's shoulder.

"Where were you? You run off and leave without a word, and there's no way to reach you in an emergency! Off with that giant whore while I'm home dealing with a *thief*. A common thief in our own house! She's been stealing from us, right under our noses, an ungrateful little thief!"

The girl's shoulders shook but she held on to herself, to the primitive dignity that rises up when the internal breaking point is reached, when the point of honor outweighs the risk of action, when it is necessary to confront.

"I'm no thief. I never stole nothin' in my life."

Robin whirled toward Adam. "She's a liar! My clothes keep disappearing. I came home tonight and I decided to try on that navy silk dress I bought last year, I wanted to wear it to the officers' club party next week, my *best* dress and it's gone and my silver shoes and my best silk nightie, scarves, all kinds of things. It's been going on for months. Things disappear, then they reappear. Some of them *never* reappear. My good pearl earrings! She's taking them. No one else in this house could be doing it. And I saw her, too. I saw her coming out of your study with my scarf in her hand! I'm going to call the police."

"Robin, you stop now!" Maybe took her by the shoulders, her plump face drawn and tense. "Nobody's callin' no police. This here girl wouldn't hurt a fly. Now, jest calm yoself down now."

Adam felt the throbbing in his head move, crossing to the side, flooding his brain with blood.

He moved past his wife and helped Trewanna up, wiping her tears away with his hands. "She did not take your things, Robin. She did *not* take your things." He spoke in a quiet voice, so quiet and so dead and so certain that it stopped the scene cold.

Points of honor. Adam stood washed in his own shame, helping the skinny, broken black girl put her pride back together.

Adam arrived at his tidy whitewashed chapel before dawn. He had not slept, his clothes were wrinkled, his eyes circled with dark, bruised tissue, as if he had smeared them with an ink-stained finger.

After the house quieted and Trewanna was sent to the relative safety of her own single bed, Adam wandered around in the stuffy isolation of his private study until Robin's sounds ebbed and faded into sleep. He wandered as his father and grandfather before him had wandered, cut off from the world of family and friend, of love given in open joyous freedom, of lives lived without fear, without secrets, hidden rooms, locked drawers, hated truths; unable to open the windows, the arms, the heart to ventilate the spirit. Finally, he took his key and unlocked the closet door. He entered and gathered his wife's stolen garments, the navy dress, the pearl earrings, the silver shoes. He had chosen things that it seemed she never wore, from the back of the closet, the bottom of the drawer. She never mentioned them and so he forgot to be careful; forgot to put away the pale yellow chiffon scarf that felt so silky and cool and comforting next to his throat. Or maybe he had wanted to be caught, punished, forced to confess.

The worst part of the whole hysterical tribunal on his front stairs, by far the most horrible part, had been that for a moment, one terrible instant, it was a choice between his lie and Trewanna's life, and he hesitated, he faltered, he almost let it be. Judas guzzling wine and breaking bread as the door was being kicked in, the caster of the first stone; he had been that afraid. Wandering, he still did not know how far his fear would have gone if he had been challenged, if Robin had not collapsed in sobs and let him take her upstairs, so overwrought with her powerlessness and hurt pride. Her double cuckoldry. Betrayed by her lover and her husband.

She did not sustain her assault, and so he was granted a reprieve, spared the final test of his own honor: "Trewanna did not take your clothes; I took them." He had been spared this time. Slowly, he gathered the clothes together and put them in a suitcase and tiptoed downstairs to Maybe's room and tapped gently on her door as his father before him had done so long ago; the door that would always open, radiating the God light of true love and compassion. As it always had, it opened, revealing a large old woman with ruddy cheeks and a blinding white nightgown, who was as close to the archangel as he was ever likely to get.

It was obvious that she had been waiting for him. Her bed was still made, her book and a cup of honey-tea still steaming beside the old wing chair that had held her with various children in her arms for forty-odd years. She smiled at him and kissed his cheek.

"I guess you've been waiting for this visit for quite a while."

"I got mo' sense than that after three generations of you folks. I just take it moment by moment and try not to be too shocked by nothin'. But I ain't too surprised to see yoself in here, tonight."

"I've got Robin's things in this case. I don't know how to return them. I can't think of how, of what to do. I've been living this lie for so long, I'm losing myself in it. I almost let Trewanna pay for it."

"But you didn't and you wouldn't! I know you better than that, Adam Richeleau. You got the strength that yo' poppa and yo' momma never had. You got the Lord in you. You would not have let no harm come to that poor girl or no one else, including yo' own self."

Adam took her warm, spongy hand and pulled her down next to him on the old brass bed. "I hope you're right, Maybe, because I'm going to need all the strength I can beg, borrow, or steal now." He sighed, rubbing at his tired, puffy eyes. "I want you to know about Lily. Lily's like me, Maybe. She was like me, anyway. She had an operation, she became a woman. She took me to talk to someone tonight, a very strange fellow; Laurel would have liked him. He runs a clinic up north, in Boston. It's where Lily went, it's for people like me.

"I'm not the only one, like I always thought. Remember how frightened we were, how ignorant. Remember what Madame Zhanna told me and I couldn't even find the words in the dictionary? Well, I have books all about it now. I'm not the only one. I've been fighting it so long. And I probably would have gone on but for poor Trewanna, sitting on those stairs, paying for my lie. And Robin, she's paying. I can't be a husband to her. She married me thinking her life would be one way and I've ripped all her dreams out from under her. I know she's not perfect, and that she tricked me with Alex, but I never gave her a chance. I lied more than she did and this marriage, this life here, is unraveling her.

"I've been a damn martyr and suddenly tonight I realized that I'm not doing it out of *selflessness*, for the sake of God and son and family. I'm doing it out of supreme selfishness. I don't want to give up *my* son and *my* ministry, but I will betray both and many people who believe in me if I don't even have the courage to be who I am. And I'm not a man. My mind and my soul, that's what this man talked about tonight, my heart and soul and brain are like yours and always have been. I have to go away and be who I am. I have to let go of all of you or I'll end up pulling you down into my despair, and that will be the true end of this family.

"I just want you to promise me one thing, if you can:

that you'll stay with Alex, stay with them both. She can't do it without you, and I don't think I can go unless I know that he's safe, that he has your guidance. You can go back to New Orleans and live in the guesthouse. I'll set the money up in trust for Alex, with you and Laurel as executors, so that, well, just to protect Alex in case Robin can't handle things, as a safeguard. I hate to think about it like that, but it's too important to make a mistake about. I'll be in contact with you, but no one, no one on earth except you will know where I am or even if I'm alive, and no one will ever know about what I'm going to do, for Alex's sake. So once again, I need your help. I have to just disappear, forever. I know I have no right to ask you to do this, especially when your job with us lunatic Richeleaus was almost over."

The large old woman stood up, her white-lashed royal blue eyes bright with tears that she would not permit to fall. She turned away from him for a moment, closing her eyes as if to clear her vision, breathing in her own private supply of air. "I be here for ya, Adam, as long as I'm breathin, and you know it. You go on and get yoself fixed. Do what you gotta do. We'll be fine. Robin will sputter a while, but she has her priorities, and a husband ain't really the main one of 'em. Everyone who'd be hurt by what you are doin' is long dead. You're free of that past now. You go on and find some happiness."

They held one another for a long time, heartbeat to heartbeat, the old woman and the young pastor, saying good-bye to the people they had loved and to each other.

When Adam opened the door to his office the sun was just beginning to edge over the stained-glass window in the chapel, casting soft morning light on his rumpled clothes and the polished wood of his desk. In the center of the desk was a note, on lavender paper, smelling of Lily.

Adam. I told him. I'm glad I did, you were right about not living a lie, but it's over. He threw me out. (I was lucky at that, he took a swing at me, thousands of dollars of brand-new plastic surgery jeopardized! Fortunately, I ducked and he broke his hand on the doorjamb.) When you read this, I will already be long gone. I don't know where and it's best if you don't either, just in case Joey comes looking for me. Please don't feel bad, because you were right. I was crazy to think any love could work started on a lie of such enormous proportions—though I guess a lie of minute proportions could unfurl the same flag. I am so sorry about Sam. Please forgive me. But I do feel that you needed to hear someone from the Other Side. I'll contact you when I've resettled. I'm not giving up on love or myself and I learned a lot. Please tell Robin I'm sorry I won't be able to lunch with her today (Miss Otis regrets, etc.). My leaving should make your *home* life better, anyway. I'll miss you. God be with you and don't forget your 'girlfriend' Lily.

He sat holding the sweet-smelling little note tightly in his fingers, turning it round and round until the sun pushed forth, covering the sky, streaming in everywhere, ending his sleepless starless night and beckoning him forth into the new day.

PART THREE
NATHAN'S
BOOK

CHAPTER 14

While Adam was settling his affairs in Shreveport, La., I, Nathan Poe, was celebrating my forty-seventh year on Mother Earth by committing my drug-addicted, herpes-infected (before it was even fashionable), eighteen-year-old daughter to an elegant loonyland in upstate New York. The year of 1977 had not been one of my better ones, either.

I stood amidst the rubble of my third failed marriage and my once promising career, watching my only living child wheeled away in a straitjacket, her bare legs flailing, screaming down the cheery, modern print—filled corridor, "It's all your fault, you selfish, no-good son of a bitch."

Mostly she was right, it was my fault. I don't mean to go heavy on the chest-beating, but since I had spent the past thirty years chasing rainbows, ambulances, world leaders, women, and my own tail with a kind of self-indulgent, gleeful gusto usually associated with bail bondsmen, cartoon characters, or psychopaths, I had managed to pretty well fuck up all relationships, people-wise, careerwise, and otherwise.

I was more than willing to be fair to myself. It was not *all* my fault. But it was a lot my fault.

I was living at the time in a second-class hotel-apartment building on the East Side, near the East River and several very good newsmen's drinking establishments. They took care of me there, the elevator man, the doorman, the lady on the switchboard, the janitor who stocked my fireplace with cords of dry, sweet pine all winter. They were all a little run-down and round about the heels and so we understood one another.

I had been living in this wrinkled bachelor limbo for the better part of a year, trying to sort through the cerebrum steamer trunk in my moth-eaten emotional attic and salvage what I could of my virtue, or at least my vanity.

Most of the time I was in a state of shock: I felt stunned, like a bird barreling into a plate-glass door; unstrung like the tennis racquet from those Southampton summers, lying in ruin on the bottom of my musty hotel closet; struck dumb by my own fate; the middle-age mayhem was leaking from my cigarette-puckered lips, flowing over my wrecked, overfed body like "lice in Egypt" (as old Clarence Darrow once put it). That was me, covered with self-pity, like lice on a camel seller's dinner. Wallowing.

It was not supposed to be this way. It was not how I started out or where I had intended to go. It was not that I was one of those methodical, anal types who writes out a life plan on their third birthday (Ph.D. at twenty, first million at thirty, cover of *Time* magazine at forty), but I had started cocky, energetic, ambitious, and virtually hyperventilating the first eight bars of the American Dream Concerto.

So how had I come to this? Passed over by Wallace, Safer, Rather, Cronkite, Reynolds, Sevareid, and the gang. A correspondent's version of "always the bridesmaid." I found myself, after almost thirty years of tearing around the world looking for The Story, and past the point where I could double my age and still be here, with nothing to show but a spastic colon, bad lungs, a liver that probably looked like the inside of Hadrian's tomb, a kid in a strait-jacket, three ex-wives who would not be too grieved to watch me free-fall from the observation deck of the World Trade Center, and a humongous case of midlife angst. No Pulitzer, no nightly news anchor, no closing commentary, no Paris bureau chief appointment, devoted family, salient love life, or self-worth.

This was not what Maxie Polinski's adorable curly-haired matza ball had planned for himself. My aunt Ida used to ask me, "So if you're on TV why aren't you rich and famous?" Well, I had just sat down to figure out a proper answer. The idea of consequences had never made any impression, now it was my favorite word. I would sit at my hotel desk, in front of my trusty machine, and type the word over and over again, as if I had just discovered it. Consequences, consequences, con se quen cessss. . . .

Somehow I had been floating around in the amniotic fluid of self-deception for forty-eight years and now, when I needed those luscious cherry-pop juices most, the damn sac had sprung a leak. Reality was oozing out and I was not prepared.

My first wife had been very big on reality. Reality meaning everything on earth that you would not like to talk about over dinner. She had been part of the 1950s American leftist socialist fervor. Elsie Frank, my young, radical crusader, could rattle on for hours about the end of the world, government, corruption, the Bomb, Father Coughlin, Trotskyists, Stalinists, Huey Long, social unrest, revolution, starving children, civil rights, and Korea; the evils of: television, *Vogue* magazine, payola, police actions, instant coffee, filter tip cigarettes, and brain-washing; the number of murders in each major city in the world, capital punishment (she was against it), free love (she was for it in theory though God knows not in practice—even I didn't get any free), and death.

She was obsessed with death. She saw mortality metaphors in everything from a *dying fire* to *dying to see* or *dying to read*, in flickering matches and afternoon naps. I thought she was mad (not to mention depressing). Death had no more reality to me than acid rain (doesn't sting when it falls). It was an abstract concept.

My mother died shortly after I was born, but since she had no reality to me, neither did her death. It was like meeting an Eskimo, curious, but not relative. Suddenly, at forty-eight, I picked up my little Jewish Red ex-wife's attraction to the subject. In fact, if we had met then we would have been a perfect pair, rattling off all the old horrors plus all the new ones. By then we had added: nuclear waste, environmental cancer, My Lai, Jonestown, nukes, Jimmy Carter, runaway inflation, Maurice Stans, Rose Mary Woods, Deep Throat (and the Watergate Revue), shopping malls, McDonald's, abortion, mass murderers, gun control, rape, race riots, inner city decay, suburban spiritual somnambulism, the John Birch Society, American Nazi Party, Why-Johnny-Can't-Read, midlife crisis, noise pollution, El Salvador, the Six-Day, Seven-Day, and Yom Kippur wars, the PLO, born-again Christians, Charles Manson, child molesters, kid porn, and a host of dinner table tableaus to keep us sobbing in our chicken soup until Armageddon or nuclear war (whichever comes first).

Elsie and I met right after my return from Korea, where I had received a Purple Heart for diving under a desk in the field press office and accidentally saving a young French photographer who just happened to be behind me. As it was described to me afterward, I risked my life, throwing myself on top of him and catching a large ball of shrapnel in my ass (that was not their word).

My tour of duty—which was not supposed to include

anything close to risk of life or limb—ended and I was sent home to sit out (though with considerable difficulty) the rest of the war, writing radio spots for Voice of America, which was just fine with me.

Elsie worked for Voice of America. She was big-breasted and round-hipped and—since my experience with women was limited, but enriched by a conception (motherless and all) of women as magical, perfect people, beyond the understanding of mere men such as I—she seemed of goddess proportions. I had never even seen one fully undressed and that was a miracle of soft, foreign loveliness; I stood before her as a caveman before fire, awestruck and afraid of being burned. That, I have since learned, is not quite the healthiest way to approach them. So, to me, she was the Statue of Liberty with tits and to her I was the young crusader out to save the world from the bad guys through the power of the mighty pen.

It did not take long for the fire to grow cold. One night I stuck my finger into it and it was out. The illusion shattered; instead of my magical maiden; there was a whiny, middle-class girl from Queens who wanted to be a Russian peasant and thought sex in particular and men in general were a necessary though evil route to saving the world. When she realized that my motives for buzzing around New York chasing injustice were far less noble and Upton Sinclair I was not going to be, she pulled her finger out of the ashes, too.

It almost broke my father's heart when I left her. Pop, having lived the most unconventional life he possibly could (a fact that he always blamed on my mother's untimely death), wanted nothing more than for me to reside in Great Neck, Long Island, in a Colonial-style house with a nice Jewish wife and three rapturous young children. I loved my father and I had married Elsie partially to help him achieve that fantasy, but in the end, I couldn't go the distance with it even for him

In that hotel-apartment by the East River I thought about Elsie and about death, how fast everything had gone and how little I had to show for my pushing fifty years here.

One night I sat, with a carton of cigarettes and a fifth of Glenlivet, and went through my scrapbook, reliving my life through my old newspaper clippings. What I saw was not very pretty. I saw corruption, tragedy, despair, unsolvable problems, and worthless solutions. I saw bad news. Day after day, report after report, story after story; bad news. I had never thought about it like that (not with Elsie's snake-eyed grasp); it was just what I did, report what was happening in the world.

Sometimes it got to me. I covered an innocent man who was accused of rape and lost his job, his wife, his entire world, spent years in jail, every cent he had, and was finally exonerated. I remember him saying to me, "The very worst part was that no one even said, 'We're sorry.' " That got to me, the possibility of that kind of blind, fascistic injustice. A car pulls up to a guy on his way to mail a letter, "You're under arrest" someone says, and your life goes down the toilet. There was a case against an automaker where a woman and her husband and their three small children were lightly rear-ended. It was the kind of crash that should end up with a tsk-tsk, an apology, and a shrugged shoulder. But this light tap exploded a defective gas tank, burned all the helpless screaming babies to death, and left the husband and wife maimed beyond human form, living like two ravaged horror-film characters on the thin edge of their will to survive. Those times I would take a long walk, drink more than usual, and even cry occasionally; but still, it would all go under the heading of Not Relative, not overwhelming, or impossible to live with. I just went on to the next story.

What I realized, while thumbing through my life's work, was that the effect was cumulative. The toxins compress, the jaundiced eye begins to yellow and ooze, the world-

view clouds, hazed over with apathy and cynicism. Alfred
Dreyfus, I was not (Émile Zola, neither). It had gotten
to me, all the junk on which news is made. The Tha-
lidomide babies and George Lincoln Rockwell and Richard Milhous and Cambodia and Malcolm X, all of it, and
I had never even noticed the effects until one morning,
shaving, I saw the oozing poison in my puppy brown
eyes. Double forty-eight and you get ninety-six—not a
chance, Nathan, not a chance.

In 1930, at the zygote of the Depression, when I was
six months old, my mother, Sylvia Polinski, stepped off
the curb at the corner of 42nd Street and Fifth Avenue
and was struck down and killed instantly by the German
ambassador's diplomatic limousine, which was en route
with Herr Ambassador to the Waldorf-Astoria. I was in
her arms at the time, but since it was evidently not my
turn, I was thrown clear. I landed on Fifth Avenue almost
in the lap of a nice old Lithuanian widow named Mitzi,
who took me home to my pop, wiped his tears, and stayed
to change my diapers and cook my pablum for almost
two years.

The irony of my poor, sweet young mother, who had
escaped the Warsaw Ghetto and the growling, anti-
Semitism, being killed by the goddamn German ambassador's goddamn decadent, bloody Hunmobile, escaped
no one, especially my maternal grandparents, my pop,
and his sister, Ida, who were the only relatives I had on
earth.

This tragedy did not make my father, Max Polinski's
(a. k. a. Maxie Poe's) life easier. My father was a first generation Polish-Russian-Jewish kid raised on the Lower East
Side of Manhattan who was orphaned in 1924 at the age
of sixteen when his parents burned to death in a sweatshop
fire in the garment district. The Roaring Twenties ground
to a halt for Pop and his sister, Ida.

Maxie was a short, wiry kid with "a nose like a light

bulb" (as he described it), a pod of slicked-back, center-parted, frizzy, carrot-colored hair, a slightly bowlegged swagger, and a little man's furious, manic energy.

He was not special enough in any way to compete in the city-school jungle. He wasn't strong enough for athletics, smart enough for scholarships, or tough enough for the gangs of misplaced youths who segued from street kids to mob members with relative ease.

What my pop did have, though, was a lightning quick, schticky sense of humor. He was funny. He was born funny. He did one-liners for pennies on Mulberry and Orchard streets when he was five years old. "Hey, Mrs. Morelli, wanna see time fly, throw a clock outta de winda."

My pop's sense of humor protected us through the Depression, failure, sickness, loneliness, hunger. "What we should do, Nathan, is get rid of that meshuga I.Q. test and replace it with a S.O.H. test, a Sense of Humor Test. Anyone who fails has to spend a year doing one-liners on the steps of the New York Public Library."

Maxie's sense of humor kept him from beatings by local thugs, got us fed, and cheered up the whole neighborhood through the Horrible Hoover Years.

Humor was his reflex, his defense, the outlet for his hostility and frustration. When my mother was killed, Maxie was working burlesque, his eye on Ziegfeld, Cuban cigars, Park Avenue co-ops, radio. But as funny as he was, he had no presence on stage. He was just a little too nervous, a tad too fast. He didn't have the magic, the God-given ability to pick an audience up, bounce it around in the palm of his cool, controlling hand, and deliver it panting and applauding back into its velveteen-covered seats.

In addition, he had me. After Mitzi left, I became part of the act, like the ventriloquist's dummy, he schlepped me around to agents, auditions, one-nighters. In between we lived on the goodwill of Aunt Ida and her *employed* husband, Jake; in the Hoovervilles and Battery dives; and even in the back of his friend Dominic's taxicab.

My nursery school was the R & W Deli on 46th Street and Seventh Avenue, an *office* for comics (would-be's and has-been's). As the thirties deepened and the presence of radio grew, accelerating the need for fresh material, the action around the R & W picked up. Now there was a new group, the joke peddlers, and my pop became the leader. These guys sat around over Danish and five-cent coffee inventing jokes, or stealing them, to sell to working comics and writers. Every hour or so the phone on the counter would ring or the revolving door would twirl open, bringing in winter cold or summer swelter accompanied by a hyperanxious agent, writer, manager, or second-string comic in desperate need of new material.

"Hey, anyone got a mother-in-law routine—we're payin' a sawbuck."

I learned to read, using an old Fred Allen script. I learned to add and subtract (still haven't gotten around to multiplication or division—and did not know how to tell time until I was nineteen years old—everyone thought someone else had taught me) tallying up the "funny money" as Maxie called it, the daily take for him and his cronies.

I teethed on water bagels and truly believed, until I was ten years old, that milk came in coffee cups.

Pop was no fool, and he realized that I had my uses (as well as my disadvantages). How could anyone with half a heart turn down an Eleanor Roosevelt joke gurgling from the cream-cheese-stained mouth of a tiny motherless tyke? It worked pretty well.

Sometimes we took our act on the road. The phone at the deli would ring and one of Maxie's street spies would whisper, "Benny's at the Sherry Netherland" and off we'd go, hitting the lobby at a run and planting ourselves by the front entrance with a 180-degree view of arrivals and departures. Doormen and house dicks knew us and let us be for the most part (I was a fairly cute little guy). Sooner or later, an elevator door would swing open and out would come a King of Comedy, cashmere overcoat thrown over mohair suit, scampering sycophants clearing the way. Up Maxie jumped, pulling me behind him. "Hey, Mr. Bergen, remember my boy Nathan, got a fantastic Hoover joke, brand-new—wrote it just for you." They almost never refused. Partly because the jokes were usually good, partly because of me, and mostly because they were all scared shitless of ending up like Pop. Buying Maxie's joke was the comedy king's version of the blind man's cup.

All the while, Maxie kept trying to break into radio. He was hampered by the Depression, me, his appearance, and the fact that he was only barely literate, having left school when his folks died without learning too much while he was there. When he had an interview or a chance to do a script on spec (they like it, you eat), he would leave me with the guys in the deli or Aunt Ida and tear across town in his only suit, slicking back his hair with the sweat from his own nervous palms.

These were the strangest of times. Maxie would whiz by bread lines (which we might be standing in ourselves later the same day), stop to comfort a pretty woman sobbing over a run in her only pair of stockings, then fly into the RCA building to the world of "Fibber McGee and Molly," "One Man's Family," "Amos 'n' Andy," "Major Bowles," "Mr. First Nighter," "Burns and Allen," "The Jell-o Hour" (with Jack Benny and Mary Livingston), "Manhattan Merry-Go-Round"; down the cool, quiet, insulated corridors where there was plenty to eat and stockings to spare and the American Dream was still recharging its national battery. One night, as Maxie left the RCA building, he was almost hit by a man tumbling from the sixteenth floor. It was not uncommon in those days, hardly raised an eyebrow at the dinner table. Maxie wanted more than anything on earth to be inside an office on the sixteenth floor, and this turkey was jumping out!

Finally, Pop did get a job in radio (though not until 1939), and we moved into a small hotel in the theater district, close to the R & W. All day long and often well into the night, he sat in a nicotine-yellowed, windowless room writing gags for "The Chase and Sanborn Hour" with Don Ameche, Dorothy Lamour, Edgar Bergen, and the Stroud Twins. After a while they moved him around from show to show, patching and filling where needed. To Maxie it was "Heeb Heaven." Money in his pocket, prestige. A radio writer. He began to plan his plans again and dream his dreams.

The dream lasted until Pearl Harbor and my feisty little thirty-two-year-old father was drafted. "If you got eyes, ears, and a throat, you're in," he said, the prototype Sad Sack. Pop checked us out of our first real home, checked me into Aunt Ida's row house in Brooklyn, and went off to fight a war that for him had been little more than a rich new source of material.

Maxie's tour was not so funny. He was a foot soldier in eastern Europe and he came home bald, blind in one eye, and broken. He never talked about it, not to my knowledge to anyone to this very day, and he could never make jokes about it again. He had been in the Occupation forces and had liberated Polish concentration camps. He never told or sold a Nazi or any other kind of war joke (or any at all for a long time). He had the G.I. bill and a disability pension and after a fairly long and silent con-valescence at Aunt Ida's, he took me from the cozy middle-class life of stickball and school days, baseball cards and model planes, other children and regular meals, back to our hotel and the R & W.

There was no place in radio for him anymore. It was not a gagman's time. Roosevelt was dead and movies were where the magic was. Crooners were edging comics off

the airwaves and shell-shocked, aging, half-blind joke
men, even if they were vets, were hardly in demand. For
a while we lived on Maxie's pension and hung around the
R & W greeting what was left of the old crowd, drifting.

I was almost fifteen by then, a nice-looking, big-nosed
kid with a cocky smile and a serious, heavy streak hidden
behind a pubescent's idea of nonchalance. I was lonely,
skinny, in the primary stages of adolescent lust, and torn
between my ecstasy at having Pop back (my father the
Jewish war hero) and my sadness at leaving the warm,
schmaltzy safety of Aunt Ida's well-organized sensible life
(it was a battle that I would fight over and over throughout
my life, never resolving to any satisfaction). So it was
back to bagels for breakfast, school on occasion, catching
acts, hustling material, hanging out at Deuces listening
to bebop till dawn; Pop and I, On The Town.

The postwar forties were a great time to be in New
York but a lousy time to be a teenager. Teenagers in those
days were like flower bulbs, a necessary stage of devel-
opment, but utterly worthless until they bloomed. We
dressed like second-class grown-ups and imitated our adult
overlords with a heartrending combination of bravado and
innocence. Since my life was certainly not the average,
I was especially vulnerable and, thus, considerably more
obnoxious (cocky, brash, and imitative) than other adolescents.

I lived at Yankee Stadium cheering on my DiMaggio,
my Rizzuto by day and inhaling Benny Goodman, the
Dorseys, The Count, or playing Glenn Miller records (he
had gone down in a wartime accident over the English
Channel) while I slept, which was rarely and heavily.

By my sixteenth year, Pop had regained enough of his
old spunk to land a job doing legwork for the nightlife
columnist of the grand old *New York Herald-Tribune*. He
ran around gathering gossip, doing interviews, making
up funny lines that supposedly fell out of unfunny famous
mouths till his good eye closed in exhaustion.

It was then that I discovered the world of news, and it was definitely a case of obsession at first sight. I would stand in the corner of the city room waiting for Pop, now and then catching a glimpse of Jock Whitney, John Crosby, or Walter Lippmann, all intense, frantic, cigarettes and coffee containers almost surgically attached; everyone racing around as if the very fate of the world rested on each story.

I started smoking to be like those great rolled-sleeved, pasty-skinned guys at the *Trib* and drinking, too (show me a real newsman in those days who didn't toss the sauce and I'll show you one without a byline). I had found my niche. For the first time in my life I began to read something other than radio scripts or baseball scores. I read newspapers, Ernest Hemingway, F. Scott Fitzgerald, Sherwood Anderson, Sinclair Lewis, Damon Runyon, *The New Yorker*, William Faulkner (never could get into him), John Steinbeck, James Thurber, John Dos Passos, Robert Benchley, Alexander Woollcott, Eugene O'Neill, and I read them all slowly, with great difficulty and a dime-store dictionary at my side.

I found out what to read by reading, and I learned how to write by copying my gods at the *Trib*, stealing discarded copy from the wastebaskets, imitating their style and syntax (a word that I had never heard). I didn't know a dangling participle from an adverb, but somehow I had the instinct and, most important, I wanted very badly to do it. When an opening as a copyboy came up, I quit school forever (token though the gesture was) and moved full time and full throttle into the news business.

This was fine with Pop, who had just begun to consider the fact that I was almost grown and would have to find some way to support myself. So he helped me. This was also the time that he began to envision a life for me like he had never known and certainly never wanted.

He hustled for me, found stories on his runs around Manhattan that no one would let me write.

One night, well after midnight, Pop came panting into my room, pulled off my blankets, and shouted, "Get up quick! I got a story for ya they gotta take!" I was up and out so fast I didn't even realize I had no shoes on till we hit the street. Well, screw shoes, I was onto a hot story. Pop led me down alleys, to the Onyx, an after-hours club on West 52nd Street known for its all-night jam sessions. A brawl was in progress. In the room were several prominent musicians and men about city hall who were swinging with the best of them (fists, not instruments). Lying nude on top of the piano was the source of the fracas, a well-known motion picture actress revered for her demure, virginal portrayals, with an empty bottle of gin in one hand and a clarinet, which she was using as a club, in the other. Luckily, Pop had the foresight to grab our camera on the way out and so, three hours later, I raced into the city editor, story and film in my steamy little hand: BEBOP AND BARE BEAUTY LEAD TO OFF-BROADWAY BRAWL. And lo and behold, they ran it, byline and all. From that moment on, I was unstoppable, at least until Korea. "My son, the reporter" became my new introduction at the R & W.

So much for the rites of passage. No long reminiscence about boyhood days in the country, fishing holes, and homemade pie. Until Korea I had never been north of Harlem or south of Ebbet's Field.

After Elsie, I set about changing all of that. Voice of America led to a job in the Paris office of the *International Herald-Tribune*. Hemingway was there, James Jones, Picasso, Sartre, the whole number. I took to it like rock salt to pretzels and I grew up. I also met my second wife.

Looking back from the Glenlivet-blurred eagle's-eye view of my forty-eighth year, it seemed hard to believe that the person sashaying about Montparnasse thinking he was one hell of a special smart fella could have possibly been so crack-brain stupid. But that's the double-edged sword

of hindsight, how-you-would-do-it-differently-with-what-
you-know-now-but-if-you'd-done-it-differently-you-wouldn't-
know-what-you-know-now. Anyway, I met an absolutely
gorgeous fashion model from Tulsa, Oklahoma, named
Norma Childes and moved from the Statue of Liberty
with tits to Greta Garbo with nymphomania.

I fell in love with the package, Bogey and Bacall, Lady
Brett and Jake Barnes, Paris in the spring, fantasy goddesses, hallucinations of ego. I forgot Pop's dictum about
the Sense of Humor test. Norma thought a sense of humor
was an ice-cream bar. What she *had* heard of was sex,
clothes, fast cars, champagne, Dexedrine, marijuana, and
Jack Kerouac. We went On the Road, French style, sort
of *The Lost Weekend* stretched into two years, which almost
cost me my job (newsmen develop an uncanny fortitude
and can continue functioning beyond their ability to feed
themselves, stand upright, and remember their first names).
I had certainly never had sex like Norma. Days spent in
dark stuffy rooms, lost in a frenzied, palsied eroticism
that would have scared the shit out of me either before
or after her.

We partied in Paris for two years, until I woke up one
morning fucked out, drugged out, drunk out, dying for
a nice hot cup of kreplach soup and a good conversation.
It was 1959, and the decade was getting ready for its
swan dive. Ike was getting ready to retire, Kennedy was
getting ready to run his black Irish ass off, Nixon was
getting Checkers out of mothballs, I was getting ready
to go home, and Norma was getting pregnant.

Part of growing up without a sense of permanence or
traditional values is that one doesn't always learn to do
the *right thing*. Pop and I had our own cowboy rules. Never
lie to an agent, never steal anyone's material, always back
a buddy, carry your own weight, get there before the
other guy, pay your bar bill, wash your hands after bodily
functions, idolize ladies and help old ones across the

street, and don't get involved in other people's problems.
That was about it. Martyr was not on our list.

So when the cold light of day cast its long shadow
over Norma's wonderful face and I realized that the party
was definitely over, I was already packing when the news
came.

Baby. You must have been a beautiful one; "Babyface,"
"Rockabye Baby," "One for My Baby." All I knew about
them was Tin Pan Alley. I didn't know and I didn't much
care. I had a plane to catch and Norma was standing
there, without a sense of humor and pregnant.

I brought her home to Aunt Ida; a skinny shiksa who
had never heard of chicken *schmaltz* and thought that
Greek was the official Hebrew language, sitting in the
kitchen eating potato chip sandwiches on white bread
with mayonnaise and crying all the time. But, with Aunt
Ida's guidance, I "did the right thing"—meaning, I stuck
around, so to speak, working for the *Daily News* and
coming home occasionally.

My daughter was born on a sticky Indian summer night.
She looked exactly like me, which caused Pop and me
to crumple into tears for the first time in memory. We
named her Greta (what else). Greta Poe, not a bad mon-
iker, considering.

By the time Greta was one year old, Norma had resumed her modeling career, going on to become the
hottest face in N.Y.C. and making more in a week than
I was getting in a month. Off she went, taking my chunky
little clone, breaking Pop's heart and bruising mine (ego
is a great protector of bawling hearts), fleeing into the
arms of an equally humorless but quite successful songwriter (he only did ballads). Little Greta was calling him
Da-Da before her diaper was wet.

The next seven years whizzed by. I trotted through
the sixties in a hedonistic, workaholic haze that I remember only through headlines: Kennedy, Camelot, Bay of

Pigs, integration, U-2 incident, the Pill, Vietnam, love children, militants, Kent State, Bobby Kennedy, L.B.J., draft dodgers, miniskirts, the Berlin Wall, the airlift, napalm, long-range intercontinental ballistic missiles, Eugene McCarthy.

I spent a year (one night) at the *Detroit Free Press*, another at the *Chicago Sun-Times*, another in Thailand for U.P.I. bouncing off barstools, broads, hotel beds, sending postcards to Pop and Greta and waiting for the big break. I was proceeding. I was gaining a reputation as smart, tough, dependable, and a terrific lead man (great first two paragraphs then downhill, a fifty-yard-dash man, not a miler). I looked like a journalist, I talked like a journalist, and I lived like a caricature of Ernest Hemingway (who had also lived like a caricature of Ernest Hemingway). Then, finally, the call came. *The New York Times* wanted me to do investigative reporting. Special features, special byline. A bowl of heavy cream placed before the starving tom.

I had made a lot of money, for me, anyway. Mainly, I made it because I never had time to spend it. The checks came in, I stuffed them in my hotel sock drawer, piling them up, living on expenses and beer money.

I came back to the Big Bad Apple with money in my jeans and a jut to my cleanly shaved Jewish jaw.

I took an apartment off Central Park West, small but classy, and bought Pop a *studio unit* at a schmaltzy senior citizens community in Miami. He went, his good eye squinting at the first sunshine and palm trees he had ever really seen. Within six months he became the nightclub columnist for the retirement community newspaper, sort of the Earl Wilson of Leisure Village, writing a weekly column entitled "Maxie's Midnight," which consisted of items stolen from *Daily Variety* and tips from the old gang at the deli. But since not one inhabitant of Happy Palms Oasis had been to a nightspot in twenty years, no one

knew the difference. Maxie was a smash. Soon after, he
met a giggly little widow from Akron with a nice round
bottom and Xerox stock, traded the studio for a two-
bedroom deluxe and got married.

As for me, I—it seemed—was also on a roll. One
night, shortly before my thirty-fifth birthday, I was invited to the CBS building to attend a private press reception for some media news giant or another. At the
party was a handsome ladylike-looking woman of about
my age whose hazel eyes I kept catching over the heads
and swirling smoke of the crowd. She was with an older
man, who I took to be her sugar daddy but soon found
out was her father, who just happened to be a major
stockholder and director of CBS. What better place for
a randy opportunist on a roll to be?

We met. We dined. We wined.. We teased. We wed.
This time, I had done it right! A bright, attractive, well-
bred woman of good family with a sense of humor and
connections.

This was how my switch from print to picture tube
came about. Frenda Weisman (she was even half Jewish!)
Poe, bless her elegant, understated heart, used her influence with Poppa and got me an audition at the Big Eyeball
in the sky. They liked me. They hired me. Good-bye
city room, hello America.

Frenda was a good sport and a nice person. I felt like
a drifter who finally thumbs the Big Ride ("I'll take you
all the way, honey").

It was the first home I had ever really had. A home
with hot fresh food, flowers, clean sheets, people coming
for dinner, tickets to the theater, a cleaning lady, monogrammed towels, Kleenex in a special dispenser and two
months' supply of toothpaste, shaving cream, and soap
in *the linen closet*. Pipe and slippers. A room for Greta to
come and visit. (Norma had left the songwriter and fallen
on hard times). Coffee no longer came in a paper cup.

There we were, my pop and me, brought into line by the love of good women, at last.

Frenda had had some practice. She was married for eight years before me, to a bright young stockbroker who, for reasons either too painful or too remote for her to deal with, lay down on his Miës van der Rohe lounge one night and blew his head off.

I was a little rough around the edges, but what she saw was what she got and she seemed to like that idea. I didn't have a stiff upper lip or an inside move in my repertoire. I wasn't very deep, but the water was fairly clear.

What Frenda really wanted, besides a home and a non-suicidal, working husband (she had her own money but she was not willing to carry a lead weight around in her checkbook), was a baby. After Greta, I had pretty much abandoned the idea of myself as father material, but now, in the glow of our Dagwood and Blondie existence, I readily agreed to try again.

This was in the days before midlife motherhood became popular, and the medical profession was wary and rather uninformed. She didn't have an easy pregnancy, both because she bled and was put to bed for the last five months and because I was off, flying around the world doing field reporting for father tube. I was in Brussels when our son was born, early and lifeless.

Somehow, that breach, that tear in the delicate bonding process of marital trust, was permanent. She buried her anger and betrayal behind her good-girl perfect-wife role modeling, but it ate at her, and at us. They told her that she could not have another child and sent her home to dismantle the Lord & Taylor layette in stale stoic silence. We went on, the coffee still came in china cups, but the fun was gone. If we had been able to fight it out then, break past our grief and guilt, clear the rancid air . . . but we didn't. I went on the road, she went to work for the Metropolitan as a volunteer, and we drifted around each other, two rubber duckies in a shrinking tub.

The early seventies were a newsman's version of the Agony and the Ecstasy. For me, it was the perfect excuse for not dealing with Frenda. I was on so many airplanes I forgot how to eat at a real table. There was Attica, Red China joined the U.N., the Olympic massacre at Munich, L.B.J.'s memoirs, India-Pakistan War, the mining of Hanoi Harbor, the shooting of George Wallace, Patty Hearst, the landslide victory of Tricky Dick, the death of Harry Truman, the signing of the Vietnam peace pact, and Watergate. After Watergate, there was only Watergate. Watergate was my Waterloo.

Every journalist in America wanted to cover Watergate. It was where the action was, as glamorous and frantic as any Hollywood version. I wanted it bad. Special assignment in Washington, covering the dog and pony show. I didn't get it. In fact, not only didn't I get it, but I was sent off in the opposite direction covering such *historic* events as Kissinger's Moscow visit, the Alaska pipeline dispute, and the Two-Germany Pact treaty. I didn't even get the Israeli-Egyptian war. I had been running steadily up the stairs toward the top of the pyramid and somebody tripped me. What it meant was that I was not A-team material, no fifty-yard-dash man was on the Capitol steps waiting for John Dean and the gang. Reality. I got the message. I had gone as far as I was likely to go, which had seemed a lot farther until I slipped over that wingtip on the way to the Watergate hearings.

Needless to say, this did not help things at home. I drank more, smoked more, and was unfaithful more. It was the time to reach out to this woman who had loved me and made a home for me, who had suffered her losses and betrayals in silence and was good for me and to me. But I didn't know how to do it. I had lived my childhood without the presence of women and the understanding of female compassion and tenderness. I did not believe it was real or that it applied to me. What I needed was mothering, and what Frenda needed was someone to mother. We were that close, and the soap slipped out of my hands.

Probably she would have left me then if one cold December night in 1975 the doorbell hadn't rung and Greta had not been standing outside our tucky little co-op, stoned out of her mind, wearing her nightgown and carrying all her blue jeans in her mother's Gucci suitcase.

I'd almost totally lost contact with Norma since Greta was old enough to take a bus and make a phone call by herself. I did know that there was not a run on self-destructive, humorless, aging models, and that time had taken its toll of her. After the songwriter she had married a struggling actor type who went through most of her money and self-esteem (whatever she had left). I also knew that her relationship with Greta was a seesaw of love and hate, Greta's jealousy at her mother's beauty crippling her ability to accept what love was available. Greta grew up standing in line behind Norma's mirror and men, not a spawning ground for well-adjusted, pleasant young women. Greta was a wreck. Wrecked by rage. Rage hiding hurt.

A shrink once told me that when you're anxious, it's always because you're expecting to be hurt.

My daughter was angry and anxious.

In she moved. Frenda had someone to take care of. They grew closer and I retreated. Frenda got her into a drug abuse program, cleaned her up, put her in group therapy, and met Norma weekly for lunch. The power of women, setting things right.

It was now late 1976. Gerald Ford and Jimmy Carter were getting into shape, Mao Tse-tung was dead, and I was teetering on the edge of a nervous breakdown. Burnt

out, bored, going through the motions. I hadn't slept
with my wife in almost six months (or with anyone else's,
either), and for the first time in my career, I was losing
my concentration. On the air, I was scared. One weekend
I flew down to Florida to see Maxie.

"Welcome to Swinging Senilesville! Come on, fill your
old pop in on the action. Nathan, I got it made here,
but ya know, kid, the older I get, and I may not be getting
any older—the quack in Miami told me my ticker's writing its own material—anyway, I sure miss the old days,
son. People had guts then, hope; now it's all caca; nobody
cares about nuthin' or no one. They don't even have real
comedy anymore. Got a lot of flippo teenage junkies
making jokes about muggings and drugs.

"When Benny died, I cried like a baby. I remember
back in the old days, you'd be asleep next to me, when
we stayed on Ida's couch or later, at the hotel, and I'd
wake up, scared—my heart'd be like conga drums, like
Krupa doin' a solo, just scared about keepin' it goin',
having the next gag, you know what I mean? Anyway,
I'd get up, pacin' around, and then I'd think about Jack
Benny and I'd say to myself, 'As long as Benny's there,
we'll be okay.' It was like he was everything nice in life.
He was safety. You'd flip him on and you'd smile and say
'Everything's gonna be fine.' I haven't felt like that since
he went. Funny, huh?"

It wasn't funny. It was right on the button. "I haven't
felt like that since Vietnam. It wasn't Jack Benny's kind
of war."

Maxie's face reddened. "Neither was Mr. Hitler's, kid."
Pop rubbed his bald head with his small fists. "You ever
have things so full inside that you're scared peeless if they
ever get out, you'll just disappear into them, gone?"

"Yes. That's why I'm such a lousy husband."

"Yeah. I guess that's my fault. You never got to see
what women do for ya. How they help ya let things out.

You just had me—runnin' around in circles holding it all down, laughin' everything up. I'm better now, since I married Helen, except about that stinkin' war. That ruined me, Nathan. I saw things . . . and I still feel, if I say it out loud, I'll make it happen again and I'll go stark ravin' round the bend. Slapsie Maxie, off to the nut crackers."

"I'm feeling like that myself these days, Pop, like everything's unraveling and I'm never going to be able to put everything back on the spool."

"Nathan, sometimes you're not supposed to. Sometimes even if it hurts like hell and it's a real mess, you've just got to let it all unwind, let it all go."

"I'll probably lose Frenda and Greta, too."

"Maybe. But it'll come back to you. Sometimes you just have to follow the thread, kid. It's scary as hell, but there's always a new suit that fits just right at the end."

"I love you, Pop."

"I love you, too, kid."

I flew back from Florida feeling better. Maxie gave me hope. Maybe there was life after "60 Minutes." Maybe it wasn't too late to pull my marriage and my career together into some realistic balance. Maybe Frenda and I should take Greta and get out of New York for a while, go to Connecticut, or the Caribbean. Maybe I'd try to write a book, maybe we'd even . . . the pleasant hum of my own hopeful fantasies lasted until I turned the key to my first and last polished wood door.

I could hear crying and loud voices from the hallway. My jaw tightened, so did my chest and stomach. Inside, I was greeted by Frenda, Norma, and Greta.

Frenda and Norma were standing like two svelte Upper East Side bookends, arms crossed before them, tears running down their rouged, angry cheeks. Greta was crouched, half-naked on my favorite overstuffed club chair, hands over her ears, chanting something that sounded like "Ice tea, fondue," rocking back and forth and shaking her head like a water-logged poodle. I half expected Elsie to leap out from behind the white silk moiré couch and bite my nose off.

When I entered, all emotion was refocused in my direction. Three hysterical women screaming abuse at my sun-reddened, newly optimistic being.

"It's all your fault, you selfish, two-timing son of a bitch! What kind of a father are you! What kind of a man are you! You left me and that baby alone, you never even took her to a goddamn movie. You ruined her!" said Norma.

"I've had enough, Nathan. I've had enough! Keeping house for you, putting up with your boozing and your womanizing, leaving me to put your daughter back together, passing the buck on everything! I want you out! Get out!" said Frenda.

"Ice tea, fondue. Ice tea, fondue," said Greta.

Apparently, as I was able to later reconstruct the events leading up to my "surprise party," Frenda had come home from a Carnegie Hall benefit with her mother and father and found Greta on the living room floor, stoned out of her mind, fucking her brains out with three of the black leather crowd. So much for her rehabilitation program. Frenda freaked and called Norma, and while she was waiting for her (having gotten the apartment cleared of frothing bikers and horrified parents), Greta related the discovery of me playing patty-cake in The Ginger Man with a blonde of about her age the week before. I had, of course, not seen Greta (I hardly remembered the blonde), but the facts were the facts. I had danced too close to the edge for too long.

That was the end of that, for the time being anyway. I was alone again. So for the next year I kept following the thread, heeding Maxie's advice, waiting for my perfectly tailored, three-piece black gab, clutching my moth-eaten tatters around me.

The black clouds settled in to stay. I sat under one while my crushed child held her collapsing little parasol over her own gray storm. I could not reach her. I felt that I had lost her, until the night, almost a year later, when she rang my bell.

The night I committed Greta, I was thinking about my favorite new subject, death. I was standing by my desk gazing out at all of the middle-aged men jogging along the river, looking as if they were trying to defecate cannon balls, their faces squeezed in a kind of bullet-biting agony. There they were in their trendy attire, panting and bouncing, checking their pulse rates on digital watches, and all I could see was that they were all running from death. There was no joy in it; it had the compulsive, frantic quality of hysteria about it. They were trying to deny death, run their way around it. There was none of the exuberance of young people using their bodies out of the fun of being alive, strutting life, belching it, sucking it in, pushing at it. This was grim, this was about death, not about life. Narcissistic, self-obsessed, and scared. It couldn't be good for you, I thought, lighting another cigarette, hypnotized by the parade of terrified, middle-aged people below me; their wobbly, knobby, varicosed limbs putting up and down. "No, no, no, I won't go, go, go." I went back to my typewriter and made a note, "Running Away from Death: The New American Pastime." I, however, personally seemed to be taking the counterattack. Casting off my Nikes and wiggling my naked, flabby, aging piggies in its fearsome face. Catch me if you can, Mephisto; I've given up the futile fight.

My doorbell rang. Outside was my daughter, who was one step ahead of me in the big race. She was reeling, blasted, disheveled. Her jeans were on backward (which is a stranger sight than one might imagine). My throat closed in pain for her and fear for myself.

"I've got a disease. I'm ruined . . . ruined . . .

ruined. . . . Pussy's all stuck together with runny red sores. God's punishing me. . . . I wanted Mommy to die . . . wanted you to die, too!"

There was not much to say. I led her in and sat her down and made her some coffee and tried to keep from bursting into tears of self-pity. Being a reporter I at least knew enough to let her talk, which was, of course, why she had come.

"I wanted to be her, beautiful. You'd come back. You'd want me, but you left her, too. Joke's on stupid me! Wasn't anything else to be. I reminded her of you. . . . I reminded you of you. You both hated me! But not as much as I do! I hate me more! But you're stuck with ugly me! Mr. Sexy Newsman. All my stupid friends thought you were so cute." She shook her head back and forth, long dirty black hair flying over her face, wrapping around her throat. Her body sagged in grief.

"Never put your arms around me . . . told me I was pretty. Never held my hand . . . never smiled just at me. Just me! That's all I wanted. . . . Told that to the shrink at Frenda's precious clinic. 'What do you want from your father?' Want him to hold my hand and smile just at me." She fell forward beating the cushions with her open hands.

"Oh, God, shit, fucking, Christ! I'm so gross . . . gross . . . gross. . . . There's no cure! No one will ever sleep with me, ever again; no one . . . put . . . arms around me . . . just smile at me! Mommy got all of them . . . aren't any smiles left . . . all used up on her. You could've come and taken me away. You never came! Never, never. . . . Just fuck other people's daughters. You pervert!

"You don't know! Having a mother like that and not being beautiful! I knew what they thought, 'Poor Greta, tsk, tsk!' Not fair! I'm a better person. . . . No one cares. I'm ugly. Disgusting. Gross! Gross! Gross! You would've loved me if I was beautiful!

"Starved. Straightened my hair. I did everything for
nothing! Fixed my fucking nose. I'm the loser in this
family. . . . That's me. You all want me dead!" She sat
up. Her face blotched with fear and anguish. Her large
dark eyes wet and vulnerable, the toughness gone.

"I can't put it together like Frenda and Mommy. I get
scared . . . get sick, get so scared. All those perfect women,
tough women, pushing me out of the way. . . . Get so
scared. Don't want to live being me anymore! Don't want
to. . . . Found someone nice. . . . I thought it was okay,
not being beautiful, because he liked me . . . and
. . . and . . . he gave me this horrible thing and he split!
Oh, shit, shit!"

Listening to my only child belch her self-hate from
across the couch, I saw a well-built, dark young woman
with a strong handsome face and lovely soft brown eyes.
She did not have her mother's drop dead lanky magazine
glamour, but who cared? I found her infinitely more attractive and appealing than women like Norma. She had
a brain and a sense of humor (though certainly not at the
moment), and while it was true that I had not been comfortable or attentive with her, I had always loved her,
truly and deeply. In fact, she and Pop were the only two
people I had ever really cared about vulnerably in that
way. Her vision of me, her childhood, herself were twisted
inside her throbbing young head like a longshoreman's
knot. I also saw that there was absolutely nothing that I
could say that she would accept or believe and to try
would unleash her guilt, and confuse her even more. If
it wasn't us, then it must be her? I didn't think she could
handle any more self-doubt at the moment, so I said
nothing. I sat choking on my despair.

What is it that happens between parent and child that
leads us off into our own mangled, tangled distortions?
We start out filled with total, unblemished passion for
one another. Maxie and I sucking our darling baby girl's

toes, one by one, Greta gurgling "Da-Da" and sticking
her fat moist fingers in my ear, my nose, my mouth, any
opening in my physiognomy, with delight. We could not
get closer, we could not love more. Then the baby goes
and the person appears and things start to get complicated.

There are betrayals of which we have no awareness
that pass and are buried for fifteen, twenty years only to
pop out some stormy night—"You never smiled just at
me! You never took me to the movies! You thought I was
ugly, stupid, a burden. . . ." Oh, God, I would have
smiled just at you if I had known; I thought I did. I made
you so miserable and I didn't even know what was happening. The hurts fester, the brain retains, distorts, issues
half-remembered, bitter reports. We pull away from each
other and call it growing up, growing old, getting on
with your life. Parents and children, shuffling off, one
arm clutching their bleeding scar and no one knowing
what went wrong, when the toe sucking turned to suspicion and defensiveness and guilt; love folded into hate
like eggs in cake batter, swirling round and round and
disappearing into a new form.

I couldn't tell her she was wrong, no one's feelings can
be wrong, and so then no one's truth can be wrong.
Feelings are the only reality we have, though God knows
we spend enough time, money, and energy trying to deny
that fact. How Greta perceived her relationship with me
was her truth. Her pain and anger were her reality. Her
vision of herself was as real as if she were in fact seeing
a monster head reflected in the hotel mirror above me.
What is a mirror anyway? Just a window with silver paint
on one side. Some of us look through windows and some
of us silver them and look only at ourselves. If I got very
lucky maybe Greta and I, together, could begin scratching
the paint off, getting a little wider view.

When she had exhausted herself, emptied all the rusted

old poison, she fell over, passed out facedown on my
studio couch. I did not know what to do.

I paced around, listening to her drugged uneven breathing. I thought about the news, images of old stories buzzing past my inner eyes. I did not want to do to Greta
what we do with the news. We use the news. We play
it up, woo it, lust after it, focus all of our immediate
attention and interest on it, until it has served our purpose,
and then we drop it. It disappears from the front page to
the third, to the back, then out. What happens in this
game is that when the story disappears we think that the
problem is gone, too. If dioxin's on page one, it's a problem, when it's in the back of the B section, the danger's
over.

What a way to solve problems in real life! The minute
the screaming stops, we put the eggs on to poach and
clip our toenails. We all have our piles of yesterday's
headlines, frosted-over crevices in our psyched cupcakes;
but they pile up, they can't stay out of sight or mind
forever, wrappers for dog shit and fodder for winter fires.
Old news has its revenge in the end. It returns to haunt
us, leering at its rejectors, and the only way out is to
solve the fucking problem. Period.

I did not want to clean Greta up and file her away. I
stood over her, watching her slack-mouthed heavy sleep
filled with black, clouded dreams and then I called
a friend, who called a friend, who called a doctor,
who called me, who called a clinic, who woke Greta,
who drove Greta, who held her down while they put
her in a straitjacket, who signed the papers, the headline
smeared with dog shit open before me demanding to be
read.

Two years passed. Greta was in the hospital for a long
time and she began to heal. Her "disease" vanished as if
the healing in her mind had dried up the leprotic sores

of her body. By the time she was discharged, I was able
to tell her what I could not have said that night and she
received it. That was the highlight of those two years.
The seventies and I staggered to a finish.

When Greta was not fucking bikers and being committed, she played the violin. She played it very, very
well. She played it well enough to get into Juilliard and
to entertain the prospect of a serious career. She did not
play well enough for a solo career, but the hope of first
or second seat in one or another symphony orchestra in
a decent-size city was not out of reach. When she returned to Juilliard after her long absence, she played better
than she had before, freed of the heaviness, the exhaust-
ing weight of her own emotional cogs. She had more
energy and concentration for her music. I had been redeemed (I even had pleasant phone calls from Frenda and
Norma).

One afternoon as I trudged in from somewhere after
covering something in which I had no interest, there was
a message from Greta inviting me to come to a recital
featuring a string quartet made up of Greta and three
classmates, who were accompanying a sextet of dancers
from the Inner City Ballet in a small performance to raise
money for some dancers/musicians fund or whatever. I
had a hot (as hot as I got anymore) date with a perky
reporter from Washington who was sprinting up the lad-
der faster than I would have liked, but who had wonderful
legs and a reputation for nymphomaniac urges for aging
journalists. I broke the date and went to hear my daughter,
not knowing that fate had just put a fork into my dead-
end road.

As it turned out, I barely heard the music. In the corps
of dancers was a pale, glowing, champagne-haired woman
who seemed to be magically lit from within. I was transfixed. I'd never seen anyone like her.

I had seen people with presence, famous people, stars,

people who stand out, set apart by a kind of radiance, a specialness that identifies them immediately as above the throng. It was a quality that often intrigued me because it wasn't necessarily something that one was born with. I had followed politicians who started without a glimmer and got it. A switch turned on, clicked into orbit; a star.

You never relaxed with these radiators; it was as if they were separated from mere mortals by their inner light. It protected them, and it was the only privacy they had. I always wondered if it clicked off when they were home alone, when it was not needed.

But this woman, for she was a woman, older in years and in manner than the other young dancers around her, she was so bright, so captivating, that it entranced me. She had a delicate but well-defined body and a physical strength unlike any I had seen in female dancers before (not that, God knows, I was an expert, having gone to the ballet with Frenda as if I were being asked to swallow sand). She had strength and grace and she danced with a passion, a joy that was contagious. She loved what she was doing and made you love it, too. She had no special part, no solo role, but as I looked around at my fellow observers, it was clear that I was not alone in my adoration. She held everyone's eye. She had it. She radiated.

I had never felt such a powerful, armor-melting attraction to any woman in my entire life. I did not know what to do about it, where to take it, what the hell it meant. I only knew that if all of that fuzzy gush about love at first sight had ever touched my life, this was it.

After the performance, I took Greta to Gallagher's for steaks and champagne and I inquired.

"Who was that pale dancer with the chardonnay-colored hair? Do you know her?"

Greta looked at me steadily over her fork. "Sort of, why?"

I tried not to blush or remove my eyes from direct contact, a sure giveaway. "I was just curious. I've never seen anyone dance with such intensity. She was impressive."

"She's a very nice person, kind of psychic. One afternoon at rehearsal I was in a real bad place, I was itchy and depressed and I got scared that the *thing* was going to come back again and I was standing backstage with my head on my violin, trying to pull myself together, and she came by. She was going on, and they're really strict about entrances, but she stopped and put her arms around me and kind of pressed her fingers over my eyes and said something like, 'It's okay. Have faith. You're going to be fine.' It was real nice. And she was right. It helped, having her understand it. She missed her cue and she got blasted, too."

Greta stopped, smiled at me, took a large sip of wine, a big mouthful of french fried potatoes, and chewed slowly and with relish, while I kept my eye contact open and my mouth shut.

"She's dancing her first featured role next week at the matinee. One of the *Sleeping Beauty* pas de deux." She swallowed and wiped her full unpainted lips with her napkin. "Her name's Eve."

CHAPTER 15

The next week I found myself just happening to be in the neighborhood of the Inner City Ballet round about matinee time. This in itself was rather astounding since leisurely afternoons were hardly my style. I don't remember how I arranged it, but there I was, *leisurely* purchasing a second row center orchestra single to see *Sleeping Beauty*, without a gun to my temple or a story angle. I was nervous. Nothing like this had ever happened to me before. I had a quick drink in the lobby and made my way through the students and ladies from Scarsdale with too much jewelry, too much perfume, and too many empty afternoons to fill, and into the theater. I sat down beside two powdery matrons with husband troubles.

"He thinks I'm a slave."

"I know what you mean."

The lights dimmed. The luxurious sounds of Tchaikovsky filled my pulsing ears. It began. It seemed to go on forever and then, there she was. This glowing, ageless creature, dressed in white, her arms like liquid glass, her face beaming.

223

I was close. I saw something shiny fall from a character dancer's costume onto the stage. The scene changed. Eve returned. I waited for her feature. A lovely, elegant duet with a dark, rather effete young man. She moved flawlessly, precisely, without effort or strain. I was fascinated. I had never before understood what ballet was, what an awesome feat, to move the human body in such rigidly controlled and disciplined ways, with such power and grace and timing. It was a miracle, this dancing; beyond my capacity to conceive. She leapt into the air, like a bird without gravity; she twirled on one long perfectly formed leg; she flew into what I now know was a grand jeté and her shoe stuck to the bit of fallen metallic fabric on the stage; her body turned, but her leg stayed in place. She fell so fast, a white cloud carried by a sudden gust. I heard the kneecap pop, a sound of bone and muscle tearing, sickening the stomach.

I jumped from my seat, stepping on the swollen feet of the ladies with husband trouble, and climbed onto the stage. Two stagehands were carrying her off while the dancing continued around us. I took her hand and she opened her eyes, clear aquamarine filled with pain, old, old pain as well as the throbbing new wound. She smiled into my eyes, my heart, the way Greta had wanted me to smile at her, I remember thinking. Then she closed them and they put her in an ambulance and took her away.

I followed the ambulance to the hospital, where no one would tell me anything until I pulled my press credentials and then they told me to wait. I waited for a long time. Mindless, compelled.

"She has a splintered kneecap, dislocation, and severely torn ligaments. She's cast, we put a pin and a metal plate in, the procedure was quite painful and she's heavily sedated. It'll be a slow recovery."

"Will she dance again?" I asked the stranger hoarsely.

The doctor looked at me steadily for what seemed like hours. "I try to be positive about things like this. But the chances are one in a thousand, optimistically. And if she did it again, she'd be crippled for life."

Tears filled my yellow, jaundiced eyes. I turned away from the purveyor of deadly news and walked down the ominous, medicinal hallway and out into the cloudy, noisy, frantic New York afternoon, filled with tender grief for this pale, azure-eyed creature who did not even have a last name.

Whatever I would have done next is irrelevant, because when I got back to the CBS building the head of news called me in and announced that the shah had been dumped and I was to be on the next plane to Tehran. A hot potato dropped in my burnt-out lap, warming the cold, dead space in my life. Iran. Another Watergate. The fifty-yard man goes for the hundred. I left that night, thoughts of the broken dancer fizzing and finally settling, calming, dwindling in my newly recharged brain.

CHAPTER 16

Adam left Robin one month after the night of Trewanna. He left a letter telling her of his malaise
and setting her free. In this letter were the terms. All
money was put in trust, with Maybe and Laurel as executors. Robin would have full use of the income from
this trust until Alex reached the age of twenty-two. At
that time a sizable allowance would be settled on Robin
for life. The only restrictions were that Maybe was to
remain with Alex as long as she was able and that Alex's
care, education, et cetera, were to be maintained at the
highest possible level. If not, the use of the trust would
transfer from Robin to the Richeleau House Foundation.
His life with her had not been honest or fair to her or
Alex; the reasons for this were better left unsaid.

Adam also left a note for Alex to be read when he was
old enough to understand.

My adored son,
I must leave you and your mother for reasons that
have nothing to do with my love for you. If I believed

that it was possible for me to stay without bringing unhappiness to both of you, I would never leave.

We must all make decisions in our lives based on what we think is right, and from the bottom of my heart I believe that it is better for you without me.

Grow up proud and strong and kind, Alex. Grow knowing that you are the wonder of my life, the best of me and of your ancestors. Grow knowing that your father loved you, that you are a work of God. Have faith, and joy will fill your life and guide you. Reach for the God within you and know, then, that you will never be alone.

The night after Adam gave these documents to Maybe, he left his house after midnight with one small suitcase and drove to the Mississippi. He parked his car near the bank, left a shoe on the shore, hitched a ride to New Orleans, and caught the next plane for Boston.

The police were called. A search took place. The possibility of suicide was, of course, strong. No body was found, but the circumstantial evidence seemed enough. ("One way or another, the guy does not want to be found," the sheriff said.) Missing, presumed dead. Case closed.

Robin, Alex, and Maybe returned to Richeleau land, and Adam moved in with Sam. Eight months later, he really committed suicide and Eve was born.

When I saw Eve dance that fateful evening, she had been alive for little more than a year. The thrill of being able to dance in public gave her the strength to deal with the constant burning loss of her son, her family, and her work. And there was also the endless loneliness. No one in New York knew about her. She arrived with a letter of introduction from a ballet master in Boston and the benefit of Sam's energetic support. All of her vital statistics were altered. She had taken the name of Eve alone. No surname, no past.

In spite of her age (twenty-six) and lack of experience, her audition for the Inner City Ballet was fine enough to earn her a place in the corps.

Eve was not Adam without a cock. Eve was Eve. A new being, no longer trapped in Adam's body. Eve had the intensity, the vibrant power that he had lacked. It was as if the freeing of his female soul had unleashed the true muscle and energy of his being. There was a focus in her, a sureness; a direct, positive truth that had been suffocated by Adam's ambivalence and self-doubt, the penumbra surrounding the umbra. Eve was an arrestingly confident, centered being of magnetic presence, drawing strangers, ballet masters, men, and women toward her force.

She had been freed of her crusty, uncomfortable skin, cracked through it and flown out, flown higher than Adam had ever dreamed. She was magical, filled with pain and light, laughter and terror, sorrow and hope, male and female, life and death. Singular, risen, clear.

All of this energy she put into her dancing. The other dancers were threatened and suspicious at first, but gradually, her guileless warmth broke down their defenses and they began to turn to her as therapist, mother, friend. She listened, smiling, touching, offering hope, keeping her own counsel, delighted to be needed. She felt her own spirit rising, her new being taking hold, beginning to fit, like a pair of new pants taking on the creases and curves of her body.

For the first few months she refused all social invitations, still raw and terrified of exposure. As her power came into balance, the dancing cemented her new sense of self and the presence of Adam loosened; she began to open her arms to the world around her.

A month before I first saw her she had accepted an invitation from the other corps dancers. She had just finished her first week of actual performances and she was buoyant, high on this fantastic dream coming true. The heartsick boy with dreams of swans and powdered arms was flying now. A streak across the sky. A dream with open eyes.

Eve went out to dinner with some ballerinas. They went to the Village to a lively Italian place with good pasta, cheap wine, and attractive men looking for pretty ladies.

Eve was quiet, still marveling at the mysterious, frank conversation of women, listening from her foreign ship, soaking up the new language.

"I need therapy more than *anyone* I know. And you *know* who I know! I'm really desperate. I've got this pain in my chest, psychic pain, just crunching my chest. I even went in and had a mammogram and an EKG, just to be sure, but I knew it was emotional. Every morning I wake up thinking it will be gone and instead it's worse. God, I need help!"

"Well, for chrissakes, see a woman. Male shrinks stink for women. It's basic biology. Their little things are outside, our little things are inside. The poker and the pokee. How can the fucking poker help the pokee! See a woman!"

"What's the pain from?" Eve asked.

"Her boyfriend's fucking her best friend, what else!"

"That's too simple. It's old pain—primal pain."

"Kitty shit! It's about fucking. That's what it's always about. Pokers and pokees!"

Someone at the bar was looking at her. She could feel it, heating her neck. Her eyes raised slightly, up over the head of the woman in pain, sideways toward the boring eyes.

Squinting eyes, behind large wire-rimmed glasses. A man in a fedora hat and blue jeans, burgundy hair shaggy beneath the rim. A man she had always loved and never forgotten. Duggan's Chinese crinkled eyes looking at her in confusion. Her mouth dried up, the moisture sucked out, blotted with shock.

He rose, lean and tan, the wary, grim smile pulling his face down. He walked over to the table of intense, frenetic femaleness and slid into an empty chair next to her.

The women stopped for one beat, accepting the entrance, then changing focus ever so slightly, cleaning up the act for the outsider.

"Excuse me, ma'am, for taking this liberty, but you look so familiar. I know it's the oldest line in history, but you . . . have you ever been overseas? Or in the South? I'm certain that we've met before. My name's Duggan O'Toole. I'm a lieutenant in the army air corps. May I ask who you are?"

"I'm Eve and I'm a private in the Inner City Ballet corps."

He smiled his tight, even, humorless smile. "Am I familiar to you at all?"

She looked into his funny, dark eyes feeling as if she would melt, scream her confession—children playing dress-up, Halloween. It's me! I fooled you! "Yes. Very familiar."

They sat for a moment, watching one another in silence.

"I'm on leave."

She nodded.

"Could I see you home? I know I'm a stranger, but I'm a Southern gentleman and there are witnesses present."

She nodded again, afraid to speak, her throat as dry and rough as cardboard.

He unfolded his long body from the chair and helped her do the same. Duggan and his pedantic charm. They left the doelike ladies exchanging knowing smiles and speculation.

Duggan saw her home, such as it was. Upstairs they went and into her spare, clean white room. A tiny place with bath off Carmine Street. "Would you like some tea?" she managed to ask.

Slowly, sorting her feelings out, Eve went about the tea making, while Duggan wandered, chatting, looking for signs of a life, of the connection between himself and this wonderful, glowing woman who moved with such sure, quiet elegance around this empty room.

There were no family portraits, heirlooms, knick-knacks, seashells, found rocks, driftwood, worn rugs, macramé, pillows—the fingerprints of experience and personal history. This small, clean white space seemed to fit her, to make it better somehow to live without pet, portrait, or memento. He could understand this place.

"I've never been to New York before, went straight from New Orleans to Nam, just about. You ever fly? Boy, there's nothing like it. When I finish with the service, I'm going to fly commercial. Good pay, great benefits. You ever been in Louisiana? Damn, you look so . . ."

She took a breath, set the steaming tea down before him, and motioned for him to sit, stopping his conversation.

"Duggan," she said, her whole body tense with memories of her amputated past. "Duggan, it's me. Adam."

Duggan's eyes opened as wide as Duggan's eyes went, popping larger behind his thick glasses. He sat motionless for several moments, then he reached out and took Eve's hand, holding it in his own.

"So you found a way to be a ballerina after all. . . . Holy-rolling rat turds! I'll be damned. Adam!"

When Duggan said her birth name, her control broke and the shuddering, shaking, teeth-chattering grief broke loose.

It felt to Eve as if a pair of protective, mothering arms had lifted her into space. A giant pair of empathetic and loving arms, holding her quaking body; as if every warm embrace of her entire lonely life, each sweet memory had surrounded and lifted her. One word. Adam.

It meant home. It meant friend. A connection, a sense

of place. From the day of her arrival in Boston, she had lived an almost dreamlike existence. She was alone in a way that even on her darkest day as Adam she had never imagined possible. She lived without the grace of history; a stranger to everyone and to herself.

At times she felt like a creature from beyond, the Thing Who Fell to Earth, wandering an alien and hostile planet, devoid of the comfort of one familiar soul, one smile of recognition. One touch of compassion. Sleepwalking.

Her life became her work. Dancing was the only part of her past that she had been able to bring with her. Dancing and God. She went to church every day, kneeling alone in the back pews of random chapels. It made no difference to her which one, God was not connected to architecture or denomination. She prayed for faith and for endurance.

At night she dreamed of her sobbing child reaching up with his soft, fat arms as she reached back, stretching toward him, straining forward while he moved higher and farther away until she replaced him, growing smaller, reaching into the same blackness, totally lost.

She had left in shame and despair and without even an old photo for company. She worked. She walked in the rain, rode buses and subways, went to the movies and endless classes. She cooked. One lamb chop. A small potato. A single serving of fruit. The contents of her shopping cart represented her future. Alone. Misfit; growing old with one boiled chicken breast and an apple.

She fought her panic at this view of her future. She loathed the mist of self-pity and tried to pretend that she was the victim of amnesia, that now was all of her existence, all that she needed.

She had been living inside a glass prison, shattered with one swift blow. One word spoken with love left her defenseless in the center of a shower of spiky shards of anguish.

"I saw you once. At the army base in Boissier. I spent months trying to track you down. It never occurred to me you'd be using another name. How silly. I thought I was hallucinating. I just as well might have been. You were always with me.

"After you left New Orleans everything began to unravel. I felt like a giant tornado was sucking us in. The Wizard of Oz without the good witch."

She paused. Aware of how absurd she must sound. "Now, don't laugh. *Please* don't. I married Robin. She was pregnant. I wanted that baby so much, Duggan. I have a son, Alexander. Poppa died. Suzette went off. Laurel remarried. My life was a total fraud. I couldn't dance. I couldn't make love as a man anymore. I was a zombie and Robin was wild. I missed you. I would say to myself, 'What would Duggan do? What would Duggan think?' Sometimes I felt you were watching me, shaking your head in disbelief. 'Will you just look at that poor soul. Get it together, Adam ol' boy! I leave you for a minute and look at the mess you've gotten your sorry self into!'

"I won't bore you with the sordid details, but what I really did, finally, was 'a Duggan.' I disappeared. They all think I'm dead, except Maybe. She knows everything. God, I don't know what I would have done without her! She's watching over my son, the way she watched over my poppa and me. I had to do it that way. I could hardly let my child see me like this. Even Southern decadence has its limits. Robin's barely coping and I get so frightened for Alex. I thought this was the only way to live decently, honestly, and to spare him, but everything has been so damn miserable and uncertain. . . . I know I sound like some old sob sister. Am I grotesque to you?" She looked up at him and tried to smile.

Duggan stroked her hand, his eyes squinting at her as if to absorb everything about this strange new creature and her passage. "God, no! I'm flabbergasted, is all. I hit

on you tonight because you knocked me out! Sometimes,
when we were together, I'd look at you and think about
how beautiful you'd be if you were a girl. In lots of ways,
I think I really related to you like that. Sort of protective,
like a big brother. Boy, girl. This seems so right, so
natural."

She shuddered. His approval releasing new tears. "You
made me want to be a boy. To be like you. But at the
same time, I loved you like a girl. I think it scared the
chitlins out of poor Maybe. She wanted so much for me
to have a friend, but she didn't quite know what kind of
friends we were." She sighed, wiping her eyes with the
back of her slender white hand.

"Oh, Duggan, you are still a miracle in my life. Remember our pledge. Your deepest secret and mine. I held
one back on you, didn't I, kiddo. Now we're even. It's
so good . . . to . . . see you."

Duggan reached out and pulled her down into his lap,
holding her close. He held her, rocking slowly back and
forth until she began to relax into his arms, his forgiveness. Her first friend, sitting in the church swearing on
her dead ancestor's bones ("I'll tell you my secret, if you
tell me yours"), he had not betrayed Adam then, and he
would not betray her now.

"I still have your hats, Duggan. I never got over losing
you. Never."

"I couldn't come back, Ad—Eve. I'll keep doing that
for a while. Jesus, Jesus, Jesus, this is just unreal. I thought
I'd *killed* my old man! I thought if I contacted you the cops
would interrogate you and find me. I just kept running.
Didn't stop for two years. I got into some heavy shit.
Drug stuff, bad company. Then I got double-crossed on
a hashish score with some small-time mob types in Florida.

"One night they came for me, picked me up under each
arm, barefoot, in my underwear—my legs dangling in

midair—and carried me to their car, tied me up, threw me facedown in the back of their brand-new Cadillac, and drove way out toward the Keys. I was so scared, I peed on myself. God's punishing me for Pop, I kept thinking. I was nineteen and I was going to die.

"They finally stopped driving and yanked me out—in my wet shorts—and turned me around with my back to them and I could hear a gun being cocked. Then suddenly the fear left, it just vanished and I felt this incredible peace, this forgiveness of myself, my father, even my mother. I turned around, I was ready to die and I said, 'If you motherfuckers are going to shoot me, you're going to have to look me in the eye and do it.'

"One of them, a great big wall of a dude, he grinned and he raised the gun and pointed it right at my heart and just kept it on me forever—and then he laughed and pulled the trigger and nothing happened. 'Let this be a lesson, sonny,' he says and they got back in the Cad and drove away and left me there in my piss-stained shorts. I walked all the way back to Miami like that and I called my father and I asked him to forgive me and he cried. Then I enlisted. When I went to Nam, I went clean inside. I wasn't afraid of anything anymore. I surrendered that whole ego trip. I flew suicide missions and I never got a scratch. It was weird. I've been home since. My old man's really changed. He says I was 'the Lord's instrument,' that I was sent to stop his sinfulness. Whatever, he's so helpless. How ironic."

It was Eve's turn to comfort him. "You were as alone as I was."

"God, you're so beautiful, I don't know what to do with you! This is very heavy, pal. May I kiss you? You know, I always wanted to. I felt real weird about it. I guess it was instinct, because I always wanted to kiss you like you were a girl. I loved you, too, Ad—Eve."

Eve watched him. Calm now, the virgin maiden, cool

and pure, untouched, waiting for the prince to warm her.

"No one has. I don't quite . . . I don't know quite what to do, Duggan. You're the first man to touch me."

He took off his glasses and looked at her steadily. "Let me show you. I always showed you. Let me be the first, so you'll know what to hold out for. Remember Kate, 'Duggle, conk of the world.' " He smiled his crazy smile and gently drew her toward him, pressing his mouth to her eyes, her cheeks, her full soft lips.

For the next week, until Duggan's leave was up, they spent every moment together, reminiscing, loving, making love. It was a gift, Eve knew, to have it be this way, a miracle, really.

Their lovemaking was playful, tender, and passionate in turn. It worked, she found out, just as she had found out as Adam, all those years before, that her male parts worked. Again, Duggan had launched her into new sexuality, with kindness and reassurance.

She knew and he knew that they could not go any farther with one another and that when he left, it would probably be over. But somehow it was okay. It was there for a reason and that was all it needed to be. He had a girl in Florida and a life plan, and he would leave Eve to return to it; but they were caught up now, the connection repaired, the end rewritten.

On the day he left, she cried, and he held her and they both knew that they were blessed by what they shared. Eve had been filled, the empty unreachable place inside had been contacted and so she could say good-bye without the pain of his first leaving. She was a woman, the damn thing worked.

"You were a pretty strange guy, but you are one hell of an incredible woman. Incredible! The best! Go conk the world, kiddo," he said, and he was gone.

After Duggan left, the loneliness became less fearsome. It had been altered and it fit her better. Duggan's love had given her hope and made her stronger. *I'll be okay,* she said to herself, over and over. *It's the way it's supposed to be.*

The pain did not leave, but it softened. It was as if in accepting it she had taken back the power. This new energy opened her and she was able to look out and see the world without the polarity of her fear. The more she looked out, the more love she let in and the more her fear dissipated. Eve looked out and what she saw was other lonely souls searching like herself. The clearer her view became, the more hopeful she grew. This was noticed by those around her.

CHAPTER 17

The interminable dusty edginess of those of us who spent the 444 days with the hostages there finally ended.

I returned home feeling somewhat like Newton's apple being raced by the train, just about the time President Peanut was shuffling off, leaving Ronnie to reap the final glory of the hostage release. I came back feeling very much like those honored captives. Confused, exhausted, out of touch. But there were no ticker-tape parades or White House receptions for freed newsmen (being divorced made me a terrific asset in Iran, I could plead nothing but criminal insanity to get out of there).

Careerwise, it had been peachy keen if I lived to reap the benefits. My gums were bleeding. My bowels were roaring. My skin was as dry as a Gucci purse. I could hardly remember who I was, where I lived (nowhere), or why I had been so eager to volunteer.

What I had gotten out of it besides the career boost, was an almost pathetic appreciation of the value of having been Made in America and a healthier relationship with

my death obsession. When you spend a year watching
people kill one another (or threaten to) on a daily basis,
you lighten up a little bit. The first machine gun pointed
at you is by far the worst. You get used to it, like anything
else, and death takes a new perspective; at least, I was a
little less phobic about it. But reentry was a bitch and it
took some time. I hadn't worn city pants, real shoes, or
a tie in so long that I felt like Tarzan hits Manhattan.

I did decide not to return to my depressive little hideout
by the river. I moved into a sunny, fancy suite at the St.
Regis to cool out and readjust. I was on leave for two
months and I intended to slog my way through every
moment of it. Part of this slog involved several hot show-
ers per day, copious room service, and continuous television.

Somehow, sitting mindlessly staring into space is more
disturbing and socially unacceptable than sitting mindlessly staring at a television (that is, if someone else were
to walk into the room, which I was in little danger of,
having pretty well severed all human contacts when I went
off to fanaticsville).

I saw Greta. She was engaged to a good-looking pros-
perous young lawyer and fellow herpes sufferer from Tulsa,
Oklahoma—living proof that the day after you jump out
of the window, something great will happen in your life,
which is reason enough to stick it out. I, of course, pointed
this fact out to my now straight, mirthful child.

Maxie came up for a week. "I told the paper I had ta
get into the city and refresh my column, be more professional, and they bought me a first-class ticket, how 'bout
that!

"So, come on, kid—tell your old pop somethin'—what
are ya gonna do now? What's the plan? Don't wanna be
morbid, but Old Man Time's startin' his closin' mono-
logue. Hey, did ya hear the one about the four worst
things about bein' an egg? You only get laid once; when

ya get excited it takes fifteen minutes ta get hard . . . can't remember the rest. Anyway, Nathan, gotta get your second act together! This is no life, livin' in hotels, chasin' crazy Arabs—"

"Persians."

"Call 'em what ya want, they're Arabs ta me! Don't innerupt! Your old man's entitled to one fatherly talk before he gets the big hook. Nathan! *Boobala!* I'm worried about ya! You're not a rookie anymore. Last time at bat's comin' up and you're still in the locker room takin' a piss. Suit up, kid! Time ta settle down. Build somethin'. Maybe you can put it back together with Frenda?"

"Frenda's remarried, Pop."

"Oh, Jeez—see! The ol' bean is dryin' up! Gonna happen ta you, too, kid; goes by so fast! 'What's the rush?' I keep askin' the comic upstairs, 'Tryin' ta get ridda me? I just barely got here!'

"Please, Nathan, hear an ol' trouper, find somethin' ta care about. Enough with the jet set and the broads! Be a mensch. It's time, kid."

"I know, Pop. I just don't know how yet."

"Nathan, let me tell ya somethin' about yourself. You're a sweet guy. All of this macho, smacho stuff. It ain't you, kid. You were the boy who helped Aunt Ida, held her *fercockta* knitting until your little arms were numb.

"Ya brought home every lost pup and kit on the block, even searched up and down alleys lookin' for the mangy little fuzz balls. You took old Mrs. Shapiro to the ball game every Saturday for two years after her husband died—took a lot of razzin' from the pimple faces about it, too. 'She's all alone, Pop,' you'd say, and there were tears in your eyes, too, kid. Ya gave me more love than any broken-down old meshuggener deserved. More than I gave back. You're a mensch, son! Like it or not. Stop fightin' it. It's a good fit, Nathan. Try it on."

It was a while before I trusted myself to speak. "Thanks,

Pop," I finally croaked out, taking his hand, which was as moist with wiped tears as my own. "I'll think about it."

Even with Pop's advice my life consisted of tossing a few with my CBS buddies in the King Cole Room, walking in the park, or hitting a movie. I was healing, like the hostages, only out of the glare of public attention. Quietly, insensibly, in my new silk pajamas (a gift from Greta), lying on my clean hotel bed, eating club sandwiches, drinking Heinekens, and watching the tube.

Then one morning I flicked on the thing, fell back onto my sleep-warm sheets, and there she was: Eve. I sat forward, memory flooding me. There before me, beaming out at America with the full luster of her sweet, shiny smile, was my fallen damsel.

She was dressed in white dancer's clothes, white ballet slippers, her hair held back with a white silk sweatband. But she was not dancing, she was standing on a black marble square in the center of a polished, bleached wood circle, a huge circle, surrounded by people—women and men in exercise clothes—and she was talking. She was not talking about dancing, she was talking in a steady, husky, loving voice about God. God? I shook my head, took a long drag, a deep hot slurp of caffeine and turned up the sound. God.

It was not like anything I had ever seen. People were quiet, a *Brandenburg* concerto or some such thing was playing in the background, and this heavenly slim ballerina was telling a huge circle of out-of-shape people in exercise clothes about God.

"We are living in a world that offers us endless choices between helpless despair and hope. Helplessness is easier, for there are so many things, frightening things, over which we have no control. It is hard enough work just controlling our own dark thoughts. But we do have control over our bodies, what we put into them, how we use them; laughing, crying, moving, breathing.

"Each time we use our bodies, breathe in fresh oxygen, bend or stretch, we are choosing life over despair.

"In Eastern meditation they teach that God is in the space between the inhaling and exhaling of breath, so that with every movement of air, in and out of our bodies, God is moving through us. Any of you who have watched me before know that I am here to help you find the God of your own understanding, the life force within you.

"We all live with many voices inside our heads and hearts, voices that frighten, cajole, confuse, that do not speak clearly or truthfully. But the authentic voice always speaks to you with love, is always your friend, your guide, your truth.

"To me, that voice is the God within each of us and is a force beyond us without denomination, church, sex, color, intellect, judgment. We are closest to our authentic voice, closest to God, when we are most in touch with the power within our own beings, using our bodies and our minds, under our own control, and positive effort.

"Let's all stand now and begin by breathing, freeing our hearts, cleansing our lungs, breathing out the negativity, and reaching for the God of our understanding."

The people rose and followed her. It was intense, mesmerizing. Chopin preludes, Handel's *Water Music,* Bessie Smith, Billie Holiday, Thelonius Monk played behind them. She led quietly, now and then commenting—giving permission to be tired, awkward; to rest; to grunt; to push harder. "The competition is with yourself, don't pay attention to what anyone else is doing, that is *not* the authentic voice, that is ego." They worked hard. The combination of exercises seemed to blend yoga, dance, calisthenics. There were no mirrors, which made concentration more intense, the experience of each individual more private.

This was not shrill Fundamentalist hell and brimstone or dopey, wavy-haired snake oil retribution. There was

no manic Mickey Mouse muscleman making fools of
everyone participating, no glitzy hedonism; it was classy,
forgiving, supportive, loving, good for your soul and your
buttocks.

I had never seen anything like it. A beautiful, ethereal
woman with a radiant otherworldly presence telling people how to love themselves and find God without all the
devil-dealing, money-grubbing, manipulating bullshit.
Someone lovely to watch, soothing to hear, who could
make you feel good and look good and wanted nothing
in return. There were no pledge numbers at the end, no
videos, record albums, cookbooks, monogrammed sweat-
suits—zip. She said thank you and faded away into a
Fireman's Fund commercial. The show was on an odd
channel at an odd hour. At the close it said simply, "Eve:
God Through Exercise."

Wow.

Aimee Semple, Katherine Kuhlman, Jane Fonda, eat
your alfalfa-sprouted hearts out.

I thought of almost nothing else for days. I even had
a brief, though searing fantasy of throwing on my tennis
clothes, trotting on down to wherever it was she taped,
and flinging myself into deep breathing, impressing her
with my easily accessible *authentic voice* and toe-touches.
But I did nothing. She had moved away from me now,
out of my ability to relate. Ballerinas were exotic enough
(especially those more than young enough to be my
daughter), but dancing goddesses, well. I passed. Again,
bad timing.

For so long in my life women had been a mystery so
vast, so remote, exotic and enticing that I stood before
them like a faithful pup waiting with paw up for any
attention. I chased my tail in circles, leaping in the air
in ecstasy at any murmur, pat, or praise from the en-
chantresses who did not burp, fart, bleed, or piss; who
were perfect and kept deserting me, turning into tooting,

belching, sobbing, dissatisfied, real people before I'd finished my doggie treat. Here was a dame, as close to the
old illusion as I had ever been, and instead of leaping
over the dog run and chasing the ambulance, I was turning
it off.

Maybe, I thought, this was maturity. A final settling
down with reality and expectation. There *were* no goddesses, and even this one was not perfect. She had her
bunions and bursitis (little did I know). I was surrendering
my infantile quest for Mother Love, perfect womanhood.
No, Nathan, too bizarre, I said to myself and switched to
the basketball finals.

I kept the set away from her till 1983, when she was
everywhere—network, *Time* magazine. *People*—and there
was no more escape for me.

Eve woke up from her accident in a three-bed room in
a dank old New York hospital, her left leg immobilized,
hot with physical agony, alone. One fast lethal moment
of panic filled her; she had changed back, confessed,
everyone knew. Her dreams had been heavy and dense
with surreal, symbolic twisting maypoles of image and
memory.

She was lost in the streets of some Latin town. It was
night and the town was treacherous. She had two small
children, a boy and a girl with her. They belonged to
her and she did not want them to know she was lost. At
last she finds a large stately building and takes the children
inside. She is messy, not well dressed, hair uncombed,
and there are two chic and stoney-faced Spanish women
sitting at a long, black, wooden desk, blocking her way.
She tries to be calm, not to upset the children, but it's
very hard for her to talk, her Spanish is poor and she
stutters. "We're lost, can you tell us how to get home?
It's dangerous outside and I have my children with me."
The women shake their heads and ignore her. Finally,

she pleads, "If I give you money will you help me?" They nod at her. One of them begins to speak, but she can't understand the language, can't read the map. She puts in more money. "Isn't there someone who can tell me? I can't understand you!" She begins to cry and so do the children. The other woman gets up and walks into a large Gothic churchlike room where several men are working. She feels relieved because they are speaking French and she can understand them. She tells them her dilemma, but no one answers, no one looks up. "Can't one of these men go with us and show us the way?"

The woman sighs. "They don't care anymore; they see so many lost ones," she says.

Then suddenly she remembers. *I have money, I'll call a taxi, a taxi will take us home.*

But there was no taxi, just an orderly and an I.V. and the sounds of suffering, whimpering human beings like herself.

She spent two lost days, easing in and out of consciousness, buffered from reality by pain-killers and sleeping potions, floating above herself like a Chagall maiden, circling the cow, the moon, the clouds, bobbing and weaving back toward earth.

When she landed for good she was greeted by her roommates. To her left was a tiny, emaciated spinster from New Jersey, Sada Hernfeld, and across the way a teenage beauty, named Revenge, with pink razor-cut hair. Miss Hernfeld had only a quarter of her stomach and ran to the bathroom every five minutes on hard, spindly little legs that looked as if they had run her ragged and worked her hard.

Revenge (née Eleanor) had epilepsy, among other problems, seemingly triggered by a slippery fast-lane young life as a roadie with a rockabilly group called something like Suck. Quite a trio. Miss Hernfeld hated, loved, was jealous of, and malicious to Revenge. Revenge played on these emotions both as a way to further alienate herself, confirming her feelings of worthlessness, and to attract more attention. Even negative attention was better than indifference to a child who had always been ignored. Miss Hernfeld was dying, though she did not know it yet, at least officially. Eve could see it in her, the maddened nervousness, the nibbly, rodentlike defenses.

They already knew more about Eve's condition than Eve did. The rest was filled in by the doctor who was about as direct with her as he had been with me. She sank into a depression. What would she do now? She couldn't work as a minister. She couldn't work as a dancer and she knew nothing else. Being a freak was one thing, but being a useless freak was something entirely different.

Before she left Louisiana, she set up the trust for Alex, but she had made no provisions for herself (how could she?). She just took whatever cash was on hand to cover her surgery and living expenses until she was able to work. There was no way of changing it now without reappearing, and that was out of the question. She felt angry at herself for her romantic shortsightedness, her impracticality, her martyrdom. But it was too late, or as Miss Hernfeld said constantly about her own wasted life, "Past gone, under the bridge." It was a time, if there ever was one, for living her philosophy, trusting God and living one moment at a time. First she had to heal and then she would see where she was.

Her day nurse was a large, brusque black woman from Tennessee who reminded her of Maybe and always had a story to cheer her up. "There was this preacher, and he was so holier than thou, even Jesus got bored. Well, there is a terrible flood in his town and he's trapped by the water. There he stands with his Bible in his hands and up comes a rowboat. 'We're here to rescue you,' the rower says. 'No, thank you,' says the preacher, 'I put my faith in the Lord.' Time passes and now the water is up to his waist and another rowboat comes along and the men say, 'We're here to save you,' and the preacher shakes his head and looks up into the sky. 'No, no! I put my faith in the Lord, the Lord will provide!' Pretty soon the water is up to his chin and a helicopter flies over and lowers a rope. 'Climb up quick!' says the pilot. 'We're here to get you out.' 'No,' says the preacher, pointing his nose up at the sky. 'I put my faith in God Almighty— He will provide.' 'Suit yourself,' says the pilot, and off they go. Well then, the water washes over his head and the preacher drowns and when he gets up to heaven he's all sputtering and upset and he marches up to God, who is sitting on His throne just shaking His head in disbelief. 'I put my faith in you, Lord, and you let me drown!' shouts the preacher. And God looks down at the poor fool and says, 'Two rowboats and a helicopter? What more do you want!' "

Eve was trying not to miss the lowered rope. She had come too far, lost too much, to give up now. Her body throbbed and her mind was dulled with sickness and doubt. She felt her light was dimming and she was frightened. If she could only move she could break loose the numbness, the cloud before her vision; but she could not move. She could not move and Miss Hernfeld could not stop moving and Revenge could not stop talking.

Eve watched her two fellow sufferers and her heart opened to them. She absorbed their pain, displacing her own. They responded, slowly. Circling closer and closer, drawn toward the center of her magical warmth by primitive yearnings for the soothing hand of love on their troubled souls.

She was a beacon and they floated toward her, unconscious of the power she possessed, but aware that in her presence they were not afraid.

She was the good witch, teasing them out of the sulks, breaking up their fights with a calm soothing word.

"Come now, sisters, all three of us together couldn't round up the energy to steal a gum ball from a baby. Stop that squalling and I'll tell you another story about New Orleans. Want to hear about Jean Lafitte the famous pirate?"

They would calm down, nodding their acquiescence like children after a tantrum. They trusted her and began to lean on her seemingly bottomless strength.

Eve saw this happening as it had happened with the dancers, and because she could not move away from it, block them out, diffuse it, she was forced to confront her own power.

One morning, when Miss Hernfeld was picking on Revenge about her hair, Revenge took off her nightgown and paraded before her, her lush, ripe young body like a pie in the poor withered old maid's tired face. Eve sat up as straight as she could and put out her arms to them. "Come on, now. Come here. Take my hands, hold on to me. Let's pray together. Let's take some slow deep breaths and feel ourselves letting go of all the fear. Hold my hands."

Revenge pulled back. "I'm a black-brained punker, lady. I hate God. I hate kindness; it's establishment horseshit. I want the Prince of Darkness, hard cocks, hard rock, junk food, and drugs. Keep away from me with your fairy tales, bitch."

But even as she said it she moved closer.

"No one tells me nuthin'," Miss Hernfeld whimpered. "I've never been a complainer, but they take tests and tests and I keep running and nobody tells me nuthin'. I'll get a disease if I hold her filthy hand." But she did.

When their hands touched, the two wounded women began to cry. It was the first time that either of them had let out their hurt. They sprung open like broken jack-in-the-boxes, tears flowing from their startled eyes.

Within a week Revenge had been stabilized and Miss

Hernfeld was calm enough to be told the truth, which came, as Eve suspected it would, as a great relief.

"She's a saint," Revenge whispered to her new friend, Miss Hernfeld. "It's a miracle. A fucking miracle."

As it sometimes is in environments like hospitals, where we are separated from the armor and delusions of our normal lives, without our rituals or even our clothes, strange things do not seem so and there is more freedom to be vulnerable, to risk without fear of judgment. After all, when you are shitting in a pot in your own bed and waiting for a stranger to take it out from under you, it is not likely that your Dun and Bradstreet rating or golf handicap is going to much protect you or impress anyone.

It was a perfect atmosphere for Eve's ministry. No one challenged her credentials, asked for her last church affiliation, or snickered at a woman's audacity to lead a spiritual flock.

In the microcosmic world of sickness, no one questioned her and she was able to discard the rigidity of the seminary training and let her true thoughts evolve. Soon people were coming from other rooms on crutches, in wheelchairs, hobbling along beside their I.V. and plasma bottles to listen to her talk. And it helped. People got better faster than their doctors, the experts, or anyone thought they would.

As soon as Eve was able to stand, they began meeting in the reception areas. She had discovered in bed what she had suspected all of her life. Physical confinement was the most damaging thing that could happen to one's spirit.

The moment she moved, stretched her arms, breathed, she could fight her own insidious depression and angst. The life force rose. She could talk to herself and to God— mostly one was the other anyway—with conviction and hope. She stood on her crutches before her audience of sallow fellow sufferers and asked them to breathe, to

stretch, to bend. Word spread, and the nurses set up a
space in the employees cafeteria to accommodate all the
patients who wanted to come. Soon doctors were coming,
first to watch, then to join in.

As Eve grew stronger and her first cast came off, they
let her stay on, moving her from spare bed to spare bed,
to keep her work going. She spent hours in physical
therapy trying to move her fused, stiff leg. The pain was
excruciating, but she kept on, and she shared this with
her flock, giving them strength, helping them heal and
not give up.

Near the time when Eve would be leaving, with absolutely no idea what she would do next, a new patient
was wheeled in to see her. She talked about God, movement, and hope and then they exercised together. The
new patient was Ivan Kimbal, a prominent television producer, struck down on a business trip by what was first
diagnosed as a heart attack, but turned out to be a virus
around the sac of his heart. Because viruses cannot be
cured, but hang around, like the Man Who Came
to Dinner, until they bloody well feel like leaving, he
was battling both helplessness and fear (if the bugger
gets worse, it's a killer). He had a private suite on the
VIP floor, far away from Eve and her flock, but his
nurse thought it might do him good and took him to
see her.

It did do him good, both because he fell madly in love
with her and because the movement, the breathing, the
spiritual awakening (this was not a man of Mass and
meditation, this was a television executive) helped his
mental and soon his physical misery. Before long Ivan
Kimbal was stretching and finding God between his in-
and exhalations, and the virus began packing its bags and
looking for a place to spend the summer.

Then Ivan had an idea. He would tape Eve doing her
thing. A demo tape, not at the hospital only, but on the

outside with other people. The idea focused his energy and he had already begun making arrangements when he decided to talk to Eve about it in person.

He was as nervous with her as a schoolboy before the new schoolmarm, entranced and enamored by her serenity and beauty.

"Miss Eve, may I call you Eve? I-I've . . . I've got an idea. I'm a television producer and I've, uh, well, been thinking. . . . Watching you with the patients . . . well, what you're doing is unique. . . . I'd, uh, like to make a demo tape, what we call a pilot, and see if I can . . . if maybe I might sell it as a show. What do you think of that? I mean we'd pay you, of course, and we'd do it your way. No compromises, I promise."

Eve stood over him, leaning on her crutch, trying to make sense of what she was hearing. In public and on television. Again, the first impulse was panic. She started to decline, and then she remembered the preacher and the rowboat; if this was the lifesaver, she could not afford to send it away.

"Well, if you're crazy enough to want to, I'm crazy enough to try."

Ivan recovered, Eve put down her crutches (though she still walked with a cane) and went home, returning to the hospital daily. The administration had found a way to pay her a small salary out of their rehabilitation budget while she and Ivan worked on the concept of the show.

They taped two episodes. One at the hospital and one with a group of businessmen, housewives, working people. It was a simple set: a large circle, no mirrors, classical and jazz music, hard exercise, pantheistic, humanistic commentary. Ivan Kimbal, who had never produced anything without hoopla, marketing mania, and show biz, sold it himself in independent markets.

It did not have a definable audience or a peg. It was not really religion and it was not Richard Simmons, but every affiliate who saw it was fascinated and enough bought to make it producible.

Ivan was no fool. This kind of response was unheard of. No flash, no splash, no anxiety message, and it was moving. He decided to hold it back, test it, build it, and let Eve get used to what was happening. He also wanted to take time with her, in spite of his twenty-year marriage and four children. She would have none of that (memories of her mother and Robin too strong to overcome), but she accepted his friendship and he accepted hers and they were able to work together fairly (infatuation often makes businessmen fairer). "Eve: God Through Exercise" was born.

CHAPTER 18

In 1983 I was in Boston covering the death throes of
the busing debacle and celebrating (alone in the Ritz
Hotel bar) my fifty-third birthday. I was tired and depressed. The old ennui had returned, settling down un-
invited and grinning at me lasciviously from inside my
overly active head. "What's It All About, Alfie?" whistled
through my head like elevator Musak, humming through
the vents in my unconscious. I toasted myself one last
time and stopped at the desk to check messages before
beddy-bye.

There was a birthday telegram from Greta, one from
Pop, one from CBS, a phone message from my current
though infrequent bedmate, and three nonbirthday messages from a Lily Smith at the Gender Identity Clinic in
Cambridge. Gender Identity Clinic? Hmmmmmm. I reread it on the way to my room. In spite of my third
Scotch it reread the same. Were they taking a survey?
Was I suspect? Before I could ponder further the phone
by my bed rang and a throaty Southern-inflected woman's
voice belonging to *the* Lily Smith apologized profusely
for disturbing me and stated her case.

"I am a postoperative transsexual, Mr. Poe, and my associate, Sam Cole, and I, working with the ACLU, have formed a committee for transsexual rights and filed suit against the state prison system for their inhumane treatment of pre- and postoperative transsexual prisoners. The conditions these poor souls are living in is appalling, and I deeply believe, if we can have an hour of your time, that you will see a valuable story in their plight. I am coming to you fresh with this, none of the papers or other media have it yet."

My curiosity was piqued and my ego stroked. Lily was right. It was a story replete with a bizarre cast of characters and sexual and psychological abuse. Preoperative transsexuals are put into men's prisons because anatomically they're still males; there they become the prize love birds, subject to intimidation, rape, sexual jealousy, humiliation, and verbal and physical harassment by guards. Their female hormones are withheld and without them even the postops who are put in women's prisons cannot maintain their feminine characteristics, throwing them back into gender limbo and despair. It was news. I scooped it. The Big Eye winked kindly at me.

Once I had worked through my judgmental superciliousness I grew quite fond of Sam and Lily. On the evening I left Boston, I went to Lily's apartment (her new husband was still at work) to bring her some posies and say good-bye. She let me in, taking the flowers gratefully but with some preoccupation. "Excuse me, Nathan, dear, my favorite show is on; come sit a minute, then we'll talk."

I came. I sat. There was "Eve: God Through Exercise." Of course I had been aware of her. She was network (mine, even). She was a star, the subject of meetings, musings, media mulling, a phenomenon. She had broken the barrier between fringe programming and mass audience. She was pulling the viewers from everywhere. The

TV evangelists were becoming rather disturbed (if one believed what one read). She was making them look silly, venal, greedy, distasteful. She had the glow of grace, of Christ, of absolution. Hypnotic and true.

"Reach up, stretch toward the light, feel the strength flow in, feel the poison flow out, feel the release and the peace," she was saying.

"We have moved from the Me decade into an even more profound spiritual limbo.

"We are groping toward the answers to unanswerable questions like cats in a bag—seeking, clawing, reaching in darkness and unable to find the light.

"The light is right there inside the bag with you.

"The wisdom is within. We are here together to help one another find the power within our own beings. To locate the energy that is released when we open to life. Life is air. Breathe in life and release the fear and confusion. Do not fear the dark. You can see."

Now she had celebrities coming to sing, to dance, to participate; but otherwise it was the same simple format. People trusted her, people loved her.

"Could you do me a great big favor?" Lily said, turning to me when Eve was finished as if being released from a trance. "Would you take her a note from me? I want her to come here and do a show for the Category-B prisoners."

"I don't know her."

"But she's on your network. It couldn't be too hard. Come on, Nathan darlin', where's your grit? Besides, she's gorgeous. How bad can it be?"

How bad, indeed.

What was the State of the Union as Eve walked toward us opening her graceful white arms wide for us to sink into, smiling her love at us, offering salvation through compassion? A pantheistic, reborn man/woman, offering forgiveness and self-love through calisthenics and deep

breathing; peaceful acceptance of God's will in the mundane exercise of weary, stiffened, cellulite-laced, flaccid,
neglected, gravity-defeated muucles? We were close to
the point of melt-down. We were making do and making
believe that things weren't really as grim as they sounded.
We were being bludgeoned to death by the transmission
of *bad news*.

Children romping through empty lots, turned bloated
and screaming with swollen esophagi and distended livers.
Nothing was safe, the smiling news teams told us daily
with our tainted coffee and nightly with our greasy Big
Macs.

Our food was poison, our air was poison, the rain was
poison, the sea was poison, the earth we stood on was poison. We ate more cancer-causing, heart-attack-producing,
calorie-laden crap in a day than whole villages in India
did in a year. Our homes were toxic with asbestos and
insect repellents. *Nothing was safe.* Lead lurked in our toothpaste and in the paint on our Contempo-Condos. Rapists
and armed maniacs roamed the freeways. Perverts dragged
young children into vans for buggery and dismember-
ment. Neighborhoods divided into paranoid war zones,
each house plastered with alarms and warnings: Beware
of Dog, This House Protected by Acme Burglar Alarms.
Every door was locked, every yard patrolled by growling,
snarling, hateful animals who began as happy pups. You
were not safe to buy an aspirin or an orange or to walk
to your car in the middle of a Saturday afternoon. Young
wives on their way to the dry cleaners disappeared without
a trace. Russian satellites armed with nuclear warheads
were whirling out of control around the planet; nuclear
power plants were leaking lethal garbage from their fault-
line locations. We were under siege from radiation on
the airplanes that whisked us and the dentists that fixed
us, the sun that tanned us, the ovens that fed us. People
were now shot and *then* robbed as an afterthought. Drunk

drivers were splattering people all over the highways.
Drug use was out of control; gun use was out of control;
Central America was out of control; Iran, Iraq, Mexico,
Poland, Afghanistan, and the South Bronx were out of
control.

And the cappers. Natural selection working its way to
the top. The Herpes and AIDS Show.

Herpes stopped the sexual revolution dead in its track
shoes. No more one-nighters with passionate strangers
who may or may not have incurable viruses on their pri-
vates. People shaped up, stopped sitting on their best
friends' toilet seats, became frightened of strangers and
more choosy about their high-priced spread.

Then, just as we began to relax again, from somewhere
in northern Africa, creeping across the world into N.Y.C.
came AIDS. First reports were calm. It only hit faggots.
Well, who cared about that? Serves then right, the im-
moral *momsers*, leaning over in public toilets; who cares
about them? Fear spread through the urban gay com-
munities like a bobsled on an avalanche. The list grew.
Haitian refugees, hemophiliacs, drug addicts, women who
slept with victims, children in close contact, and trans-
fusion recipients. A middle-aged lady on Long Island. A
two-year-old child in Los Angeles. *Holy shit!* The media
had a live one. An epidemic. A lethal, insufferable terrifying virus. A contagious cancer crackling across the
world. Suddenly it was worthy of money from NIH. After
all, now it was the Rest of Us, not a bunch of fairies
holding candlelit parades for their dying friends.

"20/20" did a close-up on a handsome, athletic homosexual turned bloated, decaying monster by the new pes-
tilence, the gay plague, as it was called. Panic spread.
"Not since polio," we newsmen pronounced. Herpes was
the disease of last month, whisked onto the back pages
by something much more terrible.

Gay leaders gave interviews fuming in outrage at the

irony. "The Reagan administration was not about to del-
egate funds when homosexuals were dying like houseflies;
it's been two years and hundreds of deaths, but not until
it threatened the general population did the government
care."

So much for free love, for the kindness of strangers.
Jerry Falwell smiled smugly, plague on earth sent to destroy the sinners, the worshipers of the golden idols.

What could the backlash be? Homosexuals tarred and
feathered? Vigilante committees set up to protect the
good citizens from the conveyors of the dreaded AIDS?
I wrote a piece for an underground newspaper under an
assumed name. In it I proposed the theory that we were
about to make homosexuals the new Jews, the victims of
our focusless primal rage. They would take the rap for
our fall. They had decayed the moral code and moved
into the top ranks of the arts, business, the film and
fashion industries. They set the taste, baked the best
pastry, looked better, dressed better, favored one another
for jobs and promotions, withheld from lonely women,
kept to themselves. Perfect scapegoat material. We were
drawn and repelled. Mothers feared it in their sons and
sons in themselves. Their numbers were growing, their
power was growing. They had their own restaurants, re-
sorts, churches, neighborhoods. My God! What would
the world come to now? Schools had them fired, gay
lawyers in straight firms played hetero with the same wet-
palmed anxiety that Hymie Schwartz became Harry Smith.

They were a perfect moving target; Hitler's idea of
rhetorical heaven. Blame this on Them. Moral corruption
was bringing us *a virulent disease that kills 80 percent of its victims
within two years and is spreading around the world faster than
grease on ice.*

We had just staggered up from the invasion of Lebanon,
the Recession, Tylenol, cancerous fish, Times Beach, the
Hillside Strangler, Miami riots, Solidarity, John Belushi,

the cocaine craze, the collapse of the educational system, Reagangate, and the creeping awareness that we were probably the first generation to reverse evolution, to produce children whose lives would not necessarily be better than ours (the chicken in every pot was wizened with chemicals).

The American Dream was "taking a meeting" with reality. George Burns was not really God and no news was the only good news available. Before we could turn off the set and toss the egg-stained morning scroll into the trash compactor, here came AIDS. "What next?" people hissed under their chemically freshened breath.

An upbeat news story was a retarded orphan being adopted, a jaundiced baby getting a liver transplant. Fred Astaire was no longer dancing and Jack Benny had been dead for years.

Jerry Falwell was blacking out everything but his own voice in Virginia and sending out "miracle request forms"— "select the miracle of your choice: ____physical, ____ financial, ____spiritual, ____emotional, ____intellectual. Send just $10 and Reverend Falwell will personally pray for you." Oral Roberts was being asked directly by God (certainly not by George Burns) to seek donations from everyone on earth so that he could cure cancer.

Into this came Eve. Smiling out at us, radiating warm, honeyed hope. A golden earth mother telling us to breathe deep and let in the universal energy, reach out and let love into our palpitating, angry, constricted hearts. In through the nose, touch the toes, clear the head of fear, give the godhead in each of us room to move.

This quiet, kind, shining soul had the magic. She helped tough men and angry, frightened women soften, slow down, feel connected, feel loved. She spoke through us, into us, as one being, as man/woman. Nonthreatening, comforting, glowing with the life force. "Breathe deep," she said, and we did.

So when I got back to New York, I took the goddamn lilac-scented note paper, like a kid with his mother's market list, shuffling down the halls of the Big Eye down the Saarinen corridors, down the elevators into the real world of TV. The one of dirty coffee cartons, tangled acres of cables, union guys, short tempers, large egos, deadlines, make-believe. People and props that seem to be one thing and are something quite else again. I trudged past the doors with red lights flashing (TAPING, DO NOT ENTER), makeup rooms, dressing rooms, assistant directors, associate producers, talk show hosts, preening and powdering, boredom and frenetic energy lapping one another. "Hi, pal, lunch Tuesday? Loved your Akron bit."

I shuffled into Rehearsal Room 5 like a good boy, the note clutched in my hairy hand, hoping the store would be closed, "Sorry, they were closed. Sorry, they were out of Porcelana, Mom." The door swung open and there she was.

She is leaning against a rehearsal piano, her hair pulled back in a ponytail kind of thing, no makeup, jeans, tennis shoes, a man's work shirt with rolled-up sleeves revealing slender white arms and long well-shaped fingers (I remember that moment when she fell, that hand in mine). She is smiling. An old black piano player was doodling and a young black bass player doodled back. She moved forward and began to dance, that old New Orleans stiff-legged street urchin dance. The musicians exchanged looks and they all laughed. They played it for her and she danced. "My brother used to watch those kids in the Quarter for hours, spent all of his money pitching change into their derbies, trying to make them smile. He never could. He just idolized those kids. To him, they were independently successful."

She stopped, laughing, wiping sweat from her neck with the tail of her shirt. I swallowed. The store was open; the note was burning my fingers. My hand, I feared, was about to start shaking. She turned and saw me. I tried to nod. She smiled and cocked her head sideways;

I tried to smile back (God only knows what it looked like from her side). The musicians, mercifully, kept doodling and she walked toward me.

"Hi. You're Nathan Poe, I like your work very much. I'm Eve." She extended one of those magic swan feathered arms toward me. I extended the goddamn note.

"I'm sorry to bother you. I was asked to deliver a note, the person who asked is a friend. I just did a story on her, so I took the liberty. I hope it won't be offensive to you, from a stranger and all. I think it's a rather odd request. I haven't read the note, of course, I just brought it down from Boston, but, well, I don't usually invade people like this, so I apologize." (Buy the goddamn Porcelana and go home, Nathan, you idiot.)

"Boston?" Her eyes widened a bit as she took my cursed missive. "Excuse me for a moment, please don't leave, if you can wait, I'll be right back."

She almost ran across the hall and through the glass door into the studio booth. I could see her face as she read the note, solemn, pale, smiling, then stern. She picked up a phone and made a call. I waited.

She talked for several minutes. When she was through, I could see her wiping tears from her cheeks. I looked at my loafers, which needed polishing. I pretended avid interest in the bass player's fingers. She was back, walking toward me, smiling, her cheeks pink with emotion.

"Was it okay?"

She nodded. "It sure was. I don't know how to thank you for this. It means a great deal to me. Lily speaks very highly of you."

"I take that as a true compliment. Then you know her?"

A shadow moved quickly across her eyes. "From a long time ago. From church, actually."

"Must have been some church." (That's good, Nathan, put the whole unpolished loafer right down your tar-scarred throat.)

She laughed. (Thank you, God.) "I have to get back

now. I hope I can return the favor sometime, Mr. Poe."

"Nathan. It was my pleasure."

"Well, good-bye. Nice to meet you." She stood very still looking at me strangely again, as if trying to remember something.

"My pleasure," I said, one extra time, just to show the range of my wit and charm. Out I went.

Upstairs I trod into the news department, into my office, into the elevator, out to Kennedy, and over to West Germany to interview the leaders of the Green Party (I told them not to send me; I cannot be fair and objective to any German living or dead, even schoolchildren—I only see the Iron Cross and the ovens—but no one paid any attention). I went, I did it, I came back, and for the entire four days (plus travel) all I thought about was her. I even saw her show in German in a Munich hotel room. I came home furious at her, Lily, myself. Everyone. I was beginning to lose a wee little bit of anal-compulsive middle-aged Jewish male-egotist control.

I called my bimbo of the moment. We went to bed, or at least we got into it, my sexual instrument lying in slumber unwakable by any previously known remedy. At one point she suggested ice cubes, but somehow it didn't seem worth it. I remembered George C. Scott's fantastically erotic ode to impotence in *Hospital* and sonorized as much of it from memory as possible. She didn't care that much either, and so we switched on the TV, poured another Scotch, and watched her favorite show. Guess who.

At the end of the program, Eve made an announcement. With the help of the network and the thousands of supporters from the world of sports, entertainment, and politics, she was going to do a telethon to be telecast live from Lincoln Center beginning on Thanksgiving Eve and continuing for twelve hours to raise money for victims of religious and political persecution throughout the world. The proceeds would be put into an international fund to help these people obtain freedom. She said good night, and then on the screen the list of participants in the telethon ran without any additional hype. The list was extraordinary. Even I was impressed.

The next day I surrendered enough to call and invite her to dinner. She accepted.

I called, made a date, then panicked, and chose what I thought would be the most offensive, alien, off-putting place to take her (she'll be insulted, storm out, and never want to see me again, whew).

I took her to see *Torch Song Trilogy*. It is the story of a young Jewish gay drag-queen transvestite. After all, a damsel of her refined and godly bent should find such subject matter horrifying.

We men are such cowards in the face of emotions previously unknown or at least previously controllable. To admit this, of course, is unmanly, so we have our male dirty tricks that are used just as often on women who overwhelm us and whom we adore as on those we don't know how to get rid of. The success rate is not bad, either (depending on what you consider success).

She *loved* the play. She smiled her serene smile and thanked me for choosing it. So much for dirty tricks.

We were almost mobbed on the street. Getting her out and into a cab required an energetic heroism that I would not have believed I possessed. I took her to the quietest place I knew for dinner.

"Listen, Eve, I'm sorry about the mob scene. I should have hired a car. You're my first superstar. I need a little practice."

"You were wonderful. Very gallant. I especially liked the way you threw your jacket over my head and pushed me into the cab."

"Omigod! Did I do that! What a guy!"

She threw her lovely head back and laughed until tears came.

"The look on your face! I really thought you would just

take off. You must have been in the army. You were seeing the enemy advancing."

"Well, I was, but tonight was *heroic* compared to my military performance. Sometime—I'll show you my scar. I was decorated. Sort of a reverse medal of valor."

"Where is it?"

"The medal?"

"The scar."

"Right next to my etchings."

"Oh, I see."

We sat, smiling at one another, drawn magnetically. It was good.

"Seriously, does it bother you? All those people? I've been on the tube for years and never had to deal with it. Maybe if I were blond. . . . Losing your privacy though, Jesus. . . . Can I say Jesus before the queen . . . if not, this will be the world's shortest relationship. I say it about fifty times a paragraph."

She nodded, her smile fading slightly. "I'm not like that, Nathan. You can even say the 'f' word and I won't melt." She paused. "Yes, it bothers me. I loathe it. I have been an intensely private person all my life. I'm the one who should apologize to you about tonight. I should have had a car sent. It's part of my denial of what's happened. Sometimes I wake up whispering to myself. 'I'm invisible. I'm still like everyone else.' It frightens me. I don't go out much. This is really my first time. Thank you."

At dinner we drank wine (at least she wasn't one of those body-purified eggplant-eating granola freaks) and talked about television. She asked me questions and listened to my answers. I talked a lot, as I do anyway, but especially when I'm so nervous I'm about to leap from my skin. I told Maxie stories, radio stories, Depression stories. I think I even told her about Elsie. She talked about coming from the South to New York, about dancing, about her accident. All current history. She did not give interviews and she talked only about now. She was an orphan. She had no last name. She felt her life had begun when she came east. Weird, mystical. When she said it to your face, it sounded better. But I had heard her with those musicians talking about New Orleans and her brother (the reporter's mind never clicks off). I did not bring it up.

I took her home to the plain white room in the Village, which moved me greatly, which in turn terrified me even more.

"So this is how a media superwoman lives? I was expecting something a little more schmaltzy, as my aunt Ida would say. Maybe you should renegotiate your contract."

"It's all I need."

"I like it. Very much."

"Thanks." She brushed her hair back. My heart did a three-and-a-half off the high board.

"Who's Aunt Ida?"

"My pop's older sister. She helped raise me—which assures her of a place in heaven and Ripley's. You'd like her. She's a helluva broad."

"I bet she is."

"So are you."

"Me?" She laughed.

"I didn't mean to be sacrilegious. It's the bad little boy in me. I've always got to kick the can. Push my luck. I meant it as a true compliment."

"You're a funny man, Nathan Poe. I like my compliment."

"Want to see my scar now?"

She shook her head from side to side. Then leaned toward me and kissed my bristly cheek. Gently. An angel's kiss.

We thanked one another for a lovely evening, standing awkwardly like adolescents. I asked if I might call again.

She said, "Please." And I fled. Ran before I crumpled on
my knees confessing the terror running through my soul.
But at least I was alive. At least I was feeling something.
The numbness was definitely departing.

When I left her that night, Eve was not in very much
better shape than I was. She made a cup of tea and sat
down on her white couch to write Maybe. Eve had been
living each moment on her faith, blinking at God as the
path before her opened and turned into a blinding white
endless road down which she could not see, taking one
step after another on faith and instinct. Somehow she
had made it into the helicopter, or had she? She *was*
contributing. The money she earned was used to set up
foundations for the needy. She would not do endorse-
ments, merchandising, or cassettes. She had no business
manager or agent, operating alone in an even more alien
world. Dread was constant, the risk of exposure like a
cattle prod zapping into her consciousness whenever she
relaxed and forgot. Her evening with Nathan had made
her aware of just how guarded and alone she was. But
she went forward.

Maybe, dearest. How's my flapjack? I miss you both so!

When the loss of Alex had grown unbearable, she began
sneaking back to New Orleans, watching him on the
playground at school, arranging rendezvous with Maybe
and Alex at the park, the movies, the ice-cream store.
She lived for these meetings. "Maybe's friend," he called
her. But the visits were no longer possible. She was famous.

Her heart ached for him. She lived in fear. Every tornado, flood, hurricane watch. Some maniac dumped cy-
anide in the water supply, a chemical spill closed the main
highway. Robin was running wild and Alex cried himself
to sleep in Maybe's arms. "I want my poppa," he said.
She longed to hold him. She waited, not knowing what

to do, where to turn. And then into her rehearsal room walked a stranger who reminded her of home. Familiar yet unlike anyone she had ever known. Something about him felt safe, felt honest. And in his hand was a note.

Before she opened it, she knew it was Lily, she could smell her smell. "I'm alive, you gorgeous dodo! I swear, the first time I saw you on TV I was so jealous I could hardly survive it! I was pretty sure, but then Sam filled me in. I'm fine, darlin'. I'm married again, and he knows everything (my God, he's a saint, I mean, I'm a spokes-woman for transsexual prisoners! He's a saint!).

"Now, you be careful. I know it's risky for you to come here, I just said that to get Nathan to deliver this to you. I've tried to get to you for months, but those assholes won't let any calls near you. By the way, darlin', that Nathan, he's okay. A little rumpled, I know, but the stuff is good."

Since then Eve and Lily talked often and it helped. Lily even went to New Orleans and saw Alex for her.

She was working very hard. Her knee throbbed. She was having trouble sleeping. The night after meeting Na-than, she had a dream about her accident and saw his face, felt his hand in hers. She woke up, startled, wan-dering around her clean white room. That was the man who jumped on the stage. She was sure of it. Dread. That was not a man who could deal with her truth. She must not think about him again.

But he called. And she had her first date and he was so nervous and she liked him so much. She felt the power of his warmth, his raggedness, his need. He made her laugh. He teased her. She felt lighter than she ever had. Hopeful. He was a survivor, limping but still spry. He made her feel that way, too. *It will be okay.* He lessened her burden.

Why this one? she asked herself over and over after that first evening. In idle moments, at rehearsal, lying

half-asleep in the early mornings, when dreams float into
consciousness and defenses are down. Why? She remembered what Laurel had said the night she had announced
her intention to marry Dr. Joe. "We make a pretty ridiculous couple on the surface of it, but under the surface
we just happen to make a perfectly wonderful couple."

Nathan felt like that to her. She had never really known
anyone like him and yet he seemed so familiar. As he
had spoken, talking fast, spewing forth in his discomfort
a zigzag, rapid-fire view from his own peculiar turret,
pictures of her family flashed through her mind.

He had, or so it seemed, bits of everyone she loved.
Laurel's sardonic wit, Clara's spunk, Zander's sensitivity,
Louis's mournful self-doubt, Hillary's sensuous energy. He
was a bit too old and not easy, to be sure, but to her,
he felt safe; he felt like home. "To have true faith one
must live through the dread"; her college Kierkegaard
came back to her. She decided that if Nathan called again
she would say yes.

I did call and she did say yes and tentatively, awkwardly, slightly out of synch, focus, and rhythm, like
two people in a movieola with a child turning the handle,
we fell in love.

"Eveala? This is Knight Errant. Throw on the scarf and
the dark glasses and some nondescript *schmata*. I've got
tickets to the fights. I'll be there in twenty minutes. Wait
inside. I'll toot. Okay?"

"Okay. I've never seen a fight."

"You'll love it! Lots of stretching and deep breathing.
Little Italy after? Tortellini for two?"

"You're a crazy man."

"But cute."

"Cute."

"You've got a hate on for tortellini?"

"I love tortellini. I'm turning into a tortellini? My leotard
is straining at its seams."

"Great! Aunt Ida said, 'She needs a little meat. Arms like chicken bones.' "

"Let Aunt Ida tell it to CBS. I'm supposed to be the ethereal type."

"You're my type. Okay, screw the tortellini!"

"No, now. Let's not be hasty. Just once more."

"Twenty minutes, beauty."

"Twenty minutes."

The times between were endless. Twenty minutes stretched before us like two hundred years. We glowed. We could not bear to leave each other's sight. I thought of nothing else.

Love.

CHAPTER 19

I was not the only man in America watching Eve and thinking obsessively about her. There was another down Dallas way who was also bewitched by the fair lass, though for rather different reasons. Our old friend the Reverend Harley Kurtz had Eveitis. His attachment to the Richeleaus had been severed for decades. But the viper remained. He was slithering about now on the fringes of Eve's life. The threat to her family was not yet over.

When Harley Kurtz two-stepped into Louis and Hillary's lives and tore them asunder, he was already a liar, a fraud, and, at least passively, a murderer. He was now on his way to becoming a dangerous force in the mainstream of American life.

The good reverend's stories of a poor bayou boyhood were as phony as his Lusiana drawl and his dead-eyed smile. In fact, Reverend Kurtz was born one Alvin Finkle in Van Nuys, California, in 1932. His father, a Russian-Jewish immigrant from Latvia, was an electrician at MGM Studios and his mother, Rifka, an overpossessive hysteric who breastfed him until well past his third birthday and bathed him until he was ten.

Alvin was a bedwetter and an Oedipal test case straight from a first-year psych course. He was ashamed of his passive, plodding father and torn between violent feelings of love and rage for his devoted but definitely unstable momma.

When Alvin was barely fifteen his father died and his mother's nerves broke, whereupon she was sent, by Alvin, to recuperate at Camarillo, the nearest state hospital. Alvin quietly cleaned out the sugar bowl, tied up his belongings, and split for good. When Momma came home to find her beloved son and her money gone, she collapsed into catatonia and was sent back to the state hospital, where she remains to this very day.

Alvin went over the pass to Hollywood, his hot young head filled with visions of trilling like Perry Como. He changed his name to "Teddy Delmonico" after a steak he had seen on the menu of an Italian restaurant where he worked briefly as a busboy.

His money ran out before he could become Perry Como, and since his personality did not lend itself to servile employment (he was not great at taking orders), he was soon hanging around the Salvation Army Headquarters begging for food and shelter. Before long he was a recruit, an "orphan," and officer-in-training in the army of salvation. He paid attention, attracted by the power of these missionaries of the huddled masses, and he learned the magic of the spoken word, the rapturous narcissism of the preacher's life.

From where he sat, it seemed to make little difference *what* was said. You could turn folks this way or that if you said it right. Soon, little lost Alvin was pitching it to the bums and drunks and lost souls (some not long home from the war) and those who would listen to anything for a bowl of watery stew and a bed. He read the Bible; he sang. He loved it.

One night a young Southern vet, six or so years older than Alvin, staggered in, a battered old banjo in his hand.

He slumped down in the back of the hall and laughed through Alvin/Teddy's whole act.

Later that evening Alvin's commander assigned the Southern man to his room. The man, as fate would have it, was a former street preacher and war hero who had fallen on hard times or, in this case, Early Times.

Alvin, infuriated by his disrespect, confronted him. "Why did you laugh during my pitch. You apologize!" cried Alvin.

The Southern man looked right through him (which impressed Alvin so much he put that piercing, intimidating look immediately into his repertoire). "Because yur bullshit, babyface. Rantin' and ravin' with some ol' Hollywood accent—'Teddy Delmonico'—yur an amateur, boy, a punk amateur. You couldn't convert a fly to horseshit. Now if y'all stick around till I dry out, I'll show yew how it's done."

"How come you know so much, you're just a drunk and a hick!"

The man fixed him with that look again, making Alvin's heart pound. "Bein' a hick, *boy*, is the best part of the whole act and bein' a drunk is just the devil in my tortured soul. You got yours, too, boy, and no shame in neither. What's yur real name, boy?"

"None of your business."

The tall young man smiled. "Mine's Harley Kurtz, out of Lusiana."

For months Alvin was Harley's shadow. The cunning, the instinct for opportunity, the ear for the right voice, the right turn was already solid in him. For hours he'd sit and listen to Harley's stories of his bayou childhood; country code of honor, the poor boy's fan dance, which he used to manipulate for survival.

Harley taught him to play the banjo and sing country church music. "Forget that Eye-talian crooner shit, never gonna happen, boy."

Harley knew the Gospel inside out and he knew how to preach. When he was dry, Alvin listened to him, on street corners and in pool halls, open-mouthed with envy. He practiced, imitating him endlessly, and kept a diary with every story, anecdote, and bit of down-home wisdom. "Jesus had to have Judas and so do we. Without Judas there can't be true faith. No Christ, no forgiveness, no understanding of the animal in us, or the struggle of the spirit over our creatureliness." Harley's thoughts poured freely like claret into Alvin's bottomless goblet.

Soon Harley was talking about leaving, heading back South and starting his own church. "Banjo evangelism" he called his philosophy. Alvin panicked. It was as if Alvin had entered Harley like a parasite. He was attached and still feeding. He wanted what Harley had. The Southerner had hit something in the depths of Alvin Finkle's frustrated being. This was the man he should have been. His own family, his own past, were a mirage, meaningless, empty, useless to him in the real world.

The night before Kurtz was set to go with a ticket to Alabama in his billfold, Alvin brought Harley a going-away present. Harley opened it slowly, touched by his young friend's thoughtfulness. The present was a quart of sour mash whiskey.

Harley sat on his bunk, his banjo between his long thin legs, the bottle resting on his bony knees, looking through Alvin. He was quiet for a long while. When he finally spoke, his voice was hoarse and his eyes were filled with tears.

"I misjudged you, boy, but then that's Christian, ain't it." While Alvin sat motionless, Harley Kurtz opened his going-away present and drank until he fell over backward on his bed.

During the night he vomited. Alvin sat beside him listening to the gurgling, the gasping for breath, but he did not move. He did not jump up and turn his mentor over. He did not call out. When the sounds finally stopped, Alvin switiched on the light. Harley was dead.

Calmly, Alvin took Harley's military I.D. card, his Purple Heart medal, his bus ticket, his banjo, his boots and cowboy hat, and his battered old Bible. Then he ran for help.

Two days later the reborn Harley Kurtz got on a Greyhound bus heading for Alabama and his destiny.

By the time the Reverend Kurtz reached his twenty-second birthday, he had his own little church in Mobile, Alabama; was a member of the chamber of commerce; a chorale coach at one of the local high schools; and the husband of a cotton candy–haired organist (whose poppa just happened to be the owner of the city's largest Chevrolet dealership and on the planning commission to boot). Passing as Harley made his official age twenty-nine, so fewer questions about his early success were raised. He was on his way or so it seemed.

There was one little mouse dropping in this perfect aspic. Harley couldn't escape Alvin's perversity or his lust for money and power. The ersatz Harley had grown into quite an unpleasant young fellow, morally speaking. He won Miss Cotton Candy the same way he later captured Hillary—with his sociopathic sensuality. Sex became his letter of introduction. He was certainly not handsome, but he had something and thanks to his dead mentor he had finally found the right package for it.

From the day he left on the Greyhound bus until he settled in Mobile he had experimented with a variety of life-styles that included pimping, among other dubious pastimes. He liked pimping. In fact, he loved it. He liked controlling women and he liked manipulating men. And he made money at it. So, after a while, the life of the small-town evangelist with big dreams and the baby-doll wife grew monotonous. Since Daddy, the car dealer, was

not coming through with any large donations or entrée
to the city politicos, Harley needed leverage. Sex for
money was leverageable.

The rat opened his trap with his wife as cheese in the
form of a basement playroom for grown-ups. A small-
town fifties version of the Marquis de Sade as seen by
Woody Allen. In the basement, Harley created a purple-
and-black plywood Gomorrah equipped with cell-like
rooms, body racks, whips, chains, branding irons, and a
variety of other erotic knickknacks.

An ad was then placed in several out-of-town papers.
"Miss Desire, sensual sadist, now allowing select slaves
to reach ecstasy in her chamber of pleasures." Parson and
organist by day, the Addams Family by night. Mrs. Kurtz
went along because she was malleable to begin with and
hypnotized by her horny husband.

The "slaves" came. Judges, state senators, bankers arrived, some flying in from as far as Houston and Memphis.
And they paid. Within an eighteen-month period, Harley
put away a luscious, tax-free stash of over fifty thousand
dollars. The church expanded; the parson bought a black
Lincoln Continental; Miss Candy got a mink coat. Harley
was on his way to the state legislature.

He lay awake at night planning his future. Religion
and politics seemed to him intertwined; no separation of
church and state bullshit, not in the South, anyway. His
heroes were Father Coughlin, Huey Long, Adolf Hitler,
and Dr. Charles Fuller (the pioneer of Christian broad-
casting). Harley wanted to build on the resurging Fundamentalist movement; to build his power base, get rich
off the people's guilt, and then use that strength to float
into politics. He had it all figured out (in the middle of
the night, anyway). Be the power behind the throne until
you learned how the game worked and then sit on it
yourself.

But there was that mouse dropping. A vice detective

in Memphis saw the S & M ad and recognized the area
code as in his old war buddy's jurisdiction in Mobile. A
phone call to said buddy was made. The out-of-town
detective then called said number posing as a businessman
and made a date for a "night of ecstasy." The local vice
dick showed up instead and confronted Harley to the
shock of both. They served on a crime prevention committee together. *Quel scandale!* If vice dick arrests Harley,
it casts a pall over the whole town from the high school
choir to the blue-haired ladies who practically cream in
their sturdy Sears and Roebuck cotton undies over the
mysterious Reverend Kurtz. The detective made a deal.
"Y'all get your things together and be out of Alabama by
sunrise and I'll forget it ever happened. Don't ever come
back here, neither, or I'll have at you, Reverend."

By sunrise Harley, the fifty thousand dollars, and the
black Lincoln were gone, and the tearful Miss Candy was
back home with her poppa. A small story appeared in the
local paper: "Evangelist vanishes. The respected young
preacher and high school chorale director Harley Kurtz,
husband of Mobile's Candy Mueller Kurtz, disappeared
from his home last Tuesday evening without a trace. His
wife is in seclusion and his parishioners are deeply shocked
by the strange circumstances. According to Ed Mueller,
Reverend Kurtz's father-in-law and owner of Mobile
Chevrolet, 'Harley has been under great strain in the last
months. It is our belief that his responsibilities got to be
too much for him and, being in an unstable condition,
he just bailed out.' "

The marriage was annulled and Harley was back on
the road. Close calls, life was full of them.

From that moment until 1983 Harley Kurtz had a lot
of close calls, false starts, and frustrations (the Richeleau
episode being one of the closest). But he kept moving
and his timing was superb. The Fundamentalist frenzy
grew like Bermuda grass, covering whole cities, offering

lost souls a ready-made printout for life, complete with all the answers.

It made sense. If someone of hypnotic presence and seemingly flawless self-assurance offered a prescription for making life comprehensible, bearable, and safe and all that was asked in return was a certain tithe each month, well, why the hell not? Small price for all the answers. That was the beauty of Fundamentalism. It provided all the answers.

If you took the Bible literally (Jonah in the belly of, speaking serpents, Garden of Eden, devils and angels), what a load off! Millions of people struggling to cope on their own frail steam with poverty, depression, anxiety, diseases of mind and body, were teased with the promise of salvation.

Literal prophecy was (excuse the pun) a godsend. The rural South, land of lost hope and broken dreams, was the perfect spawning ground. The movement was comprised of three basic groups: the Fundamentalists, who were the zealots of literal theology; the Pentacostals (talking in tongues, the bargain loaf of the three made popular by Oral Roberts and Rex Humbard), and the Evangelicals, who put their emphasis on soul-winning. The new kids in town were the Charismatics, from the Greek word relating to God's gift of grace. They were more liberal and uptown, working within different denominations, sort of the nouvelle cuisine of down-home, old-time religion.

The real turn of the screw for Fundamentalism was, of course, television. Holy-rolling superstars were born. The power was incredible. It was the perfect medium for Kurtz.

By the late seventies he had danced the dance, bouncing from politics to the Billy Graham crusade to Oral Roberts. Learning, listening, biding his time.

The guy who seemed to be the comer, the one with the shooter and all the cat's-eyes, was Jerry Falwell, who reminded Harley more of himself than he wanted to admit.

Off he went to Lynchburg, Virginia, to the Thomas Road
Baptist Church.

Falwell was moving; from a cold-water start in a rented
room, he had built a congregation of close to seventeen
thousand members. He saw the future in the crossing
over between Fundamentalist philosophy and politics and
understood who his audience was: pro-Christ, anti-Com-
munist, flag-on-the-porch-on-the-Fourth-of-July Americans.

Kurtz called what Falwell preached the "anti-agenda."
Anti: busing, abortion, gays, détente, welfare, free love,
rock 'n' roll, defense cuts, Salt II, liberals, secular humanism.

Kurtz, as he had from the beginning, took notes and
absorbed everything like the youngest sibling learning
from the foolhardiness of the older kids. He weeded out
the flotsam, refined the philosophy, honed up on the
gospel of fear, the power of the media, the big stick of
constituency. When Kurtz left Virginia, he had Xeroxed
Falwell.

Kurtz went to Dallas, following the money and the
wife of the heir to some enormous oil conglomerate (who
just happened to own several radio and television sta-
tions). By this time Harley had put his act together. His
hair was blow-dry newsman's style, his physique lean and
permanently tan, his nose reshaped, face lifted, acne scars
dermabrased, and his teeth were capped into pearly
whiteness. His clothes were more Brooks Brothers than
Fundamentalist glitz and his voice was trained low, gentle,
mellifluous.

He had his mojo working all right, and when he sat
down on the throne with his own gabardine-covered arse,
he was ready.

He moved fast, too. He called his ministry Cain's Crusaders.

"Cain was the unsaved soul, but he had the power to
be saved—he is more like all of us than his martyred

brother, for it is that energy, the possibility of good conquering evil, that we are here to harness, snatch that energy from evil and throw it around, turn it into *soul-ar* power, the power of the Soul—to be saved from the Devil. No matter how pretty, how seductive his disguise. We are here to harness the energy of Jesus Christ, the Son's Energy, like the Energy of the *Sun* for our salvation."

Not too shabby. By 1982 he had a television, print, and radio audience of almost forty million; a school system (nursery through high); a drug and alcohol abuse clinic; a weekly newspaper; a Lear jet; a sprawling modern church complex with a membership of fifteen thousand; a tax-free annual budget of fifty million dollars and a growing, solid political power base (he swung over two million votes in Mr. Reagan's direction in the '80 election). He had helped defeat "suspicious congressmen" (meaning unreliable on ERA, busing, blacks), and was rumored to have a secret pact with the president on church school taxation among other issues.

He sang, too. Which added to his appeal, especially with the ladies. He understood the power of show biz and his broadcasts were the jazziest, his sermons the most palpitating. He worked his audience to the verge of Pentecostal frenzy, then laid back, soothing, sophisticated, scholarly, to calm them down, manipulating their emotions with the skill of the true demagogue. Poppa scares the shit outta ya, then Poppa comforts ya.

"God gave us television, radio, and the printing press to preach the Gospel, so that we can reach all of God's children. The world now holds over five billion souls, and we need your help to reach these souls and that is why I need your gift. Your hard-earned, sweat-of-the-brow dollars! The electronic age costs money! To preach our *simple* message to all the children of God takes more money than we can ever raise. God needs your help. Help us save our fellowman." It worked.

Imitators soon sprung up, more and more backwoods

losers finding a new meal ticket in a wavy toupee and a
radio announcer's voice. By 1984 there were over a hundred
thousand Fundamentalist ministers on record and more
than twenty thousand alternate church schools beating
the literal truth into clean, empty young heads. "Every
eight hours a new school opens, hallelujah," cried Kurtz,
sending chills up the spines of liberals everywhere. Neo-
fascism, Hitler Youth, the march of the maniacs disguised
beneath apple pie and Captain America suits, was on.

Not that his life was easy. Harley was riding his thoroughbred through the backbiting, media-hungry fox hunt
of his peers. Competition for those hard-earned American
dollars was fierce. Every Sunday the ads in the religion
sections of newspapers from Los Angeles to Tuscaloosa
screamed for full attention.

"Christ the Lord Is Risen Today! Community Church
of Arkansas presents 'The Living Cross' (a beautiful dramatic production)"; "Christ Lives! (choral music and brass—
child care provided)"; "Jesus Is Alive! Come celebrate the
most important event in world history!"; "Christ Is Now
Here (can you accept the possibility that He is again in
the World?)"; "How Will You Know Him, What Does
He Expect of Us? Let Dr. Erwin Forbis answer this vital
question"; "Jesus and Mary have made Miraculous appearances in Bayside, New York (similar to the apparitions of
Fatima at Lourdes, only more important); the sick have
been cured and many urgent messages have been given
concerning world events."

Into all of this addlepated madness danced Eve. Eve
scared the hell out of Harley Kurtz. He sensed danger,
and his "flight or fight" neurons pulsed. She made them
all look sleazy, reptilian, greedy—even he could objectify
enough to see that. Most importantly, she began to pull
the audience. The final blow was when she went network.
His power was waning and so was the power of the others
(all 110,000 of them).

Kurtz was certainly not one to flee. He unpacked his jungle drums and called a secret meeting of the Fundamentalist hotshots to discuss the situation.

"We have no choice. We must remove this 'little Blondie' from our path, brothers. We must find the devil in her past and unleash him—preferably on the CBS television network, prime time. Go home and go to it. Rid us of this serpent."

Off they went, the aroma of paranoia wafting from their blue serge suits, to quash the threat of this gentle little lass who was pulling their followers with deep breathing and Unitarian humanism, the archenemy of evangelism—an empathetic, all-forgiving God reachable *without* them. A heaven without hell meant collection plates without booty. The "little Blondie" must cease.

Shortly after Kurtz's demonic pep rally, Eve received an invitation to speak at the Conference for Spiritual Awareness in Dallas.

Ivan Kimbal encouraged her to accept, understanding the publicity value of such an appearance. Eve agreed. Dallas was psychologically closer to Alex and she badly needed a break from the New York pressures and the tumultuous collection of feelings that her love relationship had unleashed.

The evening of her arrival she was scheduled to attend a private black-tie reception hosted by one of Dallas's most prominent businessmen and "reborns," as the press called them.

It was the first such gathering that she had ever attended, and as she stepped into her now famous biblical white gown, her anxiety grew. For the first time she allowed herself the fantasy of someone at her side. Someone who loved her. Someone to lean on at moments like this. Nathan's face flashed beside her own in the hotel room mirror. She was sorry she had come alone.

These thoughts only increased her nervousness. She had never let herself consider the possibility of living any way but alone. Solitude was her fate and part of her responsibility to her work. But there it was. The phantom second face reflection in the fluorescent light.

The businessman sent a car and driver for her. She was, after all, the drawing card of the conference even if she didn't really believe it. She slid into the plush, soothing luxury of the limousine, grateful for the feeling of protection it offered.

She sat back and closed her eyes. *Nathan.* The phantom face followed her. My mensch, she thought, and smiled, folding her long arms around herself, hugging her memories.

Their lazy walks together, holding hands in Central Park. His funny droopy grin. A Pagliaccian grin. He was always the butt of his own jokes. "I get it from Maxie," he explained.

The tenderness he gave his daughter. A shy, hesitant caring that tore at her heart. It was the same kind of love he offered her.

"You're a fucking phenomenon, Eveala. I try and try, but I just can't figure this one out. An over-the-hill three-time-loser lands in the goddamn daisy patch!"

"Me, too, Poe."

"*You!* Lovely one, if *I'm* your daisy patch, you must have been raised in the fucking Sahara Desert! . . . Let me water you . . . prune you . . . cover you with spring mist. Each petal is so fragile. I must care for you. . . ."

"Oh, Poe. You are a mensch. Your poppa is dead right. I'm not fragile. I've hoed my own garden for a long time. Don't be afraid of me. I won't wilt."

"There goes that damn mystical shit again! Tell me! Why won't you tell me about you? You know everything about me. It gives you a helluvan edge. I'm a pretty sneaky type. I can find out on my own. It's like a goddamn B movie. The reporter trailing the mysterious lady in white. Trust me."

"I can't now. Please, please, don't push me. Soon, Poe. Soon."

"Okay. Saint Eveala. Patience was never one of my virtues, but I'll try. Enough of this poignancy! Your petals are pale. Fertilizer! You need root food. Get dressed. We're going to Gino's for some nourishment."

He made love to her like he talked to her. Tenderly. With humor and sweetness. It was everything she had ever dreamed of, and she was able to relinquish her fear that her naked body would betray her and let him love her. She needed it that much. She overcame herself. But the secret was there. After the passion, it came back. Soon, she had promised. Soon.

The car stopped at the entrance to the businessman's mansion. TV cameras and reporters were everywhere. Ropes and police held back a mob of screaming fans. Fear clutched her. She fought the urge to cry out to the driver, "Get me out of here!" The old feeling of total aloneness crept over her. Her hands were shaking. She was cold. Eve leaned forward, touching the old black chauffeur on the shoulder. "Could you, please . . . would you mind, walking in with me?"

He turned and smiled sadly at her. "Miz Eve. I'd be honored to, but it wouldn't be right. I'd lose my job, ma'am."

"How silly of me. I've been away too long. The same old Southern shazam. I'm sorry." She patted his arm.

He laughed in surprise. "You must be a Southern gal, ma'am."

Her smile faded. "From a long, long line." She smoothed her hair back and opened the door. "Wish me luck," she said hoarsely.

The crowd of fans and reporters swarmed toward her. The police fought to contain them.

"Eve! Eve! Eve! We love you! Eve! Eve! Eve!"

Flashbulbs popped in her face. A hand clawed at her dress. She felt faint and panic-stricken. The lights blinded her.

A man in a black tuxedo strode up beside her, setting off the crowd again. She turned toward him, reaching out for help. "Please. Could you walk me in, please!"

The man took her arm, shielding her and waving the crowd off. "Let us pass, folks! Be Christian, now. Let the lady through!"

The smell of his cologne sickened her. She let him guide her up the marble stairs and through the towering solid brass doors.

"Eve! Eve! Eve!" the voices echoed behind them.

"You're safe now, my dear. Delivered from the belly of the beast." The man was grinning at her. She opened her eyes slowly, trying to focus. The man's face was still hazy. He was speaking to her in a sensual, intimate manner. The voice. There was something familiar about the voice. She was cold, again. So cold. She backed away from the odor of his cologne. She could see now. A face. A leering evil face that she had not seen since she was six years old. Reverend Harley Kurtz. She was close to fainting.

"Are you all right, mademoiselle? You look rather pale. I realize that you are new to the media mayhem. It is quite disturbing at first, but we veterans have learned how to make it work for us. If I can be of service, I would be honored to share my experience in these matters with you. We are all on the same path, aren't we now?"

Eve took a slow deep breath, balancing herself. "The old bullfrog," Clara had called him. She would not let him see her fear.

"Thank you, Reverend. But I am not at all sure that we follow the same path. I appreciate your help. Please excuse me."

She turned, ballerina straight, and glided away. She could feel the hate from his tar-black eyes burning into her back. She wanted to run. She was afraid that she would lose control and confront him, lash out as she had at her father's table so long ago. "This man is a snake! He destroyed my family!" She held on.

Her host rushed toward her, taking her in hand, treating her with star deference. Every eye was on her. She shone.

All through the evening she was aware of Kurtz following her with his sharp, hard eyes. His discomfort fueled her. She was no longer a helpless, confused child. She was fighting a private battle with him for the honor of her dead loved ones.

She was seated between the governor and the senior senator from Texas on a velvet-covered dais in the businessman's gargantuan private ballroom. Kurtz sat below, glaring up at her. His positioning reinforced his worst fears of her growing power.

When her host asked politely if she would say a few words to open the conference, she agreed. She was lovely, artless. Her silvery hair held back from her elegant face.

"The title of this conference is Spiritual Awareness. It is far more difficult to achieve this state in a world of champagne, evening gowns, limousines, and television cameras. But it is in this environment that we come together, struggling for meaning. It was easier for Adam and Eve in the Land of Eden. But their growth and their capacity for love and commitment came after they were cast out. We are all cast-outs and we must fight for truth and purpose in a world of endless temptations, blind alleys, and distortions.

"This only makes the road toward God and toward our truest selves more beautiful. Let us all stretch each day toward God's grace. May we all live in love of self and one another. Thank you."

For three days she basked in the glow of her triumph. People came to her in genuine sharing and respect. It gave deeper meaning to her battle and her losses. Most important of all, it was a private triumph over Kurtz. She longed to share it with her mother. With Clara and Zander. Somewhere they're clapping, she thought. It had come around again. Now it was finished.

Little did she know of the ways of the serpent. Kurtz was just warming up.

CHAPTER 20

Eve came home and we soared in blissful ignorance (don't ever let anyone tell you that ignorance isn't) thirty feet above the skyline of Manhattan. We could not have been an odder couple and yet we fit each other with a poignant, honest tenderness.

When we first made love, it was the way it had been with Eve's parents all those years before. A clamping. A melting erotic giving, beyond self; a loss of defenses that neither of us had ever known in any human relationship.

My friends were envious. Maxie thought I was meshuga ("a shiksa toe dancer; a white-bread *maydeleh* who thinks God is located in your *fercockta* lungs"). My ex-wives thought it was hysterical and Greta adored her (that made two of us).

When she came back from Dallas she told me the story of her life—leaving out, of course, the rather significant matter of her gender and her child, but including just about everything else. When she talked about her family (at my prodding, never of her own volition), it was with a combination of intensity and anguish. The amount of tragedy in her life frightened me, and she saw this and tried to balance each episode with whatever levity was available.

I, of course, was as fascinated by her life as she seemed to be by mine. I had never known a woman like her. She seemed to have been formed without female distrust. She did not have the inherent, hidden fear of men, fear of being overrun, swallowed, used, misunderstood that I had experienced in every woman that I had ever known. She understood people from both sides without judgment, but not without insight. This was no Pollyanna airhead who just thought everyone was peachy neat. Her empathy came from her own process, from what she had lost, whom she had loved, and her own harrowing plights.

As we began to come closer to street level, the first rush of romantic love giving way to the terrifying, intricate, delicate process of building a lasting relationship, I began to feel something else happening.

She was tense and preoccupied with the demands of her show, the charities and organizations she funded, and the telethon, which was rapidly approaching and being touted as the Celebrity Event of the Century. But there was something else going on. I could feel the beginning of withdrawal. She would pull away from me in bed and her whole body would shudder with sobs. I took Eve's new behavior with less seriousness than some other guy might—having had three wives, numerous lady friends, and a female child—but still, being in love makes you so goddamn vulnerable that I was disturbed and unsettled. She wouldn't talk about it. *Here it comes,* I thought, *trouble in paradise.* I had no idea how right I was.

Eve knew that there was no way to continue without telling me the truth. She had allowed herself the joy of loving and broken her own promise to herself. She was living a lie once again, living against everything she believed. Her guilt was enormous. Her whole being ached. There was me, and there was Alex—problems that were

not going away or being confronted. Problems hanging
there before her, taunting her, sapping her strength.

She knew that it was only a matter of minutes until I
proposed, and so time was running out. When she could
no longer bear the anxiety, she got on a plane and went
to see Lily in Boston.

"You've got to tell him immediately, honey bun. Just
like you told me. Listen, I understand your not doing it
at first. Nathan is not a guy to pat you on the ass and
say it doesn't matter. He is a scarred, middle-aged American man and he may freak. But you've got to do it, at
once, and y'all knows it, too."

"I feel so foolish, Lily. What a cruel, hypocritical thing
to do. I love him. I don't want to hurt him and I don't
want to live without him."

"But you will if you have to. You've come this far,
sister, you're on for the whole ride. Now go on home
and face up."

Eve returned to New York later the same day heading
straight for the studio to tape her show. When she was
through she went to her dressing room, exhausted, to
change and go through her mail. Right on top of the pile
was a cream-colored envelope postmarked New Orleans.
On the back, in gold-embossed letters, was a name and
address. *Mrs. Robin Richeleau* it read. Eve's hands were wet
and trembling. She opened the envelope and extracted a
small note written in Robin's dainty finishing-school scrawl.
"I love your show, Adamo" was all it said.

Life had just stuck a fist into Eve's slender back and
pushed her forward into the truth. That night I got the
entire unabridged story of the life of Adam and Eve.

"Nathan, I have to talk to you about something serious."
I could feel my body stiffen. I was not surprised; my own
fear had been kneaded in the rising mound of my anger.
I was losing her. I had been feeling her withdrawal for
weeks. Here it comes, the shit is about to hit.

"It must be serious, you called me Nathan. I was really

getting into Poe. I've even thought about changing my name to just simply Poe. Like just simply Eve."

"I detect sarcasm."

"A bit." I was trembling. "I've been *very* aware that something is troubling you. Goddammit. I'm angry at being shut out. I've been patient. I've been so fucking patient. I'm not a patient type!" She tried to touch me, but I moved away. Lashing out in my confusion.

"I know that, Poe. You've been wonderful."

My upper lip quivered. I refused to cry. "I know you went to see Lily. You obviously trust her more than you trust me. The deal doesn't seem quite fair! I've been on the withholding end in relationships, too, Eveala. I don't need a safe to fall on me. I'm sick of this.

"I hear you sobbing at night. I feel you pulling away from me. You and your fucking secrets! You told me your whole goddamn life story and never revealed your last name! Jesus! I love you so much, I'm demented. I want to marry you! I deserve better than this game you're play-ing with me!"

"Richeleau."

"Who?"

"My last name is Richeleau. I haven't been playing games with you, Nathan. It's not that simple. Everything you say is right. I didn't tell you the truth about me because I was selfish. I love you. I didn't want to lose you. I was a coward. I . . . it's very hard to start this. Please sit down here. Look at me."

Sullenly, I sat. Her whole body was trembling. I could see the sweet purple vein on her neck pulsing. The vein I loved to kiss, feeling her heart with my lips. I was scared.

"Jesus fucking shit! What is it with you? Are you an escaped mass murderer? What? You are looking at one guy with a whole attic full of skeletons! What could be so terrible?"

Tears slid silently down her face. When she spoke her

voice had its lovely husky softness, but it was thick, almost slurred. "Nathan. I want to show you some pictures."

"Show and tell! Terrific."

She ignored my sarcasm and reached into the pocket of her robe and handed me a snapshot. A handsome tough little guy with her eyes grinned out at me. "Whose?"

"Mine. His name is Alex. He's almost eight."

I almost gagged with relief! "What is this, some fucking medieval romance? So you're not a virgin. I'll live. So Saint Eve had a little slip, even a great big slip. That's it?"

She shook her head sadly. "You cannot imagine how much I wish that that was all of it." She slumped forward, her arms encircling her body, which was shaking in an almost convulsive way.

"Eve! Christ! Are you okay? What is it?"

She could not respond.

"A drink. Some brandy. I'll get some brandy."

She nodded. I jumped up. Stumbling past her in a state of anxiety not much less than my quivering darling's.

When I returned with the glasses, she had calmed. She smiled at me and took a long sip. It was like watching the guy on the circus platform getting ready to dive into the tiny little tub.

She took another sip and reached into her other pocket and handed me another snapshot, smiling in spite of herself, remembering Lily sitting across from her, passing the first photo, the beginning of her journey toward Eve.

I grabbed it, having moved beyond smartass remarks. "Looks like you. Your brother? Your father?"

She shot up. Her hands clenched into tight, white fists beside her. "Me. It's me! I'm like Lily. I'm Alex's father. . . . I left to change . . . to become Eve . . . to spare him. Me! Me! I love you. I didn't think I would ever have anyone. I didn't think you would love me, want me. I've done a terrible, unforgivable thing to you. I—we . . . It all happened so fast. I didn't know how lonely I was until you took me to that play. You made me laugh. I had never felt safe before. I didn't want to lose you. Can you ever forgive me?"

I sat frozen in shock, horror, and disbelief; too numb to light a cigarette or raise a much needed glass to my purple shivering lips as the only woman that I had ever truly and openly loved told me who and what she really was.

There is absolutely no way I can describe what it felt like or the clashing, smashing confluence of disparate emotions swirling through my splitting head. I think at one point I actually stopped breathing, but I don't want to get more melodramatic than necessary. I can rather safely say that it was the worst moment of my adult life.

When I was able to move and breathe again, I did precisely what Lily had warned her I might. I bolted. I left. I left my agonized beloved sitting across from me in a white terry cloth robe, her pale hair tied back from her lovely face, cheeks soaked with tears, without touching her or even saying good-bye. Stunned, frightened, repulsed, shattered. I fled.

CHAPTER 21

Mrs. Adam Richeleau, whose monogrammed stationary had started the chain reaction, had been on a pilgrimage of her own. What she was seeking is not quite clear, but the quest thrust the pretty young widow of New Orleans's finest family into the center of a chic, though dubious, circle of youngish heirs and heiresses. Her name appeared regularly in the society columns, seen at: charity balls, Junior League teas, houseguesting with, dining among. . . . Her "crowd" consisted mainly of lost sons of prominent fathers of ambiguous sexual proclivities, who flattered and pampered her, and divorced socialites given to bouts of spastic self-destruction of a chemical, sexual, or hysterical nature.

Of this crew, Robin's closest "companion" and constant escort was an effete black sheep by the name of Augustine Hicks. Augustine (Hicky to his friends) was a bisexual young sot with a waxed mustache, slick center-parted black hair, powdered white skin, and a wardrobe of crumpled linen suits, straw hats, evening capes, and two hundred umbrellas. Augustine had inherited a seemingly bottomless trust fund from his maternal grandmother and his purpose in life appeared to be finding the bottom of it.

Every shopkeeper on Royal Street knew him by name. Up and down the streets of the Quarter he sauntered, umbrella tapping on old cobbled streets, Robin in her Laura Ashley and Gucci loafers on one arm and some or another attractive man or woman on the other.

"I feel like Hermès today," he would sigh and in the trio trotted.

"Good afternoon, Mr. Hicks, so good to see you," the manager would pant.

"My luggage is boring. Send me a new set. One of each of the best, monogrammed, of course."

"Of course," whispered the manager, sweat popping on his upper lip.

"See anything that destroys you, Mo-lasses?"

"You choose, Hicky," Robin would answer, shrugging her tan shoulders.

"Very well. Send Madame Richeleau that gold cigarette case in the window with the diamond clasp and the lighter. Oh, and six of those scarves, the long silk ones, for my friend here."

"We'll see to it at once, Mr. Hicks."

"I would firmly hope so." And out they sauntered, power exercised. A moment of venal victory. Money, the upper of all time; a quick hit of materialism to slash into the slog of their unlived lives.

Their days passed something like this: Wake up—late. Phone calls to make rendezvous plans for lunch. Ablutions. Meeting for lunch. Long, serious, gossipy meals (concerning the night before). Lots to drink. Strong Creole coffee to get back up and on the street. Shopping. Sometimes dropping into a gallery or seeing friends. Nap. Phone calls about evening. Ablutions in preparation for evening. Meeting for drinks. Dining. Cruising private clubs and/or parties. Bed—late (how late depending on whether alone or not). On weekends: tennis, golf, polo. Scattered throughout were mundane necessities: manicures, barber, hairdresser, masseuse, chiropractor, psychotherapist, facialist.

With Robin, there was also Alex to consider. Robin did have Maybe—slow though she was—a cook and a maid. Maybe had let go of those responsibilities to save energy for Alex and for dealing with Robin's simmering resentment at having her in charge of the money.

It wasn't that Robin was mean to Alex, it was just that he was of no interest to her. He had been a vehicle to hook Adam, and once that had been accomplished, she really had no further use for him. So motherhood wasn't her bag? How could she have known her husband would weird out on her (he was the one who doted on Alex; he was the one Alex loved). It was all his fault! He drowned himself. He betrayed her and abandoned them, though God only knew why. Even after years of pondering, she had never come up with a satisfactory answer. He had been so devoted to Alex and so damn positive about life and people. She was always the gloomy one! It had never made any sense. For a while, because of the coincidence of Lily's canceling their luncheon date and then disappearing so soon before Adam left, she believed that he had run off with her. But that was so totally out of character that even before Maybe convinced her of her foolishness, she no longer seriously thought so. Could it have been his impotence? In the end, to stop the noise in her head so that she could go on with her life, she had decided on the obvious. Bad genes. After all, the entire Richeleau clan was riddled with lunatics. Bad genes it must be. Adam was dead and she was left with the mess. She did the best she could.

It was bad enough that everything was left to Alex, and that Maybe and Laurel were in charge of all the goddamn money, doling it out as if she were a child.

She'd be damned if she was going to give up what was left of her youth like some martyred widow in her mohair weeds, and Maybe knew better than to push her.

She tried. Alex was happier with Maybe anyway, or so she told herself whenever guilt hit, which was infrequently and easily offset by the coke spoon, the bourbon bottle, or a trip with Alex and Hicky to buy the little kid some lavish present. After all, this was certainly not the life she had planned or what Adam had promised her, so she was damn well entitled to make the best of it.

In sober, somber moments she realized that Hicky and his friends were a rather thin hull on which to set sail. "They are *gay*," Laurel said to her on one of her auntly visits. "You *must* remember that. They've become hybrids of everything wrong with men and everything wrong with women. The fall of rotting Rome. They have the basal sexual impulse of men and the vanity and competitiveness of unevolved women. Their whole society is built on pretentiousness. Face up, Robin, baby! They use women like you to fill the vacuum. The need another twenty years *out of the closet* to settle down and refine the lifestyle. Right now it's a holy mess and y'all don't belong there. They're seductive and attractive and they say what y'all want to hear, but they'll chomp you up and spit you out.

"Men like Hicks always remind me of those horrible cobra-skin telephone tables the Duchess of Windsor had this German designer make up. I have a magazine photo of her sitting in one of her overdecorated bedrooms, gabbing on the telephone to some idiot or other, perilously close to one of those little cobra-covered tables. I used to like the idea of one of them sizzling back to life and wrapping itself around her bony little ankles. The homo's revenge. That's Hicks, one of those little cobra tables. You watch yourself, baby."

Robin and Laurel were certainly not friends, but Robin

respected her and she listened with tight throat and clenched fists when Laurel made her pronouncement. She knew the truth in it, but she was stuck, caught in her own fear, and unwilling to look past it. She was scared where she was, but she was so much more afraid of where she might go. For a while she cooled it with Hicky and kept more to the Junior League set. She even did some work for Richeleau House and the historical society, but the siren song, the pop of champagne corks, the lure of golden cigarette cases was too much for her, and back she drifted into the waiting arms of the vipers.

One month prior to Eve's opening of the cream-colored envelope, Robin gave a party. Maybe had taken Alex to Washington to spend some time with Laurel, and Robin decided to use this burst of freedom to let loose.

The party began on a Saturday evening and by Monday the line into orgy had been crossed without any of the attendees paying much heed.

On Monday evening Robin came to in her queen-size bed, bookended between two casual acquaintances; she was still radiating from the effects of the mescaline she had ingested at some point the previous day.

There were naked people asleep all over her cream-and-silver boudoir. Stoned, naked people. Some of whom did not look even vaguely familiar. She sat up. Her mouth was dry and her head felt as if a small but insistent mallet were beating into it.

For a moment, a groaning desire to cry out for her mother flooded her, rushing through her tan, sleep-warm nudity. When it passed and she opened her eyes again, they focused on the large silver Sony television across the room. It was on. A picture, colors whirling without sound. Eve was on.

Robin connected with the picture tube and mescalined into it as if she and the Sony were internally hinged. She moved forward, crawling toward the golden woman smiling from the magic silver box, beckoning her. She moved toward her, across bodies, over pillows, until she sat face-to-face, squatting on her muscular haunches, zapped by the lady inside.

Something was trying to reach her. The camera crept in on the fair lady as she moved her shiny pink lips and Robin followed the camera as if it were her own eye, closer, tighter, and then she saw. A golden cross around the narrow white throat. The filigreed heirloom passed from father to son to . . .

Robin blinked. She sat still, silent, head pounding with light, color, confusion, insight. *Eve* was Adam. Pieces fell into place, the kaleidoscope of suspicion, anger, half-finished puzzles, and frustration snapped into focus. Robin crouched before her silver messenger of truth till sunrise. Then she rose, took a long hot shower, made a pot of steaming Creole coffee, and told everyone to go home.

The party was over and the clean-up had begun.

A week later, Robin was lunching at K-Paul's with Hicky when the final piece dropped into place.

"Got some red-hot gossip for y'all," he cooed, sliding a forkful of steaming rabbit stew between his carefully rouged lips.

"Goody. I need something truly sensational. I've been in one of my black holes since the party."

"Don't I know it! You remember Claude, that gorgeous little hairdresser from N.Y.C.? The one with the Richard Gere cheekbones that I whisked off on that steamboat cruise last spring? Well, we dined last night. He was passing through on his way back from Dallas. He's been flying down there once a month to cut and color that old closet number Harley Kurtz's frizzies. Anyway, while he was in the bathroom, mixing his Grecian Formula or whatever, Kurtz took a call and Claude overheard him telling one of his oafs to step up their undercover operation of Eve. You watch her, don't you? She's the end. Kurtz is

looking for garbage in the darling girl's past. Claude said
he was really all steamed up over it. I wonder what Saint
Eve has lurking around the back alley?"

When Robin was able to stop the hysterics that followed Hicky's proud little tidbit, she offered up a great
big treat of her own.

With Nathan gone, Robin's note implanted in her consciousness, and the pressures of the telethon, which was
by then being heralded as the Television Event of the
Decade, moving out of her control, Eve was hanging by
a pulled thread.

A combination of terror and despair closed in on her
with the slamming of her apartment door the night Nathan abandoned her. She had always been able to cope
with loss, as many and as crushing as those losses had
been, by turning to her dancing or God and the remaining
needy ones around her. Beginning on the day Clara died,
she had watched those remaining dwindle and shrink until
there was no one left within reach. Her arms shot out in
her sleep toward a room full of ghosts. There was no
one. She ached for her son. She longed for Laurel's starched,
no-nonsense protection. She felt more alone, after Nathan left, than she had ever felt before. The door closed
forever on the possibility of love, of acceptance of herself
as she really was.

Robin's note pulled the last pillar of support out from
under her. She would go up in smoke. A public spectacle.
A dirty joke. The people who believed in her, and whom
she truly believed she was helping in her small way, would
be betrayed. Her work would be dust. Alex would be lost
forever. Everything would be for nothing. Blind panic
seized her. She could not breathe. She could not sleep.
Nightmares claimed her as she tossed, fighting for unconsciousness, for relief from the anguish. Robin's face.
Kurtz's face. Enemies old and new.

"God help me," she whispered out loud in her dreams. She moved, machinelike, through her overburdened days. For the first time in her life she was losing her faith. She wanted the way to reveal itself. She was terrified. She prayed each morning and evening. Alone on her knees on the bare white floor of her clean little room. "I shall fear no evil . . . he leadeth me . . . his mercy endureth, forever. . . ."

There was only silence. Only the sound of her banging heart. Panic. Alone.

"We got Streisand, she's doing 'People' *and* 'The Way We Were.' " Ivan Kimbal was in heaven, barely noticing Eve's increasing stoicism during their daily meetings. "Baryshnikov and Gregory are doing a Stravinsky pas de deux, forget which one, famous, though. Pryor's a definite, Springsteen's on for 'Cadillac Ranch,' *and* Sinatra's gonna do 'My Boy Bill' from *Carousel*. Streep, Minnelli, Bacall, Paul McCartney! Ross, Carly Simon, Midler . . . I mean, we are through the roof on this, Eve! The president is taping a bit in case he can't show. Kennedy's coming, Jackson's coming, and everyone in the fucking country is going to watch it! We've got our satellite connect—three billion people, thirty fucking languages! The cover of *TV Guide* Thanksgiving week! The goddamn sponsors are standing in line!"

"That's wonderful, Ivan. But the point is whether they'll give." Eve was so tired her bones ached.

"They'll give, Jesus—cheer up! We're making . . . no, *you're* making television fucking history!"

Somehow that thought did not provide her with much ballast. Eve left her meeting with Ivan Kimbal that afternoon, exactly two weeks from the date of my departure and Robin's note, and started walking. She wore her street disguise. A hat pulled low, sunglasses closing her off and making her sad. Somehow she found herself at Penn Station buying a ticket for Washington. When she arrived, she took a cab directly to Laurel's address in Georgetown and rang the bell before she had time to reconsider. She waited on the steps of the elegant canary-yellow townhouse (Laurel's favorite color, Eve remembered) shivering with apprehension.

Her aunt opened the door without looking to see what maniac might be outside, making Eve smile (wonderful, fearless Laurel) in spite of herself. It was dinner time and she could smell baking biscuits, pot roast, homemade pie—her aunt's own perfume. Her stomach tightened. Loneliness, longing for the phantom home, welled up, filling her tired eyes with tears. Small children laughing, running barefoot through summer grass toward the safety of fresh-squeezed lemonade and the bubbling, buttery, creamy protection of innocence.

Laurel snuffed her cigarette out in her bourbon tumbler and reached out, opening her arms wide without pausing.

"Welcome home, baby," she whispered.

They stood in the doorway, holding each other for a long while, Eve's whole being shaking with relief, the power of her aunt's love loosening her dread.

"Alex is here, baby," Laurel said finally.

Laurel, Maybe, and Alex took Southern supper together. Alex, like his father and grandfather before him, was surrounded by eccentric, unique, and loving women all devoted almost totally to the survival of the child, the hope of all of them.

Late that night, when Alex and Maybe had gone to bed and Eve was settled into the guest room wrapped in one of Laurel's flannel nightgowns, there was a knock at the door.

"Come in," she whispered, expecting Maybe but not surprised to see her aunt's wryly smiling face peek in.

"Help me, baby, I've got a goddamn tray of cookies and milk punch about to crash."

Eve jumped off the huge feather-quilted bed and opened the door for Laurel.

"Thanks, baby. I thought this was a good time for a little Brennan's whiskey punch and conversation."

"Sounds good." Eve sighed and kissed her aunt's cheek.

They sat for several moments, curled together on the warm plump bed, sipping hot spirits and sweet milk, and getting used to being with each other in this new way. It felt familiar and yet understandably odd for both of them.

Eve, sensing Laurel's hesitancy with her, reached out and touched her aunt's hand.

"You know, kid, I really thought I was beyond the point of losing my aplomb over any ol' thing, but I did over you. Not about your still being alive and turned outside-inside, because, frankly, I never for one tiny moment believed you had killed yourself. Not after what you went through with Zander and your poor momma. I just knew you would never do that. No, what did me in was that you didn't trust my love enough to tell me. I was sure Maybe knew the truth because she took the loss much too well, given her total commitment to you.

"I felt real bad, baby, for a long time. Then I began to see why. There was nothing in your role modeling to help you believe in the resilience of fearless love. You saw your family destroyed by lack of trust in one another. By their inability to open, to reveal. It must have seemed to you that too much truth, or too much testing of the insides of a relationship leads to devastation and death. Your parents didn't really want to know what went on inside you, not because they didn't care, but because they were afraid of the truth. There was no way for you to know that not everyone was like that. Certainly, you couldn't have tried it out on Robin. Maybe already knew, so she was safe. It hurt that you misjudged me, baby. I don't care if y'all turns into a swamp frog, for chrissakes, and I thought you understood. It's my goddamn fault that you didn't and I've had to live with that."

Eve was crying. Laurel's words hit deep, and she felt both her aunt's pain at the betrayal and the wisdom of her insight. She also realized that if what Laurel said about fearless love was true (and she believed and needed to believe that it was), it cemented the reality of what had happened with Nathan. The truth had been too much for the love.

"I'm so sorry, Laurel. I was so confused. I just felt that the only way to go was alone. I thought that anyone who knew became an accomplice and if things got heavy with Robin or the police or whatever, that I would be compromising them—I mean, you. I can't justify the pain I've caused. I can only offer as an excuse that it was not the clearest period of my life. I made many mistakes. I missed you so! There were a thousand times I reached for the phone. Then, after the television show and all the publicity, I felt cornered and afraid to risk any contact. Until today.

"I got a note from Robin. She knows, or at least she strongly suspects; somehow, after the note, it didn't seem to matter anymore. I don't know what to do to protect Alex. I keep fighting the urge to swoop him up in my arms and take off. I needed your wise counsel, as usual."

"Well, I'm not surprised about Robin. I mean, Eve, dear, from the moment I flipped on your show, I knew. They could hide you in a scuba suit or a ball gown—I diapered y'all, for chrissakes! That face, the gestures, those eyes! Lordy. I called Maybe the night I first saw you and I just hollered my craggy old Southern head off. She never said yes, but there was a lot of acknowledgment in her silence, I may say. And then in the close-ups, I saw Suzette's necklace. I'll bet my last golf ball that's what Robin saw. It was visible in the *Time* magazine cover, all the photos caught it. You're in the turtle soup, all right, but don't fear, we'll take care of it, we always have, baby."

Eve put her arms around her aunt's broad shoulders and held her tight. "Forgive me, Laurel."

"Oh, I do, baby. But I'd like to ask a favor while you're all mellow and contrite."

Eve laughed, wiping tears from her face, the warm woozy magic of milk punch and sharing releasing the tension of the week.

"Anything."

Laurel's face grew solemn. "I want permission to tell Suzette. Your *death* was the last straw for her, beauty. She's just given up. If there is any chance of getting her out of Gorillamala before she dies, it's to let her know you're alive."

"Yes, please. I was so full of self-loathing and self-pity, I didn't think of my going as anything but a blessing to everyone."

"Well, welcome to the rest of the world. It's good to know that you ain't all saint, baby. In my declining years, I am more and more convinced that we are all as blind as a catfish in a crock. Life reveals itself in hindsight, which makes living quite a chaotic little process. You get some sleep now. We'll talk again in the morning."

Eve was exhausted. She was asleep before her aunt closed the door. It was the first night in weeks that sleep had come up and embraced her. Cool and comforting and dreamless.

When Eve left Alex the next morning, it was as "Aunt Eve."

"You look like my poppa," the child said when Eve kissed him good-bye.

"Thank you." Eve touched his soft dark head with her long fingers. "I take that as a giant compliment."

"My poppa's dead. He drowned in the river. May I come visit you someday?"

"Yes," she said and kissed him and left without turning

back for one last look. Lot's wife, given a second chance.

If Robin needed final confirmation of her discovery, it came when Maybe and Alex returned from Washington a week later. By this time, Maybe and Laurel had spoken at length and the phone lines between Eve's apartment and Laurel's house had made up for all the years of silence. Maybe went home to Robin, wary, and as Laurel put it, "Our mammy in New Orleans. Undercover." Maybe sensed the change in Robin. She was quiet and distracted as if in the midst of solving something, scrounging through the box for the last piece of the puzzle. She stayed home. Maybe watched and said nothing.

Their first Monday evening back, at 8:00 P.M., Robin switched on the television and settled down before Eve. Alex joined her. He sat beside her, his rosy face serious and intent, uneasy with the rare privilege of being close to his mother. He waited to be banished, watching her out of the corners of his dark moist eyes and, also, watching Eve.

"That's Aunt Eve, Maybe and LaLa's friend," he said, not comprehending why that made his mother beat her hands into her satin pillow and scream with laughter. Oh, the revenge would be sweet, she thought, sweet, profitable, and neat.

CHAPTER 22

I did not have milk punch, feather quilts, and good Southern women to bind my wounds. I was wallowing. Paddling across the Slough of Despond, my diving mask covered with sump, my flippers laden with the slop of self-pity and fear.

I did have Maxie. I took a few days off and flew down to the Sunshine State, bringing my rain cloud and my angst. My stepmother was out of town at a Gray Panther convention. Oh, for a Helen of my own. A woman of simple nature, motherly form, and good cheer. Adoring and uncomplicated. A partner for bridge and a maker of brisket and chicken soup!

Maxie and I loafed by the papaya-shaped pool, drinking beer and telling bad jokes—most of which he only remembered the first half of—which broke what little was left of my heart.

"So, out with it, sonny. What's the punch line? All of a sudden you show up to sunbathe? In the middle of the week? Two days, we're lyin' around like a coupla bums . . . I've gone through all my best material . . . can't even

get a good chuckle outta ya. . . . Did I tell ya the one
about the three nuns who get raped?"

"Yes, Pop."

"Okay, okay. So? Give! Unless I'm losin' it completely,
I'd say it's love troubles. You and the blondie, right?"
Maxie leaned back on his lounge chair and crossed his
bandy little legs, the curly red hairs now mixed with gray.

The sight of those wiry, bowlegged old gams that ran
him ragged to keep me alive, now so knotted with age,
pushed me over the line. I burst into tears.

"Nathan! Sonny! What is it! You're not sick, it's nothin'
like that?"

I managed to pull myself together enough to speak.
"No, Pop. Your legs, I looked down and . . ." My shoulders heaved.

"My *fercockta* legs? I know I'm not gonna model panty-
hose, but they've never started a flood before. Better cork
it now or my ego's gonna bruise."

I laughed, brushing tears away with my beach towel.
"No, your legs are gorgeous. They reminded me of the
old days. How you ran and ran. Don't get worried, now.
I've been doing this frequently. It is about me and Eve.
I really loved her and . . . you would never believe what
happened. Please don't ask, okay?"

"Me? Mr. Live-and-Let-Live? Jeez, Nathan. It tears me
up ta see ya like this. But, I gotta say, this is the first
dame that ever made ya cry. I don't know what the problem is, but love is hard ta come by, kiddo. Your mother—
rest her soul—I never, ever, got over losin' her. I really
never even had a girlfriend all those years. She was my
one true love, corny as it sounds. My Helen's a jewel,
and I'm happy and comfy, but to this day, I cry for your
mother. Whatever it is, son, find a way. A blind giant
and a Jewish midget can make it, if they're committed.
If they love enough. She ain't who I'da picked for ya—
too young. Too skinny. Too gentile. But if she does this

to ya, then go for it. You probably ain't gonna have another chance, and that's the friggin' fact."

I leaned over and kissed his sunburned forehead. "I don't seem to be brave enough—it's a real biggie—but thanks for the shoulder."

"Glad ta be of some use. You're still my *boobala* . . . till the day I do my cut and print number. One thing, though . . . lay off my legs."

The trouble with being depressed is that you lose the courage to live. Depression is safe. It may not be fun, it may not be happiness, but it is safe. If you really know the rhumba—I mean, cold—you can do no wrong in the rhumba department, risk nothing a'tall on the slippery dance floor of life and probably can just wiggle on forever with that one step, so why try break dancing? At fifty-three I should jump into the air and spin twelve times on my head?

Depression, gloom, anhedonia, melancholia, pessimism, vapors, mumps, dumps, blue devils, despair, voiceless woe—I was on a first-name basis with the whole team. Bimbos, booze, the blues, sarcasm, soiled raincoats, cigarettes, rare steaks, and common women—now I *knew* that dance. Numb, dumb, safe. An easy slide back into the dark, squashy comfort of ennui and negativity.

But, of course, I couldn't go back. Even the goddamn depression was different, more emotional, hot rather than cool, filled with racking 5:00 A.M. sobs and hollow burnings in what I decided was the locus of my being.

I missed her. Him. It. (Shit.) I liked the Nathan Poe that came forth with her. She. He. It (shit) made me feel like Pop made me feel. Pleasant inside. Relaxed. Loved. I longed for her.

God knows I fought it. I tried my rhumba routine every waking moment, flinging my frightened, stiff self onto the floor, trying to get that rhythm back. But it was gone. My feet were flippered. I couldn't move it like that anymore. I couldn't go back and I couldn't go forward. I was carbonized, dated, tagged, iced, and stuck in the gooey, ancient black quagmire of my shortcuts, skipped steps, blind alleys, and cop-outs. I was, quite frankly, a mess.

It was in this state that I padded aboard a shuttle from Dulles to La Guardia, coming off a story.

I settled in with a double Scotch and my third pack of Camels beside Harry Morris, an old fellow journalist at the *Times* and now a political troubleshooter-cum-consultant who greased my ever-hungry notepad with tips on a fairly regular basis. We toasted the good ol' days as over-the-pass former newspapermen are inclined to do and then, through my kelp-plugged ears, my friend laid one on me.

"Got a possible front-pager for you, Nathan. Fate sent you on this particular flight. I swear, I left three messages for you at the news desk this afternoon."

"No kidding," I managed to utter from under water. "What's up?"

"Well, I thought of you immediately because I'd, uh, heard a little interoffice gossip about you and the exercise evangelist—Eve."

"Just gossip, old man. She's a nice lady. We have a common friend, or a friend in common. Sorry to disappoint."

"Oh, my mistake. Then you may not be interested in an item concerning the lady and Harley Kurtz?"

"Harley Kurtz? What the fuck has he got to do with her? Is he into tutus on the side?"

"Could be, but the way I hear it he's out to bring her down. She's pulling the audience and making the good ol' boys very uncomfortable. He's called out his Crusaders to solve the mystery lady."

I managed to move my heart far enough out of my mouth to reply. "Does he have anything?"

"Well, if you're really interested, I'll give it to you exclusive? Same deal, okay?"

"Okay."

"My man inside the Kurtz gang says they got a call from some society type in New Orleans who claims to hold an ace on the lady that's worth a million big ones, or at least that's what she wants for it."

"My God."

"Thought you were just an acquaintance?"

"It's news, pal. Besides, she's a lovely person. She doesn't deserve to be trashed by some small-town slime squad." My throat was closing.

"My source says that the society type told Kurtz she'd make the trade in New York the night of the telethon so he can pop in and make the accusation on the air and get his money's worth."

"Is he dealing?"

"Well, he's got his goons digging all over the place, but since the telethon's so close and he's not finding anything, my source thinks he'll go for it. After all, what's a million bucks to that guy. He can pull it out of the poor box. The bastard's going to be president—you watch. Before Eve, he was rising like a flag on the Fourth. If he can discredit her, he reemerges as an even bigger force. I hope you do something with this. The guy is bad news."

I was half drunk, half asleep, and covered with bog, but it reached me. Eve would have said God put him there, but I prefer to keep my distance. Anyway, it sat me right up in my window seat, heart racing. My love was in deep shit and I was already whizzing toward shore, the hurricane blowing the muck from my mask, propelling my flippers into the air, forward into risk.

I got off the plane at La Guardia, called CBS and told them the story was more complicated than I had anticipated, got back on the shuttle, returned to Dulles, looked up Laurel's address in the airport phone book, and flagged down a cab.

On our last awful night, Eve had talked a lot about Laurel, "the spine of the family," she called her. I still

wasn't ready to face Eve, so I went for the supporting
vertebra first. It turned out to be a damn smart choice.

Her voice on the phone was husky, mumbled with
sleep. "Hello," she said. My knees were shaking. It was
3:00 A.M.

"Hello. It's me." My throat as dry and tight as an inner
tube in the desert.

"Nathan? Are you all right?"

"I'm downstairs. May I come up?"

"Yes."

We stood in silence looking at one another—two tired,
tense, wounded people about to free-fall without a backup chute. We were both crying.

I felt as if I were melting, as if my own personal ice
age were evaporating, like one of Louis Richeleau's dinosaurs, no layer left to protect me. Melting. I moved
toward her and put my arms around her, mad for the
sweetness of our loving, desperate for its compassion. We
held each other till morning, unable to release our grasp
of each other, even to breathe apart. Holding on, clinging
to mother love to keep from falling off.

I had never been this close, this physically intimate
with any human being in my entire life. We simply could
not let go of one another. While it was happening, I was
aware that I had never trusted any woman before, ever.
Maybe I only trusted Eve because she had been like me
(I think at one moment), but it no longer mattered. It
felt grand.

At eight in the morning, the phone rang. Eve picked
it up, listened, then gently set it down. I could feel her
pull ever so slightly away from me. "What is it?"

"Nothing."

"Bullshit."

"I've been getting calls. Crackpots. It's nothing."

It was time to tell her. "Eve, I saw Laurel last night."

"Laurel? Something's wrong—is it Alex?"

"No, no, nothing like that. I heard something on the plane from Washington yesterday. Do you know much about Harley Kurtz?"

She sat up, her wondrous blue eyes dark. "He destroyed my family. I have a great deal of trouble forgiving him, even after all these years. Why?"

"He sees you as one giant threat and he is going to try to destroy you. He got a call from Robin, your . . . you know." (I gulped air.) "She's asking for money in exchange for damaging information about you. He plans to disrupt the telethon and expose you—although he has no idea what the secret is yet."

Eve nodded slowly and said nothing. A long deep sigh passed through her. It was as if the feared thing was folded up like an inflatable raft inside her, bloating her with anxiety and fear. The sigh deflated the damn thing and let it whoosh all the way out. The fugitive's relief at being found out. "That explains the calls." She lay down, lightened now and freed of the weight inside.

"We don't have much time, but we'll stop the bastard."

She closed her eyes. "I thought I was through with all the lies when I had my surgery, but my life is still a lie. I left because I believed it was the only way to protect my son, and I feel like I've done more harm than if I had told them all the truth. I don't want to pretend anymore. I don't know what to do."

"Your kid is *not* going to find out on CBS, that's for damned sure. Just hang on a little bit longer. When this is all over, we'll have lots of time to think about it."

She opened her eyes. "We?"

"We."

She turned on her side, watching me.

"Poe, you are not an impulsive type. I know that you wouldn't have come back unless you felt pretty strongly about us. But, I don't . . . I can't . . . I can't bear the thought of my troubles ruining your life. To the world, I'm a freak. A joke. It will be hard enough, a tough enough test of our love for you to deal with it in private . . . but if . . . if I'm publicly . . . if Kurtz or Robin publicly . . . you'll be a freak, too. It would be the end of everything you've worked for. Oh, Poe, I can't ask that of you."

"I'm not going to tell you that I'm not absolutely terrified. But whatever happens, it won't be worse than what I've been going through without you. Don't take this away from me, Eveala. I like this meshuggener guy. I have a reason for being here for the first time in years. We need each other. I feel like the cowardly lion—the courage was just all tangled up in the fear. Maxie hit it. He said this was probably my last chance. I'm more afraid of blowing it than whatever we have to face."

Because of the thickness of the soup we were in, I didn't have much time to ponder the depth of that declaration. I was off. I took a week's research time and headed for Dallas to hoe up some Kurtz country. Laurel took off for New Orleans to have a little auntly chat with Robin, and Eve proceeded with final rehearsals for what might really turn out to be the Greatest Show on Earth.

I managed to arrange a meeting with Kurtz himself on the guise of a preinterview for a feature spot on "60 Minutes" and thereby got inside the "locked ward." He was good. He was glistening cool. But I was better. Egoists respond to flattery with the spastic, thoughtless immediacy of a snake and a stick.

"You're a born preacher, a master," I gushed.

"Well, thank you, Mr. Pope."

"Poe."

"Oh, sorry, *Poe*. Should have known there couldn't be a Hebrew Pope, now, could there."

"You certainly do your homework, Reverend."

"I train my people right."

"I meant what I said, Reverend. You have a great mag-
netism, unique charisma. And you sing so well. You could
have had a career in show business."

"Well, I did have briefly."

"In the bayous?"

"No, no. Hollywood."

"California? How did you land there?"

"I, uh, hitchhiked there. I was in grief for my momma
and poppa. I just took off for a while. That's all long ago.
Let's move on now."

"By all means."

Just that word. California (here I come). Off I went.

I found old Harley Kurtz all right. Death certificate
and all, which led to a gnarly old lady who had been the
cook at the Salvation Army Mission downtown when
Kurtz was there. I finally found little lost Alvin Finkle and
then Mrs. Finkle, who still kept Alvin's baby locket clenched
in her arthritic fist.

"Poor young man was heading South to start a church
when he passed," the old cook said.

"Where South?" I inquired, salivating slightly.

"Cloudy. My head gets kinda cloudy. Used to be a
drinker, got a touch of wet brain. Maybe Arkansas? No,
the song. He sang, 'Goin' with a banjo on my knee,' that
one."

Alabama.

I arrived in Mobile two days before the telethon. Laurel
was still visiting with Robin, the hawk moving into the
chicken coop.

At 7:00 P.M. the night before the show, I found the
Kurtz clip in the newspaper morgue. At 9:00 P.M. I was
slurping coffee with Candy Mueller Kurtz Frelinghouser,
who, for reasons of her own, felt the need to unburden
herself of the long-held secret. She had neither forgiven
nor forgotten, which was terrible for her and her current

spouse, but worked grandly for me. I helped her draft a holographic account of their long-ago sins complete with photo gallery. At 3:00 A.M. D-day, while I paced the airport motel room waiting for the first plane to get me back to New York, Laurel called.

"Nathan?"

"I got him, Laurel! I've got a whole goddamn Christmas list! I've been calling his thugs hourly, no one will let me through—they say he's left town. That means, if it's true, that he's already in New York. We've got to get to him fast!"

"Calm yourself now and listen carefully. I have had my death duel with the little señorita. I offered to match Kurtz's deal, even go it better. She's lost her screws over it all. Very Shakespearean, this one. Revenge seems to be the motive. I could not talk her out of it. She ran off, snuck out before I could blow up the autos or anything. However, I did manage to eavesdrop on her last conversation with Señor Scum. They are meeting one hour before the telethon goes on the air, so that's seven P.M., in the Oyster Bar at Grand Central. Robin's sense of theater, I suppose. She's got that pineapple, Augustine Hicks, with her for backup. I imagine he'll fend them off with one of his gold-handled umbrellas.

"She's in bad shape, chock full of drugs and not rational. The weather is ghastly here, and we've got flood warnings up. The ol' Miss is spouting mad and they may close the Jefferson Highway and solve all of our problems. She's got a load of circumstantial evidence and a statement from one turncoat creep who lived with Eve at the place in Boston. It's enough for the señor to play his tune to. Now, unless I can't get out of here, I'll meet y'all at the Oyster Bar tomorrow at six P.M. before the showdown."

"Okay. Great job, Laurel. I'm still going to try and find the bastard sooner, but I'll be there at six."

"We'll have to see to Robin. She's not going to wahoo

at this little twist in the plotline. Joseph's going to come up and help us. I told him to bring some bye-bye drops. We may just have to subdue her. She could go to the media on her own; she's quite demonic about this. How's Eve doing?"

"Hanging on. Praying."

"Can't hurt."

"Not unless Cain's Crusaders has the line upstairs tied up."

The endless night passed. At 5:00 A.M. I was waiting for the ticket counters to open, Laurel was making her way through pounding rain to the airport, and Robin was asleep in Hicky's black suede guest room with the eighteen-karat-gold alarm clock set for sunrise.

I hit the city at a run, disheveled, exhausted, hyper. I went straight to my office to start calling hotels. I couldn't just wait till six. What if Robin changed the rendezvous? What if Kurtz was just playing with her and already had the goods on Eve? I had numerous sources for tracking people down, but there was no way I could put the word out without my cohorts getting a whiff, and this was *not* supposed to turn into a story.

I stayed away from Eve because I knew that she would take one look at me and see what a slender string her kid's well-being was swinging on.

I called Kurtz's thugs again. "You tell that son of a bitch that Nathan Poe at CBS News called and that before he shoots his mouth off on national television he'd better talk to me. Tell him I've just returned from a little *vacation* in Alabama and California. Y'all better do it now or he'll sic the guy with the pitchfork and the red underwear on ya!" I waited. No call came. I paced. I smoked. I drank coffee until my pulse played jungle drums and my left eye twitched.

Here it comes. Here comes the massive coronary on the threshold of saving the maiden and having a happy

ending. The evidence clenched in my fist and boom the
artery snaps. Splat! Another man in his prime, snuffed.

I had to get out. Night thoughts had invaded the day-
light. Fresh air, I thought. It was noon. Six hours. I hit
the street. It was the end of November and the wind blew
cold. My poor old raincoat was in over its head. I blew
my nose and started down Sixth Avenue.

When I got down into my old neighborhood I impul-
sively jumped off the street and into the R & W. My nose
was red, my hands chafed. Pop's old crony was still behind
the counter.

"Hi, Shlomo. I'm Nathan Poe, Maxie's kid."

"You think I don't know? You think I'm out to lunch?
You see that TV there? Whattaya suppose it's for? Heating
kaiser rolls? How's about your favorite? Fried egg san' on
an onion bagel and hot cocoa with a shot of java?"

"Sounds good." In fact, it sounded so good and made
me feel so happy and so sad and so homesick for my old
self that it took a great deal of anal retentive skill not to
lay my weary head down on old Shlomo's cigarette-scarred
Formica counter and bawl my graying head off.

I ate everything and finished with a rice puddng (mit
raisins). I listened happily to Shlomo arguing about the
appointment of a Nazi banker to the Papal Advisory Board
with an old-time press agent named Big Red Rothberg,
who used to feed Pop items when he did legwork for the
Herald. I was a visitor now. This was no longer my home.
This awareness made me both joyous and terribly sad.

I called CBS from the pay phone. No messages. I shook
hands with Simon Wiesenthal and Menachem Begin and
left my old playpen to walk in circles, trying to stay away
from ultimate concepts that might lead to a vision, an
overview of the absurd situation in which I was now a
card-carrying member.

CHAPTER 23

A ugustine Hicks woke Robin at 7:30 A.M.
"Molasses, baby girl, it's late, we failed to rise, must have been that last 'lude, dear one. Come now, up, the sky is falling. I've chosen the Rolls; if that can't get us through this storm, then we'll have to find a centaur."

Robin jumped into consciousness, panic connecting with the lightning crashing against the black shimmering walls. "Oh, damn, Hicky. I'm so fuzzy. I can't do it. I'm just wrecked."

"Never fear, I've got the magic, dear one." He reached into his suit pocket and withdrew two shiny red capsules. "First we go down, then we go up. Shower time. I've filled a flask with cognac and coffee. I'll pull the car around. Rush, rush! We're off on a great adventure, don't spoil it now."

Water hit her, she opened her mouth and let it fill and placed the red devils on her tongue. She was afraid. She could not quite remember why she had wanted to do this. She shook her head to clear the haze and swallowed hard, scrubbing herself and slowly feeling the doubt breaking up. Pow. The light went on. The pill power. Energy, courage, excitement. Zoom, zoom. The motor inside the chariot of delusion was revving.

Off they flew into the thunder, Medea and Jason on the road to the Fleece. They did not listen to the radio; no storm warning reports broke through the stereo sounds filling the car with soothing vapors.

The airport road was closed. "Oh, shit! What'll we do now, Hicky?"

"Fear not, dearie, I know an alternate route." He swung the heavy white machine around and cut across the blurred headlights of oncoming traffic, off the main road, and onto the old airline highway.

"We're so late!" Robin moaned, downing her anxiety in the silver flask.

"Then we soar with the centaur!" He pressed his Italian-loafered foot down hard on the accelerator.

Lightning slashed through a dying gum tree on the side of the potholed road, toppling it over too close to Hicky's flying machine for him to stop. He braked, skidding out of control and flipping, rolling, barreling sideways into the fallen timber. A grand white toy at the mercy of an angry child. When it finally stopped, the occupants were still.

I never found Kurtz that afternoon. Finally, at 4:00 P.M., I pulled myself together enough to call Eve.

"Nathan? Are you all right?"

"Fine. Fine. Got the goods on Kurtz. You go on and don't worry. It's all going to be fine."

"Have you talked to Robin?"

"Uh, no. No. We'll get to her soon, don't worry."

"Oh, God, Nathan! I'm coming unglued. I can't stand much more of this! Every time the phone rings, I jump like a jackrabbit."

"Hey, now. A little faith, need I remind you of that? We'll be fine. Eve?"

"Yes? Oh, God, I'm glad to hear your voice."

"Whatever happens, we'll face it together."

"I love you, Poe."

"I love you, too, Eveala. I'll be with you as soon as it's over. Good luck tonight."

"We've got J. D. Salinger! He sent in a videotape."

"Hang in there, beauty. I'll sit on the smarmy bastard until Turkey Day if I have to."

I was at Grand Central at five. At 6:10 Laurel's feisty old husband hobbled in and collapsed into a chair. "She couldn't get out! She's in some beanery twenty miles from the airport. I brought sedatives, needles, pills. I could lose my license for this—not to mention my sterling reputation. I told Laurel, one goddamn phone call and some of the boys from the old neighborhood would take this prick out."

"Don't think I haven't considered the possibility, Dr. Joe. Save a dime, just in case, they'll be here any minute." We had a cup of coffee (both of us dying for a drink but knowing the importance of clear thinking). At exactly 7:00 P.M. Harley Kurtz strode in, his face hidden behind large dark glasses and a huge cowboy hat (give me a break, I thought). He carried a large leather briefcase in one hand and a walking stick (most probably concealing a saber) in the other. On all four sides he was surrounded by brutes in shiny brown suits. They scanned the room and chose a table in the corner by the swinging kitchen doors.

"Well, *Dottore*, this is it. They can't see us from here. I'll go around and pretend I'm just coming in. You keep watch at the door for Robin, see if you can stall her. If you can't, give us ten minutes from her arrival and then come in. If things look out of control, if they've pulled a gun on us or anything crazy like that, I'll put my thumb up between my eyes. If you see that, call the cops."

"Got it, I've got my needles loaded. If you want me to

stick the creep, scratch your right temple with your right index finger. If you want me to stop Robin, pull on your right ear."

"Got it." We stood and shook hands, both of us just a second away from hysterical laughter.

I ducked sideways out the door and reentered through the huge main room, quiet after the lunchtime madness, smelling of oyster stew and beer. I held my file of incriminating documents with a death grip in my sweaty hand. Humphrey Bogart meets Jesse James.

The thugs rose, making room between them. As it was, I would have my back to the room, unable to see Dr. Joe. I maneuvered around toward Kurtz, who slunk down in his seat, popping little oval oyster crackers into his thin-lipped mouth one after another. He did not seem surprised to see me. "Get me some more of these here cracker bits." He raised his eyes and a thug jumped up, leaving the seat I desired open. "Well, Mr. Poe, I had a feeling you might just turn up."

"If you had answered my phone calls, I could have saved you and your goon squad a cab ride."

"Really, now? Well, why don't we play poker, then. Let's have your hand, Mr. Poe."

His voice was calm, but I could feel a certain uneasiness. His eyes, still hidden like two tiny night animals behind his tinted glasses, kept wandering down toward his watch. It was 7:15 and no Robin. Forty-five minutes till show time.

"First, Reverend, I know all about your *dinner guest,* who most likely will not be arriving anyway, because the storm seems to have blown the Louisiana highway system off the active list. And unless she got out late last night or real early this morning before they closed the airport, you're gonna be stuck with the dinner check. You should be ashamed, Reverend. I would have thought you'd done enough to the Richeleaus *without* this."

That got to him a bit. He sat up straighter and stopped munching the oyster crackers.

"Don't tease me, pussy, show your hand."

"Why, Reverend, such talk," I replied, and slid my soiled, precious folder over toward him. He reached for it a little too quickly and I took the moment to scan the room and catch a glimpse of my watch (7:20). I could hear Kurtz's breathing, shallow and hard. Pay dirt.

I picked up a handful of his forgotten crackers and popped them into my mouth casually, trying not to gag and choke to death in the process. "I'm sure you will agree, Reverend, sir, that regardless of what the tormented widow Richeleau may have to show you, that you are checkmate on this issue. This is one story that my fingers are just itching to peck out."

Kurtz ripped my file neatly in half and then in quarters.

"Just in case you have any funny ideas, even us *Hebrews* have their cunning. I've made copies and sent sealed letters to be opened in the event of my death, disappearance, whatever, to everyone from my attorney to the publisher of *The New York Times*, so I wouldn't even fantasize about it."

Kurtz ripped off his glasses, his face mottled red, his black eyes sparking. "You heathen son of a bitch. You can't threaten me."

"I think I just have. You'll be fine, Reverend. You just won't ever be president or a United States senator or a member of Congress. Y'all hear now?" I was starting to enjoy this.

Kurtz pushed back his chair and stood up. His brutes jumped after him. "I don't want to ever see your face again, Mr. *Poe*. I am a Christian man and I will not stoop to respond to this filth and lies, this blasphemy. You had better walk a straight line, straight and quiet, or I will ruin you. There's spiders in every wood pile, mister."

"Oh, you can relax. I'll be of no concern. Just lay off the little blond lady and don't run for public office."

At that moment Dr. Joe appeared and saw me standing in the middle of a rather dark and menacing circle. He panicked, and as Kurtz stormed past, Joseph lunged forward, plunged a needle in the dear reverend's hip and, being small and wiry, escaped the meat-hook clutches of the thugs, tearing upstairs and into the lobby of the vast quiet station with me panting behind. Not elegant, but effective. Kurtz was carried forth by his guards, who battled, I am sure, the very keen temptation to toss him into the Hudson, take the suitcase, and flee in the brand-new Mercedes limo waiting patiently outside.

Dr. Joe and I threw ourselves into a cab and raced to Lincoln Center shrieking like two demented Boy Scouts. But even as we chortled and congratulated each other on a job well done, the Goliath fallen, the reality remained. Without Robin, Eve was still not clear. Robin could open her mouth in public or with Alex at any time (maybe at this very moment). Eve was not out of danger and she might never be.

When we reached the theater, the telethon had just begun. Eve was on-camera, dressed in her all-white exercise outfit, standing in her shiny marble circle before a huge live audience in the theater and a smaller celebrity one in exercise attire on the stage waiting for the first guest, Jane Fonda, to lead them in her huff-and-puff routine. Backstage I saw more famous faces getting powdered and combed than I have ever seen together anywhere at any time. I tiptoed into the control booth, leaving the doc in the stage manager's office to recover from our adventure.

Eve was wonderful, serene; her whole being seemed translucent.

"What we are doing here tonight has never been done on television. The artists who will be appearing here during the next twelve hours will not be paid. The network is donating fifty percent of the revenues for this broadcast and with the help of all of you who care about the right of every human being to live in accordance with their beliefs, to live in freedom without moral and spiritual deprivation, we can help some of the people of the world who are not as fortunate as ourselves. All of us here will be reaching toward the goodness in ourselves, toward the God of our understanding, through our art and our joy. Rise with us now and breathe in, raise your arms and stretch tall, feel the energy move through the tension, let it all go, let the hope in."

When Jane Fonda took over, I scooted down to Eve's place backstage and found her.

"It's okay, baby, Joseph and I were magnificent. Kurtz is through."

She smiled. "I knew it. Just before I went out there, I was in my dressing room looking at Alex's picture and I just felt this wonderful release. This peace. I knew that it would be all right."

They called her back and I kissed her and walked her through the frantic backstage activity. I didn't mention Robin. When she was back on-camera I found Dr. Joe, who had located a bottle of Scotch and was merry and relaxed. Laurel had left word that the rain was stopping and she was heading back to see Maybe and Alex and find out where Robin was.

I went back to Eve's dressing room and fell into a deep heavy sleep.

The telethon was to end at 8:00 A.M. At 1:30 I woke to find Eve standing over me. "Nathan, Laurel just called. She's with Maybe and Alex. The state police were there. Robin's been in an accident. The man she was with has a broken back. She was badly bruised, her arm is broken, she's in shock, but somehow she left the hospital. No one knows where she went. What'll we do?"

"Nothing. Let's just get the telethon finished, then we'll find her."

When Eve went back onstage, I called airport information. The New Orleans terminal was now open. It was back to the coffee and nicotine routine.

At 6:00 A.M., while Bette Midler was wowing the sleepyheads back into consciousness, the door to Eve's dressing room swung open and there stood a bruised and confused-looking young woman that I knew immediately was Robin Richeleau herself.

"Where is she?" She was so dopey and weak her words came out in a fierce slur.

"Onstage."

"I want to see her, right this minute. I have to see her!"

"She'll be back soon," I replied calmly, the cagey victim before the maniac with the machine gun. "Please sit down, I'll get you some coffee."

"Who are you, her *hairdresser?*" Her sarcasm hardly veiled her anguish.

"I'm her friend."

"Her *friend.* Oh, I see." She rocked back and forth laughing to herself. "Her *friend.* Good for her. She never had much luck with friends."

I prayed for Dr. Joe to race in with his magic syringe and end this.

"I could go on this show right now and stop it, *friend of hers.* I could walk out there and say something that would make all the movie stars run right out the goddamn fucking door, *friend,* and unless you get *her,* and bring her in here in the next ten seconds, that is exactly what I intend to do."

"Okay, okay. I'll get her offstage and I'll have her back in ten seconds, but you must promise not to move until I return."

"You have my word as a *lady, friend.* Get her."

I moved faster than I had since stickball days. She was introducing Ann-Margret. I caught her eye and made a gesture that I hoped conveyed urgency without panic. It worked. She cut the adjectives in half and ran to me, leaving her guest with one unrouged cheek and a frantic stage manager.

"What is it?" She was exhausted. Her fine-boned face was gaunt.

"Robin is in your dressing room. She's a wreck, but I think you can handle her. Be very careful, she's about ready to blow. How long do you have?"

"We've got several taped pieces after this number. I'm okay for twelve minutes or so."

"I'll wait outside. If she uncorks, I'll get her out."

"She'll be okay."

When Robin saw Eve, she crumpled. Sitting like a child, her matted head in her lap, whimpering. Eve knelt down and embraced her, holding her close. "Darling Robin, poor Robin, I'm so sorry. I never wanted you to know this. Please forgive me. Please let me help you."

Robin shook her head and wiped her eyes on the hem of her soiled dress.

"I wanted to hurt you. I . . . my pride was hurt. I was jealous. I wanted to pay you back. I didn't care about Alex or anyone. I almost got killed trying to make you pay. You're so beautiful. You always were prettier than I was, even when you were a goddamn guy. Oh, shit. Everything's such a mess."

"Not so bad. It just feels that bad. Trust me, Robin, I've been in that place so many times. Don't give up now. No matter how desolate it feels, it will pass and you'll go on."

"You always were such a fucking saint, Adamo. You made me feel guilty just by being alive. I was almost glad when you died, you know, when you *drowned.* I'll rot in hell for that, probably, or for any one of a number of other things I've done."

"You're already rotting in it. You don't have to die for that. I don't blame you for feeling that way. Don't blame yourself."

Robin stared at her in awe. "You know what I was just thinking? I was thinking that if you had been like this, I would have been good. I would have been able to pull it together. I started watching your show out of hate, but you got to me. I was jealous that you were giving all those other people what you never gave me. I wanted you back *and* I wanted to destroy you."

Eve stroked her hair. "I didn't have this to give you then. Adam didn't have it. But I do have it now. Let me help you. Lean on me. Let me be your guide. You have never loved yourself, Robin. You have never understood your power or your loveliness. Let me show you how. Don't keep denying your worth. You have everything you need to be happy. Free it. I love you, Robin. Don't be afraid of the pain. It's part of it. It's necessary. It's the way out."

"I want to. Oh, God, I do. But . . . Eve. I don't think I can."

Eve stayed with her until Robin was calm. She asked for a towel and she washed up. She asked to borrow some money and one of Eve's dresses, which made her giggle. She used Eve's makeup and comb. She asked for aspirin and I went to the doc. She asked for something to eat and I brought her a sandwich and coffee. When I came back from my last errand, she was gone. On Eve's dressing table was a note.

You were always kinder and you were always a better mother. I want you to take Alex. This may well be the first and last selfless thing that I ever do (and even this act is marred by the fact that I am absolutely useless

as role model or guardian and the kid is miserable). If
Maybe dies, he'd have no one to give him what he
needs. You take him. I expect you will be fair to me
about finances. I'll leave that to you.

I won't tell anyone unless I'm stoned out of my head
and can't control myself. Unfortunately, that's a risk
you will just have to take, but *Alex* won't hear it from
me. Take him soon.

I put the note in my pocket, tears pouring down my
cheeks. I was turning out to be quite a soppy guy (making
up for twenty dry-eyed years, I suppose) and waited for
Eve to finish listening to the entire stellar cast singing
"When You Walk Through a Storm" to the accompani-
ment of the New York Philharmonic led by Leonard Bern-
stein, knowing I had a glorious little Thanksgiving present
burning a hole in my slacks.

EPILOGUE

E ve and I were married in January 1984. It made all the papers. Shortly thereafter we went to New Orleans and brought her son home with us.

Robin took the substantial settlement and moved to a villa in Portofino. Word has it she is not doing well. She has planned several trips to see Alex and canceled them all. We have also heard that her friend Mr. Hicks, who has traded his umbrellas for a wheelchair, is in residence with her.

Maybe finally retired, letting out the longest breath ever held in Louisiana and settling down to face the twilight in the Richeleau guesthouse.

Many decisions were made from that late November morning when Robin left the note on Eve's dressing table. Life-changing decisions for both of us.

I legally adopted Alex, giving him back a father, though a rather puny substitute for the one he lost. By June, Eve had fulfilled her contract with Ivan Kimbal and, in spite of hair-pulling hysteria when she told CBS, she left TV-land forever. I followed suit. In my case, if there were any screams of *don't leave us*, only the commissary mice heard them. I received a polite and respectful acceptance of my resignation and a lot of wry backslapping remarks about "memoirs" and "rich wives" from my colleagues.

Everyone thought we were both mad.

We left New York soon after; a strange, smiling trio, holding hands.

We live in France for now. Our life is not like anything either of us has ever done and that is the best thing about it. I write articles for European magazines under a nom de plume and, yes, make notes for the books I want to do.

Eve is running the international relief fund established by the telethon and I help with that, too. Her aunt Suzette is coming to work with us. The telethon was an astounding success. They raised twenty million dollars overnight.

Eve still does her God Through Exercise class (in French in our barn for the local women). We are relatively anonymous here. The French, running true to character, never really watch American television.

Alex goes to a fine local school and lives happily, in a state of emotional comfort that is almost eerie. It is almost as if in some visceral way, he knows that Eve is not just a kindly aunt who took him in because his mother was ill and his nanny too old. He asks no questions and gives us much love.

I quit smoking and walk five miles (give or take two of them) every day. I eat a lot of homegrown food, much of it planted with my own urban hands, and while I still savor a glass of vintage wine, I haven't seen a quart of Glenlivet in ages. I somehow want to stay around for a while, now.

Since I stopped smoking, I am really soppy; I can cry at a letter from my old pop or a smile from my radiant, wonderful wife. I'm a grandfather (Greta's baby girl was good for two rainbuckets at least). I've been working on

Eve to let me prepare Alex for bar mitzvah. She only nods, rather doubting, I suppose, that I could find appropriate facilities or teachers in a French Catholic village anyway. I never had one, and so I thought it might be nice to . . . well, we'll see.

I would love to be able to tell you that Eve's influence changed things, that the bad guys, the Kurtzes and such, were gone, and everyone was healthy and bicycling with God. But you know that that isn't how it happens. She gave some balance to the madness for a while. After she left, a cult started up in the Midwest somewhere, the Evettes, who preached that she was Jesus Christ (direct from his miraculous appearances in Bayside, no doubt). They were quite adamant about it for a month or so.

Ivan Kimbal is holding the tapes for rerun syndication. So she will live on, hopefully not to haunt us. We have both survived to hear the giant metal doors slam shut on our former selves, lived to grieve our mistakes and edge slowly, painfully, forward into unknown new dimensions. In my own way, I feel as reborn as Eve.

Not very glamorous, really. I don't think about my wife as she was very much anymore. Sometimes I'll forget for weeks on end and then something will happen and there it is. Laurel gave me some advice just before we left. "Think about her as a woman with a birth defect that medical science was able to remove. That's all it is, señor, she was always Eve." That helps. We live each day grateful for the love and comfort we have found in each other, as living proof, in some cockeyed way, that it's all worth it.

ABOUT THE AUTHOR

A novelist, freelance writer, and editor, GLORIA NAGY was born in Los Angeles. Now living in Manhattan, Ms. Nagy is working on her fourth novel. She lives with her husband, publisher Richard Saul Wurman, and their two children.